MW00636398

Two Runs of Stone

By

Steven D. Nielsen
Historical Novel

A Beckoning Call

This book is not an official publication of The Church of Jesus Christ of Latter-day Saints. All opinions expressed herein are the author's alone and are not necessarily those of the publisher or of The Church of Jesus Christ of Latter-day Saints.

Published and Distributed by:

Granite Publishing and Distribution, LLC
868 North 1430 West
Orem, Utah 84057
(801) 229-9023 • Toll Free (800) 574-5779
Fax (801) 229-1924

Page Layout & Design by Myrna Varga, The Office Connection, Inc.
Cover Design by Steve Gray

Library of Congress Control Number: 2003108114
ISBN: 1-932280-18-9

Printed in the United States of America
First Printing July 2003
10 9 8 7 6 5 4 3 2 1

"A fascinating portrayal of a mid-nineteenth century Danish family's encounter with Mormonism. The story unfolds in the wonderfully researched historical setting of Latter-day Saint missionary labor in Denmark and emigration to Zion. Great character development!"
— Don Enders, Museum of Church History and Art, Salt Lake City, UT

"An entertaining novel that more than held my interest from start to finish! Nielsen is a skilled story teller."
— Chuck Mortensen – former High School Principal and English teacher – active member of the Methodist Church, Northridge, California

"Amazing! I'm hooked. Wonderful plot! Catherine and Peter drive the action. The writing style is so natural; I couldn't wait to get back to reading . . . action like in a movie!"
— Bennie Willis – a reader in Houston, Texas – Masters Degree in Political Science

"Two Runs of Stone captivates you in the sense that you do not want to put it down and when you do you can not wait to pick it up again . . . a truly "entertaining" book!
— Frevent Millet – dental student, husband and father, Houston, Texas

"I was so moved by Two Runs of Stone that I read it again. One of the most interesting, entertaining novels I have ever read. A must read!"
— Nardene Hall – a reader in Texas – Financial Consultant – English Major

"Brilliantly captures the feeling of conversion . . . straight forward – a real tell it like it is novel. Very refreshing!"
— Mont Mortensen – Utah reader – no relation to Chuck Mortensen

"Always anxious to see what happened next. This book really hooked me the very first day! I had tears in my eyes towards the end."
— Sharolyn Steinmetz – a reader in Houston, Texas

"Extensively researched – excellently written . . ."
— Katheryn Garver – a reader in Alta Loma, California

"Enjoyed the pace and quick style and historical documentation. I love strong women characters!"
— Jacquelyn Wettstein – business professional – Houston, Texas

"I could not put it down! An exciting and wonderful novel – the Scandinavian history is incredible!"
— Aileen J. Larson, past president (ten years) Weber North Center Co., Daughter's of the Utah Pioneers

Table of Contents

Acknowledgments

Aileen Jardine Larson is the first name to come to mind where this novel is concerned. Aileen introduced to me the vast work done in compiling the history of the noble women, immigrants and American citizens, who laid the foundation of not only The Church of Jesus Christ of Latter-day Saints but of over three hundred cities in the western United States. Aileen Larson is the past president of the Weber County Chapter of the Daughters of the Utah Pioneers, my mother-in-law and a more unique, kind, generous and strong individual I do not know.

I would also like to thank: my dear mother Carma May Monsen Nielsen for her love of the English language, and her moral strength under difficult circumstances, my wife, Susan Yetive Nielsen for her love and support during the fifteen years it took to compile this series of historical works, for the raising of our five children and her love for seven grandchildren; and for Jill Ellen Stegall who worked with me from the beginning of this project and has been an inspiration and genuine support throughout.

Further I would like to thank: Martha Hire of Ogden, Utah for believing in me, Dean Grover, also of Ogden, Utah for his teaching and love of literature; Peter Jorgensen of Houston, Texas for historical assistance, translation, friendship and moral support; my son Patrick D. Nielsen, a technical writer, for his encouragement and editing assistance, Lavina Fielding Andersen for early editing assistance, and enthusiasm for the project; Inger Lokke Jorgensen, for historical and cultural assistance, friendship and her pride in Denmark, Flemming Axmark of the Danish Minister of Foreign Affairs Office for his keen wit, kindness, love of life and tremendous support; and Janette Nielsen Garver for historical data.

I am also indebted to Julia A. Bellon for excellence in editing, Ronald E. J. Borgstedt for his creativity, honesty, and technical assistance, to Doyle Jones, Bruce Jones, Bill Keidel and John Webber for their professionalism; and also to Sheri Lin Kemp a wonderful artist, a loving person and bonding element between two long separated families; and most importantly to Don Enders of the L.D.S. Church Historical Department for all of the above.

Last, but not least, I would like to thank two people I have never had the privilege to meet: my great-great-grandfather, Niels Peter Nielsen, who at eighteen years of age joined the Mormon Church in Holbaek, Denmark and was beaten severely for his trouble and then left for dead. And finally to Kate B. Carter, author, teacher, journalist, historian, publisher, and long time President of the Daughters of the Utah Pioneers.

Synopsis

Beneficiary of her father's lands, livestock and gristmill, Catherine Rasmussen's otherwise secure life was greatly impaired by her marriage to Elias Jensen, so-called Doctor of Jurisprudence, political aspirant and know seducer. Only her sons kept Catherine on track. Her home, the mill and other outbuildings had been spared the devastation of Denmark's 1864 war with Prussia but left Catherine emotionally shattered. A precious necklace and a few thousand pieces of gold in the vault behind her father's portrait represented half of Catherine's liquid assets but doubts over Denmark's future had the heiress anxious.

Protestors thronged the cobbled streets of Copenhagen demanding answers for Denmark's war with Prussia and reform of the country's archaic, monarchial system of government. Free elections of a more representative body in the government had grudgingly been granted but the people wanted more. Adding spice to the boiling political stew, the human existence philosophies of Soren Kierkegaard had shaken the government's bed-partner, the Evangelical Lutheran Church (Denmark's state church) awake, and Catherine's eldest son Peter, a student protestor was caught up in the fray. But of greater concern to Catherine was Peter's romance with Maren Carlsen. The implications of Peter and Maren's union included immigration to, of all places the United States, itself a boiling caldron of civil strife and Catherine was very despondent.

Was Peter's desire to leave Denmark his way of ending the conflict between himself and younger brother Ferdinand or was it genuinely connected to his recent finding of peace and direction? Catherine did not know. Her own marriage was a disaster. Some days divorcing Elias, selling her holdings and then traipsing all over the globe didn't sound so illogical.

Two Runs of Stone is an epic in historical fiction set in the late 1800's and is the result of fifteen years of concerted effort. Actual journals of the women and men who lived and died during the era provide the foundation of the work not to mention their Danish, English and American ancestors. Here's to good reading!

Section One

The Necklace

Chapter 1

Whispers of the necklace circulated throughout the lavishly dressed crowd like fire strafing a dry wheat field as Catherine Jensen came up the winding stairway and entered the marble-floored ballroom. No one even remembered Elias had been with her. Women clustered about her, bedazzled by the transformation. Elisabeth Roskelle, a formidable presence in bustle and train, ruffles and lace, hair piled and powdered, linked arms with Catherine and asked delightedly, "do tell us about your necklace, my dear, new isn't it?"

Women who knew her and those who didn't, pressed closer as Catherine, smiling politely, turned away from Elias and explained, "Hr Hansen took months with it, Fru Roskelle. He finished only recently. The design is symbolic throughout you see. The diamonds represent my four sons . . . Hans, Peter, Ferdinand and Kristian. The oak leaves on the chain are the years of my life . . . and don't go counting them," she warned playfully wagging her finger at the ladies. Glancing around, she saw Elias heading for the nearest wine tray.

"What about the pendants, Catherine?" asked Casten Pedersen, a long time friend.

"The pendants represent tears my dear friends," she said touching one with her finger. She then added with a wink. "Living with any man is a trial of the first order." Her laugh was charming, infectious and the women joined in with pleasure.

Elisabeth Roskelle, wife of a wealthy dairy farmer and always the perfect hostess, then gently moved Catherine away. "Do let me present you to Countess Danner Catherine.[1] She'll be fascinated with your cleverness! I believe your jeweler, Gustav Hansen, also designed the jewels she is wearing."

"I'd love to meet the countess Fru Roskelle, but . . ."

"She is as down to earth as you are my dear," Elisabeth said delicately, sensing Catherine's discomfiture, "but I don't think she'll expect to find such a treasure out here in the provinces." Catherine felt somewhat awkward but as she looked over at Elias who was handing a waiter an empty glass and taking another full one, she bolstered courage. *'The fool'* she thought to herself, *'we haven't been here five minutes and he's already headed toward drunkenness.'*

Standing dumbly near the sidelines Elias Jensen was still completely off-balance at his wife's sudden display of beauty that evening. "She had always been so plain, so conservative," he said to himself as he downed his third sherry since arriving. With nerves and hands trembling slightly he placed his glass on the windowsill behind him.

Elias turned and almost bumped a young man eyeing Catherine. "Fine looking woman, your wife!" exclaimed a slim young aristocrat named Bent Stauning. Had he his wits been about him, Elias would have known to spend as much time getting to know Stauning as possible. Bent was the brother-in-law to the *Bondevenners' Selskab* or in English, the Society of Farmers' Friends Party Chairman. "Mind if I dance with her?" he asked Elias.

"Suit yourself," Elias grumbled looking about for a waiter.

A feeling of rage mounted in the Elias' head, followed by a wave of nausea as he watched Catherine curtsy to Countess Danner, who smiled and with a hand on Catherine's elbow drew her closer.

'How could she do this to me?' he thought. *'Wait till I get her home. I'll teach her to humiliate me! This was supposed to be my night!'* His rancor toward Catherine was building to a crescendo the more he watched his wife but for now all he could do was stare helplessly after her.

Violins lifted into a waltz, and Elias watched numbly as his wife twirled away in Baron Stauning's arms. *'Where had she learned to dance like that'* The night he and Catherine first met was at a dance where she had been just as lovely, as charming and just as light on her feet. They hadn't been dancing since and Elias had simply forgotten.

When the dance ended, Palle Roskelle the host himself waltzed with Catherine. Catherine had barely caught her breath after the dance when she heard the distinct click of heels and turned her attention to a trim lieutenant wearing gold epaulets and a tightly fit red collar trimmed in gold braid. "I'd like you to meet my brother," Palle Roskelle said as the lieutenant bowed to Catherine. "He's just back from the mainland."

"My pleasure," said the handsome officer extending his hand. "Would you care to dance? I promise not to step on your toes," he added with a wink before Catherine could answer. Those around laughed merrily, briefly.

"Only if you left your spurs outside," said Catherine cleverly. His black leather boots were polished to perfection and so high above the knee the man appeared half boot and the other half human. "They are safe in my saddlebags I assure you my lady," he said gallantly. They shared a bit of laughter then danced away.

The lieutenant showed impeccable manners by keeping the proper distance from Catherine as he waltzed her amongst other well-bedecked couples. The hall was alive with spinning ladies in lavish gowns and highly piled coiffures and Catherine felt like a princess. She had only dreamed things might be so lovely.

Meanwhile on the sidelines Elias mechanically took another glass of wine from the waiter's tray. This one he drained in two gulps.

The wine had dulled Elias' anger into a lurid sense of humor and after Catherine's dance with the lieutenant, Elias gathered courage, approached and with a dizzy grin, held out his arm to his glowing wife. "Would you care to dance, my dear?" he invited with half a bow.

Catherine stepped closer and her countenance barely changed, but her eyes blackened cold as steel. "Go to your whores," she said in his ear with an icy tone sharp as a knife. Turning on her heel and laughing gaily, she touched the shoulder of a prosperously dressed grain broker she did business with. "Hr Mortensen, so nice to see you."

Elias stared at her numbly and his feet felt like clay as he slowly turned and stumbled away. Devastated at the shock of his wife's rejection, nevertheless bolstered by alcohol surging through his veins, Elias grew more brash as the evening progressed. He blundered about the room, breaking clumsily in on conversations, and hailed party members in a voice too loud. With a leering grin he ogled various women asking several to dance. Those foolish enough to accept were held so tightly they struggled for breath.

Elias had sense enough to be discreet around Party Chairman, Otto Pedersen, but realized the man was avoiding him. The evening's ultimate humiliation came when Elias glanced about the ballroom and realized that party notables had all but disappeared and he knew not where. He was drunk but not too drunk to realize that his escapades in Copenhagen, the women and the drinking had finally caught up with him.

His blurring eyes searched the crowd frantically, clumsily. *'They must be behind closed doors in the library,'* he thought remembering past meetings at Roskelle's. However, as Elias made his way toward the door, a butler slipped quietly from the shadows to block his way.

"No admittance," he said staring expressionlessly at Elias. The rejection was clear.

It was a little after eleven when Elias and Catherine left the Roskelle mansion. The return trip home wasn't as miserable as the trip to the party but it was longer. Much longer. The slap of leather and beat of horses' hooves was much pronounced as silence reigned inside the family coach. Elias was mentally and physically sick. His chest was heaving, and he couldn't seem to get enough air. He drained a small flask of sherry he kept in his coat pocket and threw it from the coach where it shattered on the rocks, then hung his head from the open window and gagged.

Catherine, repulsed at the stench wafting about Elias, turned away from him in disgust. In the darkness outside she looked steadily toward the future. Her husband was a popinjay, a futile, foolish, and immature man; a spoiled boy who had never grown up. She had patronized and pampered him all these years and to no avail. He was probably no better or worse off than many of the ambition-driven men whom the new constitution would draw out of the closet. But Catherine would never respect or trust Elias. There was no possibility of a union of soul with him.

But the evening hadn't been a total loss. Although Elias' initial reaction to her had been extremely painful, it had shown Catherine that he really did not love her. He loved politics and it was love misplaced, because apparently politics didn't love him. While Catherine was sorry for him, she was also angry. All this time she'd been nothing more than a meal ticket; not a true companion merely a woman who had given him money and four children, one he had used but certainly not respected. For years these were things she had known but refused to accept, but no longer.

Further but more on the positive side, the evening had taught her she could move with ease and pleasure anywhere she chose, welcomed and appreciated by even the most powerful people in Danish society.

Whatever happened to Elias' coveted career in politics she willingly relinquished to him. She would turn her back on his phony world forever. Politics could have him but again it didn't seem to want. She wondered what Elias might do to occupy his time. He was incapable of anything useful around the home or the estate, but he had to something! She certainly didn't want him underfoot all the time.

Catherine must live for her sons, and that meant protecting them from Elias and his self-indulgent, tantrum-driven influence. She would not have wanted her sons to walk through any doors he could have opened anyway. To her politics was such a sleazy world. Catherine would find other avenues to expand her sons thinking.

Spending so much money on the necklace embarrassed her. What would her father have said? On the one hand Catherine was uplifted by the evening's events, and on the other she was devastated. As the carriage bumped along Catherine struggled to regain her emotional bearings, and she would regain them. It was a long drive home.

Elias, now moaning in an alcohol-induced sleep on the seat across from her, was no more than an object of scorn. The heiress stared outside her window at the passing shadows of the countryside as her mind wandered over the past.

Her maiden name had been Rasmussen, and Catherine was a creature of industry and thrift, of common sense, not of excess. Her silk dresses were always sober in hue and subdued in style. Mostly she wore plain cotton. Creating the necklace had been an experiment, a daring step into the unknown. And for what real purpose . . . to further a husband's political career? She was no longer certain of the reason.

The gemstones were part of her inheritance from her father. Normally, a miller took a percentage of the grain he ground into feed and flour as his fee; but in dealing with grain brokers, Peter Rasmussen always insisted upon cash. Or jewels. As a result, he had accumulated a glittering hoard of diamonds, rubies, sapphires, and emeralds.

Rasmussen's request was not unusual. Viking raids on England and points south plus Denmark's hundred islands and its willingness to war—Denmark had fought back and forth with Sweden for a hundred years in the seventeenth century—meant that its currency, like its borders had been in a state of flux for centuries. Gemstones were small—easy to conceal and carry. Bartering being commonplace in Danish commerce and gems the most popular medium of exchange, when they came into Peter Rasmussen's hands, they stayed.

A veteran of the 1807 war with Great Britain, Rasmussen had inherited an old gristmill from his grandfather, doubled its size and made it prosper. The mill was a tall wooden hexagonal building three and a half stories high and built on a stone foundation. When in operation, its huge wind wings turned powerfully in the breeze forcing gears and equipment inside into action. Shafts turned. Leather belts tightened. Gears, swabbed with grease, chewed into each other and millstones, fed with a steady stream of golden-brown wheat, whined as if in agony. Warm, almost hot, flour spewed from between the stones, and then was shoveled into bolting machines, sifters.

When in operation, the crude, silk-lined and oddly efficient bolting machines shook the building like a minor earthquake, filling the air with light brown dust as they processed the flour.

The mill stood on its own small stream and had a large man-made holding pond on its west side. On infrequent days, when the wind was not blowing, a water wheel, over-shot by a wooden race, provided power to the mill. Iron bound wooden gates to the holding pond were muscled open, allowing trapped water to speed down the race and turn the auxiliary water wheel. But the pond had only enough capacity to run the mill half a day and then required days to refill. The large pond and the auxiliary water wheel were only a back-up system. Under normal circumstances, the wind powered the mill but the holding pond satisfied Peter Rasmussen's Danish propensity for maximum use of resources and time.

The mill, the house, barns, and outbuildings were located in a wooded nook of Holbaek Province, about half an hour's journey from the provincial seaport town of Holbaek. With thatched roofs, timber, and adobe brick construction, they were spacious and solid. From foundation to ceiling beams, nothing shoddy had been used in their construction; and although Peter liked his beer as well as the next man, he and his workers tended the mill with passion, maintaining it and fussing over it. Like the goose that laid the golden eggs, the mill provided Rasmussen with a steady flow of wealth.

Rasmussen never left his mill until the sun went down, lest a farmer happened by with a wagonload of grain. A physically powerful man, most evenings, and every Saturday afternoon would find him in one of the several taverns in Holbaek twisting arms with farmers and mechanics or else having a laugh with local merchants. He rarely socialized with his mill hands but on occasion did wander into the inns they frequented in the poorer section of town.

As an only child, Catherine learned genteel manners and piety at an early age. She also learned to read and write, a thing rare among Danish girls. Her mother had been raised by a Lutheran priest and was well educated. Her psalm singing and Bible reading gave Catherine her philosophy, theology, and poetry simultaneously, and she developed a saintly repose a person could readily feel.

She learned hard work and knowledge of accounting from her roaring, stumping father. Still, Catherine was feminine, yet surprisingly strong. Her family's milling heritage went back three generations and Catherine passionately desired that it continue.

After his wife's death in 1820, Peter Rasmussen buried himself in work; and Catherine, fleeing the confusion of growing up without a mother, plus fear of being alone in the house, followed him around like a little lost puppy. At first she distracted the stocky miller, but Peter was flattered by his daughter's attachment. Within a few years, her quickness with numbers manifested itself, and her absorbent mind had mastered the routines of the gristmill, granary, the hundred acres of wooded ground, fertile farmland and the household.

At fifteen Catherine's sturdy body took on the flowering of womanhood. She had an ever-so-light spray of freckles across her face, dishwater blond hair, a smooth and fair complexion and was pleasant, but not overly so to look at.

By seventeen Catherine was more attractive but still in a subdued way. Confident, she could instruct the workmen about any business of the estate and had shown herself a cool head in emergencies. Like the time a fire broke out in the barn, and when Nils Holsen, a stablehand, fell from the ladder and broke his leg. Both times Peter Rasmussen had been at a tavern in Holbaek and Catherine was forced to take charge. Her solid ways and growing confidence made her a much-respected mistress amongst the farm and mill hands.

Recognizing in his daughter a maturity beyond her years, Peter Rasmussen ceremoniously bestowed upon Catherine her mother's keys to the house, desks and the gristmill. He then revealed a small safe in the study, built into the wall between the bookshelves, behind a portrait of the gristmill painted by an itinerant painter and gave her the combination. Inside were the jewels. Their beauty had enchanted Catherine. Turning them over and over in the sunlight spilling across her father's desk, she exclaimed, "Whatever would I do with such wealth Far (Father)?"

Peter Rasmussen grinned in spite of himself. Lines of worry also mapped his forehead. "When the time comes . . . you will know my dear," the miller assured her. "When I'm gone these and all else I own will belong to you. You had best prepare yourself."

The stunned girl could only stare at the jewels in amazement. "Oh Far, I had no idea you owned these," she said breathlessly. "How . . ."

"Your mother and I worked hard Catherine, very hard. What lies before you represents years of toil. That and clever bargaining. Danish currency hasn't always been a thing we could trust; whereas hard assets speak for themselves, demand no explanation and no government can print them when their treasuries become low."

Despite her maturity, this kind of talk confused her and Catherine felt very uneasy. With knitted brow she stood there listening and gently shaking her head side to side.

"First off you will tell no one of the gemstones existence," warned Rasmussen. "Not even Inger! Especially not Inger. Her wagging tongue would have every thief in Denmark sneaking up on us."

"But we have always trusted Inger . . ."

"Where these jewels are concerned I trust nobody . . . I'm beginning to be sorry I've even told you."

The comment stung but Catherine knew her father loved her and could see he was only trying to protect her.

"You hear me now girl?" he threatened when she didn't respond. "Tell no one of these. Your life could be in danger!" His voice softened slightly when he saw Catherine's lip quiver. "Y–Yes Far," she stammered. "B–But there is so much wealth here. I'm frightened . . . But I won't tell a soul. I promise."

Seeing the weight of this responsibility had taken hold and knowing his daughter didn't lie, Rasmussen's mind was put at ease. "Don't worry your pretty little head about it Catherine. I'm not going anywhere for a long time. Not for a long, long time," he added with a touch of sarcasm.

The miller completely softened then. "Come here child," he said and took her in his arms. There was a strong bond between this father and daughter, a bond of honor, and of family integrity. He could trust her and knew it.

"Keeping this a secret is for your own protection Catherine," he said gently. "And for mine. Our household could be in such danger."

"I will never divulge a thing Far," Catherine again promised. "But I really wish you hadn't showed them to me. It is such a burden."

"I know dear girl," said the thrifty and slightly aging miller. "How I know."

Inger Daryberg, a maid if she could be called such, Catherine came to think of her as a mother, was the childless widow of Peter Rasmussen's favorite cousin. With a small beak-like nose, stubborn features, pencil thin lips, and a body as stout as a chopping block, Inger was meticulous. Her scrubbed red cheeks matched her fiery personality perfectly. After stepping on a rusty nail in an old woodshed, Inger's late husband contracted lockjaw and had died from malnutrition. He went rather quickly, horribly, and left the little woman practically destitute. Inger cleaned houses to support herself and had contracted with Peter Rasmussen to go through his own at least twice a month. Then seeing the positive effects of Inger's womanly influence over Catherine, Rasmussen insisted Inger's visits increase to twice per week. And as things worked out Inger practically moved in, returning to her own house only once per week.

At first Rasmussen hoped the plump little woman might also be interested in him romantically. But a sharp slap across the face convinced the wealthy miller that money was Inger's *only* interest in him. That and mothering Catherine, so he turned his attention elsewhere.

The years came and went and Catherine almost forgot about the gemstones. They crossed her mind occasionally but she remained true to her word neither telling Inger nor anyone else about them. Thankfully she no longer worried about the jewels whereas when her father had first showed them to her she had nightmares for weeks.

By the time she was nineteen, her father's chief terror was that Catherine would marry one of the muscled, blond, brown and unschooled farm laborers who seemed to come in with every wagon load of grain. And there was a close call with a young military officer she met at church in Holbaek. However, that fellow's regiment ended up being sent to Holstein to quell a growing unrest and the last Catherine heard, he had married a local girl. Shattered by the experience, Catherine moped about the estate for weeks barely speaking to anyone. When at last she came out of her depressed state and requested that the family's home, a large, multi-gabled, two-story be remodeled, Peter Rasmussen willingly agreed. He correctly read the request as her intention of making the estate her own home for the rest of her life.

Upset at the expense and clutter of remodeling, Rasmussen was nonetheless very pleased with the results. Catherine, working with local carpenters and masons, added 400 square feet to the house by expanding the west wing. A balanced integrity was maintained and the added footage enabled builders to enlarge several rooms in the house and provide a more spacious entrance. After the walls were completed, the workers refinished the whitewashed stucco and bindlingsvaerk, brown-stained decorative wood trim, exterior of the house and inside re-did the dried clay floors in tile and polished oak.

A walkway lined with spruce trees set off the front of the house, and on the east side near the study were vegetable and flower gardens. In back of the house and to the west were apple trees and an ornamental rose garden that filled hot summer afternoons with sweet fragrance. The house opened into a large entry hall from which an oak staircase curved gracefully up to the second-story bedrooms and sewing room. A commodious dining room and elegant living room adjoined each other on the west wing of the house; and after dining, Catherine and her father would often retire from the table to sip coffee or tea in the comfort of the living room.

Peter Rasmussen's study was on the east wing of the house where Peter—really Catherine—could keep accounts and run the estate business. Naturally lit from late morning until evening this sunny room, built on the corner contained a goodly number of books; poetry, which Catherine's mother had collected and a substantial library of classics purchased or bartered by her father. The windows of the study overlooked Catherine's well-kept flower and vegetable garden. Her mother had loved flowers, but it was Catherine who could coax anything to grow. Her few leisure moments were spent either in those gardens or in the study reading.

There were three fireplaces in the house; two were often in use and during the spring a pair of storks nested on the third. A cobblestone courtyard lay out back and beyond that the family stables.

A large clay tile floored kitchen was just off the dining room and next to it the housekeeper's room and pantry. Catherine, being an excellent cook, spoiled her father, making his favorite pastries in a melting combination of fruit and butter, seeing to his comfort, and easing his business burdens with frugality and skilled management. At any given moment, she knew how much hay was in the barns and how much in the fields, which mare would foal and when, which cow had gone dry, which was ready for breeding, and when any of the animals were ready for the knacker man. At the mill she knew the workers, their wives and their children. She knew which grain broker or farmer owed money, and how much; and she always knew how much wheat, barley, and rye were in the granary.

After the day's labors, her sole indulgence was to sit in a quiet corner and read a book, then take a bath and finish out the day going over the mill's accounts. An organized person, not one to move quickly but steadily, Catherine accomplished much more than many people who threw themselves into projects with more initial energy.

She showed little interest in the steadily increasing stream of suitors who well knew the value of the thriving and orderly estate. Catherine had no illusion that she was beautiful but it scarcely troubled her one way or another. The time would come for her to marry, and when it did she wanted a man who would love her ordinary ways, love the estate as she did, and find joy in the milling business. She had a burning yet subdued romantic nature and wanted children to whom her thriftily managed property could be passed on. She would select a steady man, a hard worker, and a shrewd and practical man. However the years passed and none such presented himself.

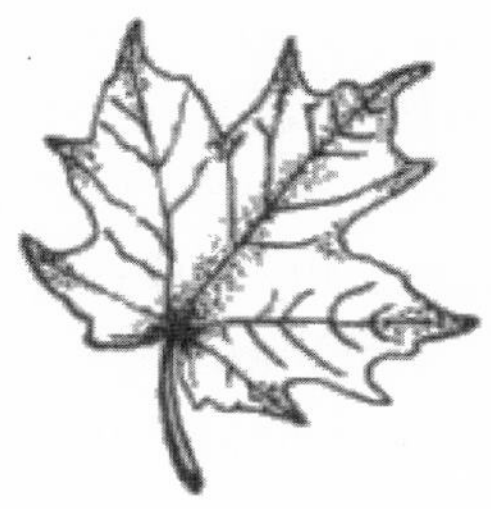

Chapter 2

In an age where men from upper-class families took titles, Elias Jensen called himself a solicitor—a doctor of jurisprudence on the strength of a few courses in law he'd taken at Copenhagen University. In an austere and military way, he was handsome—brown-eyed, brown-haired, tall, lean; but he was arrogant and carried himself with the proud, dull look of a camel. He seemed to be burning with a strange fire, driven by ambition, smoldering with confused passion, as if he could not tell his mind from his body.

In spite of certain misgivings, Catherine set her cap for him. He awakened a passion and fire within her that even years of moderation and frugality had not smothered. Her original model of the ideal man thrown to the wind, she worried Elias would be unstable. She also suspected that he would be unfaithful, inconsistent, self-indulgent, and perhaps even violent. Certainly at his age there had been women, probably several. She foresaw and scorned in advance his contempt for farm, mill, and granary; and consulting him on a business decision would probably be a waste of time. Even though Catherine fretted about these things, sadly she had fallen in love.

Her father, Peter Rasmussen, also had suspicions but he had mellowed over the years and with a vague hope of a grandson in the back of his mind, he reluctantly allowed Elias to come courting. The camel had gotten his nose inside the tent and, one evening early in the courtship with her father snoring sonorously in his bedroom, a lavish meal and heavy mead knocking the overindulgent miller senseless, things began to progress rapidly for Catherine. She stood near the dining room window, waves of heat running over her skin and as she felt Elias approach, the petals of the flower within opened gently. Without speaking, Elias removed her jeweled hairpins one at a time. In the firelight, her eyes were beautiful, her skin creamy.

Next morning Peter Rasmussen wakened to find his future son-in-law dead asleep on the couch and invited Elias to be a guest of the household, ostensibly to organize the library and to teach him about local politics and to discuss the proposed changes in the constitution which Elias bragged he understood to the minutest detail. Eight weeks later, with morning sickness and a slightly altered waistline betraying the fact Catherine might be expecting a child, the miller announced his daughter's betrothal.

The wedding was solemnized in Holbaek's Evangelical Lutheran Church six weeks later. Three months after that, laughing and drunk, Peter Rasmussen slipped into his own icy-cold millpond, had a heart attack and drowned. Catherine, in bed with Elias and intoxicated with the fire of newlywed bliss, hadn't heard her father leave the house. She would blame herself for his death as long as she lived.

When she miscarried the day after the funeral, Catherine felt God was punishing her for willful pleasure seeking. In a view as cold as stone, she stood on the shimmering edge of the millpond and knew that the days of her pleasure with the fickle, extravagant Elias were as fragile as the moon's image on the placid surface. Catherine knew she would spend the rest of her life making the best of a bad bargain. Their season of mutual indulgence would last a few months, a few years at best. Then it would be over. And whether Elias would leave her or stay, Catherine could not be certain. Other than fidgeting over political papers he was writing and talking incessantly about old family connections in Copenhagen, Elias made no attempt at steady employment.

Chapter 3

"Denmark is in an absolute state of political unrest my dear," Elias said agitatedly one morning as he and Catherine sat for breakfast. A touch of fall was in the air and the bright colored birch trees outside the kitchen window seemed to applaud the fact that Denmark *was* in a season of change. "In fact it's very disconcerting Catherine," he went on, "and yet I smell history being made."

"Oh?" she said. As Elias' head was forever in the clouds, Catherine wondered where he was going with this. But knowing she was about to hear one of his disjointed discourses she prepared herself by leaning forward, thumbs under her chin. "Isn't history always being made Elias?"

"You see Catherine," he continued as if she hadn't said a word, "laboring under the absolute monarchy of kings, our country made slow economic and social progress for centuries . . . then back in 1837 our rulers reluctantly agreed to regularly elected town councils and parish representatives."

"It was a start," Catherine interrupted feeling the sting of being ignored, "but the real gains came in 1839 when King Fredrick VI died and his handsome cousin and former King of Norway Christian VIII took over the Danish throne . . . do you know he's promising us freedom of speech and of religion . . ."

"Even voting rights for women," said Elias sarcastically taking back his conversation. It irked him that Catherine's eyes shined when she mentioned the king and that she was as up on politics as he. "As king of Norway Christian granted the most liberal constitution in the world, now perhaps he'll grant us the same."

"He will," stated Catherine wisely, taking a sip of her morning tea. "He's no fool. But what worries me, is the tumultuous state of affairs in our bordering duchies of Slesvig and Holstein. Slesvig, which is tied to Holstein by language and trade, will always belong to Denmark. But then Holstein is urging her to break away from us."

"Right you are," said Elias who rarely agreed with his wife. "But remember, Holstein consists of Danish *and* German-speaking people with strong links to Lauenberg . . ."

"And Lauenberg is of course entirely German," Catherine injected, "and unfortunately all three provinces are being courted by Bismarck's Prussian Federation." Her white curtains were billowing slightly out the open window and the fresh breeze much appreciated as Catherine spared with her know-it-all husband that morning.

"Which federation, you worry, will eventually have designs upon Denmark," said Elias somewhat condescendingly. Elias talked condescendingly to everyone. "There's reason for concern Catherine, but I don't think it will happen. Here is why. First of all Denmark is militarily strong and King Christian will not agree to a constitution that would out and out give Slesvig and Holstein a representative form of government. That would severely weaken his control over both duchies."

"But it is difficult to grant representative freedoms to Denmark, while limiting its duchies Elias."

"Very difficult," he said again and surprisingly, agreeing, but then wanting to show his more expansive knowledge of the situation added, "but what makes things even more interesting, is that certain factions in Slesvig and Holstein want their own constitution . . . a government independent of either Prussia or Denmark!"

"King Christian is a wise and experienced man," said Catherine wearily. "I understand he is working on a constitution that might satisfy all parties."

"That is also my understanding," stated Elias flatly as if he was the only one keeping up with the times. "He must draft a compromise or there could be chaos—perhaps even war."

She shook her head woefully at the thought of cannons blasting and soldiers dying. Over the years Denmark had certainly had its share of war. "Don't say even say it Elias. Something will be done . . . something must be done to keep the duchies loyal to Denmark, because the unification of all German-speaking people under the Prussian flag could become a frightening thing,"

"A very frightening thing," Elias conceded.

"And if you don't mind I would like to change the subject," said Catherine irritably. "It's such a lovely morning, couldn't we at least talk about the weather.

"I suppose," he said haughtily. "But I much prefer politics."

In the midst of the national turmoil, Elias's marriage to Catherine did much to further his political ambitions and may have been his design all along. Prosperously dressed, his purse clinking with Catherine's rigsdalers and skillings, he became a respected voice in the assemblies of Progressives that were pushing the king for a more liberal constitution. He wrote feverish pamphlets, penned ringing editorials, one of which was even published in a newspaper called the Almuevennen (the Peasants' Friend) and he made speeches at the hall where the Bondevenners Selskab gathered. The Bondevenners Selskab society later became known as the Venstre, a political party consisting largely of small farmers.

Politics well suited Elias and although he had no idea where his career was going, he pursued it with vigor. When he climbed between Catherine's lightly powdered and scented sheets at night, he talked passionately of his dreams while he traced the unstable borders between the German-claimed duchy of Holstein and the Danish-claimed duchy of Slesvig on their heavy quilt. His political passions mingled with and drove the more personal passions of the marriage bed; in fact, politics were his reason for living.

A century earlier, Elias Jensen would have lived out his life as a shopkeeper's assistant, or possibly a clerk. He might even been a reluctant soldier in one of Denmark's wars, or, had he been incredibly lucky, risen to become a village schoolmaster. By his marriage to Catherine, he became a landowner, the prerequisite for entrance to provincial assemblies, and a promising career lay ahead.

In December of 1842, Catherine gave birth to twins, who she named Peter and Hans after her father and grandfather respectively. That year Elias, to Catherine's surprise, was elected to Holbaek's parish council. Two years later, the Society of Farmers Friends paid him a small sum to establish an office in Copenhagen where they might work closer with urban liberals who were stepping up demands for a constitution. In addition, the Party would have more access to the powerful Danish newspapers for their message of social reforms to benefit their rural constituents.

Copenhagen was less than 60 kilometers away as the crow flies. However, rocky and often times muddy roads, as well as skirting the fjords, made a stopover in Roskilde necessary. One could then arrive in Copenhagen at a reasonable hour the next day.

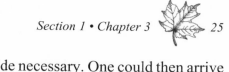

When Elias announced pompously that the press of duty required a more permanent residence in Copenhagen, Catherine, by then heavily pregnant again, agreed. But to Elias's dismay, she insisted upon going with him for a visit. She had not been to Copenhagen since she was a girl and wanted to acquire a feel for the expanding commerce, society and what her husband was to do with his time while there. She also hoped Elias might make a few connections which might expand markets for Danish flour and grist now that he actually knew where they came from. If Catherine feared there would be drinking and wenching mingled with Elias' political maneuvering, she chose not to think about it. Because of the paltry wage the party was paying, she also knew it would fall her lot to keep her politician husband solvent.

There were hard words over choice of living quarters and how much she would put in his bank account monthly, and with a feeling of despair Catherine returned to Holbaek and her responsibilities. Meanwhile in Copenhagen, Elias, giddy with power and freedom, moved a mistress into his rooms within three days.

Chapter 4

The months passed. Elias seldom wrote to Catherine and when he did it was always a request for more money. Feeling the weight of her increasing loneliness Catherine tried not to become bitter but found it a difficult task. March 12, 1845 she delivered a child into the world, a boy christened Ferdinand. The baby came on time but Catherine had torn badly during delivery. She apprised Elias of the event by mail and a month later he did return home, but not because of his son's birth. The story he told was of a large political gathering he had arranged in a downtown Copenhagen hotel. A disastrous situation as it turned out.

"The trouble was with some of the guests my dear," Elias told her innocently. "Unbeknownst to me, some had been drinking heavily before their arrival. A fight broke out between two of the more boisterous men. Glassware smashed, furniture knocked over, costly things to be sure and because I made the arrangements for the gathering the landlord is holding me responsible."

"Get your beloved party to pay it," Catherine told him angrily. "The new mill at Roskilde has taken so much of my business I have little money to spare." That Elias paused only a few brief moments at the cradle of his newborn son infuriated her. She was deeply hurt.

How could he show no interest in such a beautiful child?

"Besides," she added tersely, "I don't believe half of what you're telling me. One of your friends probably fell off his bench at a grog shop, smashed his stein and the both of you were thrown in jail. Bail money Elias? Fines?"

"Catherine," protested Elias pitifully, "how could you accuse me of such?"

Her cold stare told him there would be no money and cornered by events that *might* well land him in jail Elias conjured up a story Catherine might have believed. That he'd lost heavily at the gambling tables; had no money in the bank and was two months behind on his rent. The rent part was true, but fact was his current mistress had expensive tastes.

"I've no other place to turn but to you Catherine," he had pleaded. "You know my salary is pitiful. Curse them, and after all I do!"

Catherine stood her ground. "Enough is enough Elias. I know the root of your discomfort. Gambling indeed. Immoral escapades . . . that's what's costing you! I'll not support debauchery. Do you hear me?"

She walked out of their bedroom, slammed the door and for the next few days tried her best to pretend he wasn't around. When they did talk, they argued and for the duration of Elias' stay slept in separate bedrooms. Life became a hellish existence in the large house.

Cold as stone Catherine continued as before methodically running her business, supervising her puppy-like three-year-old twins, and nursing baby Ferdinand. While on a daily basis Elias took a dog and shotgun into the fields and blasted away at anything that flew.

Nearly a month expired and one day Elias's eyes rested longingly upon a nurse Catherine had hired to help with the baby. The nurse was indeed voluptuous, but she had a husband, children of her own and went directly to Catherine. "Keep him away from me or I'll not darken your door another single day Fru Jensen!"

The storm brought on by Elias' wild spending and her suspicions was nothing compared to the one that now raged in Catherine's home. Finally, and because of the poor example their father was setting for her sons, the heiress agreed to catch Elias up on his debts. Anything to be rid of him.

"This is the end of it," she warned after handing him a draft. "That should last six months. I know your expenses. I'll die rather than squander any extra on your women. Next time your creditors close in, they can well put you in debtor's prison!"

Elias took his ruffled ego and Catherine's money back to Copenhagen to continue his "work." Carrying on as before, with little moderation, he wrote for money occasionally but Catherine sent none. She almost hoped she had heard the last of him when oddly enough, an article Elias had actually penned appeared in the Berlingske Tidende, Copenhagen's largest newspaper. The article covered England's pressing demand for Danish grain and not only was Elias paid well for writing the article but when Catherine read it she softened greatly. She was actually very proud of her husband and immediately sent him a letter sealed with the Jensen Crest in wax.

"Dear Elias,

It was wonderful to see your name in print and on a subject of such keen family interest. I'm justly proud and upon your next visit home would like to discuss future writings that might further Danish agriculture and milling in general.

Perhaps I have been unduly harsh in the past. I have had a hard time understanding your employment and supposed my working class background to be the cause. But I've come to realize that not all men must work with their backs. I do not pretend to understand politics; so much is changing in Denmark and Europe at large. Kings giving up certain power . . . the common man having a chance to voice their opinions. I never thought we would see the day. Come home soon and let us discuss the new direction your life seems to have taken."

She signed the letter, your devoted wife Catherine Jensen and a draft from her bank was included. The letter inspired a lengthy visit from Elias, a return to the marriage bed and a truce, of sorts.

Children and the milling industry, the orderly existence Catherine had created for her household, satisfied Elias for a time, but it wasn't long before he grew restless. Anxious for the faster pace of politics and Copenhagen's nightlife, he once again lightened the purse of his faithful and wealthy wife, leaving her cosseted in the country with a fresh case of morning sickness.

In 1847 Kristian was born. Catherine was in her early-thirties. Her age, Elias's infrequent presence, and her own growing indifference of him assured her that this would be their last child. Without regrets, she looked at the ashes of her burnt-out passion and sought to reclaim her former peace. She had four sons, ample property, a gristmill as a going concern and her father's jewels locked away in a vault. It had never occurred to her to show them to Elias, nor would she ever.

Surrounded by her sons, Catherine led a relatively contented existence. She adored the boys equally and under her watchful eyes, they grew as strong and vigorous as young Vikings. She read them the Bible, taught them to pray and when the twins were of age, enrolled them in the cathedral school in Holbaek. The boys were a self-sufficient unit, a small male tribe who romped over the lawns and gardens, made huts in the forest, tunneled through the haylofts of the barns, swam fearlessly in the millpond where their grandfather had died, skated on it in winter, and haunted the mill at every hour of the day or night.

Catherine's head miller, a man named Torkil Olsen, a war hero with a crooked scar on his cheek from a Prussian Bayonet to prove it, became surrogate father to her sons. Thor, as she affectionately called him, because he reminded her of Greek Mythology's god of thunder, had massive arms, chest and shoulders, and a head and beard of thick, long reddish blond hair. His cheeks were red, chafed from frequent washings and their fiery color along with his long unruly hair gave Torkil a formidable presence that justified Catherine's nickname for him.

To her sons, with Elias absent, Catherine was the unchanging center of their universe, about whom they revolved like planets. Systematically and with occasional scolding, she taught them principles of estate management, thrift, and hard work. They learned to count by numbering sacks of flour in the mill. They learned weights and measures by watching the millers and by the time the twins were eight years of age they were sewing sacks of flour and sweeping out the mill. With or without a husband present, life was moving along for Catherine and her future heirs just as she planned.

Chapter 5

On January 20, 1848 King Christian VIII died and his son Fredrick VII took his place on Denmark's throne. Fredrick was the author of a declaration that eventually provided a Constitution granting all Danes more personal freedoms. Freedoms currently demanded by an educated and more enlightened Danish upper class. The actual document would not be adopted until over a year later but the wheels of political progress were in motion.

Elias, who had come home for a brief visit, was in a jovial mood about the situation and had actually chuckled as he and Catherine sat discussing the matter. "Tremendous pressure from Orla Lehmann[2] and Ditlev Monrad of the National Liberals, heading up a mob of angry citizens, is what it took to get the king off his royal arse Catherine my dear."

"Must you talk so crudely Elias?" she rebuked him. "I'm sure the King knew what he was doing."

"He knew all right," said Elias haughtily. "Faced with such public outcry he had no choice. There would have been blood in the streets."

"Regardless my dear," he added when Catherine didn't respond. "Absolutism in Denmark will soon be finished. The King has declared himself constitutional monarch and to appease the people he even appointed Orla Lehmann to sit on his new Council."

"Wise move," said Catherine sagaciously. "Now what do you think about the annoying question in the Duchies?"

"The new ministry has made its final offer to the rebels in Holstein and Slesvig. The Ejder Programme[3] will be followed," Elias answered authoritatively. "Lauenberg and Holstein may be given the right to join the German Confederation, but Slesvig must remain united with Denmark."

"Ha," scoffed Catherine despondently. "Neither you nor members of your infant political party, your Society of Farmers' Friends," she waived her hand mockingly, "have the faintest idea of the bloodshed and heartache which might lay ahead for Denmark. Well intended though the proposed constitution is, I believe it and the final offer made to Slesvig and Holstein will be rejected and will only intensify hostile feelings between them and Denmark."

Catherine was exactly correct in her prediction. No longer wanting to be a part of Denmark the Duchies hastily formed a provisional government of their own and led by the Prince of Nor, massed a rebel army, and in March of 1848 seized the fortress of Rendsborg which contained large quantities of Danish munitions and arms. Civil war erupted and Denmark's citizens rallied in a call to arms!

Believing the Slesvig-Holstein rebellion was part of German designs upon them, volunteers from Norway and Sweden came to the aid of Denmark. With a regular Swedish Army corps at the forefront the combined Danish forces quickly sent the Prince of Nor's army into retreat. But then, reinforced by a Prussian army of 12,000 men and volunteers from several German states, the rebels of Slesvig and Holstein fought back. What started out as an isolated skirmish soon took on international status.

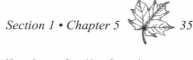

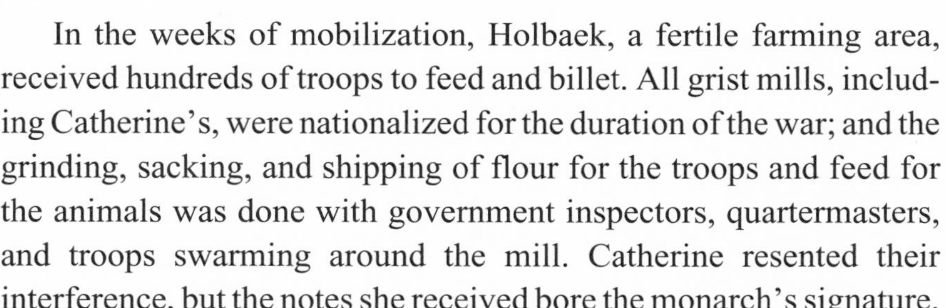

In the weeks of mobilization, Holbaek, a fertile farming area, received hundreds of troops to feed and billet. All grist mills, including Catherine's, were nationalized for the duration of the war; and the grinding, sacking, and shipping of flour for the troops and feed for the animals was done with government inspectors, quartermasters, and troops swarming around the mill. Catherine resented their interference, but the notes she received bore the monarch's signature, and helped her face the situation with tolerance and forbearance.

The war would prove short-lived. Troops made up of Danish, Swedish and Norwegian soldiers fought the rebels to a standstill by the end of June 1848. Then, because of international support from Russia, Denmark accepted a truce providing joint Prusso-Danish rule of Slesvig-Holstein. The armistice was not a permanent solution. There would be more fighting.[4]

Politics and bawdy a lifestyle had turned Elias' highbred hauteur into stridency and nervousness. His eyes darted about as he talked to people or else fixed his listener with a furious stare. He dreamed of power, wealth and fame, and was exactly the kind of man who achieves it by cunning. He wanted power for the sake of power, wealth for the sake of pleasure and neither for the good of the people.

It would be a year before the new constitution was ready for the King's signature. Elias intended to be elected to the newly formed Rigsdag (congress) when free elections were granted, and he would accomplish his designs one way or another.

Back from Copenhagen the would-be politician was more negative and sarcastic with his family than ever before. Catherine had no illusions about the cause of his bad temper and it wasn't necessarily politics. Nils Holsen, to whom Elias always boasted of feminine conquests in Copenhagen while the wiry stable-hand was brushing down his horse, had mistakenly let information slip to Inger Daryberg who after the death of Peter Rasmussen, had become Catherine's full time housekeeper and confident. *"The newest mistress is very demanding,"* Inger had relayed to Catherine. *"The quantity and quality of Elias' presents has in no way met her usual standards."*

So Elias who had come back plotting ways to wring more money out of his wife had experienced total failure and was in very bad temper. He stalked about the house for a week, barked at his young sons whenever they got near; and then every evening drank himself senseless in a chair near the fireplace.

One particular Sunday morning during Elias' visit, the flowers and vegetables outside the kitchen window in Catherine's garden were bright with color: delicate whites, bold yellows, soft violets, all trimmed with lacy green and brilliant orange. Catherine loved marigolds and planted them throughout her garden to ward off insects. They were bursting with color and pungent sweet fragrance, but sad to say, Elias' presence at the breakfast table had made the surroundings appear drab and odorless. Hung-over from wine, his foul attitude also made every bite of Inger's sumptuous scones seem tasteless—even when smothered with butter and honey.

"It's refreshing to see you dressed up for a change, my dear," Elias said acidly to Catherine as she came in. It rankled that she had refused him her favors last evening in the bedroom. "Your normal attire is as plain as the peasants' who work here."

It was all Catherine could do to keep from throwing hot tea in Elias' face. Instead she smiled placidly and took a seat next to Peter. "The mother of four sons has little time for glitter. Speaking of whom, good morning Kristian, Ferdinand, Peter and Hans," she said brightly. "Did you all sleep well?" Except for the youngest son they all nodded. Peter felt his stomach go in knots as he watched his father and Catherine could see the anger Hans felt as he and the other two boys simply chewed at their breakfast in silence.

Elias drained his tea and banged his cup on the table. "You should see the ladies in Copenhagen," he persisted. "There's color in their talcum, and something to see at the neckline. Why, at the functions I attend, women come bedecked in jewels and lace, with their bustles a 'bobbin'. It's all a man can do to keep his pants on!" He said the last while grinning lewdly at Catherine.

"For shame, Elias!" she scolded. "Such talk in front of the children. It's a wonder I put up with you at all!"

"Humph," scoffed Elias taking a bite of sausage and swallowing without chewing twice. "By contrast there is certainly not much happening in this household."

Hans and Peter, now going on seven, knew their mother had been insulted and both were glaring at their father. Ferdinand stared at him with admiration in his eyes and little Kristian began to cry. Elias paid none of them any mind.

"How can your employees hold you in respect Catherine?" he continued, jabbing as he wiped grease from his mouth. "You're a lady of substance and yet you not only dress like them, you associate."

"I don't like people to feel uncomfortable around me Elias," she said, retaining a degree of composure and calmness. Her mind was on the alert. Crude as he was Elias wasn't usually so demeaning. There was something up here. "They're like family to me . . ."

"Bah!" he spat. "Family indeed. They are only respectful because you pay them. Send them to their shacks one time without wages and watch their loyalty."

Catherine said nothing and Elias turned and glared at one of the twins. "Sit up straight Hans!" he snapped.

"I'm Peter," the sandy-haired boy spoke bravely but with quivering lips.

"Peter, then. And blast it, don't slurp your porridge."

"That was me," said Ferdinand unawares.

"My word, Catherine, have you not taught them respect? Manners? What kind of training are you giving them? They eat like a pack of animals!"

Catherine looked as if she'd been slapped in the face. She was so angry she could not speak. Would not speak. It was the Sabbath day and she would allow nothing, not even her husband's ignorance and stupidity to ruin it.

Elias threw down his napkin, pushed his chair back violently, and stood up. "Now everyone finish your breakfasts quickly," he ordered fiercely. "We'll be late for church."

Catherine took a deep breath and let it out slowly and nodded to the boys.

Peter and Hans were both stuffing a last bite of bread into their mouths as the wheels of the carriage sounded in front of the large house. "Everyone put on your coats," Catherine said pulling on her gloves, her cheeks still burning with anger. "Even though we have been ready for an hour we must not keep your father waiting."

Elias Jensen, an orthodox man without a shred of genuine religious feeling, supported the Evangelical Lutheran Church with the same grim partisanship he displayed toward politics. He traded on Catherine's genuine piety for much of his respectability in Holbaek. Therefore when he was in residence, Elias never missed church. A little singing, a little praying, a lot of kneeling, and enduring long sermons, he would position himself near the stained glass window under the west spire of the church and shake hands with anyone who got within ten feet of him. Elias had plans.

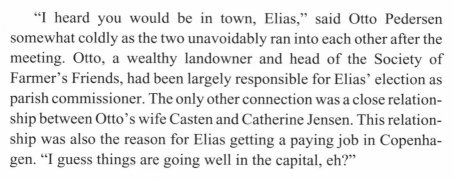

"I heard you would be in town, Elias," said Otto Pedersen somewhat coldly as the two unavoidably ran into each other after the meeting. Otto, a wealthy landowner and head of the Society of Farmer's Friends, had been largely responsible for Elias' election as parish commissioner. The only other connection was a close relationship between Otto's wife Casten and Catherine Jensen. This relationship was also the reason for Elias getting a paying job in Copenhagen. "I guess things are going well in the capital, eh?"

"We've made great strides, Hr Pedersen," Elias answered proudly. "My staff and I are blanketing the city with pamphlets . . . doing our part to keep the citizens pressing for a Rigsdag. If we're successful the monarchy should grant Holbaek parish two elected representatives."

"I'm well aware of Party goals," said Otto irritably. The chilly note in his voice was unmistakable. "Where in the world do you think the money is coming from Jensen?" he added purposely leaving out the respectful Hr.

Elias Jensen considered himself a logical candidate for one of the seats in the Rigsdag, but Otto, a sincerely religious man, had been shocked at rumors of Elias' bawdy lifestyle in Copenhagen. Hr Pedersen and other party notables anxiously awaited Elias' term to expire. "Now I must be running along," Pedersen said without so much as using Elias' name, "Good day to you."

Catherine, matronly in a long dark blue silk dress and her mother's beige shawl, stood nearby, trying to hear the conversation with one ear while she listened for her children with the other. She was holding little Kristian and watching her other three sons gleefully chase each other around the church grounds. Catherine well understood Otto Pedersen's importance in the progressive movement, and knew that his support was essential to Elias's advancement.

"What did he say to you?" she asked later as Elias, seething with tension, met her at the family carriage.

"Very little," he mumbled under his breath, then quickly smiled and nodded as Uwe Hoakensen the town banker passed. A plastic smile. "Apparently I'm slipping from grace. And after all I've done to further the party's cause in Copenhagen, you'd think our illustrious leader would kiss my feet."

"Ingratitude should be expected," said Catherine thinking she now understood his beastly attitude at the breakfast table.

Elias didn't hear her. "The swine," he said under his breath, "I know he's thinking of replacing me . . ." He broke off. "Hans, Peter, Ferdinand!" he shouted. "Get over here!" At Elias' command the boys stopped in their tracks, ran to the carriage and remained quiet as mice during the ride home. Elias grumbled and complained all the way. There would be no Sunday picnic as was generally the case during pleasant weather and with Elias in Copenhagen. With any luck, the boys could slip away from his dark presence after dinner.

Unfortunately, the dinner atmosphere was no better than it was at breakfast. Elias reviled Catherine all through the meal. He complained about her colorless appearance at church, and her lack of support for his political ambition. "Other men's wives give teas," he stormed, "they entertain, hold socials—anything to advance their husband's careers."

It was a new tactic, but Catherine didn't rise to the bait. A seed was planted however. "I do support you," she said indignantly. She was tempted to tell him his position with the party was only because of her connections with Casten and Otto Pedersen, but wisely chose not to. This mild storm might very well become a hurricane.

"If anything, you hold me back," he whined with injured innocence. "After my expenses in Copenhagen I barely have enough money for writing paper!"

Not wanting to destroy what little spirit and peace the Sabbath had given her, Catherine remained composed. Later that evening her emotions reached a point to where she would do anything to rid the house of Elias' sour presence.

Monday morning Catherine placed a thick envelope near his washbasin and to the relief of everyone in the household, Elias was gone by mid-afternoon.

Usually Catherine was philosophical about his absences. However, this time, a shadow lingered. Was the party really going to replace him? Heaven forbid! What would she do if he were constantly at home? In the past, Elias was only dictatorial with her sons if they happened to be under foot. This trip he had sought them out, picked and raged at them without cessation until they had fled his presence. Further, he'd been so vulgar and insulting with her, Catherine had nightmares for weeks.

Chapter 6

It was late August 1849 when Elias returned to Holbaek. This time he came in high spirits. Hostilities between Denmark and Germany over the Slesvig-Holstein question had again erupted earlier that year, but on July 6 Denmark had soundly defeated the combined German forces in a glorious battle. A truce had been signed on the 10th of July and public confidence ran high.

In the middle of these events, a rigorous newspaper campaign in Copenhagen, in which Elias Jensen had been published several times, helped secure royal assent to the long awaited Danish constitution. On June 5, 1849 King Fredrick VII signed the cherished document into law. A Rigsdag comprising of two chambers was created; the Folketing, or lower house and the Landsting, the upper house.

Finally, and for the first time in its history, Denmark would have a representative form of government! Freedom of speech, press, religion, and general liberties for all Danish citizens were granted. Furthermore, all males over the age of thirty who were not on poor relief were granted suffrage. The Society of Farmers' Friends would choose candidates from Holbaek to run for office to run against The Conservative Party candidates. Elias primped. Surely he was his party's logical choice to run for a seat—but there was that cold chill hanging about the pious Otto Pedersen. It was important that he reassure Pedersen. Becoming a more solid citizen in Holbaek would surely do the job, but Elias would need Catherine's help.

Suddenly very solicitous of her, Elias insisted Catherine explain everything about the estate; the crops, cattle, horses, even the workings of the mill. He felt out of place at the mill, as a clerk among longshoremen, but hung about anyway. When farmers drove up, he would ask Catherine in an undertone, "Who is that? Where is his farm? Has he got much brass to rub together?" He asked obtuse questions of bemused farmers about their harvests, animals and equipment and even lent a hand shoveling grain and lifting flour sacks. Elias refused to wear the coarse white linen breeches the mill hands wore and in suit pants and shirt after a days work he looked like an office clerk after dusting filthy shelves.

He became a changed man around the house and began to demand that the boys recite their lessons to him. Like a doting father, he patted them solicitously on the head after they did. He took Catherine on walks and discussed his dreams. He made soft-voiced speeches about the new constitution, his dream of serving in the Rigsdag and gazed ardently into her eyes. He painted a lovely picture of post-election life—how they would take up residence in Copenhagen, attend balls and rub shoulders with sovereigns and dignitaries.

Catherine cooperated somewhat cheerfully, suspicious of Elias' transparent courtship. She admitted that having a man around gave her satisfaction enough, even though the old fire was barely smoldering. She wondered if Elias really had the capability to serve in Denmark's new representative form of government. Perhaps she had dismissed him too quickly. He was such a fool in her practical world, but in his realm of politics, perhaps not. It occurred to her she might even possibly build a new marriage, based on a different and perhaps more equal partnership. Contacts in Copenhagen would do her sons no harm. It was already clear that the provincial township of Holbaek wouldn't be sufficient for the lively intelligence of the twins.

She talked it over with Inger one afternoon when Elias was in town paying calls on the city's merchants. He had actually taken his three oldest sons with him on his rounds! Inger, as wide as she was tall and crackling in a starched white apron, had never taken more than a dim view of Elias.

"What if he were to occupy a seat in the new Rigsdag?" Catherine speculated. "If nothing else, it would bring great honor to the family."

"Think of what it will cost to get `im there," scoffed Inger. "As for you, country folks have country ways and should stay in the country."

Catherine gave her a disturbed look. "You think my provincial housewife ways might embarrass Elias?" she asked calmly.

"No Fru Jensen," answered Inger honestly. "But your business is here. The mill and farm would fail without you."

"You are probably right," Catherine allowed. "But I could make Torkil Olsen my manager. He could handle the job with his eyes closed. This has been my life for so long," she sighed sweeping her hand the length of the room and looking toward the window. She turned and looked back at Inger. "And my sons . . . Elias hasn't wanted much to do with them, or anything in my world for that matter. But lately he has taken such an interest. What if there was a place for us in his world? In Copenhagen"

Inger shook her head sadly. "E' will only be using you Fru Jensen." She curtsied to her broom "And is this the wife? How charming! The little woman is it? Politics can have im'," she added acidly. "E' hasn't been worth anything to you since you married im'."

Any other landowner would have beaten the stout little housekeeper, but Catherine only sighed.

"Can't you see e' only needs your money Fru Jensen?" the little housekeeper continued. "So e' can play . . . play at 'is writing, play at 'is politics, play with 'is women," she started to sweep the tile floor vigorously as if trying to dig dirt from the cracks. "Do what you will," Inger said without looking up. "But tryin' to live in 'is world would eventually break you. An' I'm not talking money."

Catherine wasn't offended by her trusted maid's candor. She loved Inger as one would a mother. "I would never let it come to that," she said heavily.

A vague thought came to Catherine and she stiffened and said resolutely, "But I've got to try and build something better between us," she said resolutely or the marriage will more than likely fail."

'It already has,' thought Inger but she didn't express the opinion.

"Would you mind looking after Kristian for a while?" Catherine asked, looking over at the child who happened to be playing nearby on the floor.

"A' course not Fru Jensen," said Inger wondering what had suddenly come over her mistress.

Catherine left the kitchen, went upstairs and alone in her room sat at her dresser and studied her face in the mirror. She had a cute nose, a light spray of tiny freckles, but thought she was plain, definitely not a beautiful woman, however outdoor work had given her a healthy glow. Her eyes were straightforward and kindly but the eyelids drooped slightly, as if she were constantly tired. And there was a little frown between her brows. She didn't know, but it disappeared when she laughed, neither did she know how much her eyes sparkled when she smiled. Her teeth were even, white and healthy.

Her hair remained a dull, straight, dishwater-blond, far from the glistening platinum of some Danish women, but it was thick, always soft and clean. A barrel used for collecting rainwater was her media and after washings, Catherine brushed it dry. A hundred strokes and more, out on the back porch in the breeze and then she would braid it.

Would a more cosmopolitan style be attractive or make her look foolish? Despite five pregnancies, her skin was soft and fair and free of blemish. Her waist was small, her ankles sturdy, yet feminine and her bust was ample, nicely formed. Catherine was robust and well proportioned. In fact, she was one of those women whose flowering comes in later years.

She sat there, staring at herself in the mirror and wondering what would create the transformation she was dimly groping for. To her it seemed hopeless.

The thought that germinated earlier downstairs suddenly came to life. The jewels! Of course. She opened the center drawer of her dresser, took out a small key and springing to her feet, hurried downstairs to her father's old study. She still did the accounts there and locking the door behind her, she lifted down the painting of the mill, unlocked the safe, and opened the heavy little door. Inside, among documents and a metal cash-box was a small chest containing the gemstones.

It was late afternoon. Sunlight spilled across the desk, just like the first day her father had shown the jewels to her. She lifted a red velvet cloth out of the box, spread it on the desk, and poured the stones gently onto it from a chamois bag. Like tiny drops of rain glittering on a window, they sent a thousand sparkles of light dancing about the room. Catherine touched each gem, turning them over and spreading them about in a circle. There were well over a hundred gems in the mix of diamonds, emeralds, rubies, and sapphires and four large diamonds stood out boldly amongst them. The diamonds were curiously close in size and appeared to have a similar hue.

Her nerves began to tingle as she sorted these four and held each to the light. Starting with them she could create something spectacular, something extraordinary. A necklace! A queen's ransom to grace her lovely neck. *And I could be lovely*, she almost said aloud.

Ideas began to flash through Catherine's mind. Her sons. They would be the subject of the necklace, the concept and symbol. A design began to form in her mind and Catherine hastily pulled a piece of paper from the desk drawer and began a sketch. An hour later she was satisfied. All the sketch lacked was color. The necklace she had drawn would use most of the stones, and by the time a matching bracelet and earrings were made only a few would remain.

The necklace would be exquisite, and definitely expensive. Catherine folded her hands and looked out of the window. The sun was setting. Soon Elias and the boys would be back, clamoring for supper. Just thinking his name caused misgivings but Catherine faced her purpose squarely. She had fallen in love nine years ago; how, she really wasn't sure. Perhaps carnal desire had overwhelmed common sense. Now, in her steady and well-planned life, perhaps she once again needed something dangerous and extravagant. Something that spoke irresistibly to her senses again. She'd been in love with Elias before. Maybe it could happen again.

Catherine hoped what she was about to do might be a passport to a world where she and her husband might be partners of the mind as they had once been partners of the body in the early years of marriage. What, realistically, were her chances of success?

She considered the question soberly. As long as Elias had political aspirations, it was to his advantage to have a respectable marriage and family. This she had given him. She never needed to worry about his demanding a divorce, and because of her religious convictions she had never considered one either. Whether or not she could fall back in love seemed preposterous. Being an asset to Elias in Holbaek society was one thing, but how would she fare in Copenhagen? That would be another story. Well respected, she may move fairly easily in that layer of society. Would she even like living in Copenhagen? She was definitely not familiar with the elegant social currents in which Elias said he swam. Could she enter the turbulent waters and not make a fool of herself? A beautiful necklace and a new commitment to their marriage would give her initial confidence. But once involved, could she maintain? And could she make a practical, continuous contribution to her husband's political career?

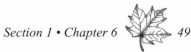

There was a third world to be conquered. And that was Elias's disorderly, sensual, self-indulgent world of drinking and mistresses. Could she ever forgive him? Even in the middle of the fairy tale she was planning, she sincerely doubted it.

But had he not returned to her? Yes and with a relatively decent attitude. She wondered how long it would last. Full time and meaningful employment could make the difference, and with the new constitution was there not the opportunity of political office for Elias? In fact there was. Adding it all together, the possibility for a renewed marital relationship existed. Catherine would do her part. The rest had to be up to Elias.

Resolutely, Catherine scooped the gemstones into their chamois bag. She prolonged Elias' self-serving courtship of her, this time entering seriously into political discussions and arguing theory with him. Although he considered her arguments as nonintellectual, and too emotional he found her grasp of politics remarkable. Here was common ground. Catherine and Elias held mutual distrust of the newly powerful Prussian Empire and both, like most Danes, were fiercely patriotic and very uneasy at the military giant lying at the border.

Catherine, for the first time since her marriage, opened her large house with its polished oak floors and clean bright rooms, to hostess social gatherings. Elias beamed proudly as the solid buergers of Holbaek with their equally solid wives came to eat exquisitely cooked food and stroll about the grounds, admiring the mill, farmyard and Catherine's brilliant late summer gardens. After one such social even the frosty Otto Pedersen smiled approvingly when they bade him goodnight, standing at their door with Elias's arm circling Catherine's waist in a proprietary manner.

Chapter 7

On Elias' next trip away Catherine summoned Gustav Hansen, one of Copenhagen's premier jewelers. Bushy eyebrows and kindly blue eyes, Gustav had served his apprenticeship in London with journeyman's stints in Belgium, Strasbourg, and Paris. Now in his late fifties, the jeweler had an impeccable reputation, a pair of experienced hands and an enviable clientele among who were certain members of the royal family. When Gustav peered through his jeweler's glass at the gemstones Catherine had gently poured on her father's old desk, his brow furrowed, his face flushed, and he started breathing heavily.

He said nothing until after he'd inspected the larger gemstones, then he learned back and took a deep breath. "These are incredible stones Fru Jensen. I've not seen their likes in decades. They are all high quality stones but these," he touched the four large diamonds he'd arranged in a row in front of him, "these are truly amazing."

With his tiny tongs, he picked up one of the stones and held it in the sunlight. "I've seen this heavenly bluish tint in diamonds only once . . . in the crown jewels. Those diamonds originated in India."

"The four large ones aside I've never seen such a hoard. It makes one wonder where on this wide earth they came from."

Catherine shrugged her shoulders. "Father never said. He did a lot of bartering; some of the gems are no doubt part of old Norse raids, but I know nothing of their exact history."

Gustav was staring again at the four large diamonds. "These are remarkably close in weight. Their rounded bevel is very old-fashioned. Cut properly, so that each facet is sharp and at the correct angle, their sparkle will most likely blind the eye." He winked at Catherine. "These four alone are worth a quarter of a million rigsdaler Fru Jensen. "

Catherine nodded calmly. "I want you to make me a necklace Hr. Hansen. An heirloom of detailed and prodigious work. I have a design in mind that will symbolize my family; the four large diamonds will be its main focus."

She pulled her sketch from the drawer and pointed out the parts as she talked. "The four diamonds represent my four sons. Like my love for my sons, rework the diamonds so they are identical, then place them in a setting surrounded by smaller diamonds and emeralds. The chain for the necklace should be made of gold and I want no clasp. I want it like a ring, the symbol of eternity. Make the chain large Hr Hansen, large enough to drape evenly about my neck and lie on my bosom. The chain will be of small oak leaves linked together to represent the years of my life. As no two oak leaves are just alike, neither were the years of my life. Each was different, each unique. Thirty-five years Hr Hansen and if you tell a soul you will lose your commission." They both smiled and she went on. "Like a dew drop, each leaf will have a small diamond at the end . . ."

"Nice touch," he said.

"And again, no two leaves exactly alike."

"I'll use the lost wax process Fru Jensen, and *real* leaves. When cast each will look as natural as life and no two exactly the same."

"Good" said Catherine, as she pointed to another part of her sketch, "Between each diamond, place long pendants of gold for ornamentation. Tears if you will. I've raised my sons in sorrow. Each pendant will bear a small ruby. The details I leave to you."

The jeweler rubbed his chin, his eyes intent upon the design. "It will be such a pleasure to create this work," he said enthusiastically. "Sheer pleasure."

"I will also want the oak leaf and diamond design for earrings and a bracelet," Catherine added.

"Of course, of course," said Hr Hansen.

"Now, as to your fee?"

"Gold will be my greatest expense Fru Jensen. I will need at least ten thousand rigsdalers to begin the project. The finished work will total near twenty."

"Agreed," said Catherine without the slightest hesitation, then added, "If I am pleased with the final result, there will also be a bonus."

One by one Catherine repackaged the gems, checking each from her inventory. Then she tied the drawstrings of the bag firmly, folded her sketch and handed both to Gustav. She then prepared a draft on her bank in Copenhagen for the stipulated advance and sent him on his way.

Torkil Olsen, following Catherine's explicit instructions to 'Strap a pistol beneath your coat. Hr Hansen is carrying valuables,' accompanied Gustav all the way to Roskilde where the jeweler caught a train for Copenhagen.

By the time he opened his shop the following week, Gustav Hansen was in love with Catherine's project. He distributed the other commissions and less important shop business to apprentices, then began in earnest. First and most critical was the work of cutting and polishing the gems. Some minor cleaving was necessary on the four large diamonds, and making them identical became an obsession with the jeweler. As he worked Gustav talked to the stones like a father to his children. "Not too much now, a little here, a little there. I won't hurt you . . ."

Oval shaped, the four diamonds would be 11.8 millimeters in diameter and 7.6 millimeters deep. *If one of them were to fracture, it would be a tragedy,* the jeweler thought as he wiped sweat from his brow. *There is no replacement on earth for any of them.* He cut the four diamonds in an exquisite `brilliant' design and polished them to perfection. Their pale blue clarity was like looking through a jeweler's glass.

"What joy working with such jewels as these," the experienced old man said under his breath. "I feel as if angels are guiding my hands." A project of this magnitude was something jewelers often dreamed. It wasn't his first but this one was for such a fine and generous lady.

When he was finished with the large diamonds Gustav was overjoyed to find all came within a fraction of weighing seven carats each. Turned to the light their now sharp and exquisite facets flashed like miniature sunbursts. The effect was breathtaking. The jeweler knew his trade.

Many of the smaller gems were given to apprentices' to cut and polish but the molds for mountings and the oak leaves Gustav prepared himself. He used real oak leaves to make his molds then labored delicately to clean each vein and stem of debris before sealing the top and bottom portion of the molds together. The workmen in the old shop scarcely dared speak to the master jeweler for fear of disturbing his concentration.

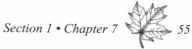

While all this was going on, Catherine made a trip to Copenhagen to visit Elias and to look in on the bushy-eyed jeweler's work. She made one or two small suggestions but no major changes.

In the small and steamy foundry behind his shop, Gustav looked like an ancient alchemist and his senses were keen as he prepared the gold alloy. Then with wood charcoal and a steady pumping of the bellows he brought it to the exact temperature; ladling off the molds with a steady hand. Cooled and opened, most molds presented a perfect leaf; those that did not were cleaned, sealed and re-poured. When there were enough oak leaves to represent the years of Catherine's life, each was buffed until it shined like sunlight.

At the same time the necklace was being made, the oak leaf bracelet and earrings Catherine had ordered were being crafted, each with a fastidious sprinkle of tiny jewels. But they were effortless compared to the intensity of the necklace. The five pendants were poured in long graceful drips, polished as sleek and smooth as rainwater then a three quarter carat ruby was placed in each pendant setting. A half-carat diamond was mounted upon each oak leaf, then pendants and leaves were fastened securely on the links of the chain. Placing the four `brilliant' cut diamonds into their mountings on the chain completed the work and when he was satisfied that each stay was secure, Gustav placed the necklace gently on a green velvet cloth on his desk near the front window of the shop. He stood motionless there for several minutes looking at it. Three of his workmen gathered in silent awe.

"The crown jewels would bow to this piece," one of them finally said.

Gustav nodded reverently, gazing at the work as though he had had nothing to do with it. "Yes," he said quietly. "It is magnificent."

The necklace was placed in his safe over the next two days but Gustav took it out often to feast his eyes on its glittery brilliance and to enjoy its fine craftsmanship. He had sent a telegram to Catherine, asking when she might expect delivery and acted thoroughly disappointed when word came back to come immediately. With that, the old jeweler reluctantly laid the necklace in a velvet lined rosewood box made especially for it, packed the box in his valise and boarded a train to Roskilde.

Catherine gasped and placed her hand above her bosom as Gustav opened the rosewood box. The gold leaves and chain of the necklace shined warm and exotic in the afternoon sun and each gem glittered with fire. Her reaction said it all and Gustav beamed with pride. "You have quite outdone yourself Hr Hansen," she said appreciatively. She did not speak again for a full minute as her eyes took in every detail. Catherine wondered if she had gone too far. *How can I wear such an astounding piece?* She asked herself silently.

At last she lifted her eyes to Gustav. "You've created a treasure my dear sir. As I requested, it's an heirloom, a tribute to my family. Oh that I had a daughter."

They spent half a day together drinking tea and eating pastry, recounting every detail of the creation. Then Gustav, and a burley coachman he had hired for protection, drove to Roskilde. An impressive bonus lined his pockets and Gustav was feeling very lighthearted on one hand yet oddly bereft on the other. *Back to routine,* he thought sadly.

As soon as the jewelers' carriage had disappeared from the driveway, Catherine went hastily to her room, locked the door and stripped off her dress. Clad only in her pale chemise, she delicately placed the necklace over her head. It glistened with a myriad of tiny lights against her skin, glowing and accenting her bosom. Her skin shivered at its touch, then warmed along with it and she had a sudden, vivid feeling of pride.

She looked at herself critically. The wreath of braids she so often

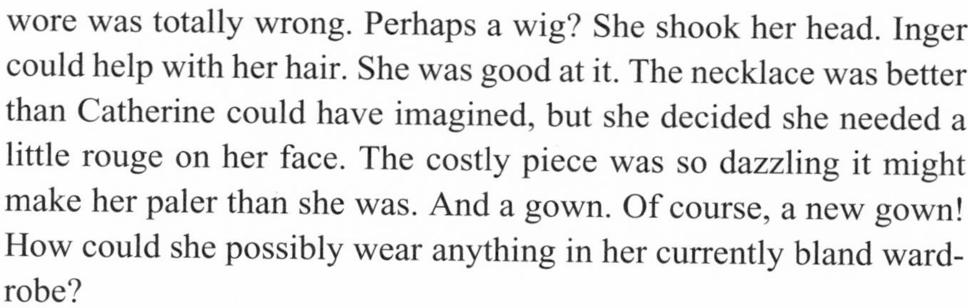

wore was totally wrong. Perhaps a wig? She shook her head. Inger could help with her hair. She was good at it. The necklace was better than Catherine could have imagined, but she decided she needed a little rouge on her face. The costly piece was so dazzling it might make her paler than she was. And a gown. Of course, a new gown! How could she possibly wear anything in her currently bland wardrobe?

For five years, Catherine had been a steady but undemanding client of Madame Merete, the best dressmaker in Holbaek. She had never lingered over decisions, simply calling by in the spring and fall to order, "Another dress. Perhaps indigo this time. Same style."

This winter, to Madame Merete's delight, Catherine had spent hours in her shop mulling over design sketches and illustrated Parisian papers. With her tiny, perfect hands the little seamstress showed Catherine sketch after sketch of what fashionable women were wearing in London and Copenhagen. Most enjoyable were the sketches of the Danish heroine Countess Danner, Madame Merete's most famous client. An obvious corset under the dress made the Countess' waist look tiny while lifting her breasts proudly. The dress had a high and lacy collar and was very distinctive but Catherine knew the effect would not work for her. She was as robust as the countess, but her shoulders and throat must be bare if she were to wear the necklace.

"Tell me about the jewelry you'll be wearing," the little seamstress said as if reading her mind. Catherine gave her the details of the necklace, earrings and bracelet and Madame Merete's eyes danced with approval. "From what you are telling me we need something very bold, and I think I have just the thing. Wait here." She ducked through the curtains of the back room and soon reappeared with a sample evening gown.

"A Polonaise design," she said placing the gown against Catherine's shoulders.

"I like it Madame," said Catherine hesitantly, "but don't you think it's a little too revealing?"

"Not at all Fru Jensen. It's an excellent choice for such a necklace as you describe. With your graceful neck and lovely shoulders it will be perfect . . ."

"I like it," said Catherine decisively. "Let's pick out the cloth and color." For the next half an hour the two women went through a large inventory of cloth from which Catherine finally chose a bolt of cream colored taffeta.

Madame Merete next had Catherine undress to her camisole and then walked around her broodingly. "Hummm . . . You must wear no less than three petticoats Catherine. The gown I'll create will transform you into a princess. It will be soft, layered and very lacy, with less than a yard of train. Yes, I think that will do it. Oh Fru Jensen this is exciting!"

Chapter 8

The spring of 1850 arrived verdant yet chilly. Winter had passed in a fever of political maneuverings with opposing parties grappling for power, and debating about the future of the country under the new constitution. King Fredrick's popularity with his people was unprecedented, but succession was currently a thorny problem. Fredrick VII was the last male in the Oldenburg dynasty, and three marriages had failed to produce a son. If the king was to die, and a foreigner assumed the throne, the country might lose everything it had gained. The ruling monarchs of Europe believed Denmark was in the middle of an experiment and perhaps a prelude to war.

"The situation with the duchies is a tinderbox," Casten Pedersen was telling Catherine as they met for lunch at a small outdoor café in Holbaek. "All it needs is a spark to ignite it."

"I'm sure you are right," said Catherine trying not to sound overly worried. "Meanwhile Prussia hovers restlessly on the borders." A balmy breeze brushed at their faces as the two women snacked at their sandwiches and sipped their coffee. It felt so relaxing to be out and away for a bit. Leaves on the trees that ringed the patio were of various pastels of green and gave the secure feel of a quiet forest.

"There are dangerous and fascinating issues occupying the minds of Denmark's newly liberated electorate," stated Casten knowledgeably in her usual direct manner. "Of our three emerging political parties, two hold similar beliefs; the National Liberals and the Society of Farmers Friends."

"Both parties support suffrage for *male* voters, freedom of speech and freedom of religion," said Catherine. "Am I correct?"

"You are," said Casten, "but one political party speaks for the poor and the other the rich, and as you know class distinction makes people suspicious of each other."

"Sad but true," agreed Catherine.

"There is hope to bring everybody together however," Casten continued excitedly, "before the Fall elections, my husband Otto and I are sponsoring a formal ball, right here in Holbaek. We are inviting prominent members the National Liberals, and the Friends of Farmers and their wives of course."

"What a grand idea," said Catherine but then she frowned. "Funny thing, but Elias hasn't mentioned it."

"Hummm," said Casten with a slight pained expression on her face. Then to maintain her positive mood added, "Otto thinks bringing the two more liberal parties together will insure the defeat of Conservative Party candidates in the coming elections."

"It does sound like a wonderful idea," said Catherine whose viewpoints aligned with those of the National Liberals, becoming mildly excited.

"Well," said Casten pleased that her friend Catherine wasn't too upset that Elias hadn't told her anything about the up and coming event, "the purse strings of the party treasury will soon open wide. A twelve-piece orchestra is coming from Copenhagen and a wealthy friend of Otto's named Palle Roskelle has offered his mansion."

"I know the Roskelles," said Catherine, "that is I know Elizabeth Roskelle . . . from church. But I've never been in her home."

"It is huge," Casten exclaimed. "On the second level is a marble-floored banquet hall lighted by fancy glittering gaslight chandeliers, and there's plenty of room for dancing."

"My," said Catherine taking a sip of her coffee, now cool from the breeze, while she watched a handsome young couple stroll past the café. "It sounds very nice."

"The mansion also has a lovely curving staircase," Casten went on, "and extra bedrooms where ladies can adjust their corsets, or even rest if necessary."

Catherine raised her eyebrows at that. She knew a few pampered ladies and didn't have too much patients for them. But sitting there watching people pass by and pondering what Casten had outlined, she knew the occasion had finally arrived to unveil her necklace. Without impatience, she would wait for Elias to announce the gala affair. One way or the other she was going. Meanwhile, there were preparations make. Shoes to buy.

"There's even a long balcony outside where men can drift off to enjoy their drinks and tobacco," Casten was saying, "and a spacious English-style billiard room where they can make their little deals . . ."

"Or talk about women and money," said Catherine with a wink. "With money taking preference." The two women laughed in spite of themselves.

Elias returned from Copenhagen four days before the ball but avoided Catherine completely the first day. "E' wants to be sure the latest French perfume 'as worn off," Inger said spitefully.

"Hold your tongue," said Catherine impatiently, but her rebuke betrayed inner fears that perhaps the dear little housekeeper was right on target.

At the breakfast table on the second day, Elias announced pompously, "there is to be a ball this Saturday evening my dear, a social gathering of Party members from principal cities including Copenhagen. The affair is to be held at the Roskelle's. I realize you have little interest in such things . . ." Catherine lifted her eyebrows. This after an entire winter of teas and dinners? The newest mistress must indeed have his undivided attention. "but it is necessary you attend with me."

"I've already heard reports of the ball," Catherine said stiffly. "I understand Countess Danner will be present," she added.

"Yes she will," said Elias haughtily.

"I can hardly believe it," said Catherine with a twinge of excitement. "Have you ever actually met her?"

"Ah," he coughed, "well no, no I haven't," Elias admitted defensively, knowing the truth would surely come out at the ball. He knew this did not look well after the many insinuations he'd made to suggest he was one of the Countess' inner circle. He cleared his throat in an effort to regain his phony composure. "The ball begins at nine," he said crossly, "and if you don't mind I'd like to be," clearing his throat, "punctual." The congenial attitude he had worn on his last visit had all but disappeared and Catherine felt a knot in her stomach.

"Have you ever known me to be late, Elias?" she returned irritably.

He made no reply then announced arrogantly. "I shall be in Holbaek for the rest of the day. Final preparations, my dear. We can't neglect a single detail. It is rumored that those who will represent the party in the Fall elections, will be informally selected at the ball. This could be the turning point for me."

"Perhaps a turning point for all of us," said Catherine serenely. She looked at him hopefully and detected the hint of a smile, or perhaps a suppression of a cough, maybe a smirk?

Saturday evening arrived and found Elias in top hat and tails, and pacing in the front room. "Hurry up, Catherine," he shouted up the stairway. "We'll be late."

The twins, Peter and Hans, peeped through the door leading to the kitchen where Inger had Ferdinand by the hand and Kristian in her arm to keep them quiet. Earlier she had arranged Catherine's hair, after Catherine had religiously visited the rain barrel and brushed dried it in the wind, then put it in a lovely pomp piled a-top her head so that her ears showed, and was held there by a long curved mother of pearl comb and hair pins. Catherine's bangs were curled and a silk flower was pinned to the right side of her head; which matched the colorful bouquet of flowers sewn along a seam in her dress. Inger was skillful! She had also applied powder, pinched her cheeks and lined Catherine's eyelids lightly with a charcoal pencil.

Inger had helped Catherine draw on silk stockings and put on her new high-heeled off white velvet shoes. She'd laced the corset, and helped Catherine step into the taffeta gown, drawing its straps over her shoulders, then buttoned the row of tiny buttons down the back. The gown's creamy off white color brought out the rosy tints in Catherine's skin. Her breasts rose roundly and velvety white next to the rich fabric. The ordeal of dressing had taken a full two hours.

The final touch came when Inger helped Catherine lift the necklace over her coiffure and position it upon her breast. Each gemstone was all a-sparkle, and each gold leaf gleamed like sunshine. Pulling the long gloves over her elbows, applying a light touch of perfume, fastening the earrings to her soft lobes, and latching the bracelet took only moments.

Catherine stared wordlessly at her radiant image in the mirror. She appeared queenly, a woman who had stepped out of a legend and into the present. "You are quite beautiful," said Inger with tears forming in her eyes.

Catherine only smiled. "Go downstairs now, Inger. Find my sons and tell Elias I'll be down in a moment."

Waiting now as she was, Inger felt her anger rise each time Elias bellowed but with Catherine's four sons clustered around her tittering quietly, she had to maintain composure for their sakes. She hushed the boys and prayed her mistress would hurry.

Just as Elias drew his breath for another roar, the door to Catherine's bedroom opened and she gracefully began her descent. Elias stopped pacing and his mouth fell open. His wife was exotic, glamorous, and virtually unrecognizable. Her face had been literally transformed. He had never seen her in a low-necked gown before and stared at her as if for the first time. He stared at the golden circle of jewels glistening like a million stars against her silky bare skin; where had they come from? And her dress, her hair! Catherine was as elegant as a queen. Indeed she appeared noble.

Could this be Catherine Jensen, his heretofore plain and efficient little wife? Elias should have been ecstatic, whereas he found himself baffled and completely out of sorts. He felt foolish. Next to her he knew he looked like an old schoolmaster and he was furious. She had completely upstaged him. *What in the world was she trying to prove?* he wondered angrily.

"You look like a prostitute, half-naked like that," he said loudly. "And where did you get that necklace?"

Inger drew in her breath with a sharp gasp. The boys froze. The twins weren't old enough to know what a "prostitute" was, but both could feel their mother's humiliation and anger and they were frightened. Even little Kristian trembled under the hideous tumult of his father's stupidity. Catherine paused momentarily. A shock like ice ran over her entire body, leaving her cold as stone but in complete control of her emotions. She took a deep breath. Elias had instantly answered her question about whether or not there would ever be a full partnership in this marriage. Whether there would ever be true love between them. Her smile became frosty, and she continued her descent, pausing again when her eyes were on a level with his.

"I believe you should keep comparisons to yourself, Elias," she said icily. "I doubt very much that party officials wish to know the extent of your acquaintances with half-naked women. Unless of course, you'd like me to mention it to them?"

His thoughts in turmoil, Elias was speechless. He hadn't meant what he'd said to her—yet he had. This was to be *his* night of triumph. Catherine would appear with him, then blend dutifully into the background while he conferred conspicuously with Otto Pedersen and other party notables. This glamorous creature would capture every eye. What would she say to the men who held his future in their hands? And what to their women?

Catherine descended the last two steps, gently moved him aside with the gloved hand and, in her elegantly draped gown, floated past him to the dining room. "Come here boys," she called to her sons. "Give me a kiss—but gently!"

Awestruck, her four offspring moved cautiously toward her. There were tears streaming down the twins' faces and Catherine wiped them and laid a finger on their lips before she stooped and kissed each of them gently. Ferdinand caroled, "Oh, Mama, you are so bee-you-tiful!" Inger lifted Kristian holding him so that his hug would not muss his mother's coiffure.

"Goodnight, my angels!" she whispered then turned and headed toward the door. Elias, puffing like an old train, stood helplessly by. His eyes were darting all over the room and in his anger and confusion he hadn't the faintest idea of what to do next.

Inger, her face brick red with fury, pushed past him and opened the front door for them. "Good night, Fru Jensen," she said, ignoring Elias completely. Coming to his senses, Elias jammed his top hat on his head and stalked out after Catherine; and as soon as he had crossed the threshold, Inger slammed the door with all her might. The windows in the front of the house shook. It was exactly what Catherine needed. She bit her lip to suppress a sudden urge of laughter and seated herself gracefully in the coach. Neither she nor Elias spoke the entire trip to Roskelle's mansion.

And now it was all over. What was to have been Elias' night of glory turned out to be Catherine's. The making of the necklace, her gown—all the preparation, and the ball itself. *Is that all there is to high society?* She wondered looking back on the evening. *The jostling for popularity, political position, power and money?* Catherine was so grateful for *her* world. As far as parties went, she would much rather be in the dusty old mill witnessing the millers process the loads of grain, making entries in already bulging ledgers, or paying bonuses, seeing her workmen off for the holidays and joining them in a toast for the new year when she opened up her house for their families each Christmas.

Reminiscing on the return trip in the darkness of the coach had hastily eaten up the miles between the Roskelle's mansion and home. The family coach was just entering the gates of the estate. The necklace and the ball had been an experiment, an exciting, and in many ways successful experiment. But it had all been so costly, and not just in terms of money.

At the house, Catherine left a staggering Elias to put himself to bed. When she put the necklace in its rosewood box and locked it in the safe, with it she locked away the last fragment of dreams for happiness in her marriage. She no longer held any illusions about Elias. All that remained was duty.

But there were her sons.

SECTION NOTES:

1. Countess Danner, third wife of the King Fredrick VI (Fredrick VI had ruled Denmark for 55 years) and a former ballerina and milliner, remained a prominent national figure even after the death of her husband.

2. Orla Lehmann an aggressive young lawyer and head of the National Liberal political party and his friend Ditlev Monrad were two progressive leaders largely responsible for the passage of the constitution not to mention a not so quiet rebellion among Danish citizenry.

3. The Ejder Programme was a policy, the adherents of which opposed the 'unified state' policy and wanted instead to incorporate the duchies, Slesvig into the kingdom of Denmark and break with Holstein and Lauenberg. Named for the river Ejder that formed the border between the Duchies of Slesvig and Holstein, the Ejder policy had the support of the Conservative Party and the National Liberal Party but knowing that it might bring hostilities from Prussia, Prince Christian of Glücksborg was decidedly against it. This policy constituted the main platform of the National Liberal Party.

4. During the lull in fighting, (battles during "the Three Years War" only took place in summer months) three distinct political groups which existed in Denmark, solidified: a conservative right, later calling itself The Conservative Party; consisting of large landowners, a center or moderate group; the National Liberal Party which consisted of well heeled city merchants, clerks and the like and a radical left; Elias Jensen's Society of Farmers Friends, liberal attorneys whose constituents were small farmers most of whom were uneducated.

Section Two

A Potpourri of People & Events

Chapter 9

As things went, the Society of Farmers Friends chose a shopkeeper named Søren Christophersen,[1] in their bid to represent Holbaek in the up and coming fall elections. Elias Jensen's efforts to ingratiate himself and trade on his "experience" in Copenhagen were ignored. He was deeply injured by the rejection of his party. Not only that, but when his term on the parish council, his second four year term, ended later that year he was told the party would no longer require his services in their Copenhagen office. Shattered by his ongoing run of bad luck Elias drank more heavily than ever and continued womanizing until his money nearly ran out.

Walking alone toward his upstairs apartment one humid morning after two days of steady drinking Elias picked up a copy of the Berlingske Tidende from a newspaper urchin and read the following;

"The Three Year's War is over!!!"

'*On July 25, in the year of our Lord 1850 some 40,000 Danish, including Swedish and Norwegian volunteers clashed along a three-mile front with 27,000 rebel forces at Isted Heath. Excluding minor scattered confrontations, the battle has ended in a decisive victory for*

Denmark!! Further; the resulting treaty has given Slesvig and Holstein back to the homeland!'

"That must have been what all the bell ringing in the churches last evening was about," he said to himself as he walked along and tried to clear his pounding head. He stopped for a moment, rubbed his eyes, took a deep breath and continued to read the detail. '*The fragile truce between Denmark and the rebel forces of Slesvig-Holstein, backed by volunteers from the neighboring German states including Prussia, ended in bloodshed. After rebel forces had surrounded the old fortress town of Frederica, Denmark's Federal Army bolstered by Swedish and Norwegian troops, launched a determined counter attack driving the rebels away and back toward Germany. Remarkably and at this writing not fully understood, Prussia had pulled its troops out of the war leaving the rebels to fend for themselves! Rebel casualties were high. Victory is ours, homeland morale is unprecedented, and the Viking spirit has returned to Scandinavia. Never before have the bonds of Denmark, Norway, and Sweden been stronger!'*

"It will not last," Elias said aloud. "Language barriers and prejudice toward Denmark is alive and well amongst the Slesvig rebels, and the question of absolute rule by Denmark's monarchy stands unresolved. They still want to govern themselves," he said as if anyone were listening to him. With that he threw his newspaper in the trash and continued down the empty street.

Out of touch with reality as he was Elias would prove right in what he had said to himself, nevertheless Denmark was about to enter an era of peace and prosperity that would last over a decade.

It was early November when the would-be politician cleaned out his desk in Copenhagen and took a train to Holbaek. Elias was out of money, very depressed, he had also picked up a nagging cough. The first week back he remained drunk and reclusive in a sick room Catherine had prepared where his coughing became incessant. The stench of vomit filled the upstairs rooms. Racking and steady coughing, Elias unnerved the household to a point of madness. In quiet desperation Catherine summoned W. H. Corneleas Mogensen, Holbaek's finest surgeon. The doctor quickly diagnosed the case as consumption—tuberculosis—the triumphant result of an immoral lifestyle.

"The signs are all there Fru Jensen: the fever, rash and nausea. His coughing . . . he must remain quarantined and everything he uses either boiled or else burned. And for heaven's sake cover your face before entering his room."

For the next two weeks Elias took little nutrition, only thin soups and plenty of wine. And Catherine indulged him. He could stay inebriated for the rest of his life for all she cared. The wine eased his coughing, helped him sleep and gave her household much needed relief. She followed doctor Mogensen's instructions explicitly. She and Inger masked themselves before taking in soup or medicine and boiled every stitch of clothing and the sheets Elias had touched. Throat rags were burned.

More than one doctor came and went, packing Elias in mustard plasters, feeding him herbs, or else letting his blood. Their potions and treatments alone should have killed him. After three weeks he'd become a rack of bones, totally debilitated but somehow he survived.

Elias was scarcely aware of the fact, but in a bedroom just down the hall from his, five-year-old son Kristian, had contracted a high fever, a hacking cough and was wasting away at a terrifying rate. Whether or not the boy contracted the disease from his father or from the doctors was anyone's guess, but in Kristian's case the tuberculosis became complicated with pneumonia. Day by day Catherine hovered over him in speechless agony but despite her tender care, the child died December 5th 1850. Through gigantic effort of will, Catherine did not cry out against God for taking her innocent and angelic son, leaving her deceptive and immoral husband behind. Instead she was deeply humbled by the incident and made certain vows.

"The Lord is my shepherd I shall not want," the minister began, "He maketh me to lie down in green pastures . . ." Gathered in the churchyard for the funeral were Catherine, her surviving sons; Hans, Peter and Ferdinand, also Inger Daryberg, Torkil Olsen, and five other employees from the mill and their wives—all dressed in black. Elias was still too weak to leave his room. A few members of Catherine's congregation, including Christa and Otto Pedersen, Elisabeth and Palle Roskelle had braved the freezing weather to pay their final respects.

Catherine barely heard the minister's words. In her injured state of mind, unsparingly she scored herself with the bitterest of condemnations. Her own pride and extravagance had caused Kristian's death or so she told herself. She had been caught up in making the necklace, wearing it, enjoying her triumph. and then daydreaming of other conquests. At the height of her pride and vainglory, God had reached out and put his blighting hand on the tender flower of her child.

"Surely Kristian succumbed to his illness that I might be brought to my knees," she had said earlier sharing her feelings with Inger as they were riding to the cemetery located behind the old Lutheran Church in Holbaek. "How else could I be taught the things that really matter in life? For months I've had my head filled with nonsense."

"You must not punish yourself in this way Fru Jensen," Inger had answered her solidly. "If God hadn't wanted the boy 'e'd still be here. Kristian was simply too good for this foul earth."

Catherine had turned restlessly in her seat, remembering. "He'd always needed extra care, Inger. He was such a frail child. But just before he got sick my thoughts were still upon the necklace and other parties, how I might bolster Elias, when I might wear *my* necklace again. How I'd wear *my* hair . . . and dresses . . . new dresses . . . trips to town . . ." she trailed off.

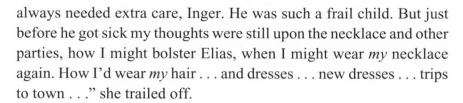

"Stop it!" Inger had shouted. "For the last time, Kristian's death was not your fault!"

"He leadeth me beside the still waters, he restoreth my soul . . ." Gusts of wind seemed to carry the minister's words and Catherine's thoughts away. Catherine's black veil flailed gently about her face as she stepped near Kristian's little casket. Tears streamed down her cheeks, her shoulders shook and she sobbed like a baby. She literally felt like dying. Part of her was being buried in the cold earth this day. Would she ever see her child again? Life was so cruel.

Torkil put his arm around her shoulders. "There, there now dear lady," his words were scarcely audible. "He's with the Father."

'How I wish Elias could be such a man,' Catherine thought bitterly as Torkil patted her shoulder gently. *'Shouldn't it be him with an arm around me? Whatever made me marry the man?'* She would need a man's strength in the weeks to come and Catherine's loneliness was suddenly so overwhelming she could scarcely bear it. Her eyes welled up red and angry. Elias had never been someone she could lean on and never would be.

Standing there she thanked God for her remaining sons and suddenly a softness came over her—a certain humility, and a willingness to let go of her burden. She slowly raised her veiled face toward the swirling and dark heavens. Without bitterness or accusation, in her mind she made a vow to God: *Father in Heaven,* her soul cried out poignantly. *I will be a better person. Any worldly plans I've ever entertained are done away. Any thoughts of parties or pleasure are gone. You have taken my little Kristian but please* . . . her gloved hands tightened into little fists, *please dear God, spare my remaining sons. Spare them the illness that took their brother.*

Catherine continued her silent prayer with remarkable clarity and fervent concentration. *Father, I pray you, if you spare them, I covenant with thee, that I will live for others. I will be more charitable to the poor. Do more for my workmen to make their lives better, and I will care for Elias. Without flinching, no matter what demands he makes, I'll be a dutiful wife. I will teach my sons to serve thee, this I promise.*

"In the sacred names of the Father, Son, and Holy Ghost. Amen," the minister said solemnly. Catherine was suddenly aware of her surroundings. She was chilled to the bone, yet her cheeks felt hot, raw from tears and the cutting wind. But her soul was resolute, alive and determined, refreshed from fervent prayer. Her lips began to tremble and her teeth chattered slightly and she had to repress a wild impulse to open the casket, take her son to her breast and once again give him life. Instead she stepped forward and calmly placed a handful of earth upon the little vessel then turned to face the people who were moving past her, touching her hands and offering sympathy.

When the last person walked by, Catherine quietly gathered her sons whereupon they made their way to the coach. Along with Inger they huddled together, tears coursing down all their faces. Torkil Olsen climbed to the driver's seat, and under his encouragement a team of black horses pulled the carriage homeward.

The days that followed were quiet ones at the large old house. School was in recess for the holidays and the twins clustered together in the nursery, talking in low voices. Inger lured them into the kitchen with Christmas cakes and an almost defiant cheerfulness that did them much good. Catherine remained in mourning. She took meals with her sons, held lengthy prayers and read the Bible to them at night. She gave short lessons on their duty to God and most important of all she loved them. Embraced them. She spent hours on her knees praying, resolutely mastering her grief over Kristian. Every day she cheerlessly but dutifully nursed Elias, who whined and complained, but gloried in Catherine's attention.

Christmas with all the bright colors, pastries and gifts that normally attended the Jensen household may not have happened at all had not Inger taken charge. She worked quickly and unobtrusively, and the occasion turned out festive despite the stifling restraint in the house. Though they felt the sadness over their brother when they stopped to think about it, Hans, Peter and Ferdinand were too busy being boys to let their sadness linger.

The bitter months from January through March were quiet at the mill. The holding pond was frozen solid, to the delight of the boys, who made figure eights on the ice or battled with sticks for a wooden puck. They skated wildly about, while the mill, like an old prisoner behind crystal bars watched them through the icicles drooping from its windows. The mill, rustic and picturesque as it stood in the snow, was like its owner, in a season of repose. A season of healing.

Like the doctors who attended Elias, traveling millwrights appeared at the mill during the winter months and dressed the millstones, made necessary repairs to gearing and wind-wings, and changed out the silk bolting. Verdant March winds caused the ice to all but disappear and farmers brought in the last of their grain, holding back just enough for planting should the seeds already in the soil fail to sprout. Slowly, ever so gradually spring leaves unfurled on the trees, tender green grasses furred the brownish ground and Catherine was once again seen walking about the estate. Tending to this, seeing to that, and it wasn't long before she was back in charge. Workmen plowed her fields and planted hay and several acres of wheat, while Catherine set to work turning the soil for a small vegetable garden and a few flower beds. For the first time since the previous June, she inspected the mill's books.

Torkil Olsen had a good head for business and had kept the mill running during Catherine's absence—her support of Elias' political aspirations and then during her mourning over Kristian's death—and in the final battles of the Slesvig wars Torkil dealt directly with government agents providing grist for horses and flour for the soldier's bread. Now the ever faithful miller had the wisdom to step aside as once again his employer took hold of the reigns. The outbursts of tears had slackened, and gradually Catherine was reading stories to Ferdinand again and helping the twins with their studies. The strongest sign of her recovery was when she spoke of Kristian occasionally. Their mother's improvement was a great relief to the boys and soon all three were rollicking about the house. Fun and laughter were again a part of life expressed freely and without guilt.

Through it all Catherine never neglected Elias. She spent an hour every morning and one each afternoon with him, coaxing hot soup and bread into him, bringing him books, reading the Bible and newspapers to him, and listening patiently as he rambled about politics.

That summer Catherine also gave Peter and Hans a colt and watched as Nils Holsen helped them train the animals. Life around the Jensen estate returned to a semblance of normalcy. Catherine, as always, was serene and far seeing. (Her spirituality had increased mightily over the ordeal of Kristian's death and was rounded out by physical improvement brought on by her work in her gardens, her service to her family and her employees, all encompassed in an organized routine.)

Chapter 10

The next few years around the Jensen household saw Catherine's sons broaden their horizons. At twelve years of age Peter and Hans entered Herlufsholm, an exclusive school attended by children of well-to-do parents and those of nobility. Three years later Ferdinand would also enter the school but although the school had an impeccable record Catherine insisted upon a tour.

"You see Fru Jensen," said Katrine Castensdatter, wife of the school's Headmaster, "the complex of Herlufsholm was originally centered around an old castle, built in 600 A.D., and a large four sided monastery called Skovkloster, or Monastery in the Woods built here in 1135. At one time the monastery housed 30 Benedictine Monks, their servants, and laborers."

"That certainly provided enough room for today's students Fru Castensdatter," observed Catherine.

"Yes, well, then on May 23, 1565 a childless couple, Herluf Trolle, Admiral for the Royal Danish Fleet and his wife, Brigitte Goye, officially established Herlufsholm as a school. But exactly twelve days after its charter, Hr Trolle was mortally wounded as a participant in a Danish Navy battle with the Swedish Fleet and died."

"My," said Catherine, "it's a wonder the institution survived."

"It survived through the valiant efforts of Brigitte," boasted Katrine Castensdatter. "And do you know, evidence of some of the school's most famous students remains carved in its benches to this very day. Let me show you!"

The two women wandered through a musty smelling, colored glass lit chapel and there carved in some of its wooden benches Fru Castensdatter pointed out names such as: poet\writer Knud Lyhne Rahber, a student in 1775 and contemporary of N. F. S. Grundtvig. World renowned sculptor, Bertel Thorvaldsen, physicist H.C. Ørsted, discoverer of electromagnetism, greatest Danish poet of the nineteenth century, Adam Gottlob Oehlenschläger author of The Gold Horns and novelist B. S. Ingemann.

There were others. Names Catherine was not at all familiar with but trusted were important people, because her guide said so. "Even great men were once boys," she mused as they next entered a large but cozy classroom with wooden floors, desks and windows pouring with sunshine. "But I don't demand that my sons to become great . . . only well educated."

"That will happen here Fru Jensen, our instructors are among the finest in Denmark!"

"I'm sure of it," said Catherine.

"Up there is where the Headmaster and I are housed," said the prim little woman as they wandered into a courtyard and gazed upon a quaint two story brownstone building. Catherine wondered why she had yet to use her husband's name. *Very knowledgeable, but certainly an odd little thing,* she thought.

"On the northern part of our campus and on the east are a few medieval buildings," Fru Castensdatter continued as they left the area. "A number of arched rooms grace the school's architecture including a hall from the middle of the thirteenth century. Let me show you."

They traversed a long pathway lined with bricked columns and decorative arches. "Beautiful," exclaimed Catherine, "and there too." She had pointed to a building then a columned walkway near the Klostergarden with eight gothic arched sections which formed a room and provided a very unusual, atrium-like, lighting effect.

"In 1812 that huge brick building over there, it was once used for cattle and to store hay, was remodeled into dormitories," the lady continued. "That is where your sons will spend many a month with their heads buried in books, especially the Holy Bible"

"Now I am hearing what I came for," said Catherine seriously. "Spiritual and mental discipline is what Peter and Hans need. They are both so . . . well so unbridled. Hans especially. I pray this institution can channel some of his energy into things of a higher nature!" Catherine hadn't realized the energy *she* had put into the statement but noticed her guide was smiling.

As they talked, they were walking along a road which was lined with trees and which completely surrounded the school. "There are lakes nearby," Fru Castensdatter pointed out, "and a moat still surrounds the castle. There is also a brook which passes through five arched columns under the main entry bridge."

It was indeed a lovely campus. Spacious lawns, kept trim by a few goats and a full time groundskeeper, and ivy covered brick buildings scattered about which gave the place all the atmosphere of a large English University.

"Nowhere in Denmark is as rich in history and tradition as Herlufsholm Fru Jensen. Every year on January 14, our pupils put on the official school uniform, with Brigitte Goye's shield of armor on the left pocket, and file by her grave."

"That is impressive," said Catherine not too impressed, "what about extra curricular activities?"

"Well," said the little lady, "we have horseback riding, fodbold, —soccer—gymnastics and handball. Summer activities include row boating, sailing . . . and in winter there's a huge frozen pond two hundred meters from the complex which looks like an ant bed as skaters dart about. Some of our students strap on their skates in the morning and don't take them off until dark!"

Fru Castensdatter did make it sound wonderful and in truth Herlufsholm was a fine school. With little other than sports to distract them, and long hours devoted to study it seemed very ridged, but late in the evenings, time was also there for conversation on matters important to a boy's mind. Matters such as: body hair, the size of one's biceps and shoulders, and of course talk of life's greatest wonder, the mystery of all men and boys . . . the female of the species. Shy fellows hovered at the perimeter of such conversations, their hearts pounding, their ears pricked and their minds on the alert.

There was also wrestling at night. Talk of females and other serious matters, brought out the beast in the young men and soon the dormitory rocked and swayed with perspiring bodies slamming into walls or rolled up in knots writhing upon the floor trying to pin each other's shoulders to the wood.

Catherine was satisfied with her tour, especially after hearing that most of the school's instructors were Lutheran Priests, and so Hans and Peter Jensen began what would prove to be an excellent education, one that truly would bless their lives.

Peter, though occasionally homesick, thoroughly enjoyed school. Everything about it: wrestling, soccer, ice hockey, but especially reading and drawing. A drafting instructor named Polottski, a balding man with the light in his eyes shining forth through thick spectacles, opened Peter's mind to the expansive world of architecture. Hr

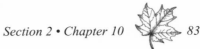

Polottski, a Jew from Latvia, was himself a draftsman\architect and before deciding to spend his twilight years teaching, had designed churches and homes and a huge textile mill in Copenhagen. Before the first year ended Polottski had his star pupil's head swimming with ideas. The walls near Peter's bed were covered with drawings of gristmills, churches, and houses.

But beyond this Catherine had spaded the garden of Peter's mind and harrowed the clods. Seeds of religion found fertile soil in which to grow. Sunday's sermons were highlighted with long robes, candles and light streaming through the colorful cut glass murals of Christ and the apostles in the windows on either side of the school's chapel. School days also brought the lectures of Arne Hammergaard, an elderly and wise Lutheran minister. He talked of: arks, lion's dens, slave's Exodus, Moses and other prophets came alive in Hammergaard's classroom. But Peter's favorites were stories of: a babe in Bethlehem, a young boy teaching the Elders in the Temple and then at maturity, his ministering to the people, healing the sick, the lame, cleansing Lepers and giving sight to the blind. Many nights when classmates were fast asleep Peter; sat in the library, an open Bible before him, a lamp lit, and his mind burning brightly.

Though he attended the same classes, slept in the same dorms, haunted the same buildings and romped the same campus, the impression Herlufsholm left upon Hans Jensen was entirely different from that of his twin brother. Only five kilometers from the Herlufsholm complex was a large army garrison. Soldiers in gray, blue and red uniforms, bedecked with tassels, brass buttons and snug collars frequently marched past the school on their way to maneuvers. Whether in classes or outside playing soccer Hans always stopped to watch.

The colorful banners, gleaming swords, polished muskets and pointed helmets shining in the sun; and furling proudly at the front of each procession, the mighty Dannebrog, the oldest flag on earth. With its crimson background representing the blood of Christ and its bold white cross, the flag was a thing of great pride to Hans. Whether outside playing soccer or otherwise engaged with friends, he always stopped to watch. He was especially awed with the massive cannons trundling along, their wheels cutting ruts in the ground, accompanied by mounted companies of cavalry.

All this plus being constantly surrounded by the ancient castles and the outbuildings of Herlufsholm stirred something in his soul. There were strict rules governing military and education, and Hans loved the order that came with them. At Herlufsholm, like in the army garrison, everything was orderly; and punishment for breaking rules ranged from beatings to confinement to expulsion.

Where some of his classmates resisted strict discipline and order, Hans reveled in it. The last thing Catherine Jensen might have expected from a snobby realm of higher education such as Herlufsholm was a military influence upon her son. Even so that is exactly what happened.

During their summer vacations from school, Peter, Hans and eventually Ferdinand also served an apprenticeship at the family's gristmill. "I'll not have any of you growing up not knowing a trade," Catherine told them at the beginning. "You will report to Torkil and do whatever he assigns you. There will be no favors shown just because you're my sons. At first you'll be sewing sacks, sweeping up and other menial tasks. Then as time goes by you'll learn all about the grades of flour and feed, how the smutter and bolting machines work and so forth."

"I will personally teach you how to keep the ledgers and deal with farmers and grain brokers but if you watch Torkil carefully you'll learn how to treat the workers. There's much more to milling than meets the eye but if you learn it, and learn it well you will always have something to fall back on."

The Jensen mill was an imposing structure and could be seen for several miles. Driven by wind-wings, its two runs of stone were remarkably efficient. One run was for milling cattle and pig feeds, the space between its bed stone and runner stone adjusted accordingly. The other run of stone was for flour; coarse brown flour popular among the poor, and also the expensive light, finely ground and sifted white flour used for delicate Danish pastries. As was mentioned, the mill also had an auxiliary holding pond and millrace to drive the machinery on rare days when the wind wasn't blowing.

Peter and Hans were by no means strangers to the mill. They had been in and around the place ever since they were children. But their apprenticeship taught them to respect hard labor rather than fear it, and by the time they were 15 both boys had legs and arms as solid and thick as oak limbs. Both handled hundred pound sacks of flour like pillows.

There was a comforting and secure feel to the mill. A feeling of industry. There were sweet tastes and smells in the air and the soft feel of warm flour spewing from the millstones. And noise! During a run of dried corn, a person could yell at the top of their lungs and be inaudible to someone standing right next to them! Lips moving, little understood. The roar of the stones at the beginning of a run of wheat wasn't near so loud as corn, and there was something very satisfying about the steady "whifting" sound when a second pass of flour was in process.

Bounteous harvests were processed at the Jensen mill with relative efficiency. Wagon after wagon laden with golden grains came creaking up the road to the mill, then others, equally laden with sacks of finished product went creaking away.

Peter, the most sensitive of the three brothers saw the hand of

God in it all. To him the mill represented life, nourishment for people and animals, and income for workers. The mill employed six regular men and depending upon the season up to twenty part-timers. Unseen hundreds also benefited; persons at the looms in textile mills making cloth for meal and flour sacks. Farmers, laborers, brokers, merchants, shippers of grain, feed and flour and a host of others. Commerce in the truest sense of the word, gristmills stood at the heart of 19th century society and young, as he was Peter instinctively knew it.

Even though of a serious nature, during his apprenticeship Peter was as much in the middle of horseplay and contests as his dark-haired fun loving brother, Hans. It was they who climbed the ladder to place hundred pound sacks of flour on workers backs during "stacking," a game designed to buckle the knees. On a good day Torkil Olsen could hold up to twelve sacks but Jens Hedemann, a farmer as stout as an ox, held the record at fifteen. Other contests included catching hundred pound sacks of flour dropped from the top story window of the mill; a missed sack created a large circle of brownish white on the ground, a choking participant and gales of laughter. There were also sack races. Some way or another Peter as well as Hans participated in most everything.

Just as he did at Herlufsholm, Hans looked at the situation at the mill entirely differently than Peter. At breaks he'd sit with the men and listen while they boasted of the women they had known, brawls they'd been in, horses they had tamed and of course battle, as most had served in the Slesvig wars. The scar on Torkil Olsen's face would redden and his eyes would blaze as glorious stories of Prussian troops in full retreat tumbled from his mouth. Hans hung upon their every word.

Hans was assertive and proud of the rippling physique hard work had given him. Being amongst the workmen gave him benchmarks to compare with. Some said he was already as strong as Mons Krabbe a young journeyman from Odense and Torkil bet ten skillings Hans could throw Mons in wrestling. The match had yet to take place.

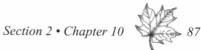

Lithe but not so physically strong as Peter and especially Hans, Ferdinand had similar experiences to his brothers while working at the mill but he shied away from physical labor. Foremost in his young mind was the money he saw produced and he was drawn to the mill's books like a moth to light. Catherine marveled at his quickness with numbers. The gift came from her and she took pride in it but Catherine felt a shadow hanging about her youngest son. Ferdinand was a stark contrast to his adventurous brothers. He stayed to himself most of the time, disliked the out-of-doors and exhibited a steely coolness regarding the mill's operation that made the workers feel a bit uneasy. What would it be like to work for him one day? Unlike his brothers, Ferdinand had cold blue eyes, light blonde hair and lean facial features that became more chiseled with age.

As a mother Catherine was justly proud of Ferdinand but his shrewd ways and intimidating manner were both stark reminders of Elias. Ferdinand was cunning, and had a propensity to manipulate people. Unless he wanted something he was not normally warm or very talkative. Unfriendly best described him. Perhaps the death of Kristian played cold upon his heart. That's what Catherine chose to believe anyway. But there was something else, and it had only cropped up recently. Ferdinand, though a studious reader, lately he purposely avoided the Bible. Even when Catherine read the beloved book aloud to the family she saw disregard and lack of interest register in her youngest son's eyes.

"I don't believe Christ really walked on water mother," Ferdinand openly announced one night at the dinner table. Catherine had just read about the incident in the 14th chapter of Matthew. "Or that he raised the dead for that matter."

"Or gave sight to the blind, little brother?" Peter chided.

"Those stories are just symbolism," scoffed Ferdinand using a word new to him. "Fairy-tales."

"Well I don't agree with you," said Catherine, shocked. "They were actual happenings. In fact Christ performed many more miracles than are recorded. The apostle John said it would take volumes to cover what he did."

"That man Peder Dalgaard you hired last month has filled his head with nonsense mother," Hans spoke up.

"He hasn't either," declared Ferdinand.

"He says the Bible is only symbolism. Like Noah and the Ark is just a story of how rain washes the earth clean."

"My," said Catherine.

"And you should hear the man, mother." Peter said over-riding his younger brother, who was about to speak. "His talk is dirty."

"I think he's funny," defended Ferdinand.

"How would you like it if mother heard the story he was telling you today?" Peter retorted sharply.

"Its just part of working at a mill," said Catherine defending that particular charge. "I heard much the same when I was a girl. I think that's why I married so late in life," she added heavily. "Men scared me."

"If I owned the mill, I wouldn't allow dirty language," said the idealistic Peter. "I'd fire anyone who used it."

"You wouldn't mill much flour," said Hans knowingly. "Every man who works there has a filthy mouth."

"Not Torkil," defended Peter.

"Did you know he fought in the Great War, mother?" said Hans excitedly. "In the battle of Fredericia, he led an entire company!"

"I think he was just a soldier," commented Catherine mildly.

"He said he was a Kaptajn," argued Hans.

Catherine just shook her head. "Isn't he supposed to be teaching you boys about grain and milling? I must have a talk with him."

The stigma of Ferdinand doubting the teachings of Christ lingered as Catherine sat in her room later that evening sipping a cup of tea. She couldn't understand why he didn't stand up for what she had taught him instead of caving in to the first wind of falsehood that came along. Hadn't she taught him those stories herself? And didn't he attend church right along with his brothers where Bible teachings were amplified? Hadn't she always taught him to pray? Maybe his working at the mill wasn't such a good idea after all. People like the new man certainly didn't help matters. "But I can't fire Hr Dalgaard just for being an atheist," she said aloud. "He's a good worker. And there are atheists everywhere. Even at Herlufsholm. All I can do is teach Ferdinand the truths of the scriptures. Whether he accepts or not must be his decision."

Catherine turned down her lamp and got into bed and as she lay looking at the ceiling, her thoughts turned to the mill. There in the forefront was Torkil Olsen, strong and wise, standing near the machinery and the millstones, overseeing the workings of the mill. His kindly eyes seemed to be upon all three of her sons. Thank heaven for his example she thought as she dozed off to sleep. "Where would the world be without such men?"

Besides being a noble example of manhood, Torkil *was* teaching Catherine's sons the miller's trade. By the last year of their apprenticeship they knew how to produce everything from fine white flour to the coarse utility blends and meal. They also knew the fine points of milling, such as how to balance the speed of the stones with the state of the grain so as not to scorch the flour, and what to do when flour would smear or ball up. How to repair the sifters, adjust the belts, work the gates and most importantly how to read the condition of the millstones.

The schooling and apprentice years weren't all work for Peter, Hans and Ferdinand. There were scheduled holidays at the seashore and visits to Roskilde where Catherine's aging aunt lived. And every other year the family took a week's stay in Copenhagen to visit art museums, the theater and to take in the bustling international flavor of Denmark's capital city. Catherine also allowed her sons time to roam the countryside of Holbaek. Time to fish in nearby ponds and streams, and time for camping in the forests with Torkil Olsen and his sons Emil and Paul. Catherine was a natural at mothering boys. She knew their needs before they did and often wondered what she'd ever have done with a girl.

"Horses need to run," she was telling Elias as she looked out the window watching the twins race about on their horses one afternoon in 1860. "Young mustangs too," she added making sure Elias caught her meaning.

"It's the Sabbath Catherine," her husband commented piously, sourly. "The Lord's day of rest. And the twins never sit with me when they're home," he complained further. "The first person they go to see is Torkil Olsen. Then they're either hunting in the forests with him and his sons or heaven knows what else."

"We see them at meals," said Catherine automatically, exhaustion tugging at her. The past few weeks Elias had been very demanding. She poured some herb tea in a cup and mixed in a spoonful of wild honey. "Here, Elias," she said as she had on hundreds of occasions. "Let me prop your head up."

"Thank God Ferdinand isn't like them," said Elias, sipping the mild brew, then pushing it away to cough. "He likes his books. You know Catherine, I see him as a lawyer. Stalking the courts . . ."

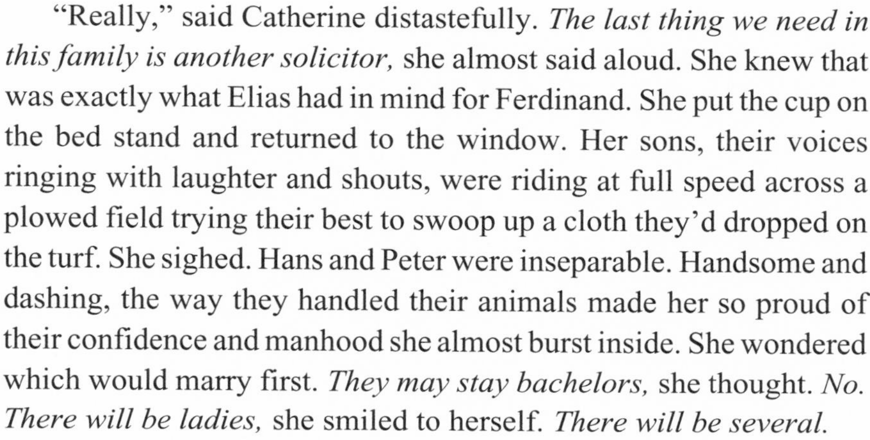

"Really," said Catherine distastefully. *The last thing we need in this family is another solicitor,* she almost said aloud. She knew that was exactly what Elias had in mind for Ferdinand. She put the cup on the bed stand and returned to the window. Her sons, their voices ringing with laughter and shouts, were riding at full speed across a plowed field trying their best to swoop up a cloth they'd dropped on the turf. She sighed. Hans and Peter were inseparable. Handsome and dashing, the way they handled their animals made her so proud of their confidence and manhood she almost burst inside. She wondered which would marry first. *They may stay bachelors,* she thought. *No. There will be ladies,* she smiled to herself. *There will be several.*

Catherine looked down at Elias and shook her head. His latest malady had been a boil under his arm. She'd drawn out the head and the gathering with poultices and the redness was greatly diminished; yet he lay as if he was dying. That year her patient nursing had finally born fruit and Elias' tuberculosis had been declared cured by the doctors. He had even moved back into Catherine's bedroom.

Ironically, Elias believed it was God, and not Catherine who had healed him. And Catherine accepted it without question, as Elias had become somewhat of a religious fanatic. His blazing zealotry was as different from her quiet faith as his earlier political enthusiasms had differed from Catherine's intelligent love of common sense and practicality. Tending to her family, mill and garden she was as down to earth as Elias was up in the clouds.

Chapter 11

It was the summer of 1860 and Peter and Hans had finished up at Herlufsholm. Things were busy at the mill and the Jensen estate, and life seemed full of anticipation. It was a time when Denmark was impatiently moving forward under its new constitution. Trade, commerce and education were rapidly expanding, and in no other place in the world, except perhaps England and the United States of America, was the light of religion burning more intensely. For decades the biased views of the Statskirken[2] (State Church) had constricted the religious viewpoint of the Danes. Now their new constitution granted freedom of religion, and there was a curious stirring in Denmark. New light concerning God and Christ was virtually flooding the country and behind the head-gates were two major reservoirs of knowledge; the teachings of Nikola Frederik Severin Grundtvig (1783–1872) a clergyman\poet, whose folk high school movement would eventually revolutionize Danish education; and the prolific writings of Søren Kierkegaard,[3] (1813–1855) a recently deceased philosopher.

Concerning our Lord Jesus Christ the writings of Kierkegaard had stirred the souls of Danish society like none before or since. As more and more Danes became literate they found in Kierkegaard's witty and deeply challenging themes due cause for personal introspection and change. Called a genius by some, a devil by others, Søren Kierkegaard stirred Denmark out of the religious stupor imposed by centuries of religious ceremony void of true Christian teachings. A gifted philosopher, his passionate attacks upon established thinking and official Christendom, had left men of the cloth and their congregations squirming in the pews.

"Some say Kierkegaard was as handsome as he was gifted," said Casten Pedersen as she, Catherine Jensen and Elisabeth Roskelle sat for tea at the latter woman's mansion. The three women, each in their own light were women among Holbaek's educated elite. Casten, wife of politician Otto Pedersen was the daughter of a Lutheran Minister and like the wealthy Elisabeth Roskelle and Catherine Jensen had been home taught. Having become good friends and very comfortable in each other's company they often came together for lunch or tea, stimulating conversation and companionship.

"He was both handsome and gifted," Elisabeth declared. "Palle and I once dined in the same restaurant with him. He was only two tables away. He was thin, had prominent cheek bones, a dominant nose and sported thick wavy hair which was combed back and resembled a wild bush in the wind."

Catherine smiled openly. She found slender men attractive, but never mentioned Elias as a comparison. "Looks aside, he was certainly profound," she said. "My father often quoted him. He also agreed with him, especially where Kierkegaard decried candles, incense and celibacy. He called them left over trappings of paganism."

"Hr Kierkegaard and my father despised the narrow doctrine of Grace as the *only* saving factor of humanity," Catherine went on. "Not to minimize the crucial importance of Grace mind you . . ."

"We understand," interrupted Elisabeth as was her habit. Elisabeth was sixty, a mite plump and always wore expensive rings and other jewelry. “Kierkegaard taught that along with Grace man’s actions play a vital role in his salvation. Like me, he believed we are totally responsible for our actions, what we say, and even for what we think!”

Casten Pedersen, a lovely blonde about the same age and build as Catherine was an avid reader of the controversial philosopher’s works and chimed in a powerful Kierkegaard theme. “He also taught that ‘some ministers and so-called thinkers, teach that guilt is a thing to avoid,’ and I quote “they say guilt is a thing harmful; but I believe guilt is a necessary condition in human existence. Guilt is God-given and painfully reminds us of our sinful ways. Guilt sometimes humbles us to our toenails and eventually inspires us to action. As dark and harsh as it sometimes is, guilt can set human beings on a course toward repentance and more noble aims.”

“Well said Casten,” Elisabeth Roskelle decried. “On my desk is a pamphlet Kierkegaard wrote, one that I’d now like you to read from. You know these old eyes.”

Elisabeth went to her desk and when she returned, Casten took the document from the wealthy lady’s aging yet dainty hands. “Right there,” said Elisabeth pointing to paragraph with brackets on either side.

Casten mockingly cleared her throat and stood to read. Lacy white curtains draping elegantly on either side of three wide rows of windows in the dining room gave a stage like back-drop with plenty of lighting. Casten wasn’t really showing off, just a bit tired of sitting. “What Christianity needs,” she began, “is not the stifling protection of the state. Ah but no, it needs fresh air, it needs persecution and . . . the protection of God. The state does only mischief in averting persecution and surely is not the medium through which God’s protection can be conducted. Whatever you do . . . save

Christianity from the state, for with its protection it overlies Christianity like a fat woman overlying her child with her carcass . . ."

"My!" exclaimed Catherine shaking her head. "He certainly was angry with church leaders."

With that Casten sat down again surrounded by Elisabeth's fine crystal and polished silver and poured herself a little more tea, stirring in just half a teaspoonful of sugar.

"And they with him," agreed Elisabeth with a wry smile.

"I heard that during his most prolific years, church outcry forced him to create the illusion he had actually stopped writing!" said Casten taking over again. "His facade included hanging leisurely about the streets of Copenhagen, strolling along popular canals with an open book in hand . . ."

"That was all true," interrupted Elisabeth. "One could see him at Kehlets, (a well-known café in Copenhagen) drinking tea and nibbling cake. And he always made it a point to stroll past the offices of The Berlingske Tidende, our most prominent newspaper as if he hadn't a thing in the world to do." Elisabeth's eyes narrowed as she spoke more seriously to her friends. "But evenings found him back at the desk in his apartment burning the midnight oil, putting words on paper. His fiery and unquenchable pen produced twenty-seven volumes of philosophy before his untimely death at age of forty two." Her saucer rattled as she took a sip of tea, set her cup down and took a deep breath.

"In addition to his books there are hundreds of papers and pamphlets," she added. "His passionate opinion and his sharp wit have made him a Danish folk hero."

"He was one of the great thinkers of our day," mused Casten. "Before his and N.F.S. Grundtvig's influence the church had a powerful grip upon the minds of our citizens, but it seems to me that grip is slipping, especially amongst our youth."

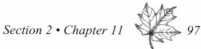

"I can already see that in my Hans and Peter," injected Catherine. "They are readying themselves for university studies and both exhibit free thinking where religion is concerned . . . anything but the Statskirken status quo. I'm not saying they're turning against the church mind you . . ."

"But perhaps the likes of Kierkegaard have opened their minds," Elisabeth finished for her.

"Perhaps," agreed Catherine.

Chapter 12

"So it's architecture you want is it Peter?" Catherine asked after Elias had finished a prayer the length of which had put a chill on the sumptuous baked ham Inger had prepared for dinner.

"Yes mother," Peter said without hesitation. Elias scowled and coughed fretfully, while Catherine smiled warmly at her son. She'd seen Peter's drawings and heard him talk often of Hr Polottski.

"Our mill has been my inspiration," Peter went on.

Catherine looked surprised and very pleased "Our mill?" asked Catherine.

"That's right mother," Peter said assertively. "It's a fine old building and when I began my apprenticeship I couldn't see anything wrong with its layout."

"There's still nothing wrong with its layout," interjected Elias peevishly, and then stuffed a forkful of ham in his mouth.

"That's where you're mistaken Father," Peter said still directing his comments to Catherine. "Working there with Torkil and the other men. . . and Ferdinand here . . ." Peter ruffled his younger brother's hair and the latter pulled angrily away and scowled at him—"we were always getting in each other's way. The basic layout encumbers production."

"Oh," said Catherine pursing her lips.

"At Herlufsholm I discussed the matter with Hr Polottski. Then at his suggestion I designed an entirely new layout for a gristmill. In my mill the stones are located in the upper level and processing done there. Then flour would be sifted down through the bolts and sacked in the first level near the doors. With my design, gravity would work for us instead of against us."

"And how would you get the grain to the upper level in the first place?" scoffed Elias.

"That would be simple Father," said Peter knowledgeably. "A long ramp could be constructed. Wagons driven up and unloaded at a dock." Though he was only 17 years old, Peter spoke with authority.

It galled Elias. "It wouldn't work with a stub-mill,"[4] he said sarcastically. "The way you are talking we may be better off to tear down the old place and start over."

"A huge project," said Catherine mildly offended herself. "Your grandfather would roll over in his grave."

"Peter has some good ideas, Mother," said Hans, swallowing hard and coming to his brother's defense. "I worked there too you know. There was much double handling."

"There still is," said Ferdinand now well into his apprenticeship.

"Architecture will suit you well Peter," said Catherine returning to the subject at hand.

Elias addressed the two boys sternly. "Have either of you considered the seminary? Becoming a minister might repay God for the many ways in which you have offended him over the years."

Hans kept his head down, concentrating upon his meal to avoid confrontation. Peter with raised eyebrows glanced over at Ferdinand, then at Catherine, who was staring at Elias in open confusion. "Whatever do you mean Elias?"

Elias cleared his throat and thumped his glass down abruptly. "Well," he said ignoring her question. "Have you?" He looked like he might be about to roar.

Catherine, seeing the impending tantrum, quickly intervened, "And what about you, Hans? Have you made up your mind what you want to study?"

"Yes I have Mother," said the more rugged of her sons quietly. Then he hesitated. Catherine put her fork down with a slight chink. Peter did not look up from his plate. He knew what was coming.

Inger, who had just washed and dried a long-handled pot, hung it on the rack just above the table rattling it slightly against neighboring pots and pans. "Sorry mum," she said addressing Catherine and went back to her work. Watching Inger, Elias coughed fussily and just then Ferdinand slurped his milk.

"I want to be a soldier, Mother," Hans said at last, his voice resolute.

Catherine's eyes opened wide. "What did you say?" she asked, taking a deep breath and placing a hand to her breast.

"I want to be a soldier," Hans repeated cautiously.

"You'll be the death of us yet," said Elias exasperated at the truth.

"Hans," said Catherine with deep concern in her voice. "Nobody is forced to serve in the military at the present. We are not at war. Why not a more rewarding career . . ."

"Such as law," Elias quickly injected.

"Such as medicine," countered Catherine, which both pleased and angered Elias at the same time. He respected doctors and yet wanted at least one of his sons in law or else the clergy.

"You don't understand," said Hans, respectfully but being stubborn. "I don't want to be a common soldier, I want to be an officer. I'd like to attend Officer's Training School at the academy at Frederica."

"It has a fine reputation," Catherine admitted. Elias forked a chunk of ham into his mouth, chewing rapidly to hide his resentment. He didn't have the strength for an argument. The table was silent as everyone worked at their plates, stealing glances back and forth at each other.

Catherine sat with her hands folded, pondering what to say. Finally she pushed back her chair and walked to a bay window. Hans' eyes followed her; relieved at the gentle smile he saw form on her lips as she turned.

"I suppose you have to get this out of your system, Hans," she said quietly. "We can manage to buy a commission for you. Fortunately your marks at Herlufsholm were high."

Her unexpected approval thrilled Hans to the core, but incensed Elias. He gathered enough strength for at least one volley. "I have heard all of this I want to!" he spat angrily. "What a way to waste your life! The military indeed! An officer . . . All pride and vainglory!" He threw down his fork and napkin and pushed away from the table. "It's not all sitting on a horse in a fancy uniform and shouting orders! You could get your fool head shot off!" Coughing and hacking Elias left the room and his footsteps slowly faded up the staircase.

At the close of his bedroom door everyone at the table gave a sigh of relief. "Graduates of Frederica are usually assigned to various posts around the country," Catherine said, then paused, and lowered her voice as if Elias might be listening from upstairs. "I once knew a young officer from the academy." Her eyes held a faraway look. "He was quite dashing in uniform." She heaved a sigh. "He was transferred from Holbaek to Holstein near the Lauenberg border and ended up marrying a German girl . . ."

All three boys looked sympathetically at their mother. She'd never before mentioned this episode from her past. If Elias' outburst had upset them, this information was calming. Of a sudden the heavy kitchen table where they were seated and the thick braided rug beneath their feet felt very secure. There had actually been another man in her life! Catherine seeing their surprised looks added. "But then if I'd have married him, I wouldn't have any of you, now would I?"

"Hans," she said returning to the subject at hand, "the only thing I don't like about your idea, is that if war comes again . . . you'll be right in the thick of it."

She stepped over to Hans and placed a hand on his shoulder. Hans slid his chair back and stood to embrace her. "I'll keep my head down Mother." He winked over at Peter. "Being an officer is the safest job in the military. And it's what I want," he added with conviction. "I'll make you proud. You'll see."

"I'm already proud," she said looking up him. "Proud of all of you. My, how you have grown Hans," she said leaning her head into his chest. "Come to me, Peter, Ferdinand," she motioned. The latter two got up from their chairs and joined Hans. All felt a bit awkward, but each loved their mother unequivocally. "My sons," Catherine said, a tear spilling down her face. "Growing up and leaving me."

"Not yet, Mother", said Peter trying to be cheerful. "There's still a lot of summer."

"He's right," said Hans. "Weren't we going to take a holiday? A vacation from the grist mill?"

"Don't complain about the mill," said Catherine holding up a finger. "I've told you before, if all else falls to ruin, you'll have a trade to fall back on."

During July, Catherine and her sons, with Elias in tow, went to Copenhagen specifically to visit the University of Copenhagen. They interviewed with the Rektor, paid tuition, inspected the dorms and prowled the grounds. "It says here that the University of Copenhagen was founded in 1479," said Elias reading from a one page oiled paper brochure the Rektor had given him. "But then burned to the ground during the Great Fire of Copenhagen in 1728. Let me read it verbatim," he added and stopped walking. Not wanting a scene more than out of respect everyone stopped and listened to him.

"Several university buildings were among those rebuilt and again destroyed during the British bombardment of Copenhagen in 1807," Elias read as if he had penned the paper, "rebuilt again, this time in restrained Gothic by architect Peder Malling, the frontage of the university's main building sports a series of lively gables seemingly supported by squared columns fashioned into the brick. Smaller columns adorn either side of the main entrance, above which are decorative marble headers. Exactly at the center of the main building rising proudly above everything, is a massive gable, underneath which arched windows and sculpted trim inform the world that here is a center of learning and center of culture!"

"My," said Catherine using her usual expression of appreciation, and her sons, following her eyes, looked around at what their father was describing.

"A novel feature on our modest campus is a small four hundred year old medieval building in the very center of the main courtyard. This charming old edifice dates back to 1420 and on days when weather permits students tend to gather near it to talk with friends or just sit in the sun. Bright and airy beech-wood trees with their soldier straight trunks, plus gnarled oak and maple trees shade the University's walkways and nearby ponds attract geese and swan."

Hearing that Catherine readily saw how Peter might easily meet a pretty young maiden in such a romantic setting. The problem however was there were none on campus. Higher education was still denied to Danish girls.

"The enrollment at the University of Copenhagen is expected to reach 1200 students this year," The paper concluded, "and we welcome you to our ranks."

"They are talking about you Peter," said Catherine with pride in her voice.

Peter felt his face flush. He really didn't expect anything more than Herlufsholm, but if expression were there would have admitted he felt very proud at the moment. He also felt a twinge of anxiety. He had to prove himself here.

After concluding their business at the university, the Jensen family toured the capital city and finished the trip with a visit to Christianborg where Elias used to haunt the hallways. He came back in a dark mood. He couldn't find a soul he knew in the corridors and offices of the massive building, and one acquaintance he encountered signaled clearly, but with mock courtesy, that he chose not to remember him. Elias was so depressed with the experience that he stayed behind in an Inn while Catherine and the boys left on the steam-driven paddle wheeler to Frederica.

"He didn't want to go anyway," said Hans. "It was the perfect excuse."

"Don't criticize your father," Catherine said firmly. "It's obvious how worn out he is. He does the best he can . . ."

"How would you like it, if none of your friends remembered you Hans," interrupted young Ferdinand. "It would make you sick too."

"He wanted to visit the art museum," said Peter. "He said it's his favorite thing to do."

'I hope that's the only thing he does,' Catherine worried to herself.

The military academy was situated near Vejle Fjord. The day of the Jensens' arrival, the senior class was on parade. In dark blue uniforms trimmed in red, the would-be graduates marched with precision; their muskets shouldered and tilting at similar angle. Hans felt a surge of pride. His chest swelled and strange emotion swept his soul. He was sure he'd made the right choice. He belonged here.

Though obviously impressed with her country's system of building military leaders, Catherine felt a twinge of uneasiness. Was it the thoughts land-bound peasantry always feels about mighty armies with their crop-trampling boots? Or perhaps just a mother's natural worry for her son in circumstances that could become dangerous; she was sure that was it.

She looked at Hans' radiant face, and her heart melted. *'It is what he wants. And at least the country isn't at war,'* she consoled herself. *'Father served in the army and came out alive. Perhaps this will all work out.'*

After registering Hans, Catherine and her sons boarded a train in a holiday mood and traveled through the green and wooded countryside to Kolding, Haderslev and finally to Flensburg. In Flensburg there was sightseeing, shopping and food. In Elias's absence their laughter was free and joyful, and Catherine in a clear state of mind resolved the last of her misgivings. Her twin sons were going on to bigger and better things and she had better get used to it.

During July and August Hans, Peter, and Ferdinand put in their time at the mill but Catherine, knowing it would be their last summer together, allowed them great freedom on weekends; for fishing, camping and roaming about with friends. All too quickly September arrived and the twins hastily finished packing while Catherine and Ferdinand made a last-minute trip to Roskilde to do some shopping. Elias, resenting Catherine's preoccupation with her sons developed another fever and carped demandingly. The day of departure, Hans and Peter were none too glad to be leaving his litany of complaints and with Nils Holsen driving the family carriage, they, Catherine and Ferdinand headed for Holbaek.

At the docks, seagulls were hovering above the surf, bobbing about the water and strutting on the sand pecking at dead crabs and fingerlings that had washed ashore. A throng of citizenry was also gathered. People of position were saying good-bye to their sons; a few of which, like Hans, were taking the steamer to Frederica while others were boarding a wind ship bound for England and then France to study abroad.

A cold wind funneled across Holbaek fjord, sending chills down people's backs. Fathers clutched at their derbies and top hats, while the tails of their coats fluttered like wash out on the line. This was an affluent gathering and mothers bedecked in mink and fox with matching muffs fussed with their son's collars all the while dabbing at the tears in their eyes with handkerchiefs. Young men, many of whom were wearing derby hats just like their father's, moved their trunks through the waving, jubilant, yet solemn crowd of sweethearts, parents, and friends. Hans and Peter stood at the edge of the crowd, their faces sober.

"I'll miss you, brother," said Peter enfolding Hans in a bear hug. There were tears in his eyes.

"It won't be bad," said Hans likewise with wet eyes. They slapped each other on the back in an attempt at being jovial. "We'll write and we'll also see each other on holidays."

"You have a bargain," said Peter wiping his eyes. "All our lives, we've been together . . ."

"Now, no more of this," said Catherine who was trying not to cry herself. "I've some final words to say to both of you. Your trunks are well packed. And hear me now. There are plenty of pens and paper. I expect letters!" She tried to look stern but suddenly she could no longer maintain her facade. Tears overflowed, and both Peter and Hans held her.

"Please write to me," she pleaded.

"We will, Mother," said Hans.

"You know we will," agreed Peter.

Ferdinand, his cold blue eyes reddening because of the wind, shifted back and forth uncomfortably on the balls of his feet. Perhaps he would miss his brothers, but then again hadn't they been gone much of his life? Regardless, he knew without them around the estate, his importance would increase.

Catherine wiped her eyes with a handkerchief and, from her large carpetbag, produced a brown leather-bound book for each of her departing sons. Each book was studded with brass rivets and filled with empty pages. "I purchased these journals for you in Roskilde and I expect you to start keeping them," she said seriously. "Life moves fast and you need to record the precious moments. A dull pencil is better than the sharpest memory. Start today; make an entry. One day you'll thank me."

Peter took his journal willingly, running his hand over its rich leather and brassbound corners. His heart was already full of things he wanted to record. "Thank you, Mother," he said appreciatively. "I'll do it."

"So will I," said Hans not quite as enthusiastically, but serious nonetheless. Hans never made a single entry.

The steam whistle blew and Hans embraced Catherine, giving her one last hug and kiss before he hastened aboard. Nels then drove to the depot where Peter caught a stage bound for Copenhagen. When the Jensen coach turned back toward the mill, there were just two passengers aboard.

The house, large as it was, suddenly became immense. *'Astonishing how much space the twins took up when they were home,'* Catherine reminisced. Like an inn in off-season, her spacious and opulent residence seemed almost deserted. Catherine threw herself into work. The season was rapidly changing, high time to prepare the lands and out buildings for winter.

Soon the sweet and sour smell of cornstalks fermenting in the silos filled the air; other silos bulged with wheat and with sweat pouring from both humans and animals, and the sounds of whips cracking— horses, mules, and oxen strained in their harnesses and work in the fields commenced. Soil turned black under the blade of the plow and lay smooth from the spike of the harrow, as all vestiges of the season's crops were turned under to decay and enrich the land. A final harvest had stocked the barns with hay; and what wouldn't fit was stacked in high mounds surrounded by empty fields laying dormant, patiently awaiting next spring's planting.

There was grain to mill, animals to care for, fences to mend, and of course a large home to maintain. Everyone except Elias lent a hand, and Catherine, with the comfort and security of routine, missed Peter and Hans terribly; but work was nature's restorative. As she had followed in her father's footsteps, Ferdinand might well have followed her, but he already knew all he wanted to know about milling and farming. Laborious is what it was and Ferdinand had other plans. He was soon to be off to Herlufsholm for studies and was glad of it. As far as the family estate was concerned, he would live off what had already been created.

SECTION NOTES:

1. In the final elections, Søren barely won over his opponent and his victory was one of few for the Society of Farmer's Friends in Denmark at large. The National Liberals, swept most of the country, winning 70 percent of the parliamentary seats and virtually taking control of the government, Søren's victory notwithstanding

2. *Statskirken* or State Church; the Evangelical Lutheran Church. With the new constitution the name was changed to: *Folkekirken* or People's Church and its clergymen were eventually supported by a national tax.

3. Kierkegaard's enlightened teachings caused at least one intellectual minister, a man named Harald Hoffding (1843–1931) to leave the clergy.

4. A stub mill or stump mill, English translation, was a building, the entire structure of which could be turned or pivoted on roller pins to allow its wind wings to face the direction of the wind. These mills actually resembled a building set on a large stump; hence the name.

Section Three

Maren

Chapter 13

København, or "Merchants' Harbor," began long ago as a small fishing village. Deep harbors and ready access to major waterways had little effect upon its growth until 1167 when Bishop Absalon, defender of the Realm, built the castle of Havn on a nearby islet. From then on Copenhagen grew rapidly into a town, eventually becoming a major economic, military, and political center. Fires, wars and various epidemics hampered growth but the struggling community survived and in 1443 finally became the capital city of Denmark, a nation comprised of over a thousand islands.

The city was intriguing to Peter and with the dormitories of the University of Copenhagen being adjacent to the city's center, from his dorm window he had a firsthand though limited view of commerce and the bustle of downtown. After classes he had a habit of wandering the streets to shake off tension and take in the sights but one particular evening found him temporarily lost in a maze of narrow streets lined with old shops and row after row of brick and stone tenement apartments. There seemed to be neither end nor beginning to the run-down area.

'How did I do this to myself?' he thought nervously as he came to an intersection with still another long, crooked and foreboding

concourse winding off in both directions. '*Surely I'll recognize a landmark soon.*'

Dirty little children were playing in the streets while their older brothers were either throwing rocks at a dilapidated fences and buildings else chasing each other between the alleyways. Washings hung on sagging lines between tenements as women bent to their tasks and pubs where their men wasted precious skillings and rigsdalers, seemed to be on every corner. On the cobbles in front of one particular grog shop, a man obviously drunk or else dead was laying in his own vomit. As Peter bent over the ragged individual, the stench was overpowering.

"Still breathing," he said to himself as he straightened up and hastened along, "just passed out. He next approached four surly looking men smoking their pipes and eyeing him suspiciously. '*Better act as if I know where I am,*' he thought and before reaching them crossed the street as if with purpose and continued along his way.

'Where is God in all this ignorance and poverty? His mind demanded as he observed tenement after run down tenement seemingly bulging with scantily clad waifs and stunted looking adults.

Dusk was settling in, everywhere mothers began shouting for their children and finally Peter saw a tall green-copper spire peeking up over the maze of crowded tenements. *'Norre Park is right across from that church. Thank heaven!'*

Shortly he was out of the "getto" like area, had hastened across Norre Park and still later had taken a seat at an outdoor café situated on the docks and ordered himself a warm beer. Sitting there catching his breath, feeling very relieved he noticed a young professor he knew taught classes in commerce and trade at the university of Copenhagen. Peter nodded his way and was surprised when the professor whose name was Christophersen, said, "hello to you my friend. Do you mind if I join you?"

"Well, not at all," said Peter. "B–bring your stein."

"You're a student are you not?" said Christophersen pulling up a chair. "Nice this time of evening, isn't it?"

"I am and it is," said Peter pleased to have company. "I've been out walking in it."

"You do look somewhat windblown."

Peter smiled slightly.

"I like it down here by the docks," the professor said before taking a sip of his beer. "Ships from the four corners of the world all right here in our harbors." He took another drink then put down his stein and wiped his goatee and mouth. "Barks, schooners, sloops, clippers, side-wheelers, screw steamers and skiffs. Their sagging sails and tall masts rise out of the mist like a naked forest."

"Literally hundreds of masts," Peter commented taking a deep pull at his beer. "Especially on the Swedish side of the harbor. A few smoke stacks too."

"Very observant," said professor Christophersen. "Looking closely, one can actually witness the transitional era between sail and steam. Do you see where all the lanterns are being lit?" he added.

"Yes. What's going on over there?" Peter asked.

"Those huge ships are freighters," explained Christophersen. "The lack of cotton due to America's civil war has left scores of them idle in the water."

"I hear their war has shut down many of our textile mills," said Peter.

"It has for a fact," said the young Professor. "My father, bless his soul, is out of work. I'm supporting him. In fact there are hundreds of people out of work in this city and many warehouses along the docks are completely empty." Overhead the shrill cries of seagulls sparked the evening. Their cries seemed to signal a warning, or perhaps a beckoning call.

"You're very up on things," Peter commented.

"My job requires it."

Peter took another sip of beer. "What can you tell me about Christiansborg," he asked. "I plan to visit there on Saturday."

"Ah the seat of Danish government," said Christophersen. Now he was showing off. "Christiansborg is like a fortress; a mighty arch laden castle completely surrounded by a system of canals. Converging upon the huge complex from five directions are various roads, bridged over the canals. On work days horse drawn traffic thunders across almost constantly. And to accommodate so many animals, at the rear of the Chancellery are long rows of stables surrounding a huge parade ground. You will definitely want to see that.

But east of the Chancellery is the Bourse," he continued, "the commodity and stock exchange. Be sure to visit there also. Everyday except Sunday men in top hats and Prince Albert coats scurry about, in and out of the famous rust colored building investing money trying to ignite the fires of commerce. All about our great university is the appearance of wealth . . ."

"But," Peter interrupted, "one doesn't have to venture far to see elements of despair."

"That is true young man, er . . .? What is your name by the way?"

"Peter, Peter Jensen."

"Anders Christophersen." They shook hands across the table.

"Yes, with all our exquisite art museums, churches, business and government buildings, Copenhagen puts on a good show for visitors but behind the façade privation is rampant. Working classes and even a large number of professional people are unemployed. Denmark under Fredrick VII, like France under Napoleon II, is suffering."

"From what I saw this evening, you are exactly right professor Christophersen," Peter said shaking his head morosely. "Do you believe in God professor?" he then added unexpectedly.

"Well . . . of course," Anders Christophersen answered hesitantly. That is doesn't everybody? I go to church, occasionally, if that's what you mean." —He hadn't been since he was christened— "Why the question?"

"Just wondering," said Peter. "Just wondering."

Neither spoke for a short while, then Peter slid back his chair. "Its getting late and I've still got studies," he said standing up. He staggered slightly. "I guess I'm not much on beer," he explained. "I'm finding myself a bit lightheaded. "

The professor was disappointed to lose his audience so abruptly but stood to shake Peter's hand. "It was a pleasure to meet you my friend. And I enjoyed our conversation. Perhaps next semester you could sign up for my course."

"I might just do that," said Peter.

He waved as he left the café and next morning alone in his dormitory after a fitful night's sleep Peter took out his journal and dipped his pen in the inkwell. *'Copenhagen has a population of a little over one hundred thousand people,'* he wrote. *'There are scores of beautiful buildings and shops throughout the city, but its back streets comprise of a nasty concoction of narrow and crooked little paths lined with old stucco houses and tenement apartments. One citizen in twelve lives in a basement apartment, and many hundreds more in upstairs flats, as they call them. Salt and peppered throughout crowded neighborhoods are pubs, taverns, brothels and pawn-*

shops; poor areas for raising children. And there are thousands.

A two room apartment usually houses eight to twelve residents, and due to high rent and the merciless brutes that collect it I hear people can barely afford food. But crowded and mean as conditions are, most Copenhageners are an industrious and meticulous people and keep their humble dwellings spotless.

There are a lot of people out of work just now but life in the capital city is not all gloomy. People are friendly and weather permitting most days find them spilling from their tenements into the streets, promenading the ramparts surrounding the city and trying to catch a bit of fresh air and sunshine.

Starlings, sparrows, seagulls and pigeons are plentiful in Copenhagen, and to add to the charm, they swoop from the sky and from ledges of high buildings to strut amongst the crowds, pecking daringly for breadcrumbs and bits of meat thrown to them. Their droppings are everywhere.

Massive stone churches with green copper-plated spires and walls adorned with colorful stained glass windows are located strategically throughout the city, also government buildings, public bathhouses, libraries, and every kind of business imaginable. Importers, exporters, tanners, tinners and blacksmiths; also butcher shops and quaint little stores selling notions, glassware and Danish pastries. We also have dressmakers, tailors, milliners, shoemakers and scattered about.

Museums filled with; paintings, Viking artifacts, gold icons, coins, decorative porcelain and other works of art grace the city. The chapel in Frederiksborg Castle, with its lifelike and provocative paintings on the life of Christ by Carl Heinrich Bloch, I'm sure rivals the Vatican. And our boulevards and parks are accented with; statues of war heroes mounted on horseback, sculptures of queens, kings, cherubs, nudes, famous scholars and fountains.

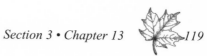

Much of downtown Copenhagen, east of the harbor was destroyed[1] in 1807 during a brutal three-day shelling by Great Britain's armada. But the city was completely rebuilt by the late 1850's and now has gas lighted avenues, wide canals and like a mooring to our island city, is the seat of Danish government, Christiansborg and the magnificent Chancellery!'

He sat back to read over his words. Much of what he had written sounded boastful but then he was proud to be Danish,. Peter was also very concerned with the crowding and squalor he had recently observed.

It was autumn 1862. Blustery winds blew leaves and acorns tumbling about the crowded markets and the parks of the city. Peter put his pen in its inkwell and stared out his window. Squirrels, their cheeks crammed full of nuts scampered up and down trees to and from their nests; "They must be ready," he mused. "Denmark's winters are harsh."

Copenhagen's crowded housing at first made the student of architecture think he had picked the right field of study; and during his first two years Peter applied himself to his books and drawings of buildings with a vengeance. He wanted to make a difference and studied hard. A paragraph midway thru a letter to Catherine dated October 10, 1862 revealed his zeal.

"I'm certain my work could one day make a difference in the way people in Copenhagen live Mother. If they only had better housing—efficient, spacious, clean housing with more parks for their children to play in—things might surely be better for them. As it goes, people are jammed together in apartments like bottled fish. The drawing accompanying this letter depicts four and five story spacious apartments with nurseries and schools right on the premises. A

complex of this nature uses no more precious land than a typical city tenement yet houses many more people."

"Isn't he marvelous," Catherine exclaimed after reading his letter to Elias and showing him the drawing.

"Bah," said Elias. "Typical youth," he coughed then continued. "He wants to take the people out of the slum, rather than the slum out of the people. That kind of thinking will get him nowhere in life."

"Oh I don't agree at all," argued a flustered Catherine as she adjusted herself on the sofa, "his enthusiasm is refreshing and I'd sooner see him fostering dreams than having his mind bogged down with the cold realities of life in Copenhagen."

"What have you heard from Hans?" was all Elias said.

"Well," said Catherine coolly, still stinging from his reaction. "Hans' experience at the Flensborg military academy has been entirely different from Peter's of course. In his most recent letter he says he has been exposed to such rigid army discipline that he's beginning to feel he can no longer think for himself. He says he has suffered as much abuse from his instructors as he has the upperclassmen. Says he must sit rigidly in all classes, then at drill when some fool can't get things right stand at attention again under the stony stare of his grizzled drill sergeant. He spends untold hours on muddy parade grounds, an aching back and an antiquated musket cutting into his shoulder." Then she smiled in spite of herself. "Let me read this part." She picked up Hans' letter from the coffee table. *"It never fails, every time we put on a lengthy drill in front of visiting dignitaries, half the cadets march as if they have full bladders!"*

"My word Catherine!" interrupted Elias cursing and rising from his chair, "It sounds as if the military has done little to mature him.

What else does he do besides march around?"

"Always the same Elias," Catherine said before she read anything further. She was determined not to let his attitude douse her effervescent mood. Here listen to this. *"I've horses to feed and groom, stables to clean, floors to mop, boots and brass to shine. Always something leaving barely enough time for studies and taking care of my uniforms. I'm not getting much sleep, and every morning am awakened by an upperclassman shouting in my ear."*

"It sounds as if Hans is stretched to the maximum Elias. By the Sabbath he says he's as wooden as a post."

"And does he attend church?" demanded Elias, pouncing on the subject like a cat on a mouse.

"Church is mandatory of course," said Catherine patiently, "but to stay awake during Mass Han writes that he sits with one leg lifted . . ." she snickered. "Why he says here he's developed the remarkable skill of sleeping with his eyes open."

"He'll do well to pay close attention," grumbled Elias.

"Food remains plentiful but tasteless, he writes," she went on calmly, *"how I long for Inger's cooking!"*

"It is a good thing Hans' regimen at the academy is more austere than Peter's," Elias interrupted again. "We wouldn't want our army full of lily pads like are in our universities now would we?"

"You make everything so unpleasant, Elias" Catherine said unhappily. "Peter writes about wanting to improve Copenhagen's slums and you immediately shift to Hans. Then when you don't like what you hear about him you return to an ugly comment about Peter. Doesn't either of our sons please you?"

Neither twin would ever please Elias Jensen and because as a father he had been out of the picture during their adolescence neither twin harbored much respect for him either. Peter's life at the University of Copenhagen may not have been as physically difficult as Hans' but it was emotionally. He had a private dorm and few friends whereas Hans lived and slept near other cadets in an open barracks, a very social setting.

'Dear Peter,' Hans wrote to his twin toward the end of the fall semester, *'Youths from all over Denmark are here at the academy. Some are the sons of officers in the Danish Royal Army. Others come from aristocratic families representing the best of society. Few, like you and I are from common stock. They are an aggressive and intellectual lot, quick of wit and prank yet somewhat studious. Most come from influence and endowment. They know who they are, where they come from, and their station in life makes many of them all the more obnoxious. Thank God for Torkil Olsen and our mother! Our un-pampered youth makes us more powerful than this lot.*

With unstable conditions in neighboring Germanic States a constant reminder, past wars are the main subject of army officers who teach us. The Slesvig wars, (Three Years' War) are discussed ad-nauseam and by now I know names and locations of battlefields as well as I do the towns and provinces around Holbaek.

Talk of females occupies large segments of free time discussion around here and many cadets are writing to one young maiden or another. Even so we discuss whether or not Denmark should "elect" its King as it now does the Rigsdag, and could education, poetry and modern day philosophy lift the masses from the quagmires of life.

And about one third of the cadets favor changes in Danish government; another third support the status quo, while the remaining group seemed unconcerned one way or the other. What say you old son? You're a fancy University student, write me your opinion and I shall share it with these aristocrats!

Your brother in bondage, Hans

Peter posted his reply just one day later.

'Dear Hans, in contrast to your exciting life with companions in the military mine is one of the serious semi-reclusive student of architecture. I have few friends but to minimize the effect of professor's lectures and after class assignments, I live a great deal of life within my head. I'm either working on building designs or else out on campus leaning against a tree, gazing into space seeking direction. For entertainment I wander the streets of Copenhagen worrying about societal malfunctions. I tend to look for problems in this society then dwell upon ways to fix them. As different as our course of study is, I think you'll agree with me that Denmark still has one foot stuck in the mud of medieval times and the other trying to pull it out. It is especially evident here.

Lately my primary concern has been Copenhagen's pitiful housing, its unemployment, poverty and ignorance of the people. Sometimes I shake myself awake asking, "what if anything can I do about it?" Then time passes and I'm back where I started, thinking of what I could do to fix things.

As to your question, I favor an elected president like they have in America. All government leaders should be chosen by the voice of the people. And please don't let anyone read this letter, I could be hung for treason!'

Where Peter might be focused upon social ills, Hans' obsession was Denmark's potential as a great political power; but only if it could build a more formidable army to keep its neighbors at bay. His thinking was somewhat skewed but did touch upon social ills too; a Platoon Leader by his third year, Hans' solution to Denmark's unemployment, and poverty was simple: "Let them all be foot soldiers."

Neither twin was afflicted with humility. Hans was confident, ambitious, and daring, but he was also arrogant, reckless, and selfish. Peter was equally bold, but more modest and put the needs of others ahead of his own. Unlike Hans he had an overly tender heart and would if he could, save the world. Both young men possessed a lively sense of humor, Peter's being more subtle than Hans', but unlike his twin, who seemed to know exactly where he was heading, Peter was searching. Something within him was terribly dissatisfied.

Christmas provided the only reprieve from university and military life, otherwise both were a year round experience. The holidays being thus cherished, Peter and Hans would joyously head to Holbaek to reunite with the family, and bask in the luxury of Catherine's comfortable home and Inger Daryberg's plentiful kitchen.

Chapter 14

By his third year at the University, the study of architecture was losing its appeal to Peter. Gradually he began to focus more and more attention upon Copenhagen's social ills. Shortly after classes began in 1863 he wrote to Hans:

My dear Brother,

This school year finds me lacking enthusiasm for my drawings, and architecture in general. One would think by now I'd have my life plan positively mapped out. But I am lost as a goose. There have been many things eating away at me in this city. Situations too complex to change. It's all very disconcerting.

Poverty and social corruption in Denmark are at the heart of my discomfiture. As boys growing up in Holbaek we lived unawares of these things, but here in Copenhagen they hit you square in the face. Copenhagen is the capital city of our country, Hans, and yet it's a place of shame. The longer I live here the more depressed I become. On the surface the city appears to be rich and filled with an enlightened populace. But nothing could be further from the truth. Slums meander throughout the city and the people trapped there live in utter wretchedness, especially so in winter. There are thousands of unemployed, beggars on every corner, and children go without proper food and clothing. But I have come to know that slums and unemployment are not the root of the social ill I see. Those conditions are only leaves on the tree. The roots of the noxious weed are the invisible shackles of, ignorance and superstition. Grundtvig's[2] folk high schools might eventually make a difference but changes in education are so slow they seem imperceptible.

The Monarchical system of government still binds us. Fredrick VII, God save him, appoints one third of the Rigsdag. Cousins and friends of foreign monarchs! If Denmark is ever to succeed as a nation this practice must change. ***All members of the Rigsdag should be elected****. We must separate ourselves completely from Europe's royal family. Our country remains more backward than Germany!*

The Folkekirken also slows our progress as a nation. As we well know, the church is replete with a pious if not hypocritical hierarchy and has far too much political influence over the affairs of state. How I envy countries such as the Australia and the United States of America! Both were founded by people who escaped the oppression of their governments and Priests! America's civil war notwithstanding, both countries have been very progressive.

Despite our constitution, true freedom remains more myth than reality. Crown and Church, Hans, between the two our people, and Europe at large, remain enslaved. The citizens of Copenhagen are anxious for prosperity and freedom from the tyranny. You can feel the unrest in the city and in the halls of this great university. It's as thick as fog in the morning.

All this has greatly affected my thinking and my plans. I'm no longer sure I want to be an architect. Who knows? I may follow father's footsteps and study law. You know I'm not serious. If you have any advice, please send it soon.

Your brother in confusion,

Peter

Hans eventually wrote back and when Peter received the letter he opened it eagerly:

Dear Peter,

I can't agree with you more about social problems and corruption in our government. Fredrick VII is a good king but his ministers and the Rigsdag are of questionable background and purpose. Yes, the Folkekirken does have backward if not obstructive influence to Danish society, but you're beating your head against the wall on that one my brother. The church will never give up its control of the people.

As for me my main concern is Denmark's military. One would think the government supports a strong army, but the longer I'm here, the less I believe it. My conclusion is that our army is dangerously undermanned. Do we need the Swedes to cross the ice again to wake us from our slumber? Our current military leaders are inexperienced, the heroes of the Three Years' War being either dead or retired.

I think Danes are suffering under the delusion that if we are invaded by the Prussians again, Russia will come to our rescue, just as it did before. Who knows but Russia herself might turn on us? We must strengthen our army. Train new leaders. All Danish young men must be compelled to spend at least a year in service to the country and the government must provide funds, especially funds for better weapons.

Let me digress a moment and address your quandary regarding a profession. Father would be ecstatic if you turned to law, but I'm sure it would kill Mother. I have no advice to offer. It looks as if you must make a decision like I did. I'm glad that part of life is behind me.

Returning to Denmark's social problems, to compare your situation in Copenhagen with mine here in Flensborg is a bit like comparing heaven with hell. There are no slums here. The only buildings of consequence are thatched-roof farm homes, barns, a large church and a few shops. Surrounding the town and the military academy are wide-open fields, hilly regions and dense forests, almost like those near our home. We bivouac among the trees and go through maneuvers and training without seeing a soul.

The crowded conditions you write about in Copenhagen don't exist here. On the other hand ignorance, and superstition abound; and some poverty also. Landowners still beat their peasants. The farmers I see are a poorly scrubbed and mentally stunted lot. I had an incident with one on Saturday night last. My friends and I were at an inn and it fell my lot to have my arms around a buxom maid who turned out to be the daughter of a soldier-hater. Stout old fellow he was. Smelled like a pig. He struck me repeatedly with his staff and would have thrashed me to death were it not for my companions. I was crippled for days but am recovering.

On a higher note my dear brother, I am seeing one maiden in particular and you should see the lady! She has heavenly blonde hair, rosy cheeks, velvety soft skin, and kisses of angelic sweetness. Her name is Evette. She says her father also hates cadets. I've not met him and rue the day. One can hardly blame locals for the way they feel about cadets but at least this one lets me see his daughter . . ..

Peter, the reform-minded student of architecture, paused and reread the last paragraph. Velvety soft skin? Angelic kisses? He was suddenly aware that his brother was living in a far different world than his; a mysterious world one removed even from that of the military life. Peter didn't remember finishing Hans' letter. Women hadn't been much a part of his life thus far. As a youth there had been two encounters with Katrina Hagemeister, daughter of Kurt Hagemeister a German who worked in the mill, in the woods behind her house. Katrina was experienced in kissing, Peter was not, and the episodes left him in an agitated state of wonder.

Before Herr Hagemeister had caught them, Peter had sampled many of Katrina's wondrous, wet kisses. To this very day he thought of her. There were even dreams. He could still hear her screaming as her father beat her. Peter had lied to his mother about his own bruises, also administered by Herr Hagemeister and had plans of retaliation. Maybe Catherine found out because it wasn't long after the incident that Hagemeister no longer worked at the mill. Shortly afterward he had moved his family away from Holbaek.

Peter wasn't afraid of women. In fact he admired them greatly. Embracing Katrina, and kissing her passionately were acts he longed to repeat. On the other hand Catherine had taught her sons that intercourse before marriage was an abomination before God and he'd accepted the teaching albeit somewhat reluctantly. During his first year of college he'd occasionally visited the harbor inns and danced with local girls, but he had never followed his fellow students in their businesslike pursuits of sexual gratification. But that afternoon Hans' graphic portrayal of this Evette, whatever her last name was, had shaken him to his toenails. He was suddenly as restless as a buck in a forest and felt a strong urge for a breath of fresh air. The evening's studies lay ominously before him, but he decided upon a long walk.

He was still thinking about Hans' letter when Peter wandered past a dark brunette, not all that common in Copenhagen, sitting on a park bench feeding breadcrumbs to pigeons. He was deep in thought, oblivious to his surroundings, and had drifted to a halt on the path near the bench where he stared absently at the fountain.

"You look lost," Maren Carlsen said in her typically friendly way.

Dragged from his gaze and dumbfounded that a stranger, a girl for that matter would openly address him Peter looked directly at her. "H–Hello," he managed to say.

"Would you like to share my bench?" she asked matter-of-factly. "There aren't many left."

As if directed to do so, Peter gazed around the park. Everywhere he looked were couples walking hand in hand or else taking up all the available benches. There were couples sitting upon blankets watching children at play; and couples at the fountains making wishes and tossing coins into the water. Love was definitely in the air. Elderly people took up most of the park benches; their wrinkled chins and gnarled hands rested upon the crook of their walking sticks while their eyes stared off into space. Perhaps they were dreaming that they were the young lovers meandering arm in arm along the paths of Norre Park.

"I guess there aren't many places to sit," Peter said awkwardly. He sat immediately on the bench with her as Maren sprinkled more breadcrumbs. He ventured a closer look at her and found himself short of breath.

"Do you live around here?" she asked easily.

"No," he said from his end of the bench. "I'm a student at the university. I'm studying architecture. I'm Peter Jensen by the way . . . from Holbaek. Who are you?" he held out his hand. Hers was dainty yet firm and Peter found himself groping for words. He felt light headed. His heart was pounding so hard he was certain the girl could hear it.

"Maren Carlsen." She said, the light in her eyes glancing briefly into his soul.

Peter found himself staring at her, absorbed by her fresh natural ways and the newness of the experience. He hadn't realized until Hans' letter just how lonely he'd been for feminine company! The girl had a healthy, youthful glow and did not seem to notice his uneasiness.

"What about you?" Peter asked, "Do you live around here?"

"Yes, I do," she answered still smiling at him. "Above that store over there. My father owns it."

Maren had pointed across the park and through some trees toward a small dry-goods store.

"Solid-looking building," he said appreciatively.

The thickly thatched, gabled roof of the two-story structure sported a stork's nest on the west end near the chimney. The store on the street level had white stucco walls trimmed with traditional brown crisscrossed trim, and multi-paned square windows. It was an older building with its proportionate share of mice and cracked walls, and had a sagging roof. Peeping through the trees the building appeared as quaint and charming as Peter's new acquaintance.

"I work for my father," the girl offered, keeping the conversation going. "I was just taking my lunch. I love it here by the fountains."

The fountain nearest them featured a sculpture of a mother holding two cherubic babies from whose puckered lips' water arched in a graceful stream. Surrounded by a walkway, the fountain was set in a large kidney-shaped pond and the sound of its tumbling water was very soothing to the soul. Around the edges of the pond were dark green lily pads, their fringes yellowed from recent frosts, and due to the lateness of the year were void of frogs. Swans and ducks swam near the fountains, occasionally diving beneath the surface to scrabble for bugs and other aquatic tidbits.

"We've got to enjoy the park while we can," commented Peter. "It won't be long before all the leaves are gone and everything is barren and frozen over."

"I do enjoy it," Maren said exuberantly. "It's so lovely here." She looked out across the spacious lawns and took a deep breath. "The instant I'm near these trees and grasses, something inside me smiles. I'm at peace with the world."

"I get the same feelings," said Peter. "Anytime I'm out here but especially when I am visiting the forest."

"Do you go often to the forests?" she wanted to know.

"I used to go all the time," he answered. "Before I came here of course."

It was so easy to talk with the girl and before he knew it, Peter found himself telling her briefly of his family, the milling business, school and his confusion about finishing his studies in architecture. He told her he was a twin, and that his brother had chosen the army as a career; and that even though he and Hans were separated, they seemed constantly aware of each other. "Women call that intuition," Maren quipped.

She was a very attractive person, and also was a good listener. Her eyes told him so; and when she spoke she had an educated and interesting point of view. She talked about many things: the life and times of Denmark, the affairs of state and also the situation in the Duchies.

Peter was enthralled with her, fascinated by her directness and common sense. She was a lively conversationalist, had a sparkling laugh and spoke with a lilting quality; hers was not a high-pitched voice but rather mellow and rich. "Where did you attend school?"

Peter asked knowing that receiving a formal education was particularly difficult for Danish girls.

"My father was a professor at the university as I was growing up. He only took over our store five years ago when his parents passed away and left it to him. The store makes us a good living but I must admit I miss studying with him. He always shared his lessons with us children. Because of him I read, and reading is to me as breathing."

"I'm very impressed," said Peter sincerely.

"I know," said she. "Most girls should be so fortunate."

They talked until the bell from the cathedral on Town Square sounded twice whereupon Maren seemed to snap to duty.

"We've got to get back to work," a stocky man in a derby hat said as he stopped in front of their bench.

Peter felt his entire head and neck flush. The fellow obviously had authority here, but where had he come from? And how long had he been listening to them? "Peter this is my father," Maren said standing and brushing a few crumbs from her lap.

"How do you do sir," said Peter, quickly rising to his feet. He bowed slightly as he shook the man's hand.

"Just fine, young man," said Lars Carlsen somewhat frigidly. "See you back at the store then Maren?"

"I'll be right along Father," she said respectfully as he turned his back and with his cane thumping the walkway on alternate steps, strode away.

His composure all out of kilter, Peter watched the father's abrupt departure. He was sure he had offended the man.

Maren hadn't moved as yet. She was looking up at Peter. She was far shorter than he, that was obvious but she had a giant spirit. Maren was a woman of peace. She blended easily with most people, both strong and weak. The white blouse she was wearing was a puritan cut, as puritan as she. The ruffles in front emphasized her soft and ample breast and the lace around her collar and the shoulder straps of her black dress were decorated in small colorful flowered embroidery. She was so utterly charming Peter could not suppress the desire to ask to see her again.

"Could we meet again?" he managed to say.

"I come here often," she said, grinning at him.

"Tomorrow then," he said politely.

"Perhaps," she said giving him her hand.

Maren Carlsen had the work-a-day look of an average middle-class Danish girl. She was the second oldest in a family of eleven children, was pretty without being beautiful, and because of a quick smile and sparkle in her eyes, was very enticing. She had thick, coarse, brown hair, and if she had a fault, it was her envy of tall women of which there were many in Denmark.

Maren's best feature was her blue eyes, which changed according to what she wore. Black darkened them, indigo made them deep and richly blue, while sky blue lightened, brightened, and warmed them. They were friendly, smiling eyes, soft and warm. She could put people at ease with but a glance.

Maren had a smooth oval face lightly sprayed with tiny freckles, a rounded graceful nose, full lips, and looked so clean and fresh she literally shined. She parted her hair across the top of her head and made thick traditional plaits that fell over her ears. An individualistic person, she departed from the day's fashions by keeping fluffy bangs on her forehead.

Maren was small but firm, obviously no stranger to hard work yet extremely feminine. She had small feet, usually adorned with thick woolen socks and clogs, and in spite of her blocky clogs had the graceful movements of a lynx.

Her loveliness lit up Peter's soul, and how he got back to the dorm was a mystery to him. He couldn't even remember looking at the statues guarding the gabled entry to the university, as was his habit. Gradually he came to himself, again in his room and staring into his journal.

Chapter 15

September 16, 1863

Peter wrote of his experience with Maren in the park, then put his pen in the ink well, closed the journal and paused to reflect. He couldn't remember ever feeling as he did at the moment! Bells were ringing in his head and he felt like running a foot race.

"She was truly remarkable," he said aloud. "I can't stop thinking about her . . . but I have a paper due in the morning!" he added suddenly coming to his senses. "How will I ever concentrate?"

As proposed, Peter and Maren met the following afternoon and to Peter's joy the father didn't seem to be around. *'Maybe the old fellow had customers,'* he hoped to himself as he took her hand. Maybe she asked him to stay home. Maren was certainly past the years of needing a chaperone.

Peter didn't ask about her father and their conversation flowed as freely as before. This time they talked about their interests, their goals, and experiences. The more they talked, the hungrier they both seemed for more conversation.

Thursday it was raining so hard Peter remained in the dorm with his books. He studied in fits and starts. He couldn't stop thinking about her. On Friday the sun was shining and they met again.

This time the stocky man in the derby hat *was* there. Seated on a bench near the pond, Maren's father could observe the proceedings if he chose to but happily he was out of earshot.

Peter didn't care one way or the other. Maren had affected him in a way he couldn't explain, and chaperoned or not, he was going to see her. "Saturday I'll bring a lunch for us," he heard her saying. "Father will be busy with wholesalers . . . they always come on Saturday, we can eat undisturbed." She was blushing as she said it and Peter thought how beautiful she was, how absolutely fresh and honest.

"Wonderful," he said not trying to check the enthusiasm in his voice. He reached over and touched her hand and she made no attempt to draw away.

That night Peter's dreams were filled with the beauty of Maren Carlsen and Saturday morning he sprang out of bed, washed, and fussed over his appearance as never before. He took no breakfast, paced the floor and though he labored at his desk his mind was too agitated for real study. Though behind in his classes and a major math paper due on Monday, Peter threw his hands in the air.

Needing something to do to kill time, he pulled a blank sheet of paper from his drawer and began a sketch of Maren. The result looked nothing like her and he wadded it up and tossed it in the corner. He'd never been good at drawing people. On the next sheet of paper an outline of the Carlsen store began to appear. Buildings came natural to him and when this one met his approval he gave it emphasis with shading. Doors, windowsills, gables; the house was drawn peeking through the trees of Norre Park just as he'd seen it. Would twelve o'clock ever come?

Drawing absorbed him, calmed him, and the cathedral bell finally chimed half past eleven. He put on a sweater, rolled up his drawing and hurried down the stairs, across the cobblestone and toward the park.

The cool moist air tasted mildly of salt as he left the campus. Autumn colored leaves covered the trees but many had fallen during the night and littered the streets. So brisk was his passage, they swirled about Peter's legs. Make way! Here came a man with purpose!

Standing on the arched bridge overlooking the fountain near the bench they had first shared, Maren was even prettier than before. Peter felt his palms sweat and his mouth go dry.

"Hello there," he said hoping she wouldn't notice his nervousness.

"Hello to you," she said smiling. "I hope you came with an appetite." Her voice was lilting and bright, sure of itself, and just a bit teasing. He felt himself grinning foolishly in response, lost in her eyes.

He pulled himself together and unrolled the sketch he'd just finished.

"What do you think?" he asked feeling quite like a schoolboy.

"Our store!" she exclaimed.

"It's a fair likeness . . ."

"Oh, but it's exact, Peter. May I have it? Father will love it."

"Of course," he said easily. He rolled the drawing carefully and handed it to her. "That's why I drew it."

He liked the way Maren said his name. He liked everything about the girl.

"Shall we cross to the other side?" he asked. He stooped for the picnic basket at her feet and rising, Peter caught the soft fragrance of lilac. It seemed to come from Maren's hair. They walked across the bridge. Fallen leaves crunched beneath their feet. Their cheeks full of acorns, a nearby pair of squirrels scampered up a gnarled oak.

"Aren't they interesting?" said Maren as she watched. Peter nodded. "I hope you're just as hungry."

"Famished," he said with enthusiasm.

They spread their blanket under a tree and Peter peeked into the bulging picnic basket filled with breads, cold meats and pastry. "How can we possibly eat all this?" he asked. Maren giggled.

"I didn't know what you'd like," she said, "so I brought a little of everything."

Peter watched every move she made as her deft little hands set out the lunch. How graceful she was! He felt awkward in her presence and sat cross-legged, tucking his big feet under his calves as if to hide them. Maren had slipped off her clogs and curled her legs and dainty little feet under her dress. The pose reminded Peter of Hans Christian Andersen's Little Mermaid.

"Father was very curious at the size of my lunch," she said smiling at Peter. The now empty picnic basket rested between them and they were using it as a table.

"I'm sure he was," said Peter, laughing heartily. "What's he like, by the way? Is he strict?" He bit into an open-faced ham sandwich and listened.

"Father? Oh he's a good person . . . a hard worker. His life is now our store. He's made a personal vow to maintain his father's legacy."

'I know something about that' thought Peter as he was reminded of Catherine.

"All he does is work." Maren paused. "What about your father?"

Peter swallowed and hesitated. He hadn't thought of Elias in weeks. "A stern man," he said bluntly. "A sick old solicitor. Narrow minded and religious to a point of fanaticism."

"Oh?" said she quite taken back. "You're very graphic about him. Is he really all those things?"

"Those and more," Peter answered. "All my life I was either in the family pew at church or at the dinner table listening to him lecture on religion. Where God is concerned, if it hadn't been for my mother, I might have turned out to be quite a cynic. "My mother is a saint," he hesitated then continued. "Though she had good reason, she never said a bad word about my father to us boys. They've argued, and she has no illusions about him . . . don't misunderstand me . . . but when Father wasn't around, my mother did not criticize or complain about him. Another thing that saved my brother and me from him was that Mother set us to working in the family gristmill at an early age. Later we were sent off to a school. I still saw more of my father than I wanted."

"Hmmm," said Maren.

"He used to be some kind of government official," Peter went on. "He worked here in Copenhagen for a time. Then he contracted tuberculosis. Though he remains unhealthy, he thinks God spared him from the disease."

"Religion has always been important to my father, too," Maren said seriously. "But not in a negative way. He always told us Bible stories . . ."

"So did my mother," Peter injected.

"But lately," Maren continued, "Father has had doubts about the church. Its political power bothers him most. He thinks the church should keep its nose out of the king's business."

"My sentiments exactly," said Peter enthusiastically. "Has he read any of Kierkegaard's writings?

"How odd you should mention Kierkegaard," Maren exclaimed. "A man is speaking about him tonight at a gathering in this very park."

"Speaking about Kierkegaard?" Peter asked.

"That's right," she answered. "Do you want to come? It should be interesting."

"Nothing could keep me away," he said.

Peter met Maren in front of her father's store later that evening in what might be called their first real date. The wind whispered soft and sweetly against their skin as they walked to the park, making them both feel fresh, free, and so good to be alive. They held each other's hand love was budding forth and Peter wondered if he would have the courage to kiss her when he took Maren home. By coincidence the speaker turned out to be none other than professor Anders Christophersen and he sounded quite the expert as he lectured on Søren Kierkegaard. But the next day because Peter had in very deed kissed Maren goodnight, and the sweetness of it still lingered on his mind, he couldn't remember a thing the man had said.

Chapter 16

For the next few weeks Peter and Maren met almost every afternoon. At least once a week they took in a concert or attended an evening lecture of one sort or another. Evenings were clear, star-studded and chilly. Days were likewise bright. Autumn was heightening, the weather cool and refreshing and the leaves full of color. Peter himself felt alive with color. Heart and soul he was experiencing a new life. He was not only falling in love but his mind was awakening anew. There were several reasons. He and Maren were energetic persons not content to sit about in parks. They took long walks together, went to theaters, visited museums, listened to concerts both open-air and in halls and frequently attended public lectures.

The subject of religion was a common interest. Both were students of the Bible and many times read passages to each other then sat to discuss and sometimes debate the meaning.

"Look here," Peter was saying to Maren one evening as he met her after work, "I found this tract near my door. There's to be a street meeting tonight. Would you like to go?"

"I might," said Maren. "Let me read the tract." He handed it to her. The printing was neat but the paper was curled and looked well handled.

"It says that the true gospel of Jesus Christ is once again upon the earth and a discourse on the subject will be held at the central fountain of Norre Park."

"It also says we must bring a Bible . . ."

"I have one," said Peter proudly showing her the leather bound book Catherine had packed in his trunk three years previously.

"Well it certainly can't hurt to hear what they have to say I suppose," she said not caring one way or another. Maren just wanted to be with him. "Whoever *they* are . . ."

That night with his Bible tucked under one arm and Maren proudly hanging on the other, Peter led the way through the park. It was a crisp evening, with just a nip of winter in the air but the glow of companionship warmed the young lovers. A sizeable crowd had gathered by the time they arrived in the park center and a certain electricity permeated the air. It almost crackled.

The fellow speaking looked to be about Peter's own age and appeared somewhat awkward in a well-worn and too-large suit. Danish words were coming haltingly from his mouth yet his face seemed to radiate. He was obviously a foreigner, an American Peter guessed correctly.

"The book I'm holding aloft is a companion to the Holy Bible," he said with respect and sincerity. "It is *not* a replacement to the Bible . . . but it does contain the fullness of the everlasting Gospel of Christ!"

The speaker paused to reach down, whereupon a younger fellow, his companion, handed him a copy of the King James Bible, the leather covering of which was blackened with use. As the missionary held both books aloft, the crowd began to murmur. Heads were bobbing up and down and tension grew with every passing second.

"Each of these books contains revealed Scripture," the young man continued. "Writings of the prophets as revealed to them by God. Each of these precious documents I hold supports the other.

"One is the stick of Judah . . . and the other the stick of Joseph.

"Let me quote," he added putting his arms down and handing the thinner volume to his friend. "Turn in your Bibles to; Ezekiel the 37th chapter and start reading with me the 16th verse."

Peter was thumbing through his Bible as were several other listeners, but grading on the curve the crowd showed every emotion from sincere curiosity to pure hatred and antagonism.

"Moreover, thou son of man," the missionary began when he was satisfied that a few in the crowd had found the spot in their bibles and were with him, "take thee one stick and write upon it, for Judah, and for the children of Israel his companions; then take another stick, and write upon it for Joseph, the stick of Ephraim, and for all the house of Israel his companions. Verse 17; And join them one to another into one stick; and they shall become one in thine hand."

"Brothers and sisters, the sticks the prophet Ezekiel mentions are scrolls. As you well know, the ancient scriptures were written upon scrolls wrapped around round wooden dowels . . . sticks! This book, the Holy Bible," he held his leather bound Bible aloft again, "is the stick of Judah."

"And this book," he took the other, The Book of Mormon, and held it up, "this is the stick of Joseph!"

No sooner had the word Joseph left his mouth than he was struck smack in the face by a splattering wad of mud.

"Blasphemy!" shouted his attacker.

"Blasphemy and lies!" hooted another as both rushed the young speaker knocking him off the box he was standing on. Books and speaker went sprawling whereupon the young man's companion came quickly to his aid.

"Stop this! Stop!" shouted one supportive bystander, a well-dressed man of business or so it appeared. But the two young missionaries and the businessman were soon overwhelmed by other members of the crowd; including a woman who was shrieking and clawing at them. "Liars!" she shrilled. "Liars!"

"You there!" shouted Peter. "Let them have their say."

"Let's get away from here!" exclaimed Maren, frightened at the growing struggle and still clinging to Peter's arm.

"Don't get involved in it," she pleaded as she tried to restrain him, but Peter pulled away and was soon amongst the tangle. He had dropped his bible, Maren stopped to retrieve it, and standing watched as Peter entered the fray trying to separate one of the young missionaries from a man who was choking him. To break his grip, he ended up slugging the missionary's attacker square in the face knocking him to the ground.

Fists and elbows were thrown in all directions throughout the crowd, and the brawl had reached a fever pitch by the time a police whistle sounded. Two large shadowy figures could be seen rushing through the park heading toward the chaos. Meanwhile, someone had slugged Peter in the nose while another kicked him in the shins with a well-aimed boot cursing hatefully as he did; a painful black and blue bruise would mark the spot and what happened next was a blur of shouts and thuds; at least it was to Peter.

Moments later with one policeman blowing his whistle, and the other starting to lead the two bleeding and mud smattered American missionaries to jail, Peter's head cleared and something went off in his mind.

"Those two missionaries were only trying to add new light to our drab state religion!" he yelled at the crowd in general, "and got themselves arrested! Do we have freedom of religion in Denmark or do we not?!"

"You're lucky they don't arrest you," someone shouted back.

People were actually shrinking away from Peter. Some probably thought he was crazy. With his hair all wild and his face bloodied, he looked the part, but many who had heard him were actually ashamed. "Should I write the King?" Peter persisted. "Or stand on street corners and shout? Where is our country heading?'

One of the missionaries was clutching his bleeding cheek, peering through swollen eyes and saying to the other, "Are you all right Elder? Are you all right?" The other turned and looked at Peter.

"Thanks my friend," he said saluting. "Thanks very much."

"You're nose is bleeding!" Maren said as she found Peter whereupon he wiped at his nose with the length of his forearm smearing blood all over his face. His knuckles were skinned and bleeding and when he again looked at Maren his face opened up in a grin.

"I got one fellow pretty good," he said proudly. "He'll have a headache in the morning."

"You could have had your front teeth knocked out," Maren scolded. "All of you should be ashamed!" she said loud enough for some of the disbursing crowd to hear.

Nobody paid her any mind, just a curious glance or two as people slowly went about their business. Maren then went to a nearby lily pond, dipped her scarf in the water and returned to clean the blood from Peter's face.

"You'd better take me home," she said shakily as she rubbed his face. "With all the commotion it's a wonder my father hasn't come for me already."

Peter was trembling slightly himself. "Sorry about all this," he apologized as they started across the park. "Did you get my bible?"

"Right here," she said tucking her arm through his.

October 12th 1863

'This evening Maren and I were attending a street meeting given by two young and very sincere missionaries from America,' Peter recorded later that night in his journal. 'What happened reminds me of something I'll quote from a pamphlet by Søren Kierkegaard: "Let us be in earnest again and stop playing; for a Christianity preached by royal officials who are paid and insured by the state and *who use the police against the others,*" he underlined the last, "such a Christianity bears about the same relation to the Christianity of the New Testament as swimming with the help of a cork-belt or a bladder does to swimming alone . . . it is mere play."

Peter went on to record the details of the tragic event in his journal and when he retired to his bed, his adrenaline still flowing, he lay awake far into the night thinking about what he had heard, seen and experienced. Peter couldn't know it yet but the delicate flame of Christianity, originally kindled in his mind by his mother, the flame fanned and kept burning, although sometimes barely by Arne Hammergaard at Herlufsholm School, was soon to become a healthy fire!

Chapter 17

Days passed and the missionary incident remained on Peter's mind. '*Who were the young men and what had become of them?'* he wondered. *'Surely they were released from jail. They probably have a rented flat somewhere. Young as they were they called each other elder, very odd. And what were they trying to get across to the crowd? Stick of Judah? Stick of Joseph? A strange message indeed.'* Peter determined to find them again.

The month wore on and one cold night he and Maren were again at a street meeting where missionaries were talking and though one looked familiar Peter wasn't sure if it was the same fellow. There was no violence this time, only a bit of heckling from one or two of the listeners. There were other compelling lectures on the streets; lectures on Kierkegaard, debates concerning the new king. Change was in the air. Religious and political upheaval was apparent and Peter and Maren were infatuated with it all; especially with the missionary's message. It was an exciting time, a time of growth, awareness and love. Peter reflected on it in a letter to Catherine and Elias.

'Dear Mother and Father;

My mind has been so much upon the degraded conditions here in Copenhagen and the political and social unrest in Denmark at large, that at the beginning I found it hard to concentrate on my books and drawings. It was a bleak year and just when things were blackest I met a young woman named Maren Carlsen. She has made a big difference in me. Where I'd been feeling lost about my studies, I now have direction and purpose. Where I'd been worried, confidence has taken over. I feel like a new man!

Maren works in her father's millinery shop, a tidy little store across from Norre Park. She is a thrifty and very energetic person, has a delightful laugh and leads me all over town to lectures, concerts, and museums. It's a chore keeping up with her.'

"Peter has a girl, Elias," Catherine said happily, handing the letter to Elias as he lay propped up in bed. "It sounds as if he's in love."

"What?" croaked Elias, looking at the letter as Catherine seated herself on a small curved love seat near his bed. "She's the first girl he's ever mentioned." Elias's weak chest was currently inflamed and congested, and he was being careful not to overexert himself.

Catherine picked up her long needles and basket and began knitting contentedly.

"Listen to this," said Elias frowning after he'd scanned Peter's letter.

"We recently attended a lecture given by a disciple of the late Søren Kierkegaard. He immediately got our attention by saying Denmark is only a Christian nation because centuries ago King

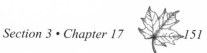

Harold Bluetooth forced baptism at the point of a sword. He said that few Danish citizens have actually made a conscious decision about Christ and that we're being led about by the nose by priestcraft. He went on to challenge the political power of the Folkekirken and said that even though the people long for freedom of speech and freedom of religion, it, the church, secretly works to suppress it. The government too. Even some citizens."

Catherine, expecting an outburst after what Elias just read, held her breath. Her needles picked up speed. But Elias only coughed and read on.

"The speaker also reminded us that that a person can't officially marry in Denmark unless the marriage is solemnized by a State-Church minister. Coronation and funeral of the king are also under the direction of the Folkekirken. In our personal lives and in our government, cradle to grave the church has its hands in the political pie."

"Where has he been, Catherine?" Elias said, scowling angrily as he leaned over the letter. "Why shouldn't the church be involved with these things?"

Catherine did not answer or look up from her knitting.

Elias continued reading. "The speaker finished his text by saying that paganism and ritual in the church keeps Danes enamored and ignorant of who God really is and what he expects of us. He said most Danes haven't the faintest idea what's really in the Bible. We leave its reading and interpretation to our ministers. He added that

Denmark is impoverished because of ignorance and the church does little to help.

The man almost caused a riot. But I agree with much of what he said. Copenhagen is in financial and spiritual bankruptcy. Thousands are out of work and are starving; yet the church, and our government, go merrily about their way saying all is well."

Elias, trembling with rage at this point, pushed the letter feebly to the floor and layback panting for breath. "What does Peter know about ignorance and poverty!?" he coughed. "And what does he expect the church to do about it anyway? What can be done by anybody? The poor will always be with us. The Bible says so. Things are just fine in Denmark."

"Out here in the provinces, yes," said Catherine, stooping to pick up the letter and placing it on the nightstand. "But apparently Copenhagen is a different matter."

"Humbug," spat Elias feeling a twinge of strength. "You'll not forget I spent most of my life there. It's not nearly so bad as Peter makes it out to be. Furthermore, Peter had best be careful when he mentions the church the way he does. He might be playing with his very salvation! I've read about the followers of the illustrious Søren Kierkegaard. They're nothing but a small pack of dissidents!"

'You're grossly uninformed and out of touch with the social affairs of Denmark dear husband,' Catherine thought to herself. *'Had you been out of this bedroom you might be abreast of society. The movement started by Søren Kierkegaard is no insignificant thing. The late philosopher's teachings are on the minds and lips of the educated public and even seeping down to those less privileged.'* At that point Catherine stood up briefly and adjusted her knitting basket. Elias was mumbling to himself as he again scanned Peter's now

wrinkled letter. Stretching a bit first, Catherine again sat to her knitting. *'Yes my dear Elias,'* her thoughts continued as her long needles clicked, *'Many Danes are genuinely questioning their Christianity. Are they following the teachings of the Savior of mankind or those of the Folkekirken? A subtle but very real change is sweeping quietly over our country. Kierkegaard's philosophies challenge the teachings of not only the Folkekirken but of other churches as well. And he virtually gave his life preparing and presenting his vast number of messages . . .'*

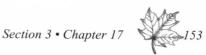

"Peter's a fool," Elias spat angrily snapping Catherine out of her thoughts. "He spends over two years studying architecture and now seems ready to scrap the whole business and for what? Some dead philosopher's gibberish. It doesn't sound to me as if he knows what in hell's name he wants."

"I won't have you swearing in my presence," said Catherine mildly. "Peter's entitled to his opinions."

"Humph," said Elias unrelentingly. "Opinions . . . more like out and out sedition. He'd better get his mind back on his studies or he won't graduate."

Elias settled into his pillow as Catherine retrieved Peter's letter and ran her eye over the closing paragraphs.

'I have personally witnessed religious oppression here in Copenhagen. Maren and I were listening to a lecture given by a Mormon missionary the other night and before he even got to finish his message he and his partner were attacked by a mob and later ran out of town by police.'

She didn't read Elias the last part. Other than furrowing her brow as she read she paid it little mind.

"He adds that he is well Elias, and . . . oh, here he asks for an increase in allowance. Peter has never asked for additional funds. But you can't have a lady without expenses." She laughed uncomfortably.

Elias shook his head irritably. He shared none of his wife's romantic silliness. "I'm sick of Peter's nonsense," he said bitterly. "Read me Hans' latest letter. You did say one came yesterday."

"Yes it did, are you sure you're strong enough?" Catherine asked solicitously.

He glared at her. "Anything will be better than what you've just read . . . yes, I want to hear it."

"Alright," she said calmly

"October 1863 . . .

Dear Father and Mother,

We've just returned from bivouac. Being in the woods causes me to know I made the right decision for my career. I thoroughly enjoy army life. It's in my very blood!

While on maneuvers we staged a mock battle. It was thrilling. I was placed in command of one regiment and Bengt Nielsen in command of another. The red army and the blue. Under my sword, half my reds confronted the enemy directly, issuing blank cannon and musket fire creating the illusion we were coming directly at them."

"Under his sword?" said Elias distastefully. "Don't you think he sounds somewhat boastful, Catherine?"

Undeterred, she read on:

"While this was going on I divided my remaining men into two groups and sent them around either side of the blue army, then rallying the first group to charge, we hit both flanks and front simultaneously.

With wad and powder we discharged our muskets as fast as humanly possible, filling the air with noise, smoke and confusion. It looked and felt like real battle. Before it ended we had surrounded the blues completely, and the field instructors gave us the victory. I received a letter of commendation from the commander for the achievement."

"Doesn't that make you proud of him, Elias?" queried Catherine exuberantly.

"Somewhat," said Elias dryly.

"Well it does me!" she said. "It also gives me confidence. If there ever is war Hans will know what to do to not only survive but to win!"

Catherine gave him a sharp look then dropped her eyes and continued:

"In my last letter I mentioned the king, and you won't believe it but he's coming to the academy to review the cadets and watch us drill. We intend to show His Majesty how an army should look. Enrollment this year has swelled our ranks to over a thousand cadets. We should make quite an impression."

"By heaven, Catherine," interrupted Elias. "This is the end! They intend to show the king? What is the matter with this . . .this strutting cockerel! The king honors them with a visit and he comes up with a blasphemous statement such as that! Furthermore I've noticed neither boy writes about test results or grades. Are they passing? I'd wager not, and I have to ask myself why we continue to waste money? Better Peter and Hans had stayed at home and worked in the mill!"

"You're being ridiculous," Catherine said. She folded the letter without finishing it returned to her knitting, only her quickened breathing betraying agitation at Elias's bad temper.

"I'll tell you this," said Elias venomously. "One word of disrespect about the king or the church while Peter and Hans are in my presence and I won't be responsible for my actions."

"Elias," said Catherine patiently. "You've got to realize that your sons are free agents with opinions of their own! And I say it's healthy. What if they were like parrots? Would you be proud if they simply repeated our words or even those of their professors? Thank heaven for free thinking!"

"Free thinking?" countered Elias, then coughed convulsively, cutting off her reply. "More like open rebellion to all we have taught them!" Catherine did not rush to his side but simply waited until his paroxysms were over. Then she continued deliberately, "Elias, our sons are becoming men. As their parents, we should be filled with joy. You've cankered my pleasure in these precious letters. Think what you were doing at their age!"

"I was minding my studies," was Elias' curt answer. "My father would never have allowed this kind of nonsense. One word, one act of rebellion, and I'd have been cut off from all money, all privileges, including letter writing!"

"Fortunately the twins live in a more enlightened era," Catherine snapped. Finally out of patience, she stood up and walked to the bedroom door. There she turned to Elais and her eyes were dark as a storm. "Peter and Hans are well educated. I've seen no evidence that they form opinions on the basis of mere whims. I'm glad they have minds of their own and are able to speak them!"

Elias began coughing piteously, but Catherine walked out of the bedroom, repressing the urge to slam the door.

Chapter 18

King Fredrick VII made his royal visit to the military academy in late October. It was bitterly cold with a light snow falling; instructors and school officials sat in the stands, while mounted on a marbled gray stallion the king proudly saluted the passing cadets. The day was as cold and as gray as the cadet's uniforms and sadly King Fredrick became chilled during the event. The chill quickly developed into pneumonia and November 15, 1863, the fifty-five year old well beloved monarch died, causing shock waves of grief to ripple throughout the country. And in the wake of public grief an unwanted guest, Prince Christian of Glücksborg, a German Prince, came calling on Denmark.

It was cold when Peter and Maren met in Norre Park and temperatures were well below freezing. The sky was clear, nearly a foot of snow covered grounds but the paths were well worn with the footsteps of skaters traveling to and from a large frozen pond off center of the park. The small arched bridge nearby, where Peter and Maren were watching the skaters was also clear of snow.

"They crowned the bugger King Christian IX just two days ago

Maren and already I feel a pall setting in over our country."

"His rule might not be as bad as you think Peter," she commented cheerily. And you should be proud to have been chosen among the few university designees to attend the coronation."

"I suppose so. My grades *have* been good this semester."

"Was it a grand occasion Peter, lots of color?" Her frosty breath hung about her lovely face in lacy clouds. Very happy to be away from her father's store catching a breath of fresh air with the man she loved, Maren was the picture of health that morning.

"Actually his coronation was a very quiet affair," Peter answered. "The was some pomp and circumstance; the royal guard in their high beaver hats, blue and red uniforms with polished boots and gleaming bayonets, but no marching band. It was not at all grandiose like those I've read about in England."

"Humm," she said. "And what does this new king look like?"

"Well, he's a rather a tallish man," explained Peter, "somewhat thin, has a high intelligent forehead and wears a heavy mustache. Like all the royal family he carries that pampered and noble air."

"You would too if you didn't have to work so hard," she said looking up into Peter's slightly blood-shot eyes. "You need to get more sleep."

"I suppose," Peter said yawning his frozen breath fogging the air. "The new king is 46 years old," he went on, "and he speaks German better than he does Danish. Young as he is he'll most likely rule for a long time."[3]

"Two days before King Frederick VII died," said Maren, "a common constitution for Denmark and Slesvig barely passed through Parliament, and to his favor, King Christian is against it."

"I know," said Peter. "He is also against the Ejder Programme."[4]

"I heard that," said Maren. "Father and I attended a debate in Aalborg Theater last night. What a crowd! Your professor Christophersen was one of the panelists by the way. My head is still full."

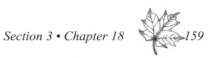

"My main concern," Peter went on, "is that the new king was educated in Germany and naturally harbors pro-German and pro-Russian sentiments. Also," he continued, "before our existing constitution's provisions have time to go into effect, I fear he may try to alter them. Limit our freedom of speech and religion for example. Who knows?"

"That was covered in the debate last night," said Maren beginning to show concern. "Ever since the war over the Duchies in 1848 we Danes have been leery of Germans."

"And now we've got one as king," injected Peter.

"Are we going to survive as a nation Peter?" she asked looking up at him. "Or will Prussia eventually swallow us up."

He looked at her tenderly. "Of course Denmark will survive Maren. All this has you very troubled hasn't it?"

"Somewhat," she answered with tears forming in the corner of her eyes. "It's just that where our future is concerned . . ." She couldn't put the last into words.

Peter took Maren into his arms and held her closely. Then looking down at her, kissed her on the mouth, then held her protectively. A few skaters paused to take a look at the couple on the bridge, but Peter went right on. "We have a future Maren," he said confidently as he looked into her eyes. "Don't fret about that. I don't care who is king, or what he tries to do to our laws. You and I have a bright future."

That evening Peter sat at the small desk in his dorm and took out a sheet of paper. He had a great deal on his young mind and perhaps some very important news to break to his parents. There was no time like the present. The letter was posted November 18, 1863 and Catherine received it less than two weeks later.

'Dear Mother and Father,' it read. *'Good King Fredrick is dead and our country is in mourning. He was the only leader I ever knew, and as you know because he initiated improvements in the constitution that improved life in Denmark he was dearly loved by the people. Giving rights to women on par with men in matters of succession was one big step and allowing farmers form retail cooperative societies another. I know I've complained about our government in the past and still believe there are flaws, but I now see King Fredrick was doing all he could to hasten reform.*

Life in Copenhagen continues as before I suppose, but the death of the King was totally unexpected and people feel uneasy. There yet remains the possibility of conflict with Prussia over the Duchies and no one is sure of the new King's ability to lead. Especially in time of war! And will this King Christian IX support our constitution or try and change it?

Some sections of the city are in an uproar. At night the podiums and halls are ringing with rhetoric over this German. It's an interesting time to be alive! It's an enlightened age, filled with worry and yet I have never been happier.

Maren Carlsen is the reason for my happiness. She has caused such a great change in me. I can scarcely write her name that my heart isn't singing. She is a wonderful person and because of her my life is fulfilled as never before. I haven't asked her to marry me yet, but intend to soon. I pray she'll have me.

I haven't told you yet but Maren and I are studying with the Mormons. We are finding answers to some of life's most difficult questions from them. Questions such as; who are we? Where do we come from? And where do we go after this life? Answers I've been getting from the missionaries are opening my mind, and very satisfying to my soul'

The further Elias read in Peter's letter, the redder his face became. "I tell you, Catherine," he roared, "the boy's gone mad!" He stood, wadded the letter, and flung it toward the fireplace. It struck the bricks just above the opening and fell safely to the floor near the coalscuttle.

"Marry a shopkeeper's daughter?!" A fit of coughing overtook him but straining his throat he continued. "A commoner, and as sure as I'm standing here, he's forsaking the church . . . Mormons, indeed!"

Catherine quietly retrieved the letter, smoothed and folded it and tucked it into her knitting basket, then continued acting serenely with her needles clicking. Inside she was shaking with anger but with the spirit of the Lord's season upon her she determined to get hold of her emotions. This Maren Peter spoke of was more than likely a capable and lovely young lady. Catherine couldn't imagine her son choosing a drudge.

Elias, who for once was out of his sick bed, was pacing the floor.

"The boy doesn't appreciate a thing we've done for him," he grumbled. "We send him to the finest institute of learning in the nation and all he picks up is what he hears on the streets and in secret religious meetings!"

"You're making assumptions," Catherine said calmly, but wrinkles on her face betrayed uneasiness. "Christmas will arrive soon enough. There'll be time to discuss all this."

"Bah," said Elias. "You've read his letters. It seems to me his mind is made up! Next thing you know, he'll write and say he's finished with the university!"

Like an iceberg floating slowly down Holbaek Fjord, a cold gray barrier was moving between Catherine and Elias. Nothing turned the heiress' heart to stone more quickly than when Elias attacked her sons.

"We also have another letter from Hans," she said desperately wanting to alter the subject. Would you like me to read it aloud?" When he didn't answer and she began anyway.

"Dear Father and Mother:

Christmas will soon arrive and it's the first time I can remember my spirits being so low at this festive time of year. The news of the coronation of Christian IX this year was not well received here at the academy. And I myself fear the future. There are whisperings of war. Prussia with her desire for German unification still has designs on Holstein and Slesvig. Having a German-minded king, and a weakling at that or so go the rumors, gives me great uneasiness.

Parliament voted its approval to go along with the London Treaty[5] *of 1852 but they have failed to see the dangerous circumstances it has placed Denmark in. Our army is weak, our military leadership is aging and our weaponry out of date. Our beloved country is in a very poor condition to defend herself. These are precarious times and we don't need a weakling as our king. More than ever I am convinced that following royal bloodlines is an archaic system whose time is over."*

Elias, who was still seething over Peter's letter, dropped his hands hopelessly to his sides.

"Your sons are going to put me in the grave, Catherine," he said despondently. "The monarchy has served Denmark well for centuries." He cleared his throat. "Fredrick VII had no sons. Following the London Protocol was the only way to maintain order; the only way to maintain peace. Hans knows Slesvig and Holstein follow the House of Augustenborg where female[6] rule is unacceptable. And having a king who understands the way Germans think can only help us. Hans should know that. Why in the name of reason . . ." he coughed again, "does he continue on his rebellious course?"

"I don't see rebellion in what he is saying Elias!"

Even though she had raised her voice he ignored her and continued rambling. "Now that Christian IX has been crowned we must all stand behind him. What else is there to do?

"And being enrolled in a military academy doesn't give Hans knowledge of the country's overall strength!" Elias added angrily.

"Oh Elias," interrupted Catherine wearily. "He'll soon be an officer in the Danish Royal Army. He is in a far better position to know the country's military strength than we . . ."

"And he called the king a puppet!" Elias choked, again completely ignoring her comment. With a dressing gown hanging limp upon his sickly frame he looked like a refugee from a hospital ward and Catherine couldn't help feeling sorry for him. He shuffled to the window overlooking the stables and parted the draperies. It was misty and dark outside, complementing Elias' attire and mood perfectly. Weak and sickly though he appeared, here stood a latent volcano, bubbling, rumbling, and ready to belch hot lava at any second.

"Your sons . . . our sons," he moaned. "Where did we fail them?"

"Wait until Christmas, Elias," Catherine said soothingly but nearly out of patience. "They'll both be home and then we can all sit down and discuss these delicate issues rationally. Letters leave so much to the imagination."

"Peter left nothing to my imagination," said Elias turning on her. "He's nothing but a forsaken rebel." His choking coughs overtook him for a moment, but he regained his strength. "I'm going to put a stop to this! Becoming a Mormon, marrying a common clerk . . ."

Catherine had stood enough and abruptly rose to her feet, startling Elias. "For the last time," she said coldly. "Peter can marry a commoner or anyone else that suits him. Why, you speak as if you're royalty. You were no more than a commoner yourself before we married!" Elias' mouth fell open but nothing came out. "Furthermore," said Catherine standing her ground, "Peter's decision about religion is also his own. Be thankful God is real to him. That's what counts, not which church he chooses to worship in."

His hands gripping the windowsill until his already pale knuckles were nearly transparent, Elias was speechless. Catherine continued, her voice level and in control. "And as far as Hans is concerned, he is right about the archaic system that chooses our leaders. Royal-blood indeed. Ha! They would have you think they descended from the gods. Warlords started the whole system! Barbarians would be more like it!"

Elias's hair stood on the back of his neck. "Catherine!" he croaked. "You'll bring damnation to this house."

"Kings are mortals Elias," she continued resolutely, "no wiser, no stronger, no better than any of us. Just because Prince so-and-so marries Princess whatever, what gives them the right to govern an entire nation? And King Christian *is* a weakling; a puppet and you know it!"

"Treason and blasphemy!" shouted Elias, trembling with rage. "None of this would have entered your silly head had it not been for

Hans' and Peter's letters! When they return, I'll beat them like dogs! I will not tolerate their rebellion!"

Catherine glared at him angrily. Any trace of calm had vanished. "You'll not lay a hand on either of them Elias! Ha," she added when the thought of confrontation hit her. "Why you will shrink at their presence. They are men now Elias. Strong—young—virile men," she enunciated her words.

"Do you think they'd stand for a beating from the likes of you!" They stared hatefully at each other; sparks exuded from their eyes like flint off of steel. Catherine knew she'd gone too far but years of frustration had finally boiled to the surface. And strangely, at least to her, Elias backed down. All he could do was take a seat on the bed and stare numbly at her.

"Oh, for shame, Elias," Catherine said and she sank back into her own chair. "Shame on us." Tears sprang to her eyes. "Christmas is coming," she added quietly. "The birthday of our Lord and Savior. And we would have violence in our home?" She shook her head silently and hot tears splashed on her folded hands.

"When our sons return, we will calmly discuss these troubling, and joyful, I might add, issues. I myself have concerns over government and church, and who my son might marry; and I wish to air them out; openly and with respect for each other."

After a bit she wiped her eyes and picked up her knitting. A strange calmness had settled over her. For ten full minutes all that was heard was the clicking of her needles. "Ever since the death of little Kristian, Christ has been the most important aspect of my life," she said at length, and softly. Catherine adjusted her knitting and raised her eyes to Elias. At the moment, she regarded him as little more than a boarder; and one that paid no rent. "When I think of Peter getting married, and the grandchildren that may come, I feel so happy, so at peace."

She took a deep breath. Elias was still her husband and after reminding herself of the fact she addressed him more respectfully. "I spoke in anger," she said shaking her head slightly, "and for that I am sorry, but we can not have the celebration of Christ's birth ruined by contention and violence in our home, no matter what the reason. You and I must calm ourselves between now and when Peter and Hans return."

When he didn't answer, Catherine got up wearily and left the room. She had said all that she would on the subject and needed to be alone.

By Christmas, Elias had another fever and coughing spell that confined him to his bed for several days. Catherine's attentions at his side were as soothing and as assiduous as ever and neither of them spoke of their confrontation. Meanwhile, she and Inger made up the beds with fresh linen, shook all the rugs, dusted, swept and cleaned every room, then decorated the large house with bright colors, boughs of greenery and ribbons of red and gold.

Extra wood was brought in so all the fireplaces could be kept burning, warming the house cheerily against the subzero nights and crisp days. Down at the stables Catherine also had Nils Holsen prepare for the return of the twins. "I want every detail perfect Nils," she told him after she and Ferdinand had given Peter and Hans' horses a morning run.

"I've brushed them down every day this week Fru Jensen, even re-shoed them. But they've fattened up . . . you and Ferdinand will need to run them every day until Peter and Hans return. If you don't they'll be as slow as mules."

Catherine loved horses as much as any man and she also handled them well. "I hardly think they'll be that slow Nils," she said. "But Ferdinand and I will do as you say. Hans is especially fussy about his mount." She rubbed the stallion's neck. "Good Vargus. Hans won't be happy if you're slow; will he now? I wonder where the name comes from Nils? It sounds mythical don't you think?"

Nils threw a pitchfork of hay within reach of both horses. "Could be," he said.

"Maybe Hans got it from an old Greek," Ferdinand answered sarcastically.

It was cold outside and the horses were steaming. As Catherine, Nils and Ferdinand took gunnysacks and wiped the sweating animals down, the straw strewn about felt comfortable under their feet, blending with the contented munching sounds of both animals. The acrid smell of horseflesh mingled with the sweet rich fragrance of hay permeated the air.

"I'm glad Peter's not so particular as Hans about his horse," said Ferdinand putting his sack aside.

"I've taken as much care with one as I have the other," said Nils doing the same.

"Oh I can hardly wait to see them, Ferdinand," said Catherine with exuberance. "It will be a grand Christmas. Nils, did I tell you that Peter may be getting married?"

"Word's gotten around madam," said Nils.

"You would have to be deaf not to know," Ferdinand said blandly.

"I could soon be a grandmother," exclaimed Catherine. "Can you imagine! Wouldn't it be thrilling to hear the sounds of a baby in the house? It has been such a long, long time." Catherine walked to the next stall, that of a speckled mare. "Look here," she said gentleness in her voice. "This one's heavy with foal."

"There are several in her condition," commented Nils with a business like air. "They'll be at least four colts this spring."

"Wonderful," said Catherine exuberantly.

"The old girl looks large enough to have twins," observed Ferdinand.

"Perhaps we'll name them after your brothers."

"Humph," said the lanky boy.

Like his brothers, Ferdinand had worked at the stables and mill, only much less enthusiastically than his brothers; and even less diligently at home chores. When Ferdinand graduated from Herlufsholm the year before, Catherine had not insisted he begin university studies the very next year as she had Peter. Nor was there even a fragment of encouragement that he attend the military academy at Frederica. Not that Ferdinand was interested in either. He seemed content to remain at home, and to her own amazement, Catherine preferred it that way. Was it that Ferdinand provided a buffer between she and Elias? Or was it that she was hanging on to her last child? Perhaps a little of both, but as Elias' burden and temper worsened over the years, she had come to rely on Ferdinand to take some of the load from her shoulders. To take meals to him, wait on him and listen to him whine.

But Ferdinand seemed to be changing with all the time he'd been spending with his father. Even though Hans and Peter had not been home in a year it seemed a certain animosity toward them was growing within him. Catherine couldn't put her finger on it exactly but clear signals were shown one morning when she and Ferdinand were back out in the barn checking on the mares.

"Horses are so demanding," complained Catherine, "always something. They need to be shod, or else fed, watered or groomed. You'd think they'd give us a little milk for our efforts right?"

"Lucky we have Nils around or this is all I'd be doing," Ferdinand complained as he curried one of the pregnant mares. Cold as it was in the barn, the old girl seemed to be enjoying the attention and stamped her hoof repeatedly as if to say so. Her nostrils flared at each stroke of Ferdinand's brush and she snorted like a steam engine. "My brothers will never be out here again," he added.

"They will once they get home for the holidays," said Catherine. "Hans and Peter have never been known to shirk their duties."

"All I know is that every day I'm out here with Nils and Torkil while my brothers are off traipsing around the country. And they are not going to come back here permanently mother. Once his studies are completed Peter will probably live in Copenhagen, and who knows about Hans?"

Catherine had chosen not to think seriously about what Ferdinand had just outlined. She knew changes were coming of course and while Ferdinand was rambling her mind drifted back and forth between her twin sons. She even imagined visiting Copenhagen and seeing Peter and Maren in an apartment, *'and, was that a grandchild over there in the corner, crying in its crib?'* And astride a fine prancing horse there was Hans, all decked out in the proud blue and red uniform of Denmark with medals on his chest. *'How had he earned them?'*

"Now they've gotten themselves all educated," Ferdinand mumbled, "they both think they are so clever. Downgrading the monarchy, showing disrespect for the church . . ."

"What was that Ferdinand?" asked Catherine coming out of her daydream.

"Oh nothing," he answered.

"Who put those thoughts in your head?" she wanted to know.

"What do my brothers care about the lands and mill Mother?" he said taking her off the track. "You and I are the ones doing all the work around here. Peter in Copenhagen, Hans in Flensborg . . ."

"You shall have your time at the university or away somewhere," said Catherine patiently as she sprinkled a bucket of oats along the horse troth. She didn't really mean what she had said. She knew Ferdinand lacked the adventuresome ways of his brothers and would likely end up right where he was. "What do you want to do with your life?" she asked just to see what he might say.

"Oh, I don't know," Ferdinand answered shrugging his shoulders. "You and father are not getting any younger. Somebody's got to mind things around here."

"And you're doing a fine job, I might add," she said appreciat-ively.

"Father said I might one day have all this," he said turning away from the mare and pointing out the open barn door with his saw toothed currying brush.

"Did he now?" said Catherine raising her eyebrows.

"Well neither of my brothers wants it."

"These are large concerns Ferdinand," said Catherine candidly as she scooped another bucket of oats from the bin. "Surely decisions many years into the future. And I'm not nearly ready for the rocking chair," she added, this time throwing the oats along the horse troth. Catherine was surprised at her reaction but her youngest son had certainly started her mind turning.

Later in the kitchen as she and Ferdinand were washing up his attitude toward Peter and Hans continued. "They never write to me you know."

"What's that?"

"Peter and Hans, neither of them writes. They don't care if I'm even alive."

"They always ask about you in their letters," Catherine countered.

"I tell you what they say. Have you written to them?"

"Well no."

"Remember the old adage Ferdinand, he who writes, gets written to." Catherine's holiday mood was such that she chose to shrug off Ferdinand's disdain toward his brothers. She was sure it would mellow out once the three were reunited. "When they get home Ferdinand," she went on excitedly, "the first thing you ought to do together is go ice-skating. The weather is perfect, and the millpond is frozen solid. Why there's probably a foot of ice by now!"

"I was there just yesterday," said Ferdinand. "It is getting close."

"I might even put on some skates and join you," Catherine exclaimed. She glanced out the barn door toward the gristmill. "It looks so peaceful this time of year. Dusted with snow instead of flour, the blades not turning. Like a graying old man, it appears to be resting. My father loved that mill; and now that all three of you have worked there it's as much a part of you as me." Tears came to her eyes.

Ferdinand seemed unmoved by his mother's sentimentality and Catherine seemed not to notice. She placed her hand on his shoulder and kissed his cheek affectionately. "Let's go to the woods and cut a Christmas tree, Ferdinand," she said, suddenly becoming cheerful again. She looked over toward the house. "We can place it in the parlor and decorate it . . . put some life in that depressing old place over there. Let's make this a Christmas to remember!"

SECTION NOTES:

1. During the Napoleonic Wars, Denmark rejected British demands that she give up her navy before Napoleon's advancing armies could seize it. In a show of force British warships converged upon Copenhagen shelling the city to the tune of four thousand projectiles every 24 hours. Over a 1,000 buildings were destroyed by fire and explosion in the spectacular fusillade and several hundred people were killed. A third of the city lay in ruins and when the smoke cleared most of Denmark's sizable armada of ships had been carried off to England. Following the cataclysmic rampage, Britain also captured over half of the markets that fed Denmark, causing economic chaos and unemployment that lasted for decades. Antagonism existed between Denmark and England that only eased after the marriage between Alexandra, daughter of Danish King Christian IX, and King Edward VII of the United Kingdom, Great Britain and Ireland in 1902 making Alexandra Queen of England.

2. N.S.F. Grundtvig, short for Nikola Frederik Severin Grundtvig, was a progressive Lutheran Priest, an educator and the driving force behind the new system. With his theme, "The national and civic life we all can and must share," Grundtvig was trying to steer public schools away from a system that had the sole and narrow purpose of training young men for the ministry, toward one whose objective was a well rounded education for all, females included. Innovative though the new plan was, because of the iron hold of the Folkekirken, (the state church) Grundtvig's work took decades for its fruits to ripen.

3. Peter's prediction turned into prophecy. Christian IX ruled Denmark from 1863 until 1912.

4. Ejder Programme—see Section Notes in section one.

5. London Protocol was a treaty signed July 4, 1850 between; Denmark, Russia, Britain, France, Sweden, Norway and subsequently Austria which in theory re-established the indivisibility of the Danish Kingdom. In it was a specific clause stating if that Frederik VII should die without a male heir, Prince Christian of Glücksborg a very distant cousin of Fredrick VII, would be the new King. Educated in Germany and fluent in the German language Prince Christian was the likely choice. The signers of The London Treaty believed (erroneously) that a German-speaking monarch would serve to keep Lauenberg and Holstein loyal to Denmark and thus keep the country united.

The London Protocol also ensured succession in the female line for Denmark

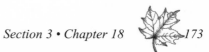

but Holstein and Slesvig were loyal to the house of Augustenborg where female rule was unacceptable. This was another reason Prince Christian was named in the treaty.

6. Denmark had not had a queen since the fourteenth century, and even though the Treaty of London maintained provisions for female succession Holsteiners would never hear of it therefore Prince Christian *was* the obvious choice. Like many Danes, Elias distrusted the new king but he worshipped the monarchy for the monarchy's sake; and once a King was installed whether for the people or against them, he was still satisfied with the system.

Section Four

A Gathering Storm

Chapter 19

Christmas 1863 was rapidly approaching. Except for a few minor details Catherine and Inger almost had the house ready for the gala event. In the living room, with its bulky stone fireplace, a large green spruce tree was brightly decorated with flags and tinsel and placed in the corner of the room. The tree was also adorned with red and white satin bows, colored ornaments, candles stuck in their own wax on select branches and a silver star on the very top branch. Under the tree were several presents wrapped in white paper and tied with colorful ribbons.

Catherine's best porcelain, silverware and fine linen adorned the oak table in the parlor while hundreds of crystal pendants shimmered from the chandelier sending blue and red sparkles of light dancing about the room. Silver candelabras with lighted candles and green pine branches decorated the shelves and fireplace mantel. The heavenly smell of freshly baked bread filled the house, while in the kitchen Inger was busily rolling out dough for pastries. Throughout the house and property, holiday preparations warmly awaited the return of Peter and Hans.

The University of Copenhagen closed its doors for the holidays on December 20th, as did the Academy at Frederica. Hans' more difficult journey across the strait meant he would arrive a day or so after Peter, but both were on their way.

It was snowing the morning Maren drove Peter to the depot where he was to catch a stagecoach to Holbaek via Frederikssund, Skibby and Agerup. With cheeks flushed and lacy white snowflakes floating softly onto her hair, Maren presented a lovely picture as she and Peter rode carefully along in her grandfather's carriage. Peter smiled at her appreciatively and after stopping at the way station, helped her down, held and kissed her.

"You handled the horse very well," he said as he hoisted his trunk.

"She's old and gentle," Maren said modestly.

The graying mare, as if on cue, raised its tail and vented a fine pile of steaming manure clumps on the ground. Maren shook her head, looked away and rolled her eyes skyward. "Such manners."

"She knew you were talking about her and put on a show," laughed Peter.

Just then a locomotive at the depot across from the way station sent two blasts of steam shrieking from its whistle. Moments later another huge blast of steam erupted from its boilers and, for a moment, train and depot disappeared. Pistons lunged into action and the train's giant wheels began to turn, spinning once or twice at first and then biting into the track. "I would have taken a train to Roskilde," Peter explained as the steam fog began to clear and the train chugged slowly away, " but after buying gifts for the family I couldn't afford it."

"The last time I rode a train I was a little girl," Maren said wistfully. "I don't even know where we were going."

"Your next trip will be with me to Holbaek," Peter assured her. "When we go to meet my family . . ."

"Father would go through the roof if I even suggested such a trip now, especially un-chaperoned."

"We've been over this already" said Peter testily. "Christmas is our store's busiest season," he added in a deep voice mocking her father."

"We've only known each other a few months Peter," she said apologetically, but slightly irritated. Her father *was* a task master, but he was still her father and she loved him. "Just give it a little more time."

"I will, I will," he said impatiently. They each took a handle of Peter's heavy trunk and lifted it. "But one day soon the waiting will be over." After setting the gift-laden trunk down at the stagecoach loading dock, Peter again took Maren in his arms. "I'll miss you terribly," he said in earnest.

"And I you," she said looking at him through moistened eyes.

"But I'll be back before you know it," he added. "The holidays always pass quickly."

"Too quickly I suppose," said she.

It was busy at the way station. Coaches for Frederikssund, Roskilde, Holbaek and beyond were coming and going about every half-hour. Snorting horses with their jingling bridles were everywhere, leaving clumps of fresh manure and yellow pools of urine in the melting snow. Stepping gingerly around the mess, other would-be passengers and loved ones were saying their good-byes.

"This one to Frederikssund," called a driver as he pulled up to the loading area. "First call!"

"Perfect timing," said Peter trying to be cheerful. "I may as well climb aboard. I do wish you were going with me Maren."

"I know," she said kissing him on the cheek. "Just have a good time with your family and remember I'll be waiting."

"How can the holidays be filled with such joy and pain at the same time," Peter whispered in Maren's ear after kissing her unashamedly once more. "It's good to be going home, I suppose; at least to be free of studies for a while." He gave her a last embrace and handed his trunk up to the driver.

"Last call for Frederikssund!" the driver shouted as he tied down the trunk. He may as well have saved his breath—a family of five was already climbing aboard. They along with Peter filled the coach. "Last call!"

Peter stepped into the coach and leaned out the window. "I'll be back in two weeks Maren," he said blowing her a kiss. "No later."

"Farewell," she said brushing at her eyes.

It was still snowing only lightly as Maren drove homeward. The atmosphere around the carriage was as peaceful as a quiet prayer. As if in respect, even the sound of the mare's hooves were muffled as she clopped along in the white fluff. The carriage approached Norre Park with its snow-covered paths and Maren pulled back on the reins. In a state of melancholy she gazed across the tree studded landscape, thinking of the pleasant days so recently gone by. In her mind, the fountains were still bubbling, swans were still gliding smoothly across the water, and she was sitting on the grass holding Peter's head in her lap. She was very comfortable with him. They had such fun together and could talk for hours on end never tiring of one another's company. Maren loved him so deeply she felt her heart would burst.

"His family probably thinks of me as poor and uneducated," she murmured miserably. "Rich and uppity people I'll bet. How would it be to have so much land and such? His mother doesn't sound so bad I suppose. Oh, I hope they'll accept me one day." The gray and lifeless trees looked as bleak as Maren's thoughts. Only Peter's love could bring in sunshine. She clucked to the mare and slowly drove away.

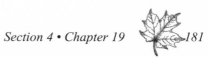

On the stagecoach, a large stern-looking man wearing a thick beaver cap, waistcoat, and fur-collared overcoat was seated next to Peter. Over-dressed as he was, he left little room and on the seat across from them, a thin sallow-looking woman with pinched cheeks and a haunted look was holding an infant. Seated next to her was a small boy. Peter judged him to be about four. The boy and his little sister were still fidgeting with excitement. It wouldn't last. The stern gaze of the father would eventually subdue them, or so Peter judged.

'Why can't men simply enjoy their families?' he wondered, his thoughts immediately turning to Elias. He had to repress a shudder. He glanced up at the woman and she smiled at him. Could she read his mind?

The coach rocked and jolted along. Temperatures were dropping. It would be a long trip but at least Peter was certain of arrival. Reports in the Berlingske Tidende told of a train that had been stalled by snowdrifts for two days earlier that month. But traffic was heavy on the roads from Copenhagen to Roskilde to Holbaek. Enough farmers' wagons, commercial rigs, and individual carriages traversed the rutted way to keep it clear.

By now the snow in the air had reduced to a light powder and only a few inches covered the road. Puddles of water revealed the deepest holes in the road; they would freeze solid later that night; even so two hours into the trip Peter and the other inhabitants in the coach felt as if they had been beat up. Everyone except the children. Constantly standing then sitting, up and down they seemed unaffected by the continual bouncing.

The coach stopped three hours later at Lindenborg Kro, an inn overlooking Isefjord where drivers watered or else changed horses while their passengers drank beer and snacked on pickled herring, smoked salmon and pumpernickel bread. Peter wasn't hungry and wandered around the inn to examine its architectural beauty. Lindenborg Kro had been built a decade or so previously, but its impressive size and rock-solid construction gave him the feeling it would remain there forever.

'Forever, that's what I want with Maren,' he mused, *'a relationship that will last throughout eternity. Even after these rock walls are gone,'* he added still absently examining the Inn's sturdy construction. Maren was everything to him. Her companionship, her freshness, already Peter missed her warm and tender kisses! The very fragrance of her soft and gentle breath lingered on his mind. Lately it had become so difficult to control his passions for her. He wanted to possess her, protect her and provide for her.

Still roving about, killing time Peter ventured out back of the Inn to take in the spectacular view and vast blue depth of Isefjord. The fjord's rocky shores, pounding surf and sheer magnificence took his breath away! Like a gigantic blue gash in the land, the fjord cut a path directly toward the ocean. *'Roadway of the Vikings,'* he thought. *'I wonder if Maren has ever seen this place. I must bring her. What a perfect place to honeymoon!'*

Later in the afternoon, as the coach sped across the hilly, white countryside toward Holbaek, Peter felt as if he were going to visit strangers. Except for Catherine that is. Her presence was forever a shadow, forever attached to him. He loved his mother, but Elias was a recurring nightmare and Ferdinand only a vague memory. Inger? In reality Peter could not wait to taste her cooking, but not necessarily her salty personality. Torkil, of course he wanted to see the man of strength. He was the steady voice at the mill. Nevertheless, all in all, Peter felt somewhat estranged from everyone.

'I guess it's because I've been away so long,' he thought. *'Or*

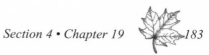

maybe it's because in my mind I've already severed family ties. I've asked Maren to marry me. She has agreed but . . . there is so much to work out. Still all I can think about is being with her.'

The road was smoother now and Peter kept his mind on Maren. Holding her, talking to her, loving her. He scarcely spoke to the other passengers, or they to him.

Contrary to what Peter had hoped, the children in the coach never did settle down. They were obviously not afraid of their stern-looking father. Their continued poking at each other and rude behavior even after many of his warnings proved their father's stern demeanor was simply a false front. When not getting up and down from their seats or exclaiming about this cow or that bull or horse in the fields, his children were whining to their mother that they were hungry or about when they might arrive at their destination.

Where he and Maren were concerned, children had never entered Peter's mind. Were his thoughts not so intent upon her, he might have taken notes on how not to discipline children. But his concentration was not so great that the children's antics didn't finally bother him. Greatly. He was about to scream at the man and his wife to get control of their offspring when, to his blessed relief, the stagecoach stopped at Brømølle Kro[1] and the entire family got off to spend the night, leaving Peter alone on the coach.

With its rich leather smell and polished wood the coach's interior was pleasant enough, especially without children jumping around inside. But its rocking, jolting motion was far from restful. Regardless, Peter leaned his head against the padded outer wall, curled his legs against his chest and fell asleep. It seemed but a few moments later when dead stillness wakened him abruptly. There were muffled voices outside the coach and a man was leading the horses away. Snow was falling and Peter pulled out his pocket watch; it was almost seven o'clock at night.

Under the lantern light at the way station and magnified by falling snow, he recognized Ferdinand sitting atop a buckboard; his silhouette hunched against the cold. Peter, still groggy from his nap, stepped unsteadily from the coach. “Ferdinand, that is you isn’t it?” The frigid air hit and caused a shiver to ripple down Peter’s spine.

“It is,” called Ferdinand.

“Let me collect my trunk.” Peter returned.

“I’d have brought a carriage but Nils left this old work rig ready and waiting,” said Ferdinand when Peter threw his trunk aboard.

“It’s fine,” said Peter shaking his brother’s hand. “Have you been here long?”

“About two hours,” said Ferdinand sourly. “I was here yesterday too. We weren’t exactly sure of your arrival.”

“I didn’t mean to be such a bother little brother,” said Peter troubled by Ferdinand’s disdain. Ferdinand didn’t reply.

“So how have you been?” asked Peter still trying to clear his head as he climbed aboard the wagon.

“I’ve been alright,” he held out his hand and Peter shook it. “All settled in?” he asked.

“Ready for a warm bed,” Peter replied with a shiver. “Let’s get going.”

“Gid’ up,” said Ferdinand flicking the reins.

Peter was amazed at the reception he had just received. Hadn’t it been months since they had seen each other? He wanted to reach across and smack his younger brother. Instead he hunkered into his greatcoat and tried to get warm. He needed to be more fully awake before attempting a serious conversation with Ferdinand; otherwise the drive to the Jensen estate might prove very unpleasant. They had little in common anymore, that was certain, but there was something eating away at the youngest of Catherine's children. Before Peter returned to the university, he determined to find out what it was. For now he would keep the conversation light.

"How is our mother?" he asked sincerely interested.

"Well enough considering holiday preparations," said Ferdinand. "She has nearly killed herself getting things ready for you and Hans."

"The house looks nice does it?"

"Very. Get up there!" Ferdinand called as the team approached a snowdrift across the road.

"How about father? How is his health?"

"He's doing fairly well at present," Ferdinand said above the clamor of the buckboard and team. "He's had a long battle, but he finally appears to be rising above things."

"Good," Peter said not sure if he meant it. Intuitively he felt the influence of his father strong upon Ferdinand. He was about to explore just how strong when the thought of actually facing Elias hit him squarely in the face. *'What will I say to the man? I've been thinking so much about Maren I haven't planned a thing. What would set him off first?'* Facing Elias was going to be difficult, and talking with him about Maren Carlsen very touchy. Peter *had* thought about that. *'Father will want to know what I'll be doing to support her after marriage. He will probably encourage my employment in Copenhagen. But that's where Maren and I plan to live anyway. Isn't it?'*

Now he was so close to home Peter wasn't sure. He wondered about the estate, about his mother and about the mill. Even though he was studying to become an architect, deep inside Peter believed that somehow he would always be involved in the family business. There was something about milling. It was in his blood.

"Is Hans home yet?" he asked mechanically.

"Of course not," was the reply. "Else he would be here too."

Earlier Peter noted how tall Ferdinand had grown and with a slight twinge of jealousy, how skillfully he handled the team. *'Mother's got all the support she needs right here,'* he thought. *'She can get along fine without me. She can also get along without Hans for that matter. Ferdinand does look a little soft though,'* Peter concluded.

"Where are you headed with your life?" Peter asked over the ruckus. "I mean since you've been out of school and all?"

"Well, I've spent a lot of time at the mill this year," Ferdinand lied. "Who knows . . . I might actually make a career of it."

"It would be a good one," said Peter encouragingly.

"Yeah, me an ol' Torkil grinding away at the wheat."

"Do you want to work there or not?" asked Peter suddenly becoming irritated. "That mill has blessed our family immeasurably over the years and I don't appreciate your flippant attitude about it."

"Unlike you Peter, I don't have my life plan all mapped out," he said as the buckboard went into a turn. *'If you only knew,'* Peter was about to say. The road straightened out and became a bit smoother and Ferdinand seemed to settle down himself. He became more serious, almost apologetic. "Maybe I'll just work about the estate taking care of what's needed and do some writing. Father says I have a great talent for it."

"Really," said Peter. He hadn't seen a single letter from the boy and hadn't heard anything about Ferdinand's literary abilities at Herlufsholm. In fact Peter had the impression that his younger brother had struggled at school. "What kind of writing?"

"I don't know. Father has some ideas we've been discussing. Danish politics, you know."

'An ambitious topic for one so lacking in ambition let alone experience,' thought Peter. He made a mental note to discuss the subject with Catherine and Ferdinand later.

The brothers were home in less than thirty minutes, stiff with cold from the open-air ride; their noses and cheeks were red, and eyebrows frosted. Peter's snow laden beard quickly moistened as he entered the house and warm air engulfed him. Catherine was there to greet him and threw her arms about his neck. "Oh Peter," she exclaimed. "It's so good to have you home. Its just wonderful!"

"Wonderful to be here mother," he said kissing her on the cheek. "And I'm starved!"

"Good thing," said Catherine exuberantly, "Inger's got roast beef cooking in the oven . . .we'd all better have an appetite."

She stood back and looked him in the eye. "My, but I've missed you," she said. "And look at you! Your beard is as thick as wool; look you've soaked my blouse. Here let me get you a towel."

"It's all right mother," he protested, enjoying the attention. She took his muffler and coat, shook the snow off, and handed everything to Ferdinand.

"Hang these up will you dear?"

"But of course. The prodigal returns; shall I kill the fatted calf mother?" asked Ferdinand as he hung Peter's wraps on a peg in the hall.

Catherine ignored him and went to get a towel from the linen closet. Peter might have picked up a bit of tension between the two of them. "You've become such a man," Catherine said proudly when she returned.

"You said the same thing last year Mother," he said hugging her again, "but being tied to your purse-strings as I am, leaves me wondering."

"What ever are you talking about?" said Catherine.

"Having you pay for everything is a strain on my self-confidence."

"That's ridiculous," said Catherine. "What are parents for if not to help their offspring when they can? Come into the living room dear. Your father's waiting for us."

Elias was sitting near the fireplace with his legs wrapped in a comforter despite the cozy warmth of a fire in the hearth. "Hello, my boy," he said formally. "You're looking well."

"How are you, sir?" Peter asked respectfully. The Christmas tree, which dominated the scene, seemed to lose some of its brightness as father and son shook hands.

"Fine, son," Elias harrumphed. "Just fine. A bit chilly."

"You're right about that," said Peter taking the chair nearest his mother. "Let me throw another log on the fire." He did so moving the log in place with the poker.

"So how is Copenhagen?" asked Elias.

"In a word sir, turbulent," Peter said authoritatively. "Hundreds of citizens are out of work . . . If the Americans don't end their damnable civil war soon, many of the textile mills will close permanently. There are more and more panhandlers on the streets and the government is at a loss as to what to do."

"It's not really the government's business," said Catherine.

"I quite agree mother," said Peter.

"Well I don't," said Elias. "There could be institutions set up to give relief, and help people find jobs."

"There are workhouses," stated Ferdinand.

"Quite frankly I think the Folkekirken could do more to help the poor," said the highly opinionated Peter. "Where do all the tithes go?"

"Tithes?" said Catherine. "There are no tithes anymore. The government pays the church a portion of our taxes."

"Regardless of where the money comes from," Peter continued, "The church could do far more where the poor are concerned, and I'm not happy about it. Nor am I happy with our new government . . ."

"So you've written," said Elias, his temperature steadily rising. He'd been hoping this subject would come up.

"Wait a minute," Catherine quickly injected. "What are we doing here? Let's not get into this. You've just gotten home Peter and it *is* Christmas."

"I'm sorry mother," he said as he held his hands toward the fire and rubbed them together. "I apologize. Looks like I started things out on the wrong foot." There was silence in the room for a moment; everyone seemed to be collecting their thoughts.

"Don't worry about it Peter," said Catherine finally. "And you're right. Sometimes things do get off on the wrong foot. And sometimes it's totally innocent. Why just the other day I had a misunderstanding with Nils Holsen over wasted feed—I'm still not sure where it's all going—but the point is I started our conversation in an accusing rather than an inquiring manner. Nils became very defensive and I was unable to discern anything, other than I had made him angry."

Peter looked over at Catherine. "I won't say another thing about the government, I promise. Plenty of time for politics, so they say. By the way you look radiant in the firelight. I don't believe I've ever seen you quite so pretty."

"Why thank you Peter . . . such a charmer." Catherine *was* all-aglow; wearing a full-skirted, puffy sleeved dress with a cameo set just below her high collared and lacy blouse. She was the picture of elegance and poise. Her hair was set in ringlets—American style and she looked very much the noble woman she was. She reached over and took Peter's hand. As quickly as it appeared the tension was gone from the room.

Elias coughed and mumbled something to the effect that indeed his wife did look nice. Then sat staring coldly at Peter. He'd get a shot at him soon enough.

"But I do wish Hans were here," Catherine went on. "Oh I can't wait until tomorrow."

"Nor can I," said Peter. "I'll bet he's grown two inches and put on ten pounds of muscle. According to his letters they train very hard."

"I doubt there's been that much improvement," said Ferdinand sarcastically, his attitude throwing a damper in the room. In the absence of his brothers Ferdinand had taken on a territorial disposition of a Doberman Pincer. He believed he was in competition with his brothers, which although natural with siblings, was altogether unnecessary in the case of the twins.

"I've an idea Peter," he said as he sat down next to Elias. "When we go get Hans tomorrow, let's take our horses and have Nils Holsen follow us in the buckboard to carry Han's trunk. We'll bring Hans' horse and that way we can race back home."

As of late, Ferdinand had spent a great deal of time in the saddle and was certain he could best either of his older brothers. He was anxious to prove it.

Elias wore a smirk. There was nothing he would love more than to see his favorite son humble the rebellious twins. "It might be interesting at that," he said.

"It's a good plan, Ferdinand," agreed Peter. "Well thought out. Let's see if the military has improved our brother's riding ability."

At that moment, Inger, wearing a holiday folk dress with red, white, yellow and green patterns stitched in its suspenders and hem, came in from the adjacent parlor. She had timed her entry. Her white blouse and apron were starched, and her face bore the look of a plump red apple. She touched off a holiday spirit—that so far had been lacking—the minute she walked into the room.

"I've got dinner waiting ma'am," she said wiping her hands with a towel and purposely ignoring Peter.

"What's this," said Peter rising to his feet. "No greeting, Inger? No kiss?" He went immediately to the stout little housekeeper and put his arms around her.

"You're as skinny as a stick," she said pushing him away. "Aren't they feeding you?"

"I've been away from your excellent kitchen far too long, Inger," he said cheerily.

"Aren't you the charmer," Inger said blushing in spite of herself.

"That's what mother called me!"

"It is grand to see you Peter," Inger continued. "Your ravenous appetite 'as been greatly missed at our table. Why you should see the food I throw away. It's shameful!"

"We've done just fine," said Elias cheerlessly. He seemed disgusted at all the gaiety and determined that everyone become as somber as he.

Peter turned to look at him instantly feeling more like a guest than a member of the family. It would be pleasant having some of

Inger's fine cuisine, he supposed. Then again, eating at the same table with Elias, he knew his stomach would tie up in knots, just as it had when he was a boy.

"I'm starving," said Catherine putting her hands to her knees and standing abruptly. "Peter, I hated the thought of your traveling in this weather. I've worried this whole week." She took Elias by the arm, and helped him out of his chair.

"It wasn't so bad, Mother," said Peter moving to the other side of Elias. "Here let me help you Father," he said taking Elias by the other arm.

"I'm not an invalid," said Elias sharply, wresting his arm free from Peter. The move was insulting. It cut Peter to the core. Elias still held tightly to Catherine however.

"As I was saying," Peter said stepping aside and recovering a bit. "There was a family in the coach; sitting close as we were, kept off the chill."

Catherine slowly walked Elias into the dining room. Peter hung behind, his face drawn up painfully. He looked over at Inger, who shook her head slightly and quickly mouthed something unintelligible. Ferdinand acted irritable. It was as if he wanted to get this visitor fed and on his way, so he could be back in charge of the house.

Soon all were seated around the table talking about the mill, the workers, meal and flour production, and other light subjects. Nothing was said about government, the death of the king, and especially nothing of religion. Catherine was anxious to talk about this Maren Carlsen person but determined to save this most interesting, and to her, exciting subject until a later date. Elias did bring up the subject of Søren Kierkegaard, and the second he did, Catherine shot him a look so dark and withering that he refrained from further comment

Peter saw the exchange as he took a bite of Inger's roast and made a mental note to avoid the infamous philosopher at all costs. He had not heard from his father by mail and therefore wasn't sure where he stood on anything. He was certain it was on thin ice. And he wondered what Hans' status was with Elias. Catherine had written several times but her letters were always upbeat and of a motherly nature: How are you eating? Do you have enough money? Harvests are bounteous. We've plenty of workers this year. We are caring for your horse, etc. She kept her sons up on everything about the estate but information on Elias was scant.

The dark pumpernickel bread Inger had baked earlier tickled the nose with its spicy fragrance and there was plenty of butter. As the meal progressed, Catherine, Peter, and Ferdinand continued to talk around Elias' silence, eating heartily of Inger's fluffy mashed potatoes, fresh garden carrots, red beets, and liver pâté, all after the main course of succulent beef. After the meal came apple layer cake, topped with fresh whipped cream. Peter was bursting at the seams but Elias had barely touched his food. Instead he sipped at his coffee keeping his eyes fixed on whoever was speaking. Like his father Ferdinand picked at his plate.

Their poor performance toward her cooking, plus waiting on them hand and foot, Inger felt like taking both Elias and Ferdinand by the seat of their pants and throwing them out in the snow! She almost mentioned the fact.

Peter hadn't eaten so well in months and could have gone on forever. Catherine, who worked physically hard each day, also ate heartily. Finally, Inger brought in some wine and this Elias drank greedily. With little on his stomach the spirits hit him hard. Soon he was nodding, unable to focus.

"I'm afraid to say it," he stated as he laboriously slid his chair back. Coughing and wiping his mouth with his napkin, "but I'm exhausted. I must excuse myself."

"So early, Elias?" Catherine said, trying to hide her pleasure. "There's cheese and Christmas cookies coming."

"The conversation's been dragging, my dear," he said boozily, "I'm tired and muss' get some rest. We've a busy day tomorrow." He harrumphed to clear his throat, and his darting little eyes came into focus. They rested significantly upon Peter. "A very busy day. Goodnight, everyone."

"Good night, Father," Ferdinand said, rising respectfully. Peter also rose and echoed the sentiment somewhat awkwardly, "Good night, sir."

Elias nodded at them, patted Ferdinand on the shoulder and shuffled through the living room, into the hall and slowly ascended the spiral stairs.

When they heard his bedroom door close, Catherine and Peter relaxed, Ferdinand too and just then Inger came in with a plate of Danish pastry. She finally sat down to sample her own cooking and the conversation sprang up spontaneously. There was much to talk about with laughter dancing about the table, Catherine even got to hear of Maren Carlsen and even Ferdinand could be heard laughing occasionally. It was a warm reunion, minus Hans, and at two o'clock in the morning the four of them left empty plates and partially filled wine glasses to make their ways to bed. Everyone except Peter retired with merry expectations of the morrow. Mildly numbed with wine, he still felt a storm brewing but had no idea of its intensity.

Chapter 20

On a clear, cold afternoon at the docks in Holbaek, the Jensen brothers were mounted and dressed in their greatcoats, knitted caps and high leather boots, with their pants tucked in for riding. While their horses breathed clouds of steam, Peter and Ferdinand stood in their stirrups and searched the horizon. Torkil Olsen not Nils Holsen had come with them bringing the buckboard to carry Hans' luggage. His wise old Viking eyes were first to see smoke from the stacks of the steamer.

"I'll bet that is it," he said, as he rubbed his bearded face and pointed across the gray and choppy water.

"God gave you the eyes of an eagle, Torkil," said Peter, remembering their camping days when the miller was always first to see a deer, and where his musket could split the branch of a beech tree at fifty yards. "I pray its Hans. Anything can happen out there."

"I have to admit that water looks dark and a might too choppy," said Torkil. "I had a friend get washed overboard in such as this and before anyone was able to throw him a line, that frigid water sucked the heat outta' him. He was gone before anyone had the time to spit."

"No time for tales like that," said Peter as he and Ferdinand dismounted and tied their horses to the railing. "Hans will get here alright."

Half an hour later with several other people gathered at the docks to greet their loved ones the water looked even more treacherous; but the steamer, apparently with an expert at the helm, crunched safely against the wharf. Ropes thrown from her decks thudded near mooring posts as several cadets including Hans stepped down the short gangplank. With his trunk on his shoulder he looked trim and strong in his dress uniform and although very pleased to see his brothers and Torkil coming his way, his somber demeanor and dark, neatly trimmed beard told the world he was serious about his chosen profession.

"I thought you'd come home in regular clothes," said Peter as he and Torkil took Hans' trunk and set it on the dock. Peter and Hans then put their arms around each other.

"I'm now the property of the Danish Government brother," boomed Hans his rich baritone voice distinctive amidst the welcoming crowd. "Would I not wear the colors?

"How are you, Ferdinand?" he then asked, hugging the younger brother.

"Overworked," Ferdinand replied somewhat stiffly, and pulling away. "But none the less for wear I suppose."

"Has Father given you such a tough time?" inquired Hans.

"Not so bad actually," said Ferdinand.

"I wish I could say the same," said Peter. "I hadn't been in the house three minutes before his genteel nature manifested itself in my behalf. Hans and Peter laughed, Ferdinand did not, and Torkil pretended he hadn't heard.

"What's the matter, Torkil? Lost your sense of humor?" said

Hans. "And by the way, haven't you got a word for me?"

"Family first, young Hans," said the miller.

"And who says you're not family?" roared Hans, as the two embraced and pounded each other on the back.

"I'm beginning to wonder if *you* belong to the family," Torkil teased. "Here you are in a beard dark as night your brother's is sandy brown. Are you sure you had the same father?"

"What about me?" Ferdinand chimed in.

"You look like your mother, Ferdinand, there's no doubting," said Torkil. Then more seriously added, "but you belong to your father." It was obvious there were negative feelings between Ferdinand and Torkil, as the former—who fancied himself heir apparent to the mill-resented taking orders from the latter as well as the reference to Elias. "He's almost quit working for me at the mill since you two went off to school," Torkil explained as Peter and Hans looked at him. "Now when you see him his head is in the books."

"Somebody has to keep the accounts straight," said Hans trying to be congenial. "I'm glad Mother has you around for that Ferdinand."

Ferdinand nodded. "I do my best Hans." He gave a hint of a smile but was obviously uncomfortable knowing that it was Catherine who really kept the books. All he did was general accounting.

A few carriages were pulling away as the small crowd sorted itself out. "Enough of this," said Peter looking at Hans with great respect. "We'll freeze if we stand about much longer. Let's get Hans' trunk loaded and get home. As you can see we brought your horse Hans, there behind the buckboard. Ferdinand and I wanted to see if the academy has done anything for your riding."

"Ho, ho" exclaimed Hans. "So you two want to race me and

Vargus, do you?" he said looking from one brother to the other.

"It was his idea," said Peter his head nodding toward Ferdinand.

Hans' eyes were filled with excitement as he went to and untied his horse; as glad to see the chestnut stallion, as he was his brothers. "Have they been good to you Vargus?" he said patting the nervous animal as it snorted and stamped. "Let's give them a lesson."

Hans loved a challenge and hated losing, at anything. "What are we waiting for?" he asked after he and Torkil threw his trunk aboard. Torkil climbed up into his seat as Hans slipped his left boot into Vargus' stirrup and threw himself into the saddle. "Let's get after it."

"We ought to get away from town so we don't run over anybody," said Peter unshaken by his brother's confidence. He and Hans had competed all their lives, and in sports such as soccer Peter could beat his brother. Where hunting was concerned, Hans had always bested him, but with horses they were dead even.

Ferdinand who had also mounted believed his horse could outrun either of his brother's. A Danish light bay, the horse was quick off the mark and had a great heart for distance. And Ferdinand *had* become a very good rider over the last year, a little too stiff in the saddle but good nonetheless. He looked confident on the bay but truth be known he was very nervous.

"Torkil you can start us at the end of the road," said Peter, untying his horse, swinging into the saddle and leading the foursome through town at a steady trot.

"It's a good bet the stretch of road from here to home will be empty of people," said Peter as they trotted along. "We didn't see a soul when we came."

"If anyone is coming they'll have to get out of the way," said Ferdinand.

"It will be fine," said Hans. "Plenty of time to get around anyone." Torkil followed closely behind the brothers and at the signpost with the word Holbaek on it, he lined them up. The horses sensed something and were skittish and hard to hold. Torkil held his arm high, dropped it, and shouted, "Go!"

Hans, Peter, and Ferdinand simultaneously dug their heels into their horses' flanks, spurring them into full gallop down the winding country road toward home. The horses were high-spirited in the cold weather, and their flying hooves churned a mixture of snow, brown earth, and dead grasses as they thundered along.

Ferdinand led for the first quarter of a mile; but shrouded in steam and a flurry of snow, Peter was soon at his side and knew Hans was purposely hanging back. Peter grinned over at his brother, and to his surprise found an angry face.

"Hah! Hah! Get up there!" Ferdinand shouted as he spurred the horse's withers. "Get up blast you!" Quirt in hand, as if the race was for money he furiously whipped either side of the unfortunate animal's rump.

"Get up!" he shouted. The whistle of Ferdinand's quirt cut dangerously close to Peter's face and out of self-defense he slackened the reins and his horse quickly obeyed falling back behind Ferdinand's. Squinting to keep snow from his eyes Peter shook his head in amazement. *'So that's how it is, eh little brother,'* he thought. *'That important to you is it . . . well next time I'll run you off the road.'*

Hans and Vargus, at first incompatible with each other, eventually synchronized their movements with such fluidity that rider and horse appeared as one. Down the long country road they galloped and soon the snorting of Vargus came within Peter's earshot. Peter spurred his mount to greater effort and once again caught up with Ferdinand. "Let's go!" he shouted to his mount. " Go! Go!"

Drifts were high on the right side of the road and brush lined the left, leaving scarcely enough room for one horse let alone two. But as the riders approached a bridge, the road opened up and Peter, with Hans close on his tail, went thundering past Ferdinand.

Hans heard Ferdinand curse as Vargus muscled past the less experienced light bay horse and looking over his shoulder with concern, Hans saw the same angry expression on his younger brother's face Peter had seen. It troubled him, but only momentarily. Hans then set his sights on Peter.

The wind had picked up, blowing powdered snow across the trail; the road narrowed again giving Peter the advantage. Close behind him, his exultant face splattered with bits of muddy grass and ice, was Hans. He was gaining. Grinning ear to ear at the sheer joy of the contest, Hans was in his glory. Vargus was strong, far from winded and with hooves pounding, steadily closed the gap between the twin brothers. Vargus could sense his master's joy and when the moment was right, at Hans' urging, the mighty animal plunged into the shallow drift to Peter's right, passing him, albeit with some difficulty.

Peter took the lead back at an open space one mile later but had the distinct impression Hans let him.

Half a mile further Hans and Peter were head to head, leaving Ferdinand fifty yards behind them and mad as a wet hen. At a gentle bluff overlooking the frozen Holbaek River another bridge crossed the road and with that in sight, Hans pushed Vargus to the hilt. He crossed the bridge a full fifteen seconds ahead of Peter and almost a full minute ahead of Ferdinand; then slowed his horse to a trot so his brothers could catch up.

"You've proved your point," panted Peter as his mount cantered alongside Hans'. Ferdinand rode past them several yards, and then reluctantly returned.

"You have taken very good care of these animals Ferdinand," said Hans offering a conciliatory word.

"Yes, you have," added Peter, still confused at Ferdinand's attitude. Hans appeared not to care one way or the other. "They're all in top condition."

"It was my superior riding that did it?" quipped Hans with exuberance.

"It wasn't bad," Peter admitted.

Ferdinand had nothing to say.

"We ride often," Hans added, still a little breathless. "I feel I've taken advantage of you two."

"I don't understand it," said Ferdinand angrily as his horse pranced about. "Let's race till the Roskilde crossroads."

"No sense killing good horse flesh," said Hans quickly serious. "Quit while you're ahead, I always say."

"Both your horses look as fresh as daisies," argued Ferdinand, "like they're just catching the spirit of things." Indeed, Peter and Han's horses were quivering; their powerful necks and leg muscles as taut as piano strings. "Let's race to the crossroads."

Peter leaned up in the stirrups and patted his horse's neck talking softly into its ear. "Steady now, easy, easy. Want to race some more? I didn't think so."

"I don't want to give either of you a second chance at me," Hans said good-naturedly, but serious just the same.

"I expected you to beat me Hans," Ferdinand said bitterly, "but not Peter."

"You haven't been on a horse in months have you?"

"Once or twice," said Peter cautiously.

"Let's just ride along and talk," Hans said with finality. "I haven't heard much from either of you and would like to catch up on a few things."

The brothers finished the ride home at a trot, with Hans and Peter chattering away like chipmunks, pleased to be in each other's company. Both included Ferdinand with a word here and there but the latter said little in return. As of yet Ferdinand's attitude hadn't bothered Hans but Peter was truly upset about it. There was a certain darkness hanging about the younger brother.

In spite of their action-filled reunion, Peter also sensed something might be troubling Hans and when they were alone Peter intended to find out what.

At the house, Torkil, who had caught up with the three brothers and followed them the last mile, took their horses to the stables and turned them over to Nils Holsen, who unsaddled them, groomed them, and forked down some hay.

Hans entered the house ahead of Peter and Ferdinand, where the fresh smell of Christmas pine and baked bread filled his nostrils. Catherine gasped with pleasure at the tall, dark, and handsome son in the uniform of Denmark, and took him in her fond embrace. Hans held her respectfully, kissed her cheeks, then stood back and pulled off his leather gloves. The tops of his ears were cherry red, his cheeks were flushed, and his hair messy, but he was truly dashing.

"Don't you look smart!" Catherine said proudly, "and my, how you've changed!"

"Has it been so long Mother?" he grinned.

"Longer than a lifetime," said Catherine kissing his face again.

Hans' eyes next found his father. Elias was standing on a rug near the hearth in the living room, with his hands clasped behind him. In dark pants and coat he maintained the lawyer's dignified image but his face held a gaunt expression.

"How are you, sir?" Hans asked, extending his hand.

There was a tense moment, and then Elias slowly took his son's hand. There was weakness in his bony grip and Hans' nose caught the familiar smell of stale alcohol on Elias' breath. *'Some things never change,'* he thought. He felt sorry for his father.

"I'm well, thank you," Elias answered slowly, coughing slightly. "Yourself?"

"The same Father."

Turning to Inger, Elias said, "Bring out some wine so we can toast my son's safe return."

He wobbled unsteadily back to his chair and sank into the over-stuffing. Turning back to his mother, Hans caught a flicker of uneasiness in her face, but she smiled reassuringly and pulled him over to the sofa. Peter sat in a chair nearby.

"Put another log on the fire, would you Ferdinand?" Elias asked solicitously, looking fondly at his youngest. Ferdinand scowled. The fire was already roaring up the chimney, but he nodded silently and threw on a log. Sparks flew inside and around the stone hearth where they glowed momentarily then extinguished themselves.

"So tell us Hans," Elias said loudly, interrupting a tender conversation Hans and Catherine were having. "How're things at the academy?" Elias' words were slightly slurred.

Hans finished answering Catherine's question, then turned to him. "Just fine, Father. A bit hectic with all that's going on, but all right."

Catherine squeezed his hand and smiled at him.

"A terrible shame about the king's death, wasn't it?" Elias continued. Knowing it was loaded, both Peter and Hans took particular notice of the question. “The paper reported he took sick the day he visited your academy.”

“That’s exactly what happened,” said Hans heavily. “It was a shock. Such an excellent man.”

“Let’s not dampen the occasion so soon, Elias,” said Catherine patiently. “The country will survive. It has before. I think I’ll have a small glass of wine Inger,” she added turning to her.

“Oh, we’ll survive there’s no doubt,” persisted Elias, peering owlishly, first at one twin, then at the other. Inger had refilled his glass and he took a long pull, shuddering faintly at the impact. “Especially with our citizens so loyal to the crown. Right, Peter? Eh, Hans?” Peter looked to Hans. Catherine felt herself becoming sick and took a sip of wine.

“The country could be in for hard times, Father,” said Hans with deep concern in his voice. “King Christian the ninth is German minded, and because of his sympathy towards them, many Danish citizens are uneasy. Especially our military leaders.”

“How’s that?” asked Elias wiping his mouth on his sleeve. “Speak up, will you Hans?”

“I said most Danes are uncomfortable with the new king.”

“They are,” agreed Peter.

“That isn’t what we hear,” said Ferdinand. “Business as usual. Loyal Danes have accepted him without question.”

The remark was inflammatory and without foundation; however both Hans and Peter passed it off as the stupidity of youth.

Inger passed around a tray of warm pastry. Elias ignored it but allowed her to splash more wine in his glass. Catherine was about to say he’d had enough but decided against it. Peter asked for tea. It

looked like it was going to be a long evening and he wanted a clear head.

"Tell us more about Maren Carlsen Peter," said Catherine deliberately shifting the subject to something at least mildly controversial. She wanted to take the conversation away from the new king before Elias got himself all stirred up over politics. "What is she like?"

This might have been the spark that ignited Elias' flame but Peter answered boldly, "She's a pretty girl, Mother. Small, extremely feminine and very bright. She has lovely hair, which doesn't have a thing to do with anything except that I like it . . ." Catherine smiled in spite of herself. "But you'll like her."

Elias appeared to be staring into his glass. Tension was easing. Hans drained his own wineglass and asked Inger for a refill.

Peter forged ahead. "Since I met Maren, life in Copenhagen has been a joy for me. We have become such friends. And she has taken me to places I'd have never gone myself. Just didn't have the mind for, such as Christianborg." Elias perked up at that. "She drags me all over Copenhagen."

"So you've written," said Catherine delighted.

"Women can definitely make a difference," said Hans looking at his wineglass and swishing the contents expertly.

"There'll be other girls, my boy," Elias stated blandly.

"It doesn't have to be that way, Elias," interjected Catherine instantaneously. "People in our family have been known to fall very quickly and very strongly in love before." It was a clear reminder of their courtship, but Elias missed the point completely.

"I do love her, Mother," affirmed Peter. "She is everything on earth to me. Wait till you all meet her. She's vivacious, genuine, but more than that, she's a true companion. From a fine family, I might add."

"You indicated that in your letters also," said Catherine. "They run a dry goods store, is that right?"

"It is," said Peter. "It's right across the street from Norre Park where I met her. The father Hr Carlsen keeps the store open six days every week except from Christmas Day until New Years. Maren would have come with me to meet you both, but busy as they are at the store she could not get away."

Elias fidgeted restlessly. He leaned forward and banged his glass down on the table at his elbow. Ferdinand jumped. "What does *she* think of the new king, Peter?" he demanded.

"You will have your way, won't you?" Catherine exclaimed, much exasperated.

Elias then sat back, picked up his glass and sipped his wine, grinning satisfactorily with himself. He looked toward Ferdinand's for acceptance but the boy had his head down.

"Neither of us knows much about the king yet, Father," Peter said patiently. "Only time will tell. That's the way I look at it."

Elias's eyes darted back and forth between Peter and Hans. Peter faced him uncomfortably, and while sipping his wine enjoyably, Hans disregarded Elias as he might a first year cadet.

Catherine raised her eyes heavenward and shook her head in frustration. Elias ignored her and coughed to show he still had the floor. "Though Christian the ninth wouldn't have been my choice," he said, more clearly than anyone expected, "lest any one of us forget . . . he is still king!"

Hans and Peter looked to their mother. Her brow furrowed and she cast them a quick, forbidding glance. Both remained silent. Elias

continued, “We could have had a queen, you know.”

“Heaven forbid,” exclaimed Catherine sarcastically. “And if you continue on this subject Elias, I’m going to leave the room! Our sons are all safely together for the first time in months and you act like this. I’ll remind you once again that it is Christmas and I won’t have it spoiled! I’m sure we can find a better time to discuss politics. All of you.”

Elias smiled boozily and refilled his glass. For a moment the only sound in the room was the crackling of the fire and the popping of cinders.

Hans, quite forgetting that he hadn’t had anything to eat all day had already drunk three glasses of wine, and was feeling a bit light-headed. “What have you been doing with your life, younger brother?” he asked wryly as he turned to Ferdinand. “Anything exciting going on around here?”

“Not a thing,” said Ferdinand lifting his head. “Just working at the books for the mill . . . and trying to keep up with the horses.”

“Like I said you have done a fine job there,” said Hans.

“And what’s going on at the mill?” Peter wanted to know.

“We sent the men home two weeks ago,” Ferdinand said authoritatively, obviously enjoying the attention. “All except for Torkil and one other. They’re sizing the stones and changing out the bolting on the sifters. We received a shipment of silk two months ago.”

“It sounds as if our brother is managing quite well, doesn’t it, Peter?” Hans said matter-of-factly.

“I have to say he has,” Catherine agreed, taking a sip of wine visibly relaxing at the direction of the conversation. “Especially the ledgers. He’s taken that task completely off my hands.”

Catherine then frowned at her own statement. She did appreciate

Ferdinand's performance with the day to day accounting, however she was somewhat uneasy with the fact he knew how much money the mill brought in. As a direct result of it, he had lost any inclination to seek a higher education. There had been many confrontations over it and to add fuel to the fire, as of late Ferdinand had taken up with Kristina Holsen, or "Krista" as everyone called her. She was the fifteen-year-old daughter of Nils Holsen, the stableman. Dark skinned like her Gypsy mother, Krista was a listless girl, subtle and yet very manipulative. She was number three of a family of 10 children and had a very poor childhood. Krista was nonetheless attractive, but in a sleazy sort of way. Fluid movements and a trim figure, she could stir the animal nature in a man by merely passing by, or with but a glance from her dark brown eyes.

A small house east of the gristmill was part of Nils Holsen's pay and because Krista occasionally brought her father a flask of warm beer and a scone for his lunch, she and Ferdinand had met on many occasions. With the lovely girl's recent flowering, had come Ferdinand's carnal interest. Barns, lofts and stacks of hay provided nooks of privacy and over the past few weeks he and Krista had become very well acquainted. The sullen, defensive, attitude Ferdinand had adopted was Catherine's first clue that something was amiss and when she confronted him about Krista the explosion was something akin to dealing with Elias.

Ferdinand's unwillingness to seek additional education was amplified by his involvement with Krista Holsen, but just like politics and religion, Catherine intended the topic remain in the background during the holidays. Afterward, she would deal with Ferdinand's insolence even if it meant forcing him to enroll at the University of Copenhagen or sending Nils Holsen and his daughter packing, or both. Lately with Krista's growing influence around the Jensen household, Nil's work had been slipping; and he had put on an arrogance that irked Catherine to no end. Perhaps he knew something she didn't. After the holidays she determined she would fire the man regardless.

"I have learned a lot about milling," Ferdinand was saying boastfully. "Since you two left I've done everything from balancing the books to inventing new blends . . ."

"Really," said Peter.

"That's right," Ferdinand continued. "With the books definitely taking precedence. You heard mother. I've completely taken over the ledgers. " He watched for his brother's reactions and noted with satisfaction the alarmed tint in Peter's eyes.

"Milling grain, and the host of problems connected with farmers, brokers and machinery never had much appeal to me dear brother," Hans said cheerily from his comfortable place next to Catherine on the sofa. "I'm glad you're watching over things. You make the flour and my friends and I will see to it you're protected." With the warmness of wine all over his face, Hans had showed little emotion over Ferdinand's incessant bragging. Soon to be an officer in the King's army, the world was his oyster and all he cared about the estate was it was a nice place to come home to.

Elias listened casually to the conversation. He too cared little about the mill. As long as the money continued to flow what mattered the source? Staring into the glowing fire, the alcohol taking effect and anger growing within him over Peter and Hans' November letters; every time he thought of what they had said about the king, about Søren Kierkegaard and especially about Peter's interest in the fanatic American sect called Mormons, his mind glowed as red as the coals in the hearth. Sooner or later, he'd have his say with the rebellious twins. He was simply biding his time.

Catherine naturally sensed all this but her own glass of wine had taken effect and for the moment the living-room seemed to radiate warmth and love. Yes, she read the respite clearly, but for the time being completely ignored it. She knew things were boiling just under Elias' surface. The truce might last through Christmas Day. All she could do was hope.

Chapter 21

The evening went on, many logs had been placed upon the fire. The living room remained as cozy as an Inn. Meanwhile, Inger was in and out of the kitchen with snacks, cold cuts of ham, sausage and thinly sliced beef. Seeing to the family's every whim, she brought, pickled herring, hot bread and warm beer to wash it all down. All the while she kept Elias' wine glass brimming.

"Inger," Catherine said at length, "let me help you clean up."

"It's not necessary Fru Jensen, I can handle it."

"I simply won't let you do the work alone," said the heiress as she rose to her feet. She was reluctant to break the spell of peace in the living room but knew dirty glasses and plates were mounting in the kitchen. She motioned Inger out of the room, hoping in her absence, her sons might reacquaint themselves with their father.

A few minutes later, with plates rattling, glasses tinkling and laughter lilting from the kitchen, Elias lifted his stare from the fire and found his targets. The look on his face resembled the anger of a winter storm out in the fjords. "Peter . . . Hans," he said firmly. "I have something I want to discuss with you"

He rose from his chair with obvious difficulty but oddly enough was steady on his feet. "I will see both of you in my room." There was no doubt he meant what he said, and the brothers out of respect, reluctantly stood to follow.

Ferdinand had a smirk on his face as his brothers left the room to follow Elias up the winding stairway. He and his father had talked often about the twins' so-called rebellion. Part of him was sad, but the rest of him was unnerved with anticipation. As ridiculous as it was, Elias made him feel used by Peter and Hans. *'They won't be coming back Ferdinand. They've left you all the work,'* Elias had said it a hundred times. At first he hadn't bought into it but now with the influence of Krista, Ferdinand was formulating plans that didn't include the twins. The mill would be his legacy, not theirs.

"He'll ruin everything for mother," the boy said under his breath as he listened to the sounds of joy and love coming from the kitchen. Part of him didn't want to see it, and part of him didn't care. Guiltily, Ferdinand had a slight impulse to enter the kitchen and tell Catherine what was happening, yet feeling tension in the air, and liking what he felt, he shrugged it off.

Upstairs in Elias' room, the door was shut, and for a while nothing could be heard below. Then suddenly a loud thump reverberated against the walls. Responding to the noise she both heard and felt, Catherine came quickly and anxiously into the living room. "What's going on Ferdinand?" she demanded as she looked around. "Where are they?"

He shrugged and looked upward just as another thumping sound, like furniture moving or someone pounding his fist on a table, sounded from upstairs

"I didn't think he would do this to me," Catherine said looking hopelessly toward the stairs. "We talked long and hard about it."

Suddenly the door to the upstairs bedroom banged open and

Elias' voice shrilled throughout the house. "I won't stand for this rebellion! You're bringing shame and disgrace upon our good name!" A short fit of coughing seized him.

"You're as backward as the monarchy!" Hans shouted back as Elias wiped his mouth of spittle. "You'll hold to the fool system 'til you're cold in the ground!" With raised hand Elias made a swipe at Hans but the latter was too quick and backed out of the door.

Catherine's eyes were pinched with anger as she arrived at the foot of the stairway. "What's going on up there?" she shouted.

"I'm going to get some fresh air!" said Hans coming down the stairs two at a time. "The man is crazy!" He surged past Catherine and burst through the front door. Hat and coat-less but intent upon getting as far away as possible, Hans slammed the door behind him and headed into the night.

Upstairs, with arms outstretched as if to block Peter's escape, Elias remained in the bedroom doorway. "And you speak of marrying," he sneered. "How will you provide for the girl? You have no profession, nor even the courage to finish school!" He stopped to cough. "Another thing," he choked, "you can't marry *anyone* in Denmark unless the church sanctions it! And if you continue to meet with these fool Mormons, you'll be excommunicated. I'll see to it!"

"How can I be excommunicated from something I no longer believe in?" Peter said defiantly. "You'll never understand Father . . . you've been shut up in this old house so long you've become out of touch! It's a new world out there. There is new information available. New light, and if you would just take enough time to listen to me I could explain everything."

"To hell with you, and your new information. I know something of the Mormons!" He paused and cleared his throat with a loud haruumph, then coughed a few times. It seemed he was literally choking on phlegm and the look in his eyes was one of frustration as well as hate. “Gold bible,” he finally managed. “Joseph Smith . . . a latter day Prophet! Why the man is no more than a latter day charlatan! All he wants is your money!” He paused in his tirade to cough again repeatedly. “Your mother’s money to be more accurate!”

At that Peter grabbed Elias’s bony wrist and pulled his hand off the doorjamb. He had heard all he wanted. In a way he admired his father’s pluck, firm in his convictions, choking between each sentence, yet forging ahead.

“Let me pass,” Peter said angrily.

Swinging his fists with all his strength, Elias struck him once in the face and twice in the chest, glancing blows and feeble, yet they stung like bites of a wasp.

“Stop it! Stop it!” Catherine cried lifting her skirts, and hurrying up the stairs.

Good sense over-powered anger and Peter refrained from striking his father back. Elias stumbled as he took a last swing whereupon Peter caught him around the waist and held him till Catherine pushed her way between them.

“Fru Jensen, Fru Jensen! Do you want me to come?” Inger stood wringing her hands in her apron and pleading from the foot of the stairs.

Catherine didn’t hear her. “You are such a damned fool Elias!” she said as she grabbed his arm and pulled him away from Peter, who was shocked, never having heard his mother swear before.

“You’ll not lay another hand on him! Do you understand?”

Elias tried to push past her, but Catherine easily pulled him toward the bed where he stumbled awkwardly and fell upon the mattress. Seized by a paroxysm of coughing Elias reached out at Peter as if to strangle him.

"Go find Hans," said Catherine turning to Peter. "I can handle this from here." Highly energized she was nonetheless in total control of herself.

Peter hesitated. "Are you sure you'll be all right mother?" he asked protectively.

"I'll be all right," Catherine insisted. "Your father and I need to be alone. You go now . . ."

"All right mother," he said realizing Elias' strength was no more than a child's and that all but spent. Catherine would be safe. He left the room, shut the door firmly and slowly descended the stairs. As he neared Inger and Ferdinand, both still at the foot of the stairs, Peter was unaware of the tears streaking his face. "Where is Hans?" he asked huskily.

"He went outside," said Ferdinand trembling slightly.

"Get our coats," Peter commanded. "I know where to find him."

Ferdinand hastily complied and the two brothers followed Hans' footsteps through the thin layer of snow and toward the barn. "Put this on before you freeze to death Hans," said Peter finding his brother and throwing him a coat. Hans was leaning against a support beam with his arms folded tightly. "Thanks," he said putting on the coat; he then climbed the wall ladder into the loft. "Come on up," he motioned to his brothers. As boys, the loft had been Hans and Peter's "secret" place; a quiet nook where hours on end they sat in the hay discussing the mysteries of life. It was only natural they sought refuge there now.

Hans pushed the hay hook aside and opened the loading door. Bluish light from the moon and stars reflecting off the snow dimly flooded the loft. There was a sharp nip in the air and the dry hay about them felt like a warm blanket. The warmth and smell of the horses in the barn added coziness to the otherwise freezing setting, and the brothers settled in for a long conversation.

"You've never mentioned you were going to change religions, Peter," Hans said finally.

"It's a long story," answered his twin.

"I thought our dissatisfaction over the king and the monarchy caused enough trouble for one night," Hans went on. "But when you told him you were going to be baptized a Mormon, he went berserk!"

"Politics and religion. Best to leave them alone around Father," said Ferdinand sagaciously.

"Apparently Father hasn't told you about my letters," said Peter despondently.

"Nor mine," said Hans equally sunken.

"Father says very little about your correspondence," lied the younger brother. Elias, being estranged from Catherine as he was, shared everything with him *especially* the content of their letters. Ferdinand had become Elias' ally, an accomplice even. In many ways he and his father were peas in a pod, thinking only of themselves and little else. Since his involvement with Krista, Ferdinand had also begun to regard his mother with irritation; as little more than a nuisance, but he had no idea what to do about it. He was after all, barely eighteen and was very much into himself. He was reluctantly respectful to Catherine; she would tolerate little else, but there was a breech growing between them; caused by a selfish young man still in the nest, a young man who wanted to rule the nest.

And it was odd sitting there in the loft. As Peter and Hans talked, really talked, analyzing what had just happened between them and their father as well as catching up on the past year away from each other, Ferdinand hardly listened to them. That is he only listened to what he wanted to hear, and that was that neither of his brothers talked of coming back home permanently. Instead their words were all wrapped up in their lives in Copenhagen and in the military. Whereas his thoughts were upon these very surroundings, this very barn, the mill, horses and a few fleeting thoughts of Krista.

Inside the house, Catherine and Elias were still upstairs. To keep herself busy but stay within earshot, Inger was in and out of the kitchen seeing to the main course of roast pork, mashed potatoes, and steamed vegetables. She slid all three dishes toward the back of the stove to keep warm because she knew the boys would be very hungry when they returned. Then Inger positioned herself within view of the stairway and nervously did some tatting. Like a sentinel, she sat knotting the fine yarn into intricate patterns. Catherine might need her and quickly. Inger was ready to run up the stairs at a moment's notice.

An hour later when it was obvious there would be no more violence Inger finally banked the fire in the hearth, put the screen tightly in place and retired to her quarters.

Half an hour after that the three brothers, having talked themselves out, and being driven in by the cold, returned to the house. In the hearth, the fire had died into a bed of ash. Peter, added kindling then kneeled down to blow, and shortly brought it back to life. He then added a small log or two. The fire grew hot and the brothers turned their backs on it first, then turned around and held out their hands, rubbing them briskly. In the warm silence they stood listening for any noise from upstairs, and hearing none they all found a seat.

Other than their breathing and an occasional pop popping from the hearth, the room was quiet; and despite the upset, the smells of Christmas filled the air. In the kitchen Inger's sumptuous meal, not to mention a pumpkin pie awaited.

Before long Catherine came quietly down the stairs and entered the front room. She sank heavily into the sofa and sighed. "It is finished. There will be no further problems this holiday season." She slowly and sadly shook her head. "Someone put more wood on the fire, please. Its' chilly in here." Ferdinand and Hans were closest to the hearth and while Hans pumped the bellows Ferdinand fed in more logs. There was soon a healthy blaze, meanwhile Peter had moved next to Catherine. "It will be all right, Mother," he said affectionately. "Times like these are bound to happen."

"Your father has been very sick," Catherine said as Ferdinand and Hans sat down, "but there was absolutely no excuse for his outburst tonight." She paused. "And none whatever for him striking you Peter," she added while inspecting for marks on his face. "I told your father I would petition for divorce if he causes another such incident, and I *will* follow through. Because of his continual illnesses' I have asked little from your father; only peace and harmony in this home. Especially at Christmas time; if the Lord paid us a visit, I want our home to be a place where he'd feel welcome."

Catherine lowered her head and cried softly into her handkerchief for a moment. Hans moved to the couch and put his arm around her while Peter took her hand and murmured soothingly to her. "It will be fine mother, everything will be fine."

"Hans, Peter," Catherine said as she wiped her eyes. "You must understand, your father is a very stubborn man. He likes things the way they have been in this country. To talk perversely about the king or the monarchy is near treason to him. He believes in our system of government . . . believes it was God-given and will prevail. Political discussions, or talk of a weak military, do nothing but upset him. I'm asking you both to avoid them.

As for religion, Peter. Where the Folkekirken is concerned your father is as immovable as granite. Anything you do or say against the church will immediately incite him. He'll never hear of or sympathize with outsiders. He has however agreed to say nothing one way or the other regarding the Mormons; and for my sake I'm asking you to leave the subject alone."

She paused, took a deep breath, and continued more forcefully, "As for myself I'll say this. You and Hans are free to choose your path in life. To think or do what you will in regards to: religion, the king and his Rigsdag, the military or whatever else that pleases you. I won't interfere with your lives. Truly I won't. But please do not impose your opinions upon your father; especially during these holidays. No arguments between the three of you either. None." Peter and Hans nodded respectfully while Ferdinand seemed to be looking at the rafters.

"I do want to speak privately with each of you concerning your future plans and desires," Catherine continued. "And if there is any way I can assist any of you, yourself included Ferdinand," she said turning to him, "then I will do it.

As for myself, I am not afraid of new ideas and new thinking. One can't bury their head in the sand; especially when you own a business. I've always kept up with the times. Changes in society and government have always affected grain, especially wheat.

It's an odd thing," she said reflectively, "but wheat is a river that flows on its own. It holds no allegiance to any specific nation or government, only to capital. Wheat operates in tandem with capital. In fact wheat is capital. People want bread and regardless of their particular government: dictatorship, monarchy or whatever else, they will have it. Fish is important, meat, fruit and vegetables too, but wheat rules the day.

But back to what I was saying about keeping up; why I love keeping up with the times. I love learning—especially from my own sons. We live in such a remarkable age." She turned to Ferdinand about to say something to the effect that he too should seek higher education, but Catherine stopped short. There would be no further contention in the home, and that included any started by her. "Don't you think so Ferdinand?"

"Yes Mother," he said respectfully. "It is a remarkable age."

As far as Peter and Hans were concerned there would be no problem avoiding further conflict with Elias. The barrier between the three of them had been up for years. As for Ferdinand, he knew his mother had included him in her comments only to be fair. For the past several months he and Elias had gotten along famously.

The fire crackled and the room became warmer. The four of them sat quietly enjoying each other's company and the solitude. A smile eventually crept across Catherine's face and a deep sigh signaled she was feeling better. A queenly aura settled over her as she sat with her sons and soon the upset Elias had caused began to fade.

"If we don't go in and eat some of Inger's dinner she'll quit the house," Catherine said at length.

"I'm as hungry as a wolf," said Peter suddenly enthusiastic.

"My sentiments exactly," Hans said. "I haven't had a good meal this year."

"Is army food that bad?" asked Ferdinand.

"You should try it little brother."

"Let's do eat," Catherine said thoughtfully, "and then lets bundle up and attend midnight Mass. That would so please your father. You don't have any problem with that do you Peter?"

"Why would I Mother? The Lutheran Church still holds great meaning for me. I haven't totally apostatized." Peter's comment struck Catherine in an interesting way. The Lutheran Church was it? She had grown up not thinking of the Folkekirken in a sectarian way. Wasn't the church, *the* church and wasn't her salvation somehow

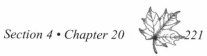

linked to it? Although part of her taxes went directly to support the state church it hadn't really occurred to Catherine, that Lutheranism was just another sect until that very moment. The point was missed on Hans, but not on Ferdinand and the scowl on his face showed his hostility.

Chapter 22

On Christmas morning, the spirit of the holidays had finally, fully settled into the Jensen household. Catherine had been correct about the late Mass. The invigorating eleventh hour ride in the family carriage to the little chapel in Holbaek, with its lighted candles and beautifully stained glass windows, colored an otherwise solemn service with the brightness of the season. There were prayers, a sermon on the birth of Christ, and in their red robes the choir sang beautifully. The Jensen family drove away much revived, the spirit of Christmas as bright as snow under lamplight. Elias hadn't attended of course. Anger and alcohol had rendered him incapable, but the next day knowing that Peter had gone to church was like a balm on an open sore. There was hope for this wayward son after all. Until he tanked up on wine later on, Elias was actually civil.

Hans seemed pensive throughout the morning, but Christmas gifts were exchanged round the tree, and feelings of love and warmth, although somewhat strained, were altogether present. Like snow under a winter sun, the tension had partially melted.

After exchanging gifts, washing up and dressing for guests, there was a four hour long feast of: smoked salmon, pickled herring, rye bread laced with caraway seeds and layered with various cheeses, all washed down with plenty of beer. Laughter, songs and conversation permeated the yuletide atmosphere while a variety of sweetbreads, pastry, chocolates and other treats were consumed in volume. Visitors came and went. Hired help were treated as family, nothing new for Catherine, Peter and Hans but Elias and Ferdinand felt above the working classes and passed around forced smiles and insincere words like wooden coins, partaking in all the above, plus wine or steaming mugs of coffee whichever was preferred.

It was mid-afternoon when Hans announced to his brothers, "If I eat or drink another morsel I'll explode. What say we go ice-skating? There's still two hours of light, maybe we can work some of this down."

"It sounds like a good idea to me," groaned Peter. "I'm stuffed like a goose. The millpond is frozen solid. Have the skates been sharpened Ferdinand?"

"They're all set," said Ferdinand efficiently. "Another thing I took care of in your absence."

"Always a barb eh Ferdinand," said Hans. "Do you mind if we leave you, Father and Mother?" Hans added respectfully.

"Why should I?" said Catherine much relieved to have them away from Elias. "Have a good time. You three have a lot to catch up on."

Even though there were still a few guests lingering about, Elias had the audacity to raise his wine glass to his sons in mock toast. "Don't break your behinds'," he slurred as he turned and stared stupidly at the fire in the hearth.

Nils Holsen, who along with Torkil Olsen and their wives, had stopped by for a drink was dressed in a pair of britches and waistcoat that may have fit him in the past, but currently had him in a miserable state of affairs, also raised his glass but lowered it quickly as he saw disapproval in Catherine's eyes. "Torkil and I would join you," Nils then stated, "but the years are telling on us."

"Speak for yourself Nils," said Torkil laughing. "I can out skate any one of them. I just don't want to leave all this," he added looking over the sumptuous dining room table Catherine and Inger had earlier moved over next to the window. The table was a bit messy but still had plenty of Christmas foods and treats.

The brothers donned their skates, and wearing heavy sweaters tramped through the snow toward the frozen millpond. The air was crisp, the sky blue and heaven an open and glorious expanse. For the moment, all was well with the brothers three. Hans looked over at Peter and Ferdinand. "I was certainly glad to get out of there," he said through steamy breath.

"So was I," agreed Peter. "I could feel Father's wrath building with every glass of wine."

"That's ridiculous," defended Ferdinand.

"Forget the old man for a while," said Hans impatiently.

"Agreed," said Peter. "Let's have a little fun. Our time together is quickly passing."

As the trio walked through the snow toward the mill, a flock of sparrows shot across the sky swooping and diving as they went. Others flitted among the leafless trees and bushes looking for a last berry or bug. Disappointed, they bunched up like little fur balls. "We need to put out some feed later today," said Peter.

"Absolutely," agreed Hans. Keep up the tradition."[2]

"I'm so full I can hardly put my skates on," groaned Hans after they'd reached the pond and were sitting on the snowy embankment.

"Me too," said Peter taking a deep breath.

Ferdinand was first to try the ice. "Watch this," he called. He headed for the center of the pond. He dipped and turned, dipped and turned, then skated back toward his brothers spraying them with ice as he turned his blades sideways to stop.

"Not bad," said Peter wadding up a snowball and throwing it at him as he skated off again.

Peter turned to Hans. "Something besides Father has been bothering you, hasn't it brother? Ever since we picked you up at the docks you've been distant."

"No I haven't," protested Hans.

"You have," argued Peter. "Back at the house when things were merriest you seemed a thousand miles away."

Hans shook his head. "Let's not get into anything distasteful," he said as he stood to follow Ferdinand. "Remember what Mother said." He reached down, took Peter's hand and pulled him up. Peter brushed the snow off the back of his pants and looked his brother square in the eye. "You've never withheld anything from me Hans. What is it? Have I offended you?"

Hans frowned and shook his head.

"Do you have a young maid in trouble?"

With that, Hans laughed out loud. "Like yourself I do have a lady in my life Peter, but she's not expecting."

Peter raised his eyebrows. "What's her name?"

"Whose?"

"Your lady's?"

"Oh . . . It's Evette, I've written you about her. We're doing fine."

"What is troubling you then Hans?" Peter demanded. "Tell me. Something is on your mind."

Hans became more serious. "You can't tell Mother."

“Don’t worry,” said Peter.

“I left the academy amid talk of government troops being called to the borders of Holstein,” Hans began. “Our spies report that the Prussians may be massing troops.”

“Just like the barbarians to come at us during Christmas,” Peter said venomously. “But how can you keep such news from Mother?”

“Because,” said Hans with a touch of foreboding in his voice. “If there is conflict on the mainland, the cadets will be called up.”

“We’d all be in it,” Peter interrupted.

“I suppose,” said Hans.

“Are you saying you don’t want to fight? That’s not like you my brother,” he added in an attempt at levity. The instant he’d said it Peter regretted his comment, but it didn’t seem to offend Hans.

“This isn’t about not wanting to fight, Peter.”

“What is it then?”

“The Prussians are mass producing a most effective rifle Peter—a needle-fire rifle.”[3]

“Come on!” called Ferdinand as he skated past his brothers again.

“I’ll tell you about it later,” said Hans. “It’s more than a five minute discussion.” He pushed off to follow his younger brother.

Peter watched them go. The words needle rifle hung in the air like his brother’s frosty breath. “Needle rifle,” he said aloud. What did it do, shoot needles? His fearful thoughts immediately shifted to Maren and a surge of protectiveness and longing engulfed him. He shook his head. Life could be so complicated. All he wanted to do was marry Maren, get a place to live, and maybe even raise a family. If there were a war, every eligible male would be called to serve in the army. It happened during the Three Years War, and Peter began to think his nuptial plans might lie in waste.

His brothers skated past him, and absurd as it sounded after what he'd just shared with Peter, Hans was actually laughing. If he can do it so can I, thought Peter. He shook his gloomy thoughts aside, stepped onto the ice, and was soon darting after his brothers. The pond was thirty yards across, the ice a foot thick, and there was plenty of room for a game of hockey. Using an old boot heel and broom handles they'd brought, the three brothers played two on one for a while, and rotated till each had stood the other. They raced around the perimeter of the pond slapping at the make-shift puck and knocking snow off the nodding cattails with their sticks. They could have gone on for hours but with winter days being so short in Denmark by five in the afternoon the exhausted, but exuberant trio sat in a snow bank removing their skates.

"A great time," said Hans.

"It was," agreed Peter, "but we should be getting back."

"Let's stop at the barn on the way," Hans said, standing and draping his skates over his shoulder. "I want to look in on Vargus."

The warm smell of large animals and dry hay tickled their nostrils as the brothers entered the quiet barn. Halters, harness, bits, and saddles hung in the tack room and next to it were pegs holding a variety of pitchforks, scythes, and shovels. The barn was as one large room with over three feet of hay covering the floor. On the outer perimeter were stalls for the horses and cows and as the brothers entered, a large brown cat came right up to Ferdinand and wrapped itself around his leg. Above the main floor was the loft where the brothers had been the night before.

"I love it here," said Hans as he dropped his skates. Horses stir something within me." He put a straw of hay in his mouth and began to chew the end. "We almost live with them at the academy. Feeding, watering, grooming, and running them are a big part of each day."

"There are no younger brothers?" teased Peter also dropping his skates. Hans bent down to his knees and tackled Peter into a pile of hay while Ferdinand who was scratching the cat's head watched with a sour expression on his face. Sooner or later he knew they'd pull him into the fray and for some reason he was in no mood. Right as rain, Hans soon had him by the legs, skates went one way, the cat scurried the other and three brothers were rolling and wrestling.

Peter groaned under the pain as both Hans and Ferdinand were upon him, then he and Ferdinand turned on Hans. No one was given the advantage. A genuine free-for-all, as three stout bodies, at times in a tangle, wrestled and dove at each other. Peter and Hans, whose strength and size were near equal, were just having fun but Ferdinand wrestled with earnestness. Seeing this, Peter and Hans turned full attention toward him and together quickly pinned his writhing body deep into the hay.

"I quit, I quit," came the muffled cry. "Get off me!!"

"What were you two trying to do, smother me!?" he gasped as they let him up. Ferdinand's hair was full of hay and he was so angry he could barely speak. "You call that fun?" he said angrily as he climbed out and brushed himself off.

"But of course dear brother," puffed Hans.

"Well I don't!" shouted Ferdinand and with that stormed out of the barn.

"Calm down little brother," Peter called after him. "We were only playing." Shrugging he then felt the weight of Hans again driving him back into the pile.

A few minutes later the two were lying on their backs, gasping for breath, and looking up at the loft. "He needed that," said Peter. "The little snot has been strutting around the house like he owns it."

"I've noticed," replied Hans. "What's gotten into him?"

"Don't ask me," answered Peter. "He is different though. He's not the respectful little boy he used to be."

"Remember when we used to jump from up there, Hans?" he said pointing to the loft as he caught his breath.

"I remember," said Hans himself still winded. "That and tromping hay during harvest time. Lucky someone never left a pitchfork buried under all this."

"Atcchh," shuddered Peter. "Don't make me think of it!"

"I still can't figure our little brother," said Hans still looking up. "Life is too short to be so bloody serious. Did you see him?"

"I did," observed Peter. "Going at us as if his life depended on it. That's why I held him down so tightly."

"Why not have a little fun in life?" Hans allowed.

"A sound philosophy," agreed Peter.

Peter's worries about war and about marrying Maren had temporarily fled, but the incident with Ferdinand had brought back negative emotions.

They lay there a moment longer, then Peter sat up, a look of worry creeping across his face. He tousled his hair to shake out bits of hay then with his fingers roughly combed it back. "At the pond you said something about a new rifle the Prussians have developed. Tell me about it."

Hans' brow furrowed as he sat up.

"Come on," Peter urged. "Tell me."

"The needle-rifle," Hans answered gravely, "is a breech-loader, meaning it loads entirely from behind, not at the muzzle. It's a bolt-action weapon and loads a single self-enclosed cartridge with the flip of a wrist. Self-enclosed cartridges Peter. Can you fathom it? No powder, no wad and ball. No ramming. Just flick and its in there ready to kill."

"So why the silly name?" Peter asked incredulously.

Hans explained. "In 1835 a Prussian bullet maker named Johann Nikolaus von Dreyse figured a way to detonate self-enclosed cartridges by building a long needle-like firing pin, and action to handle it, inside of a rifle. Being a stinking Prussian, he no doubt stole the idea from his employer, a Frenchman named Clement Potter. Regardless of where he got the idea, the needle is a spring-loaded affair inside the rifle bolt and when triggered, strikes an igniting cap built into the cartridge. An explosion results and a projectile is on its way. Because of Dreyse, the Prussians have had needle-fire rifles since 1840, but they haven't been very successful. Long firing pins can't take the heat produced in the breech, and they melt. But rumor has it Prussian arms manufacturers solved the problem with a new kind of steel and the rifles they're producing out-shoot standard muzzle loaders three rounds to one. Accurately and without jamming."

"Whew!" said Peter shaking his head. "Needle rifle, such an innocent sounding name . . ."

"For a weapon of horror," Hans finished the sentence for him.

"How do you know so much about them Hans?"

"They've been around for years Peter. The ones I've seen are of French manufacture . . ."

"The French have them too?" said Peter alarmed.

"They've done most the work on needle-fire guns," said Hans. "Like I said, the pig Prussians stole ideas from them."

"I'll bet the Americans would like to get their hands on them," said Peter. "With their civil war raging . . ."

"Americans are the most unfortunate and stupid people on this earth," injected Hans his mood continuing to deteriorate. "Fighting over slaves for pity's sake. I'm glad we outlawed[4] the evil practice decades ago."

"I've several friends from America," defended Peter.

"Is that so," said Hans with little interest. "Anyway Peter," he added disparagingly, "We hear the Prussians have entire regiments equipped with needle-fire rifles. Meanwhile we're marching around with our under-hammer muzzleloaders. I'm scared sick about it. And Father gets angry with me for criticizing the government. I could spit! The fool. Neither he, the king nor the bloody liberals in the Rigsdag have any idea the gravity of our situation. They think that because we won the Three Years' War, Denmark is invincible. Old generals and out of date weapons—we could be in serious trouble Peter."

"If things are as critical as you say Hans, why in the name of reason would you go back to the academy?"

"What would you have me do, desert? The military is my calling in life, dear brother. My calling."

Peter rose slowly to his feet. "Let's give the horses some oats and get to the house," he said just as discouraged as his brother. "I need to give this all some serious thought."

"The horses are fine Peter," said Hans taking his hand and pulling himself up. "Nils said he had them out earlier. I'm sure he fed and watered them after their run."

"Don't mention our conversation to Mother," he cautioned.

"I think she should know," said Peter. " . . .but I'll leave it to you."

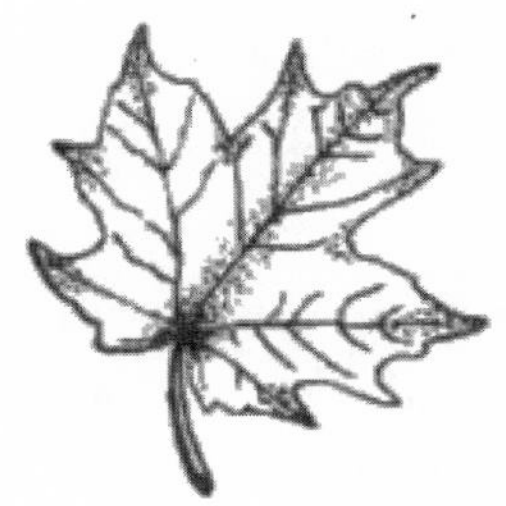

Chapter 23

Peter slept fitfully that night. Scenes of flashing cannons, exploding projectiles, and soldiers running through smoke-covered battlegrounds troubled his dreams. Explosions and musket fire sounded in his brain and in one very real scene, an army of grim-faced Danish soldiers, with bayonets fixed upon their empty muskets, were marching forward only to be mowed down in a hail of bullets shot from needle fire rifles!

He wakened in a sweat, his muscles as taut as metal bands around a barrel. "A nightmare," he said as he tried to get his bearings. "Just a nightmare." He lay there a moment or two, letting his head clear. The dream had been so real. "If this is what we face, where is a future with Maren?" he said aloud. At the moment his mind seemed as dark as the room.

He sat on the edge of his bed and tried to think, but couldn't. How long he sat there or when he got back under the covers he could only imagine but when Peter awakened early next morning, his mind was still dark and distressed. Sleep had done little to comfort him. War with Prussia and what it might do to his and Maren's plans were his main concerns, but Hans, Catherine, Ferdinand, and even Elias were all part of the dark picture. His mind burned with worry and seemingly few answers.

Something else weighed heavily on his mind that morning. Something he'd never voiced, not even to himself. And he could still hear his father's voice screeching at him. "If you do marry the girl, how will you support her?"

How, in fact, *would* he support Maren? Architecture no longer held its old fascination. Working at the mill was the only logical choice and yet he knew there wasn't really a place for him here at the estate. Certainly Catherine could provide work for him to do; busy, non-productive work or else he would be taking another person's job. The thought of either circumstance was repulsive.

Peter had great need to be alone that morning and mentally sought a place where he could think without interruption. Being a morning person, Catherine would be up and might be calling him at any minute. He dressed quietly and left the house. The morning was draped in fog and at first the barn seemed a likely place to go. Peter paused at the door. Immediately the horses, thinking it was feeding time, began to snort and stomp about in their stalls. *'No,'* he thought. *'I'll go to the mill. Nobody will be about. They're all on holiday.'* He walked purposefully, confidently as though the friendly old building in the distance, barely visible in the dense fog, were calling to him.

Creaking in the misty breeze like those belonging to a ghost ship, the mill's huge wind wings, empty of their canvas, were turning slightly; first this way, then that. The old building might well be a paddle wheeler stuck in the mud; along its side, awaiting the spring thaw, the auxiliary water wheel sat locked in the ice of the millrace.

A foot of snow had drifted against the mill's heavy doors. Peter disengaged the bolt, then struggled to force them open enough to allow passage. Inside the mill, the sweet dusty smell of grain lingered. Except for the intermittent creaking sound in the upper story shaft, all was quiet, just as Peter had hoped. He closed the heavy doors behind him.

The mill was as much a part of him as his bones. Memories of his apprenticeship flooded his mind and eased his pain for a moment; free and strong in those by-gone days, he hadn't a care in the world. Shoveling flour, laughing with the men, horsing around at break time. It seemed so long ago. Ages! Oh, to be a boy again.

The leather belts, which drove the gears, hung loosely on the main shaft, disengaged from the millstones; the huge stones themselves lay as if resting for the busy season surely ahead. *'Or will it be?'* his mind questioned. *'Of course,'* he answered himself. *'War or no, people must eat.'* Tools hung from pegs, the sifters were silent. Things were just as they should be at the end of a workday.

'Too bad the stream that passes here is too puny to power the mill year round,' Peter thought as he looked around. *'A water wheel gives a much stronger, smoother force against the gears than the gusty wind. Wind is more or less constant in Holbaek, but we need something even more reliable . . .'*

He thought of the huge locomotive he'd seen near the stage depot in Copenhagen when Maren had dropped him off. Steam, of course. 'Who knows,' he thought, 'One day we may power this mill by steam.'

Peter felt his anxiety return. What was he saying? He'd never work here again. Wasn't the country headed for war? And Hans—what must he be facing? *'This old mill,'* he said to himself, *'why it's no more my concern than the man in the moon. It will always be mother's business . . . no Ferdinand's . . . Ferdinand was taking over wasn't he? I could never work with him.'*

"So why does this place draw me like a magnet?" he said aloud.

Peter paced the dusty and smooth wooden floor trying to think.

'Milling is only to fall back on,' he thought miserably. *'Isn't that what mother taught us?'* "I'm supposed to be an architect, aren't I?" he said, as if asking the mill for an answer. The empty burlap sacks stacked near the door muted his words and the mill ignored him. "I'm to marry Maren and work in Copenhagen as an architect!" Peter shouted this last as if he were angry. He was angry. Even as he said the word architect he knew he was only trying to convince himself. Architecture wasn't in his bones like milling was; he couldn't *feel* it!

'If there is war', his thoughts went on sadly, *'what does it matter? What does anything matter? I won't be working anywhere . . . I'll be carrying a musket.'*

Including his feelings for the lovely girl from Copenhagen, Peter's mind was hot with turmoil that morning. He'd catch a plan then lose it; and then wasn't sure of anything. Threatened war notwithstanding, Peter had temporarily lost hope of anything. Standing in the center of the mill near the grinding stones, he raised his eyes toward the rafters. "Dear God, what am I to do!?" he pleaded. "What am I to do?" He dropped to his knees, with shoulders shaking and hands cradling his face, he wept silently.

Peter was no stranger to prayer. Catherine had taught all her sons how to pray. 'Now I lay me down to sleep, I pray the Lord my soul to keep, if I should die before I wake, I pray the Lord my soul to take . . .' That's how it all started, but as they got older Catherine taught her sons that their Father in Heaven didn't like repetition. He could hear her words. 'Don't pray as the heathen. With their much speaking, they think they'll be heard. Pray in specifics.'

When Peter was six years old, he had fallen from a pear tree and broken his arm in two places. Two months passed and the arm refused to mend. Surgery meant amputation. 'I believe we must ask God to heal your arm,' he remembered Catherine as saying. And with a child's faith he knelt beside her and listened as his mother plead their case. Peter could still hear her voice and feel the sweetness of the experience. Next morning the incessant fever, which had plagued him, had subsided. His head was cool and the angry red swelling in his arm and elbow had disappeared. A week later the bandages were removed for good, and a happy little boy returned to play.

'Miracles do happen Peter,' Catherine taught him first-hand. 'Always thank Heavenly Father for your blessings, then tell him your problems specifically, and ask for solutions.' Ever since Peter had made religion a serious topic of study, he had taken his mother's council more to heart. His prayers were often lengthy, detailed, and they were specific.

That morning on his knees in the mill, after long and earnest prayer, a certain peace descended upon him and Peter's soul filled with light. His eyes filled with tears and gradually all fear dissolved from his mind. He then reviewed his concerns with God, 'Is the milling business not for me Heavenly Father? If Maren and I marry, couldn't we could start a mill? Mother would surely finance us, and we could live somewhere near here. And what safer place?' Peter's prayer began to feel good, but was he listening to the spirit? He had yet to trust the concept.

'How can I think of marrying at a time like this dear Father in Heaven?' his prayer continued. 'If there's war surely I'll be called . . .' one by one as each worried question tumbled from his lips it was answered by the calm assurance that all would be well. Peter heard no voices, saw no angels, but his mind relaxed, cleared and he felt a profound deliverance. He still did not know what the future held, but all anxiety had left him. Like the little boy who had prayed, trusting that his arm would heal, Peter the man now grown, had again cast his burdens upon the Lord and again with no lesser faith.

The cold was now seeping through his coat. How long he'd been on his knees heaven only knew. Peter rose stiffly, giving little heed to his protesting joints. Prayer was real, the sensation remained; Peter's heart wasn't lying to him. He no longer worried about war, marriage to Maren, what he'd do for a living, nor was he worried about Hans, or other members of the family and their various life situations. What would be would be. He couldn't change things, he could only trust in God. "Thank you Father in Heaven," he whispered with deepest respect. "Thank you."

He looked again at his surroundings. Nothing had changed. "Lucky no one came in," he muttered. "They would have thought I'm crazy."

As he looked around the mill, Peter did make one small decision: *'When I return to Copenhagen,'* he said in his mind, *'I'll design the perfect flourmill. I may as well do something with my education. My plans will detail every convenience of operation and I'll send them to Mother. She ought to get something for all the money she has spent on me.'*

He walked about the mill again and paused to observe both huge sets of millstones. "Two runs of stone," he said, his mind turning in a positive direction. "Crude but efficient." The building felt as cold as a cave, and once again Peter thought about steam. "Steam is the future," he said out loud. "I'll work around that. Excess heat could even warm the work areas."

Wading through the snow, and at peace with the world, Peter made his way back to the house. While he had been in the mill, the sun had risen and was hard at work burning off the fog. Patches of blue broke through the morning sky and Peter felt more alive than he had in weeks.

Chapter 24

Peter's joy continued throughout the day. And that evening, in compliance with long standing tradition, he gathered with the family around the fireplace to converse and to read from the Bible. Catherine started things off by reading about the birth of Christ from the Book of Luke, while Elias, who had wanted her to read from Jonah where God chastised the prophet for his disobedience, sat in his chair by the fire sulking and steadily drinking sherry. Catherine, noting her husband's deteriorating mood, asked, "Hans why don't you read something other than scripture tonight? Something light-hearted. I'm sure you won't mind, will you, Elias?" Elias turned his inebriated stare in her direction but made no gesture. After a moment, he attempted to pour another glass from the decanter at his elbow, misjudged and spilled a few ounces in his lap.

"Let me help you Elias," said Catherine handing him a towel and pouring the sherry.

"For example," Catherine continued without skipping a beat, "How about `The Ugly Duckling,' by H.C. Andersen. It's as though Andersen has captured my life with his little tale."

"You are always pretty, Mother," protested Hans.

"It takes work to keep myself presentable," smiled Catherine obviously pleased with the compliment, and watching out of the corner of her eye as Elias dabbed at his mess.

Hans got the popular author's work from the shelf, thinking how out of place the story seemed at Christmas time, but understanding his mother's ploy he read dutifully.

Catherine finished off the evening with a chapter from David Copperfield,[5] "by that fellow who lives in England," as she called him. Despite the name Charles Dickens was very popular among the Danes. By then Elias was only semi-conscious and had to be steered upstairs by Catherine and Ferdinand. Staggering, swaying, he glared malevolently back at Peter and Hans as he stumbled from the room.

"I think I'll retire myself," said Hans momentarily excusing himself. "I've eaten like a pig all day and can barely keep my eyes open . . . Good-night brother," he said leaving Peter alone near the fireplace. A few minutes later Catherine came down the stairs but without Ferdinand, the latter having also gone to bed.

"I can't sleep just yet," she said sitting on the couch and taking up her book. She lowered her voice and added; "Your father is slowly killing me Peter. I'm at my wits end with him, but at least he didn't spoil the evening nor the day." She patted the place next to her. "Come and join me Peter . . . Don't let me talk about him another second. I get so little time to see you. This is the first time we've had a chance to be by ourselves since your homecoming."

"Of course Mother," Peter said as he came and sat down by her. He was so grateful to have Elias' eyes finally off him; he didn't know where to start. He was somewhat tired but had nothing to drink and really wanted to talk to Catherine. He had much to tell her, but would not mention his earlier talk with Hans about needle rifles; bad news comes soon enough.

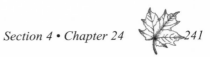

"Does father drink that heavily every night?" he asked.

"Most every night," said Catherine very much discouraged. "Ever since his party shunned him. I suppose he is justified . . ."

"Maybe so," said Peter. "Just as long as he never hits you. Or hurts you in any way."

"Your father has never raised a hand toward me," she said placidly. "In this day and time, I guess that's saying something. But again I'd really rather not talk about him . . . if you don't mind Peter."

"Not at all Mother," he said.

The coziness of the situation put them both in a pensive mood. Having little to drink that day Catherine was nonetheless glowing with pleasure at having this time with her son. And to him she looked just as beautiful as the night she'd worn her magnificent necklace. Peter could still remember.

"A lot has happened to me over the past few months Mother," he began presently. "Social and religious upheaval abound in Copenhagen; and everywhere you go someone is quoting Kierkegaard."

"So you said in your letters. He's made that much impact?"

"He has," Peter nodded. "Changing how people feel about our Lord Jesus Christ. He's becoming very important to many people again.

"The new king is also a subject of debate. His policies have brought uncertainty to Denmark and on the mainland the Prussians are restless . . ."

Even though the last part of his statement was a popular cliché, furrows deepened on Catherine's brow. "The best of times, and the worst of times," she said quoting Dickens. "But Peter aren't all those things a bit out of your hands? Best left with God don't you think?"

"Good advice," he said half-smiling, remembering his prayer in the mill. "Mother I'd like to talk to you about architecture."

"Go on," said Catherine masking her alarm at the abrupt change in conversation. She sensed there was a great deal behind his words and decided to let him talk.

"I'm not sure it's what I want in life," he said looking down at his hands. "I've hesitated to tell you for fear of upsetting you. I know how much you've spent on my education . . ."

"If not architecture, then what?" said Catherine somewhat impatiently.

"I don't know Mother, but I'm working on it."

Catherine was about to ask what he meant when Peter lifted his eyes to her. "Mother, I desperately needed this trip home. Time away from my studies; time to think. And time to plan. It has been very good for me."

"And it has been grand having you here," she said gently wondering where this was all going.

"Along with all the turbulence in Denmark, there has been equal upheaval within me," Peter went on. "And because I've had some decisions to make, I've been grateful for some basic things you taught me."

"Such as?"

"Well . . . prayer for one. You taught me that God hears and answers our prayers, and I now know that is true. I've had first hand experience." Peter then told her of his experience in the mill that morning. He covered everything, how he felt his mind in such a state of turmoil and so on. He ended up by saying he had no idea what course he was going to take in life but that he was no longer concerned. God had given him peace.

"I had no idea you'd been so upset," said Catherine at length, "and so worried. But I'm very pleased you knew what to do. Does your Mormon Church also encourage prayer?"

"It's not my church," he said mildly, "I haven't been baptized a Mormon, but yes they teach about prayer. So far the church's teachings agree with everything you've ever taught me. And incidentally, many of the things Kierkegaard taught as well."

"For instance?" she asked.

"That God is a god of love . . . a personal god."

"And," she said encouraging him.

"That man is responsible for his own actions . . ."

"What about marriage?" asked Catherine altering the subject. "Do Mormon Priests practice celibacy as do the Catholics?"

"No Mother," he scoffed but hoped she wouldn't probe further, "They don't. Marriage and family are what they teach."

Peter wasn't about to address polygamy, the most incendiary issue connected to Mormons. He had heard rumors that the practice was taught by them, but had no first hand knowledge. He was reading the Book of Mormon and liked it very much, and he also admired the Mormon Elders but he was far from being a convert.

"So tell me," said Catherine getting to *her* agenda. "What do you intend to do about Maren?

"What do you mean?"

"You know very well what I'm talking about. Marriage."

"Well," said Peter slowly, "I love her. I really do Mother."

"So? What are you going to do about it?"

"I want to marry her . . . and very soon."

Catherine laughed in spite of herself. "Oh to be so young and reckless," she said aloud. "You haven't an idea of what you will do to support her, yet you're going to marry her." She put down her book. "What will you do, sneak her into your dormitory? Put her up there?"

"Her father has a spare room behind the store," he explained. "Maybe we could live there until I graduate."

"Have you talked to him?"

"Of course not," Peter confessed. "But I intend to as soon as I return to Copenhagen."

"You'd better," she said looking at her impetuous son and patting his face. She took Peter by the chin and made him look at her. "If you're convinced she's the girl you wish to share your life with, then don't hesitate. Marry her. I'll help you and you won't have to live in her father's store. Why, we could have the wedding right here!"

Peter couldn't believe what he was hearing. He also felt a twinge of feminine pressure but the love he had for his mother at the moment eclipsed all other emotion.

"What about my allowance?"

"What about it?"

"You couldn't support the two of us," he ventured.

"Your allowance will continue until you're gainfully employed," she said without batting an eye. "But what if the girl turns you down?" She added with a twinkle.

"She won't," said Peter confidently, then his face fell slightly. "I wonder what Father will have to say about it."

"I'll speak to him if you want," she said casually.

"That's all right Mother," he said apprehensively. Suddenly

things were moving a bit too fast for Peter. "When the time is right . . . I'll do it myself."

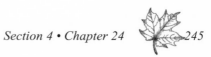

"Peter," Catherine said looking him directly in the eyes, "Nothing you've covered so far has me very concerned: architecture, getting married, Søren Kierkegaard, nothing. Your letters have been very clear . . ." Her face then took on a pained expression. "I must admit however I've been truly upset about your negative feelings toward the church. What is it the Mormons teach that has put you at such odds with your Lutheran heritage?"

There was a moment of silence between them broken only when Peter could see his mother's inquiry was sincere and not judgmental.

"I'm not at odds with the church," he said respectfully. "Studying the Mormon faith has actually given me greater respect for the Lutheran church. I also have a greater respect for Martin Luther than ever before. He was a very brave man Mother, a great reformer and the world owes him a debt of gratitude. I did find out Luther never intended to start a religion, or that is a church. Men did that, and they formed the church against Luther's will. They had no authority . . . especially any authority from God. Luther knew it. He understood it. Apparently his followers didn't." Before starting what could become a debate over doctrine, Peter stopped.

"No I'm not at odds with the Lutherans Mother," he said gently. "I'm not at odds with anything or anyone. As to what the Mormons teach, they teach of Christ. They teach powerful things Mother. Things of joy and peace. A few years back something very profound happened in America. Something that has not only helped me, but will yet help many."

"What or should I ask who, started this church Peter?" Catherine wanted to know as her son's countenance held a luster. He may not be a Mormon yet but something had changed within him. If in the past Peter had been gentle, he was gentler, if patient even more patient. If he'd had faith, it now appeared he had knowledge. Catherine was very curious as to what had caused these changes. She then sat attentively as Peter outlined the story of a fourteen-year-old American boy who had gone into a forest to ask a specific question of God.

"His name was Joseph Smith Jr., Mother, and he having read in the first chapter of the Book of James where it says; 'If any of you lack wisdom, let him ask of God, that giveth to all men liberally, and upbraideth not; and it shall be given him . . . But let him ask in faith, nothing wavering.' He stopped then continued. "The boy went in simple faith, Mother. And the question that was troubling him was; which of all the churches were true? The year was 1820, and the place was Palmyra, New York. Not that long ago, Mother."

"Two heavenly beings appeared to Joseph Smith," Peter said as he brushed a tear from the corner of his eye. "And one said to the other, "This is my beloved Son. Hear ye him. God, our Heavenly Father, and his Son, the Lord Jesus Christ, appeared to this fourteen year old boy, Mother and what has transpired since, has been nothing short of miraculous."

It took much of an hour for Peter to tell Catherine everything: of the coming forth of the Book of Mormon, Priesthood authority, and many important things pertaining to this "restored church" as he called it.

Peter spoke with reverence and sincerity, telling her everything he knew about the relatively new American sect. In parts of his testimony, Catherine was as thrilled as he was, in others she was defensive, challenged, and somewhat uncomfortable. This was definitely new information spewing from her son's mouth, still by the time he'd finished speaking Catherine had almost totally reverted to her earlier convictions: Lutherans, Catholics . . . Mormons . . . what did it matter a person's religious persuasion, so long as they believed in God, all else would be fine. Still something deep within her heart whispered that what Peter had told her was vital.

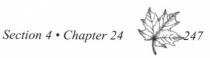

"Now," said Peter when he had finished his rejoinder, "my situation with religion is not the only thing bothering you tonight is it?" She looked at him in mock surprise then she took a deep breath and sighed.

"You are very perceptive, aren't you?"

"I don't know Mother . . . I just love you. Is it Father?"

Her face became sad. Ferdinand and not Elias had become her most pressing concern. Catherine had needed to confide in someone concerning him. Inger wasn't the person and although involved, neither was Torkil. Seeing Peter's maturity, Catherine decided that he might hold the solution to her concern. The time and conditions were right and at least he would provide an excellent sounding board. She went straight to the point. "I think that your younger brother might have a young lady in a motherly sort of way."

"Is that a fact?" said Peter a light going on in his head.

"I said might have her in trouble," said Catherine. "I don't know yet. This all came upon me a week or so ago. Its been building . . . Ferdinand has seen her quite frequently . . . he's been so sullen lately. So much like his father as of late."

"I'm sorry to hear this Mother," said Peter sincerely.

"Can you imagine the complexities Krista Holsen's being pregnant could cause me?" she continued. "The loss of Nils Holsen for one. He's a good stableman Peter, very competent. However, because I'm running a business, so to speak, I can't have such close ties to an employee. I like Nils, but don't really want to be related by marriage. He already seems to be dictating to me."

"I can see the problem," said Peter.

"Then there's Torkil Olsen. He and Ferdinand don't get along, and you know how much Torkil means to me."

"I do indeed Mother. He means the same to me . . . and to Hans."

They talked until the wee hours of the morning and both finally retired, satisfied, each having aired out to an interested party what to them was crucial information. On Peter's side of the ledger, he knew he had Catherine's support, both emotional and financial. Emotionally because Catherine had never met Maren and yet she talked about her as she might a daughter. Peter couldn't quite understand it but accepted it gratefully.

Where finances were concerned Peter longed for independence away from Catherine's purse, and wanted it as soon as possible. How to accomplish the thing would nag at him until he graduated. After that he would find a way, come what may. That he was certain. For now he could go on with life, and that is what mattered most.

On Catherine's side, she had only needed to be heard and, to her delight, found that Peter was a very good listener. She would work out her problems with Ferdinand; she hadn't the slightest worry of that; but talking openly to Peter had given her the chance to sound it out, plan a strategy.

The experience was very pleasing to Catherine and through it she gained new pride in Peter; also the realization that some very big changes were developing within her family.

SECTION NOTES:

1. Brømølle Kro was a large and spacious inn that until 1777 was a gristmill.

2. Feeding wild birds is practiced throughout the winter months in Denmark and no Danish person worth their salt would ever throw stale bread crusts anywhere but in the yard. At Christmas time birds are especially well treated. Strips of fat are hung on the stark branches of trees and bushes and crushed grain is scattered everywhere. This goes on throughout winter and because of it hundreds of thousands of wild birds are saved each year from starvation.

3. In Europe, a milestone in the development of breech-loading infantry weapons was achieved by Johann Nikolaus Dreyse, a Prussian. His Zündnadelgewehr or "needle-fired gun" used a paper cartridge with a priming pellet located at the base of a solid egg-shaped bullet. A long, needle-shaped firing pin, shot forward by a spring, pierced the cartridge and powder charge to detonate the primer. A bolt-action weapon, simple in concept and yet requiring precise workmanship, the needle rifle constituted a revolution in small-arms design. Prussian soldiers lying prone were able to fire six shots from their needle rifles for every one discharged by opponents using standard muskets.

4. In 1792 Denmark abolished the slave trade in all its overseas colonies. Denmark was one of the first countries in the world to take such a humanitarian step and a commemorative medal showing the side view of a handsome young African male was struck in remembrance of the occasion.

5. Nikolas Sondervig had recently translated David Copperfield into Danish at the translator's tender age of 79.

Section Five

War

Chapter 25

The holiday season ended quickly and no one particularly welcomed the fact, no one that is except Elias. Tired of sharing Catherine's attention with the twins and seething inside because he'd not been able to completely vent his wrath their direction, he'd sulked around the house, a glass of beer or wine his ever-present companion. Peter and Hans, prior to leaving for the university and the academy, dutifully climbed the stairs to bid him farewell. Both paused in their ascent to look around Catherine's sturdy and comfortable old house. The stone tile floors covered with oval braided rugs, the heavy ceiling beams, overstuffed chairs and expertly woven white lacy curtains on the windows made a welcome setting. Hans and Peter would dearly miss it.

"Good-bye, sir," said Hans, reluctantly entering the sick room and reaching for his father's pale hand. "It has been a wonderful time."

"It has," agreed Peter right behind him.

Elias nodded to both, and then said with grudging formality, that he would miss them both. But on the other hand they'd better well stay up with their studies else their allowance would be cut. He warned them to see to their prayers and fired a final volley regarding loyalty to the crown. The twins said, "yes sir" to everything he said, nodded when appropriate then quietly slipped out of the room. Relieved of their filial duty, they escaped down the stairs into the foyer where their mother awaited.

Catherine was wearing a green velvet dress and looked as if she had something important to do. "You're not going to Holbaek are you mother?" Hans asked protectively, as he hugged her.

"It's too cold for you to travel," Peter added. "Torkil can get us there."

"Oh I wasn't going," she said as they kissed each other on the cheek and embraced.

"I just didn't want your last glimpse of me looking like an old house frau." Catherine embraced them both again just as Inger and Ferdinand came out of the dining room. "I've packed you both some food," the sturdy little woman said efficiently. "Leftovers and good ones if I say so myself."

"Looks like we won't starve after all Peter," said Hans, taking the basket. "Is the carriage ready Ferdinand?"

"Torkil's waiting out front with it. I wanted to say my good-byes here."

Krista Holsen was with Ferdinand that morning. Peter was sure the slinky and cunning little lady had slept over but she acted as if she had just shown up that morning. She'd been peeking in and out of his and Hans' rooms while they finished packing, saying good morning more than once and moving about the house as if she owned it. Earlier she had taken breakfast with Ferdinand, eating noisily and talking incessantly. Flirting, laughing, and when the meal was done, leaving the mess for Inger.

Ferdinand had introduced her to his brothers as they'd passed through the kitchen and since meeting her, Hans had the overwhelming urge to wash his hands. The girl seemed unclean.

"I hate long good-byes myself," said Peter shaking hands with Ferdinand.

"As I," agreed Hans likewise shaking Ferdinand's hand.

They all went outside, Catherine in tears and dabbing at her cheeks with a handkerchief.

"As tall and handsome as you both are I shouldn't be turning you loose on the world as I am. I don't see how the ladies can stand it. And you better write more often," she warned. "Your letters were scant to say the least!" Both Peter and Hans held her again, and then walked to the carriage.

"Take good care of Mother, Ferdinand," Hans called back.

"You may depend on it," said the younger brother stiffly.

Krista was smiling solicitously, peering from Peter to Hans then back again only to look up at Ferdinand when either of the twins caught her eye. She may have acted warm and friendly, but the cold ambition in her was unnerving. Both twins felt it, but neither worried. Catherine could more than handle the little sneak even with one hand tied behind her back. "Mother will eat her for breakfast," Hans told Peter earlier.

"It was a pleasure to meet you both," Krista said a little too loudly.

Peter and Hans nodded, looked at each other then loaded their luggage; and while Peter was talking to Torkil, Catherine called Hans back. She'd been watching him perplexingly all the while he'd been at the carriage.

"What is it, Mother?" Hans asked as he came up to her. Peter, brows knitted, watched from afar as Catherine took both Hans' hands in her own.

"I have something to tell you Hans," Catherine said as she looked deeply into his eyes. Hers were filled with tears.

Hans, wearing his blue dress uniform with the red stripes down each leg, polished brass buttons on the coat and freshly blackened boots, was shuffling on his feet uncomfortably. Up until now he'd been in command of his emotions but at the moment felt like a boy again.

Catherine wanted to tell him to quit the academy, that she needed him home to help her run the mill, that she missed him and Peter so badly at times it was all she could do to stay sane. She wanted to tell him anything to get him out of that beautiful uniform!

Deep in her bones she knew Denmark was in trouble and that soon the military would cease to be schooling, cease to be physical training, cease to be an adventure and would become the monster that it truly was; old men's greed and ambition gained or lost at the expense of its country's brave young men. Pomp and circumstance; propaganda, lies and abject waste, that's what Catherine thought of the military.

Catherine was fearful that morning—had been so for the past few days, and for a reason she couldn't define. How could she communicate her feelings to Hans in front of everyone and on the very morning of his departure?

"Nothing, son," she said shaking her head. "It's nothing." Catherine rose on tiptoe and tenderly kissed his cheek. "Just take care of yourself that's all, and remember how much I love you."

Peter, Hans and Torkil arrived at the docks to the disturbing news that Prussian troops had entered Holstein the day before Christmas and that Danish forces had withdrawn to Slesvig without so much as firing a shot. Ten thousand troops, plus equipment had beaten a hasty retreat and while it looked to the Prussians that the Danish were fearful, nothing was further from the truth. The move would bolster Danish encampments at Husum, Dannevirke and Slesvig and prove to be a work of tactical genius.

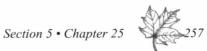

"What did I tell you Peter?" Hans said bitterly as he handed him the freshly printed newspaper. "Prussian swine! An attack right in the middle of the Lord's season."

"What should we do Hans?" said Peter very much alarmed. "We can't leave mother and father at a time like this . . ."

"Ridiculous," said Torkil as reassuringly as possible. "The men and I will take care of your parents. You young fellows must get about your lives. Besides they're going no further than the border. Norse gods protect that land. "

"I wish I was as superstitious about it as you," said Peter as he looked at Hans.

"Sacred ground," said Hans confidently. "Bring them on is what I say."

It was a typical January day, iron cold and gloomy. It wasn't snowing but the sky was overcast, streaked with low hanging clouds and the temperature was hovering near zero. For a moment Hans, Peter and Torkil stood by the carriage, each engaged in his own thoughts. Maren was uppermost in Peter's mind. He wondered if she knew about the Prussian move and if so what she was feeling.

Hans' irate demeanor easily betrayed what he was thinking. He hated the Prussians with all the vigor and anger of youth, and like his Viking progenitors, loved a good fight. Or so he imagined. Fiercely patriotic, Hans was actually anxious to return to the academy.

Torkil, the seasoned veteran of the Three Years War looked at the situation soberly. At fifty-eight years of age he was still strong and virile, he would fight if he had to, but the last place on earth he wanted to be was at the front lines. Cities were the targets, out in the country was the safest place to be; regardless he might be called to enlist, but because of age he'd be in the last wave of defense.

"I have no option but to return to the academy," Hans said at length. "I've told you that Peter, but perhaps you should go back with Torkil."

Peter shook his head. "No, Hans," he said resolutely. "Like you, I've made my decision. My place is with Maren in Copenhagen. If there's a call to arms, it's where I need to be."

"You're right about that Peter," said Torkil as he unloaded the luggage and set it at his feet. "Protect your little bird. If the Prussians invade, Copenhagen will be first on the list. They'll come by sea, through the strait. As for myself, and your parents, leave us out in the hamlets. If the Prussians want us, they can come and root us out. Me and the workers will give them one awful fight."

"Maybe I should go back with you," Peter said testing Torkil's resolve but very comfortable it was there.

"I'll never hear of it," replied Torkil. "You take care now. I've got to get back," he added with some anxiety in his voice. "There are preparations to make at the mill. If there's war you can bet the government will come calling for grain . . . just as they did last time."

"Take the paper back to mother," said Peter handing the newsprint to Torkil. "Let her know all will be well . . . and, if there is an invasion, reassure her I'll be back in Holbaek as fast as a horse can run. And tell her I'll bring Maren with me."

They parted company amid handshakes and back slaps. Later, as Peter sat alone in a coach bound for Roskilde stewing about Prussia's move into Holstein and Hans' tale of needle-fire rifles, he reflected upon the situation at home. *'Now I know why mother didn't call me*

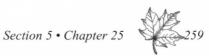

back as she did Hans,' he said to himself. *'She sensed all this! Women have a way of knowing things; still I wonder what she said to him?'* He shook his head sadly.

The coach bumped along as the snow-bound countryside passed in review. Peter was its only passenger and thoughts were tumbling in his mind like spokes on the wheels. And oddly, at least under the circumstances, the dark face of Krista Holsen slipped into the picture. *'What an unpleasant little thing she was,'* Peter mused. *'Though a mere girl, she certainly has influence over Ferdinand. But is it her that has driven the wedge between we brothers?'* His thoughts had turned to the incident in the barn. "It's not the girl," he answered himself aloud as re-lived the explosion between Hans, himself, and Elias. Clear as day Peter thought he now understood his younger brother's surly attitude. *'It's not the girl at all,'* his mind exclaimed, *'its Father. Elias is the gardener of the acrid soil. Month by month, week by week; every time Ferdinand goes into his room Father plants seeds of jealously, animosity, and greed in my younger brother's mind. Bit-by-bit, slowly but surely he's poisoning the boy. No, Krista is not the wedge pushing between us. Sure as I'm riding in this coach Elias is behind Ferdinand's vain imaginings.'*

Peter's thoughts continued. *'The boy has such a need for recognition, and that's not all bad I suppose. Everyone needs recognition, but my younger brother carries things a bit too far. Ferdinand thinks he's lord over the family's business,'* Peter thought shaking his head. But with that, and because he also saw himself as part of the family business, for a moment Peter felt himself slipping into the same depression he felt the day he'd gone to the mill.

"I won't let *that* happen again," he said sitting bolt upright. "Regardless of my concerns, I won't sink that low again."

Talking to himself when alone was a habit Peter acquired during those long nights in the dormitory before Maren had entered his life.

Talking aloud helped to calm him; the occasional crack of the whip and the whistle of the driver above, also proved soothing. Every jolt of the coach, every turn in the road took him further away from the depressing thoughts of Ferdinand and memories of Elias as well and closer to his bright life in Copenhagen with Maren Carlsen. Her love was as soft and moist as a soothing balm on the raw hide of life. Peter bowed his head to pray, and again the clouds of worry forming about him began to dissipate. Slowly, the feeling he'd had in the mill returned. Denmark may be in trouble but all was in God's very capable hands.

It hadn't snowed in a week so rather than take a coach back to Copenhagen, Peter decided upon the newly completed rail from Roskilde to the capital city. It was mid-afternoon and after buying a ticket and boarding he took a corner seat in one of four passenger cars of the rocking, smoky, rattling, unheated conveyance and closed his eyes. The tufted leather upholstery beneath him was cold and unfriendly at first, and to warm himself he sat sideways on the seat and pulled his legs up against his chest. Then he tucked his head beneath the lapels of his greatcoat. Soon his eyes grew heavy and just like the final leg on the coach trip to Holbaek, he planned to make it to Copenhagen fast asleep.

The train took on coal and water at Hedehusen, which delayed it four hours, and interrupted Peter's sleep. Because of the delay, the return trip took about the same time as the coach to Roskilde. "Trains will never replace the horse!" a disgruntled and no doubt frugal passenger shouted at the conductor as he stepped onto the platform in Copenhagen.

Maren hadn't any idea of Peter's arrival that evening and, after leaving his things in the dorm, Peter went immediately to find her. The Prussian move on the mainland had given him an overwhelming protectiveness toward Maren and for the next several days he stayed glued to her side.

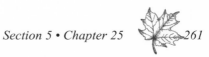

The streets of Copenhagen were bustling with people and all of them talking about the possibility of war with Prussia. Cold as it was, crowds gathered at newsstands; inns and cafes also buzzed with conversation. As news from the mainland slowly trickled in, every bit was well chewed and digested. Peter and Maren stayed in the very center of things riveted to every word and every article that came in from the front. They read everything they could get their hands on about Danish weaponry, gunpowder and the strength of Denmark's Navy. Surely Copenhagen was a prime target. Still meeting with the Mormons, Peter wondered what their church thought of war.

"Does the church believe its members should fight in war?" Peter asked a missionary point blank.

"We believe in being subjects to kings, presidents, rulers and magistrates, in honoring, obeying and sustaining the laws of the land," the missionary answered. "That includes fighting if the government deems it necessary. Yes, Mormons bear arms and yes, there are some enlisted in the army."

"Fighting in your civil war?" asked Maren as she tucked herself under Peter's arm. As of late there was nowhere she felt safer. And also as of late she and Peter had found themselves more and more interested in America's internal war, a subject heretofore distant, unreal and even barbaric to them. With what Hans had told Peter and he shared with Maren, ever since returning to Copenhagen, war and soldiering was a coming reality. Peter would gladly lay his life on the line for God, for country and of course for Maren Carlsen.

"Most likely there are members of the church fighting for the North and for the South," the missionary's companion added. "Brother against brother, father against son. It's been a bloody conflict in America, and we pray it will soon end."

Besides information gathered at church, Peter and Maren also participated in lively debates and conversations in pubs and cafes. Because of what he knew first-hand from his brother, Hans, Peter's views were not only listened to, but were sought after.

"There he is," a well-dressed merchant said as he and several business associates descended from an upstairs meeting room into the crowded café where Peter and Maren were having dinner. "I heard you the other night at Glostrup Kro, young man. Would you mind sharing with us what your brother told you during Christmas?" The merchant wore a top hat and spoke through a beard so thick one could barely see his lips moving. He was surrounded by a cadre of prominent businessmen just adjourned from a retail associates meeting. "Here young man," said an associate, "kindly stand on this chair and tell us what you know."

Being put in such a position was embarrassing, but Peter did as instructed and not only told what he knew about Prussian weaponry and the move on the mainland but added some fiery opinions of patriotism and Danish pride. He answered questions and, amid murmur and mild applause, stepped down to find several rigsdalers and a few skillings on his table. Maren, as frugal as her father, gathered up the coins and tied them in her hanky. "For our future," she said smiling proudly at Peter. "The man who asked you to address the crowd also paid for our dinner."

Over the next week or so Peter found his opinion much sought after, then interest in him faded as more and more information came pouring in from the mainland. There had been sporadic musket fire but no major battles as of yet.

Chapter 26

Anna Evette Ericksen or Evette as Hans called her, loved her father. As a successful farmer and land owner Evette also greatly admired how her father managed his holdings. The spacious home he'd built for the family with its stone fireplaces, thickly thatched roof and manicured fields surrounding it; the large barns filled with hay where scythes and pitchforks always hung orderly in their racks and the teams of draught horses he used for plowing housed in one barn, riding horses and cows housed in another and a hired man to keep them all well fed, curried, and their hooves filed and shod. Yes Evette admired her father's sage management of things but she loved him more for the freedom he'd given her.

Like her older sisters Anna Evette was tutored at home from the time she was six until sixteen years of age. She was well taught, talked incessantly and read from her Bible each and every morning. For bestowing the treasures of prosperity and education upon her, Evette loved her father but she fairly worshipped the man because he liked Hans Jensen, the rugged cadet from the academy at nearby Flensborg and as often as Hans was on leave Hr. Ericksen allowed him to visit!

Barely over five feet tall, Evette was as dainty on her feet as a fairy and like many Danish girls a platinum blonde. Her pale blue eyes shone with light, and one had to force his gaze away from them to observe her perfectly fair complexion, full and well-formed mouth, smooth rounded nose and a delicate chin that was irresistible! Other than a pale and pinkish medium sized wart by the right side of her nose Evette was without a facial flaw. She ate modestly and thus had a lovely figure, and tiny though she was, possessed an inner will as strong and resilient as tempered steel.

There had been many delicious kissing sessions in her room with Hans, also behind the barn where she kept her mare. In Hans' strong arms Evette felt protected, knew he loved her and with all the lofts and hay stacks about the farm, things had become considerably passionate between them a time or two.

Bedridden with dropsy and waited upon hand and foot by her daughters Fru Ericksen suspected things were becoming quite serious between her youngest child and the trim, dark haired and handsome cadet, however Hr Ericksen with eyes in the back of his head where his daughters were concerned, had no doubt where it was going between Evette and Hans. The prosperous farmer took it all in stride. That's the way it was in Scandinavia and after all didn't every cadet at the academy come from money?

During spring there were long walks over meadow and field with Hans enjoying Evette's quick little feet moving effortlessly to avoid rocks and ruts and her trim figure floating, or was she darting about like a pixie on wings? Hans wasn't sure but it wonderful to watch her and when she allowed him to capture her in his arms it was heavenly. But the situation between Evette and her would-be soldier was far more than just love making. The two were very good friends and when they found themselves alone, more often than not settled into long satisfying conversations.

Evette generally prattled along about her sick mother, her love for her father and often the wedding of a friend or the like. Hans was a good listener, not an interrupter but when he took his turn it was usually current events and he could match her word for word. A physical bond established between the two, their shared and lengthy conversations welded them emotionally as well. Not much of a letter writer as of late, Hans hadn't elaborated to his twin brother Peter, but Evette Ericksen was now the only girl he was seeing and had become everything in the world to him. He loved her passionately, confided everything in her and planned to marry her as soon as he graduated from the academy.

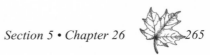

"What started our tension with Prussia was when King Christian IX signed the constitution his predecessor had drafted, into law," he was telling Evette one day as he picked at his front teeth with a straw of hay, then bit into its joint to taste the sweet juice. They were snuggled into a dry bed of hay in the horse barn loft and as cold as it was outside were quite warm and cozy.

"His predecessor being Fredrick VII, right?" said Evette.

Hans nodded reflectively. "You know I actually saw King Fredrick."

"Really?"

"Just before he died and was laid to rest at the Cathedral in Roskilde, he was at the academy on the reviewing stand. I passed by not ten feet from him. Stocky fellow. It was bitter cold that day and the king later caught pneumonia. It's what took him."

"Terrible to lose such a great man," commented Evette sadly.

"He was a great man," Hans went on, "but his constitution is what put us at odds with Prussia . . . France, and Great Britain as well."

"Denmark will be at odds with Britain until one of us conquers the other," said Evette. "All of Europe seems to be calling for our constitution's repeal," she continued as up on current events as Hans. "They claim it is a breach of the undertakings given Denmark after the war of 1848–1850. Europe's monarchs say our constitution also jeopardized the Treaty of London, and that Denmark's experiment in democracy will keep us industrially bankrupt."

"Trade will continue to suffer," said Hans sagely, "but it's unlikely we will starve. What's really bothering Europe's kings is that our constitution gives their own subservient masses ideas they shouldn't have!"

Evette laughed at that. "You are so right."

Hans became very serious then and leaned forward, slightly away from her. He looked at his hands and clenched his fists. "As a result King Christian talks of repealing the constitution knowing no European monarch will send troops to our aid should Prussia attack Denmark."

"I wish you wouldn't talk this way Hans," she said as she moved over against him. "It frightens me."

"Then there's Duke of Augustenborg," he continued disgustedly.

"Who I think is a flash in the Danish history frying pan," injected Evette wisely.

"The ink from Christian IX's signature had no sooner dried on the constitution," Hans went on, "when in open defiance to London protocol, which incidentally gave our king the right to rule Slesvig and Holstein, the good Duke of Augustenborg proclaims *himself* ruler of the Duchies."

"King Christian had predicted just such an event," commented Evette, "I think he's a man of great vision."

Highly exercised at this point Hans fairly blurted, "but to the

Prussian dragon lying at our gates, Denmark is nothing but an irksome little gnat it would just as soon swat with its tail. And what could our king do about it?"

Calling Prussia a dragon was common talk and truth be known, it wasn't Denmark's new constitution alone that had the dragon belching smoke and snorting fire; it was lust for the Duchies of Lauenberg, Slesvig and Holstein. Driven by a vision similar to American's Manifest Destiny, Otto Von Bismarck would if he could unite the many separate German speaking states into a single[1] empire of great power and glory. Being in the military Hans was keenly aware of this obsession and it affected every aspect of his life especially where Evette was concerned. How could he really plan anything with her until the future of Denmark was secure? As it was he made every second with Evette count.

"Prussia already controls Lauenberg," injected Evette.

"It certainly does," said Hans shaking his head disgustedly. "But Holstein and Slesvig remain part of Bismarck's land lust."

At that point Evette snuggled even closer to Hans and shortly leaned up to kiss his neck, a sweet, moist and tender kiss. Instantly distracted from his fears Hans looked down at her and Evette kissed him on the lips. There came a point where love making was the only thing that could sway her soldier boy from passionate discourse. Hans was one of those men who thought the world revolved around him and that given the power he could fix everything, the larger the mess the better. "You don't want to hear more?" he teased aware he'd been somewhat overbearing.

She shook her head and Hans kissed her on the mouth. Forceful at first, which thrilled Evette, then more tenderly which thrilled her even more. In reality, all Evette wanted was to be Han Jensen's wife, to have his babies. But with war on the horizon who could think of such? It was crazy! Was feminine courage in operation here or simply Evette's intense desire have a part of him always. Who knew? She loved the swashbuckling cadet more than life itself and that was enough for her. Being alone in a warm and quiet hay loft with him was stimulus enough. Soon all talking ceased, and were a person to pass within fifty yards of the barn a soft giggle or two might have been heard.

It was a week later, another winter's day at the Ericksen's farm, snow on the ground, overcast, and chilly to the bone. The day found Hr Ericksen in the kitchen enjoying his pipe, Fru Ericksen in bed having just been served a late breakfast and Hans and Evette in Evette's bedroom. Wearing thick skirts, chemise, a heavy blouse, long woolen stockings and wrapped up in a comforter sitting crossed legged upon her bed, Evette looked like a plush doll. Hans was sprawled out in a chair, black riding boots slightly steaming, hugging a thick quilt under his dark beard and looking complacently at the heavy ceiling beams above which was the attic.

The home's center fireplace was roaring away and with its back side to Evette's room had the chill knocked out of the air and under comforter and quilt the young lovers were having a quiet conversation about religion. Hans was aware of Evette's naturally religious nature a thing he also respected in his twin brother. Their overzealous father on one end of the spectrum and angel mother on the other, Hans and Peter also had their contrasts and where Peter was actively engaged in finding God, Hans was at best only passively interested.

"The two missionaries said they were from America," Evette was explaining, "curiosity is probably why father let them in . . . and he was surprisingly cordial to them."

"Were they Mormons?" asked Hans offhandedly.

"You know about them?" asked Evette surprised.

"They seem to be everywhere these days."

"They do, don't they? I've seen them in town or out on the roads walking farm to farm. After their message we ate dinner and Father let them sleep in the barn. They also joined us for breakfast," she went on, "and afterward we had a lively discussion about the nature of God. My oldest sister asked them many questions . . ." she wasn't sure Hans was listening and concluded with, "and then they went on their way."

"My brother is interested in the Mormons," said Hans.

"What a coincidence," exclaimed Evette.

"But I'm not," he said. "I've got enough to worry about these days."

"I am interested," said she. "See . . . I even bought one of their books." She reached over to her nightstand and handed Hans a thick, black, leather-bound book the pages of which he ruffled with his thumb.

"No sketches," he said disappointedly, "just words. You know Evette, if there is a God I wonder why he allows war on this old earth."

She thought about that for a moment then said, "Wars are started by men Hans, not by God."

"Yes, but you'd think He'd put a stop to them," he persisted. "So much death and misery . . ."

"Last night the missionaries us taught that there was a war in Heaven," said Evette altering the direction he wanted to go. "And that it is still going on today. It's a war for the souls of men. The missionaries said Satan was behind it all then and he is behind it all now." When Hans didn't comment she added, "I think Satan is even behind Prussia's vile expansion plans."

"Something evil is certainly behind it," said Hans, "greed most likely. So what else did these Mormons tell you?" he added surprising her.

"Well, they told us all men must repent of their sins before God and then live the commandments. They insisted it's the only way to true happiness. They said that sin darkens our countenance, holds us back and makes us unhappy."

"Everybody sins Evette."

"That is true . . . but we don't have to. And the missionaries said that if we repent of our sins, and have faith in the Lord Jesus that His atonement takes care of . . . even those sins we can't repay . . ." she faltered, watching Hans closely.

"Sin we can't repay . . . like what?"

"Well," she said hesitantly, "like lies that hurt people, or things we should have done but due to laziness or selfishness didn't do. You know when we put ourselves before others . . ." Evette became quiet at that.

"What's the matter?" Hans asked at length.

Evette's eyes were large as saucers, liquid and peering deeply into his.

"The missionaries mentioned fornication Hans."

She had said a mouthful with that and the conversation, what little would be left of it became very strained. Evette had hung her head and was looking into her hands when Hans came over, lifted her chin and kissed her. "I love you Evette," he said tenderly. "We've done nothing wrong."

He wasn't very convincing. Even though it was common practice in Danish society both instinctively knew intimacy before marriage was wrong and unlike returning a stolen coin or a neighbor's rake the sin couldn't be repaid under normal circumstances. For his part Hans hadn't felt much guilt about it, until now that is, but the night before, the message from the missionaries had definitely pricked Evette's conscience. She had at first been angry with the "Elders" as they called themselves, and had treated them coolly, but by morning her heart had softened greatly. Being so deeply involved with Hans however, she was confused and really didn't know what to do.

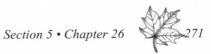

They talked quietly for a while longer each feeling the other's heartache. Because he loved her so truly being the cause of Evette's shame troubled Hans. He was also confused by this doctrine of atonement she had mentioned. Not that he hadn't heard about it but wasn't there something about "grace" where mankind's sins were concerned?

Finally Hr Ericksen rapped on the door, "your mother needs you Evette," he said somewhat sternly, "and there are chores to do!"

Hans, his emotions raw, his head swimming with questions, rose and reluctantly kissed Evette goodbye. Was she a bit less open to him? Her kiss dry and firm? It was so but he shrugged it off. In the front room he pulled on his greatcoat, bid the Ericksen family farewell, untied his horse and rode to Flensborg.

Spurs glinting against white countryside, Hans Jensen the rawboned, learned young lover of Anna Evette Ericksen was in an agitated state of affairs and urged his mount toward town. His leave didn't expire until twelve o'clock that night, he wanted the comfort of a warm beer and the company of friends; peers who often times, on days such as today, found themselves in a warm, dark, smoky pub called the Battered Ax, getting slowly stoned while elaborating upon the exciting and dangerous times of the day, not to mention rejoinders on girlfriends, females in general but war always at the forefront.

"Otto von Bismarck is a political and military genius," Bengt Nielsen was saying as Hans stomped in threw off his coat, lifted a stein of warm beer from a tray and held it in the air. "I'll drink to that," he said.

"Hear, hear," said a cadet seated on the bench across from Hans. "I'll drink to anything," he added boozily.

"Seriously now, gentlemen," said Nielsen trying to maintaining the integrity of his discourse, "sit down Jensen," he invited. "Bismarck has a brilliant legal mind, hated Napoleon III, that is Frenchmen in general, and despises greedy little potentates and clutching monarchs . . ."

"Such as our Duke of Augustenborg," interrupted Hans acidly. "He hates him . . . and I hate him!" With that Hans looked around through the smoke and din of the Inn to see if his friends were with him, then banged his stein upon the table sloshing beer all over the arm of a fourth cadet.

The cadet stood and quickly brushed the frothy liquid off his sleeve, "What's the matter with you Jensen?"

"Women," said Hans as they both sat down.

"I see. Drink deeply my friend."

"As I was saying gentlemen," said Nielsen eyeing Hans cautiously, "Bismarck believes the solution to the fragmentation problem of the German states, and other complexities of our day such as; Russia's competition for the Baltic, the Polish rebellion against Prussia, and France's constant threat, is . . . in his words, 'Blood and Iron'".

"That's all well and good," said Hans angrily and rising slightly, Evette's parting kiss still cold upon his lips, "but if he tries anything against Denmark, we'll kick his arse all the way back to Berlin!"

"Well said," called out a fifth cadet.

"Hear, hear," called another. "How come you know so much about the man Bengt?"

"Studied him my man, like you and our drunken friends here are supposed to be doing. "Know thy enemy!" Bengt smiled and Hans rolled his eyes knowing a lecture was coming. Bengt was famous for his know it all discourses.

"Otto Edward Leopold von Bismarck was born to a family of nobility in 1815," Bengt was showing off, "studied law at the University of Göttingen and the University of Berlin, and was admitted to the bar in 1835. He served as a lieutenant with Prussia's Life Guards, a crack army unit." At this Hans perked up his ears. "A few years after he left the service, he was elected to the Prussian Diet, he's an able orator by the way and cunningly moved up the ranks of Prussia's government. Between 1851 and 1859, he served as a representative in the Germanic Diet. In his current position as Chancellor of Prussia, has persuaded Austria to act with him in uniting Germany."

"Are we being tested on this tomorrow?" Hans quipped. He was beginning to forget about Evette . . . for the time being.

"King Christian believes he can pacify Bismarck and avoid war over Slesvig and Holstein by simply having out constitution repealed," Nielsen continued unabated, "and he also believes that because of the marriage of his beautiful daughter, Alexandra, to the Prince of Wales, that he has a strong ally in Great Britain."

"Alexandra?" said the fourth cadet. "Now you are talking."

"And don't forget that a movement of 'Scandinavianism'!" said the fifth. An alliance between Norway, Sweden and Denmark is finally afoot."

"And it's about time," grunted Hans to the fellow at his left. "It's only taken two hundred years . . ."

"Not only that," continued Bengt Nielsen, anxious to have the attention again, "but Christian IX also thinks Russia will help Denmark stave off the German threat." Bengt knew his subject and enjoyed having the floor. He wasn't much of a drinker and to compensate, could talk his friends under the table.

"Denmark sees herself in a strong position," he concluded uneasily. "But I personally believe Bismarck has little intention of negotiating with our scrappy little nation of islands, nor anyone else for that matter. He believes Great Britain has her expansive, bloody little hands full, Sweden will mind her own business, and Bismarck is currently working on a treaty with Russia. He will have his United Germany, which includes our duchies and he's building his forces."

"Let them build," said Hans Jensen seriously. "I'm counting on a united Scandinavia and like I said, we'll kick his britches all the way back to Berlin!" He took a swig of his beer. "The Germans don't have their heart in a program of expansion the way Bismark does," he added. "They're too busy drinking beer!" At that he toasted Bengt Nielsen's stein with his. "Thanks for the history lesson my friend . . . now what do you say we get drunk together. The evening is fast slipping away."

The alcohol was beginning to hit Hans but his mind was still clear enough to know that Bengt Nielsen's assessment of Prussia was accurate; living on the mainland and so close to the tense situation he could feel it, smell it. But the perilous situation notwithstanding, the citizens of Denmark at large, having been freed from 190 years of absolute monarchy, were enjoying their romp. The king's talk of repealing the constitution angered them. The late Fredrick VII, the people's king, had given them the cherished document and most Danes would rather die than see it repealed; if anything Denmark wanted more freedom. Newspapers were aflame. Flyers circulated on the streets. At all costs, keep the constitution! Who is Otto von

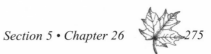

Bismarck? What of the Prussians? We've beaten them before!

Denmark's bravado stemmed from the fact that ninety percent of her citizenry lived upon the islands and felt insulated from problems Hans Jensen and his friends were facing on the mainland. Also a strong faction of pacifists in Danish society added further confusion. Let Bismarck have Holstein and Slesvig, was their cry. Peace at any price. Who needed the Duchies? Their opinion, along with mixed views from an enlightened student-body at the University of Copenhagen, added spice to an already boiling stew.

Chapter 27

On two occasions during Peter's first week back in Copenhagen, Christian IX's life was publicly threatened and mobs stormed the Royal Palace. To protect the monarch and maintain order, guards with fixed bayonets were doubled and redoubled.

"The king has the city in an uproar," Peter was saying one evening as he and Maren met at Norre Park. "Repeal the constitution indeed. Is the man crazy?"

"I don't know what to think of him," said Maren. "He's doing his best I suppose."

"Too many ties with foreigners for my liking," said Peter. "Like a puppet, they've got him dancing on a string."

Having rained earlier, the weather was damp and a fine mist hung about the air. Peter was feeling very frustrated this particular evening. Not being able to have Maren inside his dormitory, nor be alone with her anywhere cozy, was becoming maddening. With serious issues and complex feelings to discuss, the need for privacy was crucial. Theater and church certainly didn't provide a place, nor did Maren's flat; too many brothers and sisters. The only time Peter and Maren had ever engaged in any serious talking or kissing for that matter was within the confines of Norre Park. But it was winter and the lack of warm, dry, spacious lawns only heightened Peter's frustration.

He longed sit on a blanket amidst a sea of green grass and watch as Maren undid her braids letting her luxurious brunette hair fall. Her hair was such a rich contrast to her fair skin but blended delightfully with the spray of freckles across her cheeks and nose. "I would like to draw you," he had once told her. "But then how does one improve upon perfection."

"You do go on," she had said blushing.

There had been a passionate encounter that day and Maren had wanted to give herself completely to Peter. But she had remembered a pledge she had made to herself and she would not break it. *'Peter would think me as common,'* she had assured herself, *`and I'm not common.'*

"We could rent a room," Peter had once suggested, but Maren's frosty reception to the idea quickly showed him she didn't share the popular Danish belief that sex before marriage was harmless. Maren followed Biblical teachings rigidly and if Peter wanted her intimately he would just have to wait.

And Peter respected Maren's virtuous ways. That he'd be the only man to lie with her was a 'pearl of great price' to him. Still, such as on this particular night he sometimes felt frustration.

"What's more," he went on, and there was irritation in his voice, "if the king actually succeeds in repealing the constitution, there'll be a blood bath in Copenhagen! I'm sure of it."

"Oh I agree," said Maren as they walked along—Peter loved it when she bit her bottom lip when she had something important to say, "but when all is said and done, we must come to terms with Prussia over Holstein and Slesvig. I say, if Holsteiners insist upon doing most of their trade with Prussia and don't mind paying homage to them, let Holstein join the proposed German confederation. Good riddance to it."

"But what of Slesvig?" asked Peter. "Holstein and Slesvig must always be one. History says so. The people there speak Danish and are loyal to the crown."

"I'm sure you're right," said Maren. "Slesvig would rather be a slave to Denmark than be governed by Prussia. These are dark times in the history of our country," she added despondently.

"But somehow we'll pull through it Maren," Peter assured her. "We always have."

They came to the edge of the park near a lamppost, and were about to cross the street when Maren held back. "What if there is war Peter?" she asked looking up at him. "The country will fall to ruin . . . W–will that change our plans to marry?" The cobbles on the streets were shiny, wet from rain and the melting snow. What snow was left lay in patches about the ground and near the trees. Cold as it was, for a moment Peter was back in Holbaek province kneeling in the old flourmill. Once again a feeling of light and peace descended upon him. Like a halo above their heads the gas lantern softly hissed.

"Nothing will change our plans Maren," he said resolutely. "Not war, not a different form of government . . . nothing."

They stood looking into each the other's eyes until the chill of the night began to penetrate their clothing. "I'd better get you home," he said seeing her shiver. He took her in his arms and kissed her.

They crossed the street and when they reached the door to her upstairs flat Peter again took Maren in his arms. "I love you so," he whispered. "You're part of me. One with me." He bent and kissed her tenderly, longingly. Her mouth was sweet, her breath soft and so inviting. He kissed her again.

"With all that is going on lately, there's no way I can get into serious study," he said when their lips parted. "My books gather dust. All I can think about is you." His confusion over a career was another major frustration, but he didn't mention it.

She smiled up at him and put her head into his chest. "I have the same problem Peter. You're *all* I think about. But you must graduate," she added. "What would your mother think of me if I were the reason you quit . . ."

The window above them suddenly opened knocking snow from the ledge and onto Peter. "Maren!" Lars Carlsen, called. "Time to come up now."

"Coming Father," she answered. Behind Hr Carlsen the sound of giggling could be heard as the window slammed and more snow fell from the ledge.

"I must go love," she said brushing the snow off Peter's shoulders. She kissed him quickly. He kissed her in return and she pushed him gently away. "Sleep well," she said touching her finger to her lips and blowing a kiss. "You must be ready for classes tomorrow."

Peter sighed heavily. He wanted to remain with her so badly it was killing him. "I know," he said. "I know."

Maren went inside and when the door closed, Peter took off his leather cap and shook the snow off. He then wrapped his woolen scarf tighter around his neck and headed across the Park. *'Tomorrow early after class,'* he said to himself, *'I'll take her to that restaurant at the far end of the docks. We need time to really talk things out.'*

Chapter 28

For the next few days newspapers were void of any mention of the plight of the constitution. Instead they concentrated entirely upon the Prussian threat to Slesvig. In a letter from Hans, postmarked Fredericia, Peter received the following alarming letter:

Dear Peter,

War will soon commence. Scouting reports confirm the Prussians are moving artillery to the borders of Slesvig. People are spilling out of Holstein as well as Slesvig like rats from a sinking ship. The roads are full of carts and wagons, heavily loaded and going in both directions; some towards Germany, some towards Jutland. The docks at Kolding and Fredericia are teeming with refugees. It's pitiful to see people with their meager belongings huddle against the cold, but at least we know who is friend or foe.

I received a frantic correspondence from Mother yesterday in which she demanded I quit the academy and return home. God bless her, she knows it's not possible. I've a half a letter to her and must finish, but don't know what to say. Mother is such an angel. I don't want to worry her.

Where women are concerned, you may remember Evette. I've written you about her. Anna Evette Ericksen, a beautiful girl and like you she is studying the Mormon religion. It has all made me stand up and take notice. You never know dear brother, I may look into it myself. I haven't written Mother about all this but please allow me first mention.

Coming back to present reality, the Danish army is in full mobilization. Two divisions landed on the mainland this week and by now have joined Danish troops already in position at Dannevirke on the border of Slesvig, just two days march from here. Forces on the front lines now number 40,000 strong and increasing daily. During the Three Years War, there was little fighting during winter but current conditions have the ground frozen solid. Troops and equipment, especially cannon, are easily moved. Our leaders are very concerned.

If the Prussians had launched an all out attack during Christmas, they would have caught us napping. The whole of Jutland might now be under their control. As it is, all they have is Holstein. It may be rightfully theirs, but we will not give them Slesvig!

Here at the academy we've been practicing with powder and ball and shoving fixed bayonets into straw dummies. How would it be to kill a man in such a manner? I shudder to think, but we cadets are well trained and earnest. Bring on the Prussian dogs!

One last thing, the Danish regular army high command is seeking orderlies from among the cadets. These young men to serve as aid-de-camps for regular army officers. My name is on the list of candidates, and I pray I'm chosen. I'll black the boots of those officers, anything to get myself closer to the front lines!

The rest of Hans' letter was replete with bravado and talk of military strategy; of how Danish troops had more experience than the

Prussians and were defending their own soil etc., but this crazy desire to serve as an attendant to an army officer, could very well put him on the front lines and Peter would never forget Hans' chilling report on Prussia's modern weaponry.

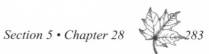

After finishing the letter Peter knew what he had to do. Announcements in the Berlingske Tidende and posters everywhere beckoned the country's young men to either enlist or they would be drafted. Long lines outside Christiansborg were stark reminders. Peter was no coward, but being a realist he knew full well that if the powerful Austro-Prussian confederation really wanted to, it could crush tiny Denmark like a grape.[2] Peter put on his greatcoat. He had decided to enlist and the sooner the better. Like his twin, he would soon be wearing the uniform of his country, fear for Hans' life and not patriotism was his motivation. Now he had to explain his decision to Maren.

"Hans has always talked of famous battles, Maren. When we were boys all he wanted to do was play war games in the woods. Then when we started working at the grist mill, Torkil Olsen and other veterans filled his head with the glories of the Three Years War." It was late afternoon and Peter was watching Maren as she worked at the linen tables in her father's store; tables and shelves were a mess, stock was low, but business-wise it had been a good day.

Maren felt very apprehensive as she listened while Peter told her of Hans being on a list of those who might leave the academy to serve as orderlies to officers. She felt herself becoming as nervous as he. Her deft little hands moved quickly folding first one piece of cloth then another, patting each firmly as she stacked them.

"He sounds so reckless Peter . . . so daring. I hope he keeps his wits about him."

"He is reckless," said Peter almost angrily. "He probably thinks he can beat the Prussians all by himself. I'm very worried about him."

"So am I," said Maren anxiously. "But I'm also worried about us Peter. What if the Prussians invade Copenhagen? Father says they'd make slaves of us!"

"That's not going to happen," scoffed Peter. "If they come at us we'll beat them back into the sea." Things got quiet for a moment as the young couple looked at each other intently.

"What is it Peter?" Maren asked.

He hesitated a moment then said soberly, "I've enlisted."

Maren's hand went to her mouth. "Oh Peter . . . "Why didn't you wait till you were called up?"

"My place is with Hans," he said huskily, then added. "But if I'm really going to be able to protect you, and our fair city I'm going to bear arms."

"That's very gallant Peter, but you don't know if you'll stay here in Copenhagen. You have no idea where they'll send you."

"Probably not," said Peter shaking his head. "If not here then somewhere on the mainland I suppose. We must contain the fighting there or all is lost."

"I don't want you fighting," she said. "I would die if I lost you Peter."

There were tears in her eyes as he held her to his breast. "I'm not going to die Maren. We have plans, remember."

Lars Carlsen was dusting a shelf and watching the young couple from the front of the store. He knew exactly what was going on. Accounts of Prussia's build up shouted from every newspaper and Lars had also read the draft notices. There was first hand evidence as well. Just as it was before the last war, his business had picked up markedly. Then as now, people were beginning to hoard items they knew would be in short supply. He could hardly keep pace. Blankets, candles, cloth, needles, thread, wax, all were in great demand.

Lars' feelings were bittersweet that late afternoon. Here was his daughter, courted by a handsome young fellow, and his store bustling with people from the time he'd unlocked the door that morning until he closed up at night. Why couldn't it always be like this? He'd enjoy the surge of prosperity as long as it lasted, but Lars knew full well if there was war, the streets of Copenhagen, and his store would be void of people, especially young men. His business and his dreams of Maren marrying into a wealthy family might all go up in smoke.

"Maren," he called, "best to tell your young man good-bye. We've got shelves to stock. There's a busy day expected tomorrow."

"You had better go love," Maren whispered as she touched Peter on the cheek.

He wiped at her eyes touched by the bright sparkle that was always there. He loved her so deeply her felt his heart might break. Peter then took her hand and kissed it. "See you tomorrow," he said. "Let's take a very long walk."

"Good day, Mr. Carlsen," he said putting two fingers to the brim of his cap as he passed his aisle.

Lars barely returned the mock salute. It was a bad omen as far as he was concerned. "Good-day young man," he said reservedly. "Come again." The merchant wasn't about to show Peter that he'd already been accepted into the family. Until after the wedding, if there ever was one, he would remain distant. It was just his way.

Chapter 29

Dear Hans,

I received your letter today and answered post-haste. Newspapers echo your correspondence. The conflict with Prussia is upon us and every man who can carry a musket is called to enlist. I signed up today but it took three hours. Ordinance is clogged with enlistees. There are no specific orders for us as yet but it won't be long. An assignment is forthcoming.

The mood in Copenhagen is precarious. Christian IX can't see past his royal nose. All he cares about are the proposed changes in the constitution! If he doesn't rally behind the country soon, he might be bowing to Bismarck. The king is a hated man. Last week there was a riot at the palace gates. Bricks and bottles were thrown and there was musket fire. Word has it Christian IX fled the country. Who knows; he's probably in Holstein sipping tea with the Duke of Augustenborg! Maybe even with Bismarck!

As to the subject at hand, Hans I plead with you. If there is war and you are called as an aide-de-camp don't do anything foolish. Stay by your officer, stay in the trenches. Keep your head down! You and I are one. Our blood is the same; our hearts beat in unison.

Please be careful. With any luck I'll see you on the mainland and we will fight together.

God bless and keep you.

Your brother Peter

By late January Catherine was beside herself. Peter had also written her of his enlistment. He had told her that at present the army was having difficulty organizing. There weren't sufficient arms to fully equip the regular army let alone the new recruits who he said were marching around with broom handles. There were no barracks and each night after training everyone simply went home, only to show up next day and work at the docks unloading federal supplies or else throwing up breast works near the ramparts.

Peter wrote a few lines concerning Maren, a few about the king and the constitution, but little else. The letter was void of anything about the Mormons, and concluded with regards to Elias, Ferdinand and Torkil. Catherine was extremely relieved to know of Peter's situation, however nothing could calm her fears regarding Hans.

"I want him as far away from Frederica as humanly possible Elias," she pleaded. "There must be something we can do to get him ousted from the academy . . ."

"I, don't think there is my dear," he choked. "Once he put on that uniform . . ."

"Can't you contact some of your old friends!?" she scolded sharply.

Pride wouldn't let him admit it, but Elias' old political connections had all but dried up. But he had never seen his wife quite like this and for a moment truly understood Catherine's feelings. He had to say something comforting to her, only what?

"My dear, if the Prussians do attack, our forces will drive them back to Germany in two weeks time." He stopped for a coughing spasm as he did when he needed time to think. When he'd finished he added, chokingly, "There'll be no need to call up green troops. Hans will be safe," he managed.

"And don't forget," he added, "there are no civilian ships sailing between Holbaek and the Jutland just now. Even if we got him out of the academy, how could he get home? The government has nationalized everything."

"Hans is hardly a civilian!" said Catherine angrily. "I've been at Holbaek's docks. Military people are thick as fleas. Maybe one of your former acquaintances could get Hans a special pass."

"Perhaps so," the former politician whined. "Only I can't imagine Hans sailing this way in uniform. He'd have to be wounded or otherwise disabled, if he left Frederica under any other circumstance, he'd be treated as a coward." For all his coughing Elias could barely finish the sentence.

"I don't care how he'd be treated or what he'd be wearing!" Catherine said angrily. "People can think what they will. I want him home!"

"You're worrying needlessly my dear," Elias said as soothingly as possible. "Surely the academy is not a target."

"Fort Esbjerg is only a few kilometers away, Elias," she said knowledgeably. "What about cannon fire? I don't care what it costs or whom we have to pay, I want Hans out of there!"

"All right, all right my dear . . . I'm sure I can . . . do something," he said, and none too convincingly. "Otto Pedersen is still Party head. Maybe I can get him to pull some strings."

There was no way to pacify her except to do what he could. Elias loved Hans as much as his selfish heart was able. On the other hand he also knew his son well enough to know he'd want no special favors.

Otto Pedersen, who was no friend of Elias Jensen's in the first place, had moved to Copenhagen two years previously, but a former party member, a fellow named Arne Mortensen, who lived in Holbaek, claimed he might be able to get Hans kicked out of the academy. "Get him accused of stealing. That's all it would take Elias. Get me the passage and a little extra to spend . . . on the right people of course . . . and I'll take care of it."

Elias paid Mortensen a handsome bribe but the man never left Holbaek. Other than getting himself and a group of friends drunk on Catherine's money, nothing else was accomplished.

Three weeks passed. Due to a harsh winter, fighting on the mainland was sporadic at best and news from the front less than encouraging. Letters from Hans were non-existent and Catherine worried incessantly, lost weight, and did her weeping in private. Hans had not written because he and six other cadets on horseback were on their way to Dannevirke and the Danish front-lines. Led by a regular Army Sergeant, the seven cadets would serve Danish officers by writing and delivering correspondence, seeing to uniforms, boots and the care of horses. They would see the art of war first hand and if they lived to tell about it would be on their way toward future leadership.

January 30, 1864 the Danish Rigsdag formally declared war upon Prussia and on February 1st, hoards of men in pointed helmets, under the direct leadership of a Prussian General named Friedrich von Wrangel, spilled across the river Ejder and into Slesvig. Because the normally marshy land between the river and Danish fortifications at Dannevirke was frozen solid, von Wrangel moved men, horses and heavy equipment easily, and once in position Prussian artillery opened fire. Following a heavy bombardment, overconfident Prussian forces then stormed Danish bunkers.

The bunkers were cleverly constructed with enclaves and tunnels and forcing the Danish out would take some doing. Advancing Prussians fell into many entrapments and hundreds were killed, wounded or else captured. Then just as the invading Prussians thought they might be getting the upper hand, Danish troops sallied forth from their fortifications. Inspired by their leader, a dashing and pompous General named Christian Julius de Meza, Denmark's forces met the Prussian charge head on. Under a murderous hail of musket and cannon fire, a desperate battle ensued in the wide-open fields of Dannevirke and remarkably, the Danes succeeded in breaking the Prussian attack.

Abandoning field pieces and hundreds of needle rifles, von Wrangel's army retreated back across the Ejder with Danish cavalry in hot pursuit. Hundreds of Prussian soldiers were taken prisoner and all of Denmark was in celebration. There was dancing in the streets and newspapers rang with accounts of Danish fighting superiority. As Catherine Jensen read and re-read the accounts she took heart. Maybe Elias had been right. Perhaps this would all be over in a matter of weeks.

As for Prussia's chancellor, Otto von Bismarck, when news of the bungled assault reached his ears, he threatened to have General von Wrangel hung. The Prussian defeat wasn't von Wrangle's fault. The Danes were defending a mythical, and to them invincible area; and despite being out-manned and out-gunned, had fought with such savagery that no army of comparable size could have possibly defeated them.

Under Christian de Meza's inspired leadership the Danes were victorious on two major fronts, while on a third front, Prussian forces remained more or less entrenched.

Chapter 30

However sweet, Denmark's' frenzy of jubilation would prove short-lived. Earlier, also on February 1, 1864, Danish Prime Minister D. G. Monrad and a delegation of politicians left Copenhagen to visit the snow bound front lines near Dannevirke. In spite of the public's keen interest in the war, news traveled slowly and unbeknownst to Danish citizens, things were about to take a nasty turn. The entourage arrived on the front lines finding General Christian de Meza's troops hunkered down to wait out the winter or at least for better weather in which to fight.

"You're in danger of being flanked here at Husum, and near the river Treene, General de Meza," insisted the spokesman for Monrad's entourage, a square-headed and graying politician by the name of Henning Borch. "Additionally, Prussian troop carriers have been spotted in Flensborg Fjord. A successful landing there and you'd be completely surrounded."

Borch, like his colleagues, with the possible exception of Monrad, had never worn a uniform. A squinting man, whose mouth was constantly open revealing spaced and squared, yellow-stained teeth, Borch had poor vision, couldn't breathe well through his nose and a person didn't want to be too close when the man was speaking.

Rotting teeth had given him the breath of a warm open sewer.

The moment he met Christian de Meza, Henning felt contempt for the good-looking and dedicated General. Of Portuguese descent Christian de Meza was as handsome as Henning Borch was ugly, and as wise as Borch was foolish. Courtesy was not among Borch's traits either. Protocol ruled, and being the eldest in the group of delegates from the king, the thin, yet pot-bellied man felt compelled to be its spokesman. Monrad, though he was actually in charge, let him.

"The way we see it General de Meza," continued the egotistical and squinty-eyed politician in his raspy voice, "Dannevirke is virtually impossible to defend. It is therefore the recommendation of this committee that Danish forces withdraw to Dybbol."

"Orderly . . . get me my sword!" demanded Christian de Meza as he raised his arms outwardly and tried to remain calm.

Hans Jensen stepped behind the general reached his arms around de Meza's waist and buckled a heavy leather belt and scabbard in place. The sword's blade sliding into the scabbard was steel on steel as de Meza faced off with Borch.

"Are you completely mad?!" de Meza then exploded. He was simply unable to stave off his anger any longer. "Retreat? Move a well-entrenched army and all its equipment in the middle of this bitter cold weather!? It's suicide! Utter madness!" de Meza was square in Borch's face. His feet were planted like trees, his eyes were on fire, and had he acted upon his emotions he'd have drawn his sword and killed the man. Hans Jensen watched the scene in rapt fascination. In the few das he had served Christian de Meza he had grown to worship the decisive mustachioed supreme commander of the Danish forces.

"Retreat is a rather harsh word, General de Meza," Borch stated shakily looking to move behind Monrad's coat tails. "It–it's not what we're asking . . . relocate would better cover it."

de Meza grabbed the politician by the lapels and shook him violently. "You foul smelling pig," he growled. "You'll cause our deaths! The men are safe here. Look around at our fortifications. The devil himself couldn't dig us out of here . . . and you would place us in Prussian gun-sights?!" He shook Borch again for emphasis, "not only that but the citizens of Denmark see it as a retreat. Call it what you will!"

"Now see here," D. G. Monrad finally spoke up as he pushed between de Meza and Borch. "You can't manhandle his majesty's emissary like this. Release him or I'll have you arrested!"

Hans was immediately at de Meza's side trying to decide whether or not to push Monrad back. Wisely he decided against it but the gesture did not go unnoticed by de Meza. He was proud of Hans and wanted to say as much.

de Meza slowly let go of the pot-bellied politician's coat lapels and shoved him back. He then walked to the entrance of the partially underground headquarters, placed his fists to his hips and stared back at his guests as if thunderstruck. "For the love of might gentlemen," he said shaking his head incredulously, "I do believe you are serious . . . You want me to pack up and leave . . ."

Borch's legs and his will were beginning to buckle, but Monrad stayed in charge. "I'm afraid we are very serious, General de Meza," he said more respectfully now. "I–in a meeting with the King and his advisors prior to our coming, sources privy to such information reported to us that the Prussians plan to launch a major offensive by sea. Not only will they land near Flensborg, as Hr Borch has tried to explain to you. They plan to establish a beachhead at Als.

Moving your armies to Dybbol could thwart their plans and not only that, Dybbol being a hilly region would give your troops better cover. Should the Prussians succeed in landing at Flensborg we'll break their advance before it gets underway. If you look at the map General, you'll see our logic is sound."

de Meza, who knew the area in question like the palm of his hand, and whose lack of tact was legendary, was staring holes through Monrad. "The Prussian advance is broken as things stand!" he shouted. "And as for the Prussian operation at sea, what in the King's name is the Navy doing!?"

"All it can," Monrad said defensively.

de Meza snorted. "We're entrenched at the narrow most neck of land on the peninsula gentlemen," he said through clenched teeth. "We've three entire divisions in place, more than 38,000 men, plenty enough to keep the Prussians at bay. A few of the enemy may get behind us . . . but if we relocate to Dybbol, thousands of miles of open country becomes instantly available to Bismarck! The Prussians will take advantage of our withdrawal and launch an army against us the likes of which the world has never seen! Thousands of our soldiers will be butchered . . . our cause will be lost." de Meza almost whispered the last. He could already see battlefields strewn with dead bodies.

Listening to the cold logic of his newly acquired hero, Hans Jensen was sick to his stomach. His fists were clenched; he wanted so badly to speak that he couldn't stand it, but again, held his tongue.

When he realized he wasn't reaching the politicians General de Meza's frustration seethed as bitter as stomach bile. He felt enraged and yet totally impotent. Either these fools had blindly made up their minds before their arrival or like most government employees, were incapable of thinking. Just blindly following orders. Whichever it was de Meza was through trying to reason with the gathering of idiots and slammed his fist against the table to show it. His face was stony, black as a flint, and he chose his words carefully. "For the love of might!! You don't just pack up and move an army and all its equipment as you would a holiday trunk! We either make our stand right here at Dannevirke gentlemen . . . or Denmark is finished!"

He had stated his case and to emphasize, de Meza withdrew his sword from its scabbard and using it like a spear, thrust it into the map on the table. Remarkably the tip pierced the word Dannevirke. The white-faced politicians were shaken by the fiery display and eyed each other nervously. Dressed comfortably in their heavy overcoats, fur caps, and well-oiled boots, with carriages and an armed escort impatiently waiting outside, they were far more concerned about returning to the warmth and safety of Copenhagen than they were about uprooting thousands of Danish soldiers who were currently like rats, holed up in muddy trenches huddling over small fires, all along the front.

Finally making his presence known and wanting to re-arm the general with his sword, Hans Jensen stepped forward and pulled the still swaying blade from the map. Grateful Hans had done so, de Meza re-sheathed the weapon and then tapped his finger forcefully at the map upon their present locations.

"It has taken months to prepare the fortifications here at Husum, Slesvig and Dannevirke gentlemen," he said jamming his finger at each spot. "We'll be forced to leave heavy artillery and shell behind. The Prussians will confiscate it at their leisure and turn it upon us. We'll be killed with our own iron . . ." It was his final plea, "for the love of God do not make me do this!"

"We have direct orders from the king, General de Meza," D. G. shouted back. "Either you make preparations to remove to Dybbol at once, or we will have no choice but to relieve you of command immediately!"

"I think you are lying Hr Monrad," said de Meza with words as cold as steel. "I think King Christian has left the matter in the hands of you politicians, and that you all agreed long before coming here to Dannevirke upon this army's removal. Protecting Copenhagen and your own behinds is your sole interest. The mainland can be sacrificed!"

Sweat seeped from every pore of young Hans Jensen as he listened to the courageous General. He wanted to scream at the politicians; to at least strike one of them with his fists. He felt as impotent as his general.

Christian de Meza kept his command for the time being, and during the dead of winter 1864, moved nearly 40,000 men, thousands of horses, hundreds of cannons, and wagons full of supplies and equipment, to Dybbol, some eighteen hours north of Dannevirke. Hans and his companions returned to the military academy a sad but wizened band of young men. War had lost its glitter, its excitement. The cadets felt like pawns in a wicked game of old men's chess, and none of them liked what they felt. Being young they hoped a rally was coming and that somehow they might be part of it.

Sketch by Simensen

The relocation proved a disastrous move; howling winds and temperatures well below zero gave the Danish army a head start but the Prussians were soon on their heels. A bloody battle occurred at Sankelmark, but again the Danes repulsed the enemy and by the grace of God and a bitter winter, further fighting was sporadic and finally suspended for two months allowing Danish troops to regroup, somewhat. Weeks later when the citizens of Denmark became aware of what had actually happened, panic hit the streets. Just as de Meza had predicted the withdrawal was seen by the populace as cowardice, a retreat.

In Copenhagen, mobs bearing rocks and clubs once again stormed the palace. At the academy near Flensborg, Hans trained with new determination. Being on the mainland he was more than aware of the danger. While on the islands, try as they would nothing Elias or Catherine did enabled them to remove their son from the clutches of the military.

General Christian Julius de Meza at the left

Chapter 31

In Copenhagen, citizens thronged the streets demanding the ouster of Christian IX because of his poor leadership in time of crises. Many wanted to see his head on a staff. To quell public outrage, the king openly chastised Prime Minister Monrad, blaming him for the retreat. While Monrad, needing a scapegoat himself immediately had General Christian deMeza[3] removed from command. In his place Monrad put a veteran from the Three Years War, a near disabled general named Gerlach.

Bismarck was beside himself with glee. If the Danish withdrawal to Dybbol weren't enough to bolster the confidence of his heretofore beaten troops, de Meza's removal was. Experienced, arrogant and though somewhat odd, Christian de Meza had proven himself a courageous and able commander and the Prussians feared him.

Hans Jensen never wrote to Peter or Catherine of his experience with General de Meza at Dannevirke. With all that was going on he had decided neither his mother nor his twin brother would believe him anyway. And after all what would he write? He was far from proud of what had happened. Upon his return to the academy he'd been given a platoon of cadets to lead and had been extremely busy with drills. His time with Evette had included just two visits and he was without formal leave on one of them. The lull in fighting barely gave him time to pause and reflect.

Like Hans' had, Danish morale sunk to the lowest ebb in history. With politicians calling the shots, the army was in a state of disarray and because of it, Otto von Bismarck, heavily financed by Rothschild money, knew it was time to launch a major offensive at Dybbol. On April 18, 1864 his combined Austro-Prussian forces with their modern breech loading cannons, plus captured Danish artillery, let loose a barrage the likes of which had not been seen since the British fleet had shelled Copenhagen in 1807.

During the first week over 70,000 explosive Prussian shells crashed into the hastily constructed fortifications at Dybbol and mortars rained shrapnel upon the valiant Danish defenders killing hundreds. In addition to the heavy artillery fire, Danish soldiers were under a constant hail of bullets from the deadly needle rifles. Accurate at long distances, the bolt-action breech loading weapons could easily be loaded as Prussian soldiers crawled or else lay in shallow trenches. With the ability to shoot four to five rounds to every one fired from antiquated muzzleloaders, Danish casualties mounted at a terrifying rate.

But on the high seas, the Danes maintained superiority. Danish Corvettes, as maneuverable as Viking warships of old but manned with cannons, turned back invading troop carriers, cut off supplies and kept the islands of Funen, Zealand and Copenhagen secure. The speedy Corvettes had the waters lively and succeeded in turning enemy man o' wars back to German ports. Unfortunately they could do little to check the Prussian advance on land.

"Fall in!" Hans Jensen shouted as the cadets under his command poured from their barracks. Danish battle flags with their white crosses on blood red backgrounds whipped in the wind, while across the parade ground bugles blew assembly. A trio of drummers beat out cadence as Knud Eliassen's platoon formed up behind Hans'. Assembling to the rear in scattered disarray were the lower classmen led by Kurt Moller and at the front of the three platoons, Sergeant-Major Preben Holberg, commander of regular army forces stationed at Fort Esbjerg, was mounted on a gray stallion. A red-faced, angry, and rather short man, Holberg looked nothing like Christian de Meza, but Hans began to idolize the man as well.

"Our orders are to march toward Als!" shouted the rough little Sergeant Major. "A plea for reinforcements has come by courier. We are sorely needed to help arrest the Prussian advance."

"A worthy foe, the Prussians, but they will die at our hands!" His propagandized speech written and memorized the night before, Holberg, his fierce eyes scanning the ranks, continued. "May God bless you cadets, one and all . . . may he bless you for your bravery and your willingness to fight! Your numbers approach five hundred strong, fresh troops ready to defend the crown!" He raised one fist. "God save the King!" he then shouted. "God save Denmark!"

"God save the King! God save Denmark!" The shout reverberating along the lines of men was deafening, and thrilled Hans to the core. This is what he'd waited for his whole life! He was frightened but he was ready. Perhaps in some small way he would avenge the disgrace Christian de Meza had suffered.

"Forward march!" shouted Sergeant Major Holberg turning his gray stallion against the wind and pointing his sword southward. "Forward march," echoed Hans and the other platoon leaders.

A late frost had the countryside looking as white and peaceful as a frozen lake as the long lines of cadets marched toward the island of Als. The sun was a faint spot in a steel gray sky and the temperature hovered just above freezing. Tall weeds whipped at the soldier's legs and above their boots their pant-legs became wet and steamy. Flocks of geese flying in V-patterns passed overhead before settling into harvested fields and distant marshlands. Nobody was looking at them and when the magnificent birds made their honking cries few men heard. It was indeed a good day for hunting, certainly a good day to be home by the fire! Nature's routine would continue just as it had since the dawn of time; ignoring the fact men had their foolish wars to fight.

The cadets moved through the fields on the outskirts of Kolding and shortly they encountered what looked in the distance to be a small squad of Prussians coming out of the woods. "Reconnaissance!" shouted the Sergeant Major as he pointed toward the Prussians. "After them!!"

As soldiers and cadets broke ranks to cheer, a platoon of mounted cavalry spurred their horses to gallop chasing the Prussians into the woods. An half hour later they were back, but empty-handed.

"How do you lose a pack of red coats in God's green woods?" demanded the Sergeant Major.

"They had horses waiting your lordship," was the corporal's reply.

"Horses?" The Sergeant Major shook his head sadly. This was going to be a tough assignment. "Move to the rear then," he shouted. "Back in your ranks! The rest of you—fall in there. Let's be on with it."

The small incident sent ripples of excitement throughout the ranks of the green cadets. Their blood pumped hot, morale ran high and victory was certain. "On to the front!" They called in cadence as they marched. "On to the front!"

'Poor fools,' thought Preben Holberg. *'If they only knew what was coming.'* Prussian artillery had shot defense lines at Flensborg to

pieces, and with bayonets dripping in blood, enemy forces had streamed through the city, cutting soldiers and civilians down like wheat to the scythe. Women were raped, the town sacked and buildings were burned to the ground. The Danish withdrawal to Dybbol proved a disaster, and because of it, similar scenes of carnage would occur all over the mainland.

Some of this had been reported to Sergeant-Major Holberg, but regardless he would get his men loaded on the troop carriers waiting at Kolding, transport them up Als Sund (strait), and have them on the island of Als and bolstering front lines before morning. It was his duty.

Boarding the cumbersome troop carriers went without incident and within two hours the brave little army of cadets had left the mainland and had later disembarked on the rugged coast of Als. The thunderous wake from distant cannon fire greeted them and bright eerie halos from exploding projectiles lighted the night sky. Thick clouds of smoke hazed over the deadly scene as hundreds of mortars and rifles continually discharged. And above the gloomy din, flaming rockets, like low shooting stars also lighted the way.

Earlier that day Dybbol had fallen to the Prussians making the island of Als the last Danish stronghold but to get to it, retreating troops had had to cross the bridge at Als Sund near Sønderborg. A one hundred gun Danish warship had been there to provide protection for the retreating troops but after firing a few volleys at the pursuing Prussians, the ship mysteriously sailed away. Resulting Danish casualties were heavy never the less hundreds of retreating soldiers did make it safely across the bridge.

Bolstered by success and like bees to the hive Prussian soldiers were also swarming across the bridge. With little or no heavy artillery to hold them in check, Danish positions might soon be overrun. Fighting went on throughout the night and the sun had no sooner made its dull orange appearance when Hans Jensen and his companions were hastily forming up and moving through a muddy battlefield, and helping the cadets truly get their bearings they were joined by an advancing brigade of Danish regulars marching toward an on coming army in red coats, blue pants and pointed helmets!

"Skirmish lines!" Preben Holberg screamed at the top of his lungs.

"Form skirmish lines!" Hans Jensen shouted.

"Skirmish lines!" repeated Knud Eliassen and Kurt Moller. Bugles sounded, bedlam ensued, and after much hollering and screaming the cadets were organized into three irregular lines facing the enemy. Regular army troops flanked their right and a few were intermingled with cadets.

"Fix bayonets!" the Sergeant Major commanded.

"Fix bayonets!" shouted Hans. Metal on metal like the sound of so many swords being pulled from their scabbards clattered throughout the ranks as bayonets were locked in place. A few muskets discharged. Smoke betrayed the culprits. "Idiots!" Preben Holberg screamed at the top of his lungs. "You're out of range! Out of range! Hold your fire!"

Mumbled words tumbled from the trembling lips of regular army and cadets like prayers from the damned as they pressed forward. How they'd come to be in such a hotbed of activity so early on seemed surreal, but no one had time to think about it; only to numbly react.

"Forward!" an angry and grim-faced Preben Holberg growled as he mounted his horse and pointed his sword toward the red coats steadily advancing their direction. Drums beat the cadence and Hans' platoon, along with a platoon of army regulars comprised the first skirmish line, led the unsteady advance. The occasional crack, crack of Prussian rifles on an adjacent field of battle could be heard and shortly erupted into bursts of withering fire. In spite of their fear the cadets held their line of march, there was no turning back.

"Kneel and take aim!" commanded Sergeant-Major Holberg as he monitored the Prussian advance. The first skirmish line immediately responded. Knees in the mud, eyes at the sights . . . "Ready," hollered Holberg as he squinted hatefully at the Prussians and held his sword aloft.

"Fire!" he shouted as he dropped his sword. The roar of muskets was deafening. Smoke filled the air and many advancing Prussians screamed and fell to the earth.

Roaring with defiance, Prussian rifles answered in a veritable firestorm. Bullets smacked into Danish lines like thousands of rotten eggs, splattering blood, tearing flesh and killing soldiers wholesale. Cadets and regulars alike buckled and fell backwards, some fell forward on their faces in the mud.

Knud Eliassen's platoon moved ahead of Hans Jensen's as what was left of it stood to re-load. Someone was crying. "Slap his sorry face!" Hans shouted looking in vain for the offender.

"Ready . . . fire," shouted the Sergeant Major again. Knud Eliassen's platoon complied and once again the roar of muskets filled the air. Smoke thickened, like London fog. Seeing more than a few yards became impossible. The third skirmish line moved forward, as the first finished re-loading. As efficient as the Danes were, Prussian riflemen returned volley for volley . . . another volley then another, and another. Then like thunderclaps in a billowing storm, Prussian artillery opened fire. The very earth shook with each concussion. Grapeshot showered Danish soldiers like rain felling men like insects. Shrapnel flew in deadly diffusion as smoke completely enveloped the area.

"Fire at will!" Preben Holberg screamed at the top of his lungs. "Fire at will!"

Bullets from both sides were whistling through the air like the freezing rain, and men were dropping on both sides. Screams and shouts of the wounded and dying were everywhere. Any semblance of order amongst the three cadet platoons all but vanished but oddly enough Prussian lines were also beginning to crumble. Through the smoke and mist, the silhouettes of human beings appeared as ghosts wandering aimlessly around a graveyard.

Hans Jensen picked up a loaded musket from a fallen comrade, fired it into a cluster of Prussians and was ramming a second charge. Intent upon his purpose, only vaguely aware of a wound in his side, he loaded quickly. His head was numb, his fingers cold but he cocked the hammer, put the firing cap in place, took aim and shot a Prussian not ten yards away.

"Sound the charge!" Sergeant-Major Holberg commanded his bugle-man. A fourteen-year-old lad standing in the grizzled sergeant's shadow, raised a brave little brass instrument to his lips and blew till the veins in his face looked like they'd burst. The Danish soldiers took heart.

"Charge!" Hans shouted as the tinny echo reverberated in his ears.

"Charge!" echoed Knud Eliassen.

Kurt Moller failed to respond. He'd been shot in the throat. Eyes wide open and a ghastly pallor on his face, he was gasping for air, reaching up as men ran past him.

Drummers speeded their cadence, bayonets flashed, muskets fired and in the mist of the blood and horror, cadets and regulars pressed forward. Some had dropped their empty muskets and were running in the opposite direction.

"Charge you bloody cowards . . . Charge!" screeched the Sergeant Major as he rode at them, swinging his sword above their heads, or else with the flat of it smacking them across their backs.

Bolstered with reinforcements the Prussians had regrouped and within moments opposing forces collided in deadly hand-to-hand combat. Two armies blended into one. Steel clanged against steel, bayonets dripped in blood, empty muskets were swung like clubs and amid the thuds were; grunts, groans, cursing, and screams. Dead and wounded mounted rapidly on both sides.

Vaulting over bodies strewn about like so many logs, the Prussians were gaining; their storming troops kicked and stomped the fallen Danish like dirt clods in a field. Slashing swords, jabbing bayonets and bashing rifle butts, the Danes fought like savages but all the while, and with deathly precision, Prussian sharpshooters found their marks.

'Dear God!' thought Hans as a bullet crashed into his chest. His breath was taken but he still managed to thrust his bayonet into the soft belly of an onrushing Prussian soldier. Dizzy then, Hans fell backward in the mud. Men ran past him. Heavy boots kicked and stepped on him.

As he lay there the reality of being mortal and thus subject to death, forcibly entered Hans Jensen's brave young mind and he was thoroughly insulted! He tried to get up, but simply could not move.

Hans' head then exploded in pain at the steely thud of a Prussian rifle butt. His vision blurred and the last feeling he experienced on

Sketch by Simensen

this earth was the warm, salty-sweet taste of blood in his mouth. Quickly as it had come the pain was gone and a peaceful, radiant light gently engulfed him.

Estimates put Danish losses in the carnage between Dannevirke, Dybbol and Als above eight thousand. Whatever the actual numbers were King Christian IX conceded defeat and Denmark surrendered.

In Vienna, Bismarck's representatives were arrogant and demanding and late in June, 1864 a humiliating treaty was negotiated[4] making Lauenberg, Holstein, Slesvig, and all of Jylland (Jutland) officially part of the German confederation. Denmark lost over 800,000 of its citizens and over one third of its land mass to Germany making her the smallest nation in Europe. "The cocky little bird has been knocked from her perch," Bismarck was reported to have said, and with that the warmonger turned his attention toward France.

Peter Jensen's only participation in the war had been helping the militia construct sandbagged fortifications along the coasts of Copenhagen. He did witness an encounter between a Prussian sixty gunner and two Danish Corvettes. The sound of cannon fire as it rumbled across the deep waters of the strait was both thrilling and terrifying and half an hour into the battle, the Prussian ship was ablaze and eventually sunk. Two other enemy vessels sailing toward the corvette promptly turned tail and ran.

Peter had waved his shovel and cheered with the rest of the men from atop a bunker they'd been building but that was the sum and total of his involvement in the war. The sandbagged fortifications he'd strained to build would never be used.

Copenhagen, Roskilde, Holbaek and other principal Danish cities were spared the war's devastation, and the most unusual thing about the war's aftermath was the fact King Christian IX eventually became very popular in Denmark. All blame for the war's disastrous conclusion was heaped upon the heads of the Liberals in the Rigsdag, most of whom were ousted in subsequent elections.

Under the slogan, "What was outwardly lost is inwardly won," the new government led by the conservative Venstre Party began to rise, albeit shakily, to its feet. Because of the land and people Denmark had lost, the new legislature made plans to extract the lowlands of Copenhagen and other islands from the sea by using dikes similar to those built in Holland. The tiny country had to make maximum use of its remaining resources to accommodate existing population and make provisions for growth, otherwise it might not survive.

Chapter 32

Elias' Jensen's correspondence dated June 27, 1864 was chilling, straight to the point, and void of emotion. *Hans is dead. Word came in from Flensborg. Hans and every cadet in his platoon were murdered near Als by Prussian invaders. A memorial service was held in his honor yesterday. Come home as you can.*

Your father,

Elias Jensen.

Most of the bodies of fallen soldiers were buried near Als, however, Hans Jensen's casket was eventually shipped back to Holbaek for burial. The rich still had privilege. A wrinkled and dirty note was pinned to its blood stained uniform. "Hans Jensen," it read simply. "He died with honor."

Catherine had lost another son to the grim reaper and Elias' terse correspondence may as well have come from the mortician who'd prepared the body, rather than the man who'd sired it. A tear-stained journal entry that night revealed Peter's troubled mind:

Hans has been killed at the slaughter near Als.—It can't be. It is untrue. When I get home again all will be well. Father and Mother will be there, Ferdinand . . . and Hans.—It won't be so. My brother is dead. Part of me is dead.—I should have been fighting near his side. If I could, I'd kill every politician in the Rigsdag for the way the war was handled. If de Meza would have been left alone thousands of young men, including my brother might yet be alive!

"I want to go with you to Holbaek Peter," Maren insisted when he had shared the tragedy with her. "Maybe I could be of some help to your mother." When he hesitated to answer she pleaded. "You need me Peter. I can only imagine what you are feeling."

Having had little sleep and almost nothing to eat since he'd received Elias' terse note, Peter looked haggard. His eyes were red and his face was a pale shade of gray. Maren cradled his head against her bosom.

"I think I knew the second it happened Maren. A few weeks back I had such a dark feeling come over me. I was going to tell you about it but thought it silly. Just having a bad day . . ." He was looking at her as if for answers.

"I wish you *would* have told me about it," she said leaning over and kissing his tear-streaked face. The salty taste was as bitter as the moment. "What good ever comes of war," she said angrily.

People passed their bench occasionally but to Peter the park seemed as lifeless as Hans' body. Having Maren share his grief was of inestimable value. He felt strength exuding from her, a strength he hadn't known until then and it bonded him to her as never before. He now knew he didn't always have to be the strong one.

"What a grand person you are Maren," he said sincerely. "Do

come with me to Holbaek. You can't know how much it would mean to me. How much it might mean to my Mother."

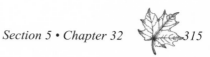

The trains were running well the day they left Copenhagen and the trip took only half a day. Peter's mind was so distraught he barely remembered traveling. To him the lovely countryside was painted in gray, dull and darkening gray, and when he and Maren arrived at the Jensen home, they found the residence also shrouded in black. From the death wreath on the front door, with its pale white roses, to Catherine's black dress and veil, everything was void of color.

The living room where Hans' memorial service had taken place looked dusty. Its yellowed curtains sagged like the skin of an old man. There were traces of funeral weeds on the floor but Catherine, who was sitting on the sofa and staring out the window, had forbidden Inger to wash the curtains or clean the room. "Leave it be until this desperate feeling leaves my heart," she had told the faithful housekeeper.

Inger politely introduced herself to Maren, said hello to Peter, but avoided any expression of joy at his homecoming. *She's grieving,* Peter thought as he took off his leather cap.

In the living room, Ferdinand was standing near Catherine as if guarding her. "Welcome home Peter," he said without moving.

"Where's Father?" Peter inquired as he sat next to Catherine and put his arm around her whereupon she wrapped her arms around him, buried her face in his chest and cried softly. Catherine needed his strength, needed to see him alive and like a life preserver clung to him as if she were drowning.

"Father's had another spell," Ferdinand explained. "The doctors have isolated him upstairs."

"Let me take your cape," Inger said to Maren. She also took Peter's cap and as Peter touched her hand Inger did smile at him. She took their things to the closet near the kitchen and went outside to the barn to get milk for supper's gravy. 'Thank heaven 'e's here,' she said to herself as she headed for the barn.

"Mother," Peter said as he gently kissed Catherine's cheek, "Maren came to comfort you, and to assist you in any way she can. I thought it high time the two of you met."

Maren dropped a bag she was carrying and went straight to Catherine. "Fru Jensen," she said with genuine sympathy as she sat beside her. "I'm so sorry about Hans . . . so very sorry."

Though they'd just met Catherine fell into Maren's embrace and sobbed like a child. Peter was touched and his eyes filled with tears. Women spoke a language with each other very difficult for a man to understand.

The two women held each other for quite a time, then leaned away and looked at each other. With eyes glistening, brimming to the point that more tears spilled down their cheeks, a thousand words and a million emotions passed between them. The bond between them was instantaneous and Peter breathed a sigh of relief. He stood and looked over at Ferdinand, then motioned toward the door.

"Let's go outside," he said quietly.

Ferdinand gratefully complied. All the tenderness and emotion had made him uncomfortable.

Women can be so blasted sentimental, he thought as he and Peter stepped onto the porch and closed the door.

The countryside was peaceful. Summer was on the wane but the trees were still full of leaves. Birds twittered here and there bending the branches slightly as they hopped from one to another. A soft damp breeze, cool and refreshing was coming in from the east. The

grass was a greenish brown and there might have been a hint of Fall in the air; a beautiful day, calm and tranquil, as if nothing out of the ordinary had even happened to Denmark. Only the sound of Catherine's gentle crying from an open window served as a reminder.

"He was just twenty-two Ferdinand," Peter said as a tear rolled quietly down his cheek and into his beard. "He had so much to live for."

"I know," said Ferdinand stiffly. "A terrible, terrible waste."

"How is Father taking it?"

"Very hard," answered Ferdinand distantly. "A few days before the memorial service, he had an attack and has kept to himself ever since. We take him meals, but he wants no guests. He only sees Mother and I."

"Good thing," said Peter flatly.

"What's that you say?" asked Ferdinand defensively.

"It's just that he's so utterly cold to me," answered Peter. "You should read the letter he sent me regarding Hans' death."

"He almost died himself," said Ferdinand maintaining his defensive posture.

"You know Ferdinand," said Peter ignoring his brother's attitude and his comment. "I've never had such a low opinion of myself." He walked a few steps and leaned against a tree.

"And why pray tell, is that?" asked the younger brother.

"The only weapon I carried during the war was a shovel," Peter answered. "I should have been at Als—right in the middle of it—fighting with Hans."

"Then three of mother's sons would lie in graves," Ferdinand said wisely, haughtily.

"I'm sure any treaty they strike in Vienna will be a disgrace," Peter went on as if talking to himself. "We should have given up Holstein long ago. Holsteiners have leaned toward Germany ever since old king Christian II sailed away in 1520.Now the Germans have the whole of Jutland!"

Ferdinand had no opinion on the subject or upon the talks in Vienna. Living in the lap of luxury, so to speak, he'd been completely insulated from it all. The mill had been busy, very busy. Money from government and individual farmers was flowing in like water. And because of her worries over Hans, Catherine had once again relinquished her responsibilities of running the mill to Torkil and the books almost entirely to him. Now, because finances were in such plump condition, Ferdinand actually fancied himself responsible for the boom! His thoughts that morning were not so much of his dead and buried brother, as they were upon his growing importance in family affairs.

Catherine was slowing down, Ferdinand was thoroughly convinced of the fact, and he could actually see himself riding around in a fancy carriage, the wealthy owner of a thriving milling business. He was sorry about Hans but really had not seen much of him over the last three years. Consequently, Ferdinand had gotten over his death rather quickly.

And for the moment Ferdinand had other situations to deal with. Yes, here was Peter, his religious fanatic brother, going on about the government, home to grieve over the loss of Hans, a touching situation to say the least. *Let him ramble on about politics, his Mormon religion or whatever he wants,* Ferdinand thought to himself, *any wealthy processor of the king's grain can deal with it for a few days. Peter will soon be on his way back to the university, once again leaving me to run the estate so his tuition can be paid!*

Then of course there was Kristina Holsen. Ferdinand also had a head full of her that morning. *Krista is getting rather plump; there is no doubt about it,* he had thought more than once, *and not quite as lively in the hay as she once was. Perhaps she's not the lady for a man of my growing importance.*

Krista was staying with the Jensen's at present. Nils Holsen didn't care. "Let her stay as close to the situation as possible," Nils had confided to his wife. "There'll be a marriage between our little girl and Ferdinand, mark my words."

Fru Holsen had reluctantly agreed. It wasn't far from her home—which again was part of the Jensen estate—but so far there had been no marriage. Ferdinand viewed matrimony as such a limiting thing, especially since there were so many beautiful girls running around Holbaek Township. He and Catherine had heated discussion over the matter and in light of Krista's condition, Catherine, maintained the puritan viewpoint that marriage was the proper thing to do.

'The only option open to you,' she had insisted.

'And yours has been so successful,' mocked Ferdinand before Catherine had slapped his face.

These issues and a few others, including the love of wine—Elias shared more than conversation with his youngest son—were a part of Ferdinand's distorted picture of life, part of his immediate thoughts. So as it was that morning, dull hangover, headache and all, he just stood there barely listening to his bereaved brother drone on. And were it not for his grieving and anger toward the government, Peter might have picked up on Ferdinand's indifference; he hadn't as of yet.

"Government stupidity threw us into Bismarck's lap," Peter was saying. "Citizens at large wanted no part of it Ferdinand. The Slesvig-Holstein question could have been resolved by negotiation.

Think of the lives it would have saved. But no, we declare war on Prussia! Can you imagine . . . the strongest military force in Europe and tiny little Denmark takes them on!

Our pompous leaders! You know Ferdinand, something is terribly wrong in a country where thinking people desire one thing and their government hands them quite another."

"You're probably right," Ferdinand said disinterestedly. "But Peter, one way or the other Denmark will survive. You will see."

"Exist, is more like it," Peter countered. "The German confederation now includes nearly one million Danish speaking people, our former citizens. And leaders are in such a state of confusion you wouldn't believe it. The King wants to go back to appointing all his ministers rather than follow the constitution that provides for elections! We could lose every freedom we've ever gained. It's chaos my brother, simply chaos. No Ferdinand, Denmark will never regain what it's lost."

"I'm not entirely ignorant of current events," said Ferdinand defensively. "The treaty hasn't been signed. Prussia might not get Jutland."

"Ha," scoffed Peter. "They'll get it. They occupy every square foot of it; and what's left of our little country may yet be swallowed up by the neighbors."

"It will never happen," said Ferdinand slightly alarmed.

"Don't be so sure little brother," Peter responded despondently. "If Russia had a mind to, they could take us in a minute; Sweden too for that matter. Our defenses are so weak . . ."

"You worry too much about things," Ferdinand said airily. "Russia has mellowed toward us and Norway and Sweden are all caught up in Scandinavianism . . ."

"You have a point there," he said, surprised his eighteen-year-old brother could understand anything so intricate. "From now on any unity between the three Scandinavian countries will be romanticism, never a political allegiance. The governments of Norway and Sweden showed their true colors. Unlike during the Three Years War, this time our fair-skinned neighbors to the north turned their backs on Denmark. Other than a few Norwegian and Swedish volunteers we stood alone."

"Hans understood these things," Peter lamented. "Oh how I wish he were still alive." Again his eyes grew wet.

"Peter," said Ferdinand abruptly, "I've got things to do at the mill." He was shaking his head. "The war is over, and as you say the government is now probably in good hands. I don't understand it completely, but I trust the king. And I hate to say this, but there's nothing you or I can do about Hans. We have to get on with our lives."

Peter's mouth fell open and he stared dumbfounded at Ferdinand. His words were so indifferent, so terribly empty. He had to mentally suppress the urge to grab his little brother and wring his neck.

"I say quit brooding about things you can't control," Ferdinand continued somewhat cockily. "You'll get over them faster. Live and let live, I always say."

"What on earth is wrong with you Ferdinand?" Peter demanded, at last finding the words. "Our brother is dead. It's just the two of us now! Shouldn't we be able to discuss things of this nature and achieve a little mutual comfort? Can't we have a bit of understanding here?"

"I don't like to talk about things that are out of my hands Peter," Ferdinand stated flatly. "I really don't. Now you ought to get back in to Mother. I've got a few pressing matters to take care of. I'll have to talk with you later."

With that he headed off toward the mill leaving Peter bewildered, angry and feeling as if he'd been hit in the stomach.

Whatever has come over him? he wondered as he watched his brother walk away. *For one so young there was some wisdom in what he had said but, it wasn't what I needed to hear. Shouldn't he and I feel closer now that Hans is gone?* he demanded of his mind. *Shouldn't we be able to talk? Was it the wrestling incident at Christmas? Or is it because Ferdinand's the youngest child and no doubt spoiled rotten?*

"We've become more like cousins than brothers," he said aloud. "And what a cousin. So utterly indifferent about everything and his highbrow attitude . . . he got that from Father. I saw it at Christmas. It's territorial that's what it is."

Peter was certain that he had put his finger on the problem, and was now determined that before he returned to Copenhagen he and Ferdinand *would* have another talk. An in-depth talk—of parents and a talk concerning legacy!

Maren hadn't been in the Jensen household an hour before she too became benefactor of Ferdinand's territorial behavior. It had spread, or perhaps originated, from Krista Holsen. Maren had gone to the kitchen to get Catherine a cool glass of water, when she ran headlong into the girl. Krista was standing near the kitchen door with her arms folded over her stomach and she appeared embarrassed. Her cheeks were red and like a child who'd been caught with her hand in the cookie jar, Krista looked very uncomfortable; she'd been eavesdropping.

At first she stared coldly at Maren, then putting on a fake smile she thrust out her hand, as a man might and said, "I'm Kristina

Holsen, everyone calls me Krista . . . and who might you be?"

As if you don't know, thought Maren. Maren was confused, a little angry, and her flushed cheeks betrayed it. But she also felt a twinge of pity as she took Krista's hand. "I'm Maren Carlsen," she said kindly.

"I'm living here now," Krista announced. "Ferdinand and I will be married soon."

"Congratulations," said Maren taken aback, "I–I'm very happy for you."

Krista made no attempt to hide her swollen stomach as she moved clumsily toward the larder and cut herself a generous slice of bread. She slathered it thickly with butter then took a huge bite. "This child is eating me alive," she said patting her stomach and chewing loudly.

"Are you wanting a little boy, or a girl?" Maren asked.

"It don't matter to me," said Krista taking another large bite and wiping her buttery mouth with the back of her arm. "Long as it hurries. You and Catherine enjoy your little visit," she added curtly, cutting things short. "Don't mind me, I'm going upstairs an' lay down."

"She's a very crude person," Maren was saying later that night when she and Peter were alone in Peter's room. Maren had taken the room next to it but whether or not she used it nobody particularly cared. Catherine normally would have, but she was so out of sorts at present that she was numb to serious issues.

"She's more than that," said Peter wisely. "Krista is ambitious. If anything ever happened to Mother she'd try and take over this household quick as a minute."

"She's got Ferdinand in a pickle that's for sure," said Maren knowingly, to which Peter frowned and shook his head.

"I'm not sure he's liking it, Maren. I don't know what to think about him. His head is so filled with nonsense right now I can hardly talk to him."

"You failed to mention Krista to me Peter . . . why?"

"To tell the truth I'd forgotten about her," Peter apologized, "or maybe I just hoped she'd go away. It's no wonder Inger's not herself," he added as if a lamp had just been lit. "Like Denmark, her territory has been invaded."

"I hope your mother can handle Krista," said Maren somewhat alarmed.

"There's no worry there," said Peter unconvincingly. "You don't know my mother. Given time she will be back to her old self, and nobody, not my brother nor especially his little bride-to-be will run over her."

Chapter 33

Over the next day or so Peter wandered slowly about the fields and outbuildings of the estate like a ship without a mainsail. And like such a ship, he felt he might well go adrift. He was grieving over Hans, troubled over Catherine's lethargy and so angry where Ferdinand and Krista were concerned he could not put it all into words.

He sought seclusion in the loft of the barn and in the forest where, as boys, he and Hans had romped and played. Maren was taking good care of Catherine's emotional needs. Just being home, Peter helped as well but he was not right with himself and needed time to think. In the hayloft he sought Hans' presence. The place looked the same. Cozy, quiet and warm, it felt the same; and it still smelled of sweet hay and sour horses. But there would be no more long talks with his twin. No more wrestling in the hay, and no more laughter.

"There would be no more races either," Peter said as he climbed down and went to the horse stalls. "And you know it don't you Vargus?" Peter could see it in the stallion's dulling eyes. "Maybe you're just getting old," he added.

"And what do you think of Ferdinand and Krista?" he said as he patted the powerful animal's nose. "Will they sell you when they take over?"

Peter smiled painfully. Hans had been such an anchor to him. He'd know exactly what to do where Ferdinand was concerned, if the situation were reversed. *If I'd been killed in the war,* he thought as he stood by Vargus, *and if Hans were here . . . he'd kick Ferdinand out of the house. Make him do right by Krista, get a place of his own and start providing. But I just sit by and do nothing. What in heaven is wrong with me?*

There's no commitment between Ferdinand and Krista as far as I can see and soon Mother *will have a grandchild to raise.*

He was beginning to see that Ferdinand and Krista had no concrete plans, but Peter still felt their deceit. That wasn't confusing at all. Mainly, Peter didn't want to see his mother taken advantage of. On the other hand, and of great comfort, he knew for certain that once Catherine was through mourning she'd be back in charge of her affairs, perhaps even stronger than before.

In spite of a well-stocked pantry, clean linens, and comfortable furniture there was little solace for Peter in Catherine's lavish home. Ferdinand and Krista maintained their controlling attitudes and vigilance. When they were together they were always whispering, lurking about, acting aloof and doing their level best to make he and Maren feel like outsiders.

That morning as Peter wandered the forest behind the barns, unconsciously he was seeking Hans' strong voice. Perhaps it might whisper out of the trees; his spirit maybe. There would be no more camping with his brother, and in winter no more skating on the frozen millpond either. Seasons would come and go but Hans Jensen's reassuring voice and courageous ways would never again cross the ice. Peter longed for his brother's sage advice, longed for someone to look up to and missed Hans so badly he felt he'd never be comforted.

On the morning of the third day Peter did find a little solace at the gristmill. Here things were just as they used to be. The wind blew as before, the great stones turned . . . here there was commerce! In a routine as solid as eating, wagons came filled with grain, and then left loaded with sacks of flour. At the mill there was life! Activity and, in the center of things, Torkil Olsen still shouted orders, adjusted equipment, and like the head chef in a dusty old kitchen, checked batches of flour with his fingers and tongue.

Torkil did seem smaller. Peter attributed it to age but the head miller's loud presence and solid confidence was like manna from heaven. The very second Torkil laid eyes on his former apprentice, he knew exactly what Peter needed.

"Hard work heals wounds!" the grizzled old miller told him as he pumped Peter's hand. "Balm to the soul. My, I'm glad you're here! Glad the war didn't claim you . . ." his voice trailed off at that. "But there'll be no moping about in my presence," Torkil warned. "Soon as you're ready I'll put you to the sifters . . ."

"Are you sure you need me?" said Peter as he rolled up his sleeves.

"Need you?" shouted Kev Monsen a fair-skinned and powerfully built man who was about to shovel wheat into a bin, which fed the millstones. "Denmark is hungry Peter; in sore need of flour. Hundreds of farms, thousands of acres of grain and all the gristmills on the mainland have been confiscated. "Need you?" There was little joy in his laugh. "Yes, we need you."

"We can't get help Peter," Torkil explained more soberly now. "There's no one to work the farms, so many young men were killed . . ." his voice trailed off.

"What about Ferdinand?" Peter wanted to know.

"Does nothing but the books," said Torkil spitting on the floor. With his flour dusty boot he rolled the spittle into a small ball and kicked it aside.

"The demand for flour is overwhelming," said Kev who also held a low opinion for Peter's younger brother. "We're working from dawn to dusk. Throw the lever Torkil."

The head miller wrestled a long, stout, wooden lever into its slot and the thick leather belting connecting the main shaft and the shaft which drove millstone gearing began to turn in unison. Hands, arms and lives had been lost in heavy belting and gearing such as this. Torkil himself was missing an index finger.

The floor shuddered under foot and the mill's huge millstones came to life. The smell of belting, the squishy sound of grease in the gearing, and the roar of the stones as Kev Monsen poured in the wheat, were like old friends to Peter. He could hardly hear himself think, but being in the dusty bowels of the mill satisfied him to the core. He felt home at last. Or did he? While Peter loved everything about the mill, when he thought of the loss of Hans and of the uneasy feeling Ferdinand, Krista and Elias put inside Catherine's otherwise warm and stately home, he felt like a stranger.

But working at the mill for the next few days proved just the prescription for Peter. Shoveling grain and flour, filling sacks and throwing them on top of wagons bound for market, firmed his muscles quickly and like Torkil said, helped heal his soul. By week's end Peter felt like living again. The thought of returning to the university was so unpleasant he cast it aside.

Maren also found herself looking for something to do during the visit. With Peter working at the mill, she felt totally out of place. Especially while Catherine was upstairs nursing Elias, or had simply chosen to be alone in her room. Inger was civil to her too but she didn't want anyone helping with the housework. Since Krista had 'moved in' so to speak, Inger guarded her domain jealously, so for a day or two, to keep herself occupied Maren read books and wandered around outside.

"If you want to do something productive, you can work in the garden," Inger told her one morning. "Fru Jensen 'asn't touched it since we got the terrible news about Hans, and it's overgrown with weeds."

To save her sanity Maren gladly complied. She'd had some experience at her grandmother's garden and there was a shared patch of ground in her neighborhood where a few industrious people grew flowers and vegetables.

Hoeing and plucking till the rich brown earth in Catherine's garden was free of weeds, Maren next attacked the rose bushes, clearing them of brambles and pruning them back. She then set the pile of weeds and brambles on fire creating a sweet yet pungent smoke and when the fire was out, she buried the ashes to start a compost. She then continued her work until the garden's rows were as neat and orderly as the shelves in her father's store. Hands black with dirt, her arms aching and her back sore, it was still very satisfying work and gave her something to talk about when Peter came home each evening.

Krista made herself scarce during this frenzy of activity. She rarely turned her hand at anything resembling labor, and from an upstairs window watched Maren in the garden with abject fascination. Officially Krista still lived with her parents, but since she'd begun to show, her dark little presence waddled around the estate like a duck near a pond. She'd have her day in the Jensen household. Time and circumstance were on her side.

Despite the depressing, yet productive atmosphere around the

Jensen estate, Maren enjoyed her visit. The sights and sounds of chickens pecking around the barn-yard, rabbits nibbling at greens, horses neighing, pigs grunting, and cows stamping impatiently while waiting to be milked, may have been mundane to country-folk but they were new and exciting things to a girl from Copenhagen. The pungent smells of manure, silage, and swill contrasted by sweet grain, fresh cut hay, warm milk squirting into pails, and wild flowers in the fields presented an odiferous bouquet the likes of which a city girl rarely encounters.

The whole experience of country living was as fresh and alive as Maren herself and she dreamed of one day having a farm of her own; perhaps one close by.

Despite his foul demeanor, Maren also pitched in with Elias during the visit; taking in meals and drink occasionally when she saw it might ease Catherine's burden. On those brief visits she tried to gain her potential father-in-law's friendship, but found it very difficult. Elias was as cold to her as he was warm to Krista.

"It was you who got him involved in that cult, wasn't it?" is how the sick and aging man greeted Maren the first time they were alone. He had been pleasant enough when Catherine introduced them but when she went downstairs Maren, at Elias' request to 'stay and chat', remained behind.

"With Christ at the center of our worship, isn't Christianity at large but a cult Hr Jensen?" she answered gently and without malice. Her question galled Elias, possibly made him think, but he didn't answer; only coughed and cleared his throat.

"If giving its heart and soul to Christ makes the Mormon Church a cult, Hr Jensen, then I suppose it is. It is certainly not a sinister organization, but one of brightness, hope, charity and very faith promoting. Faith in God, our Heavenly Father and Jesus Christ, his son; Savior to us all. Peter and I have not been baptized yet but we *are* thinking about it." At that Elias grew restless in his bed. Never one lost for words, with this young lady he was, momentarily. "The Mormon church takes nothing away from the beautiful teachings of Luther, Wesley, Calvin, and other brave reformers," Maren went on, "and what attracts me to it is that it claims authority directly from Christ. Prophets . . ."

"The Mormons have created a real stir[5] in Denmark lately," Elias finally interrupted sharply. "Popping up everywhere. People have to run them off their property. You all must have quite a tale to tell."

"Well," said Maren a bit shaken, "As I said, we haven't been baptized. Perhaps you might want to read some of the literature. You may find you like what Mormons teach about Christ. Maybe you could show Peter and I where they are wrong."

"Bah," spat Elias. Then he coughed. "I'll never read a single word of their lies . . . look what it's done to Peter. His mind is all messed up . . ." At the sound of Catherine's footsteps on the stairs he said nothing further, just glared at Maren. When it came to anything other than the state church, Elias' mind was as closed as a tomb. He'd never study Mormon doctrine or any other church's teachings and as far as he was concerned there would never be a friendship with the pert little shopkeeper's daughter either.

Having Maren about the place for the next few days was an answer to Catherine's prayers. A bright and welcome relief from the crafty, slovenly ways of Krista Holsen, Maren was full of quiet energy and the times she and Catherine were alone, she was also a good conversationalist. More important and like most women, Maren was an excellent listener.

"After their marriage, I'm having a house built for them in the corner of the west fields," was Catherine's candid communication to her on the subject of Ferdinand and Krista. "They don't know it yet but that's how it's going to be. After that they must make their own way in life; not that Ferdinand won't be involved with the family business. He will, but Krista has tried to force her way in and it's not working. At the present time I tolerate her being underfoot, but shortly I'll be asking her to leave. She's upsetting Inger."

That was all Catherine said concerning Krista and Maren admired that. The conversation then shifted to Peter and Hans. What it was like raising twins, how much they were alike and yet so completely unique.

"Both were adventurous but where Peter took time to think things out, Hans would bolt ahead. Many times I wondered how he didn't end up killing himself." Catherine laughed at that, then the irony of what she said hit her and she headed off on a different track. Wiping away a tear she added, and more for Maren's comfort than her own, "They were bright, handsome children, inseparable from the beginning; and if anyone at school wanted to fight one of them he knew he must also fight the other. Hans always started things . . . Peter would get so angry with him." She shook her head at that, and Catherine smiled as she thought of her son's youth.

She then told Maren how she had guided her sons throughout their education, both secular and spiritual. "I tried to balance it all out Maren. Sometimes I felt very successful, yet other times I wondered if I knew what I was doing. Ferdinand is a clear example of the latter."

"I thought it critical that each boy should learn their grandfather's trade. Serve an apprenticeship at the mill. I'm more proud of that accomplishment than anything. Both Peter and Hans love the milling business." She spoke of Hans as if he was still alive and to Maren it was good. "I'll never stick my nose in your business young lady, but teach your children that they need a trade. And if you have any girls;

for heaven's sake, see that they get an education. Even if you must teach them at home. Now that's all I'll say to you on child-rearing. I'm not one to meddle but if you follow *that* advice you'll thank me."

Later in the visit Catherine even told Maren how she met Elias and of her painful life with him. She concluded that her sons had been worth all the pain and heartache Elias had caused, but Catherine left Maren unconvinced. She felt a wayward, controlling man would be so destructive to a woman's soul.

Maren's wholesome honesty, purity and industry stirred something deep inside Catherine. This lovely young girl would soon marry her son and then, by the grace of God some day bear a grandchild. New life to replace that so recently lost. And a welcome grandchild, not a wedge like Catherine feared Krista's baby might be. Maren gave new hope to Catherine, but of greatest value to the grieving heiress was her sincere caring, her natural womanly compassion. She and Catherine became real friends during the visit, spending as much time together as circumstances allowed.

Chapter 34

"Not having my father to contend with has been one good thing about this visit," Peter was saying to Maren early one morning. "I've hardly seen him." They were sitting at the breakfast table, the sun was just beginning to stream in through the windows, and the house was quiet. "For the first time in my illustrious upbringing," he went on, "I've been in my father's presence and no arguments have erupted."

"He is a very cantankerous person," she sighed.

"You've noticed?" Peter said as he looked across the table at Maren. With the sun highlighting her rich brunette hair she was truly beautiful.

"I've tried to be a friend to your father Peter," Maren said sadly. "I've wanted to tell him about the gospel. About the Book of Mormon and what a wonderful history of Christ it is. But he won't hear a word of it. He's so distant and abrupt with me. I hate going in his room, I only do it for your mother." Her face at first a study of contempt, softened at the mention of Catherine. Then she knitted her brows. "By the way, Ferdinand sees him quite often, and I find that unusual . . . an eighteen-year-old boy sitting with a crotchety old man?"

"They're drinking partners Maren . . ."

"I'd guessed as much. Ferdinand smells of it . . ." she stopped herself.

"The boy is a thorn in my side," said Peter. "I don't know what to make of him."

"Your father's illness has actually proved a blessing to your mother," Maren said changing the subject. "She's so busy with him it lessens her grieving."

"I haven't noticed," said Peter rubbing his face and taking a deep breath. "But I do know what you mean by being busy. Working in the mill with Torkil has certainly helped me. It's so intense in that place I've scarcely had time to think." He wanted to say, think about Ferdinand, his cunning little wench, Krista and their obvious ambition to take over the estate but left it alone.

"Peter," said Maren bringing him back to reality. "We need to be getting back to Copenhagen. I told my parents a week, it has been nearly two."

"I know," said Peter. He got up and went to the window.

"What's the matter?" she said wishing he'd stayed close to her.

"I don't know Maren," he said rubbing the back of his neck. "I just feel so restless . . . so completely without direction."

Maren didn't respond. She knew he was hurting and that he was lost. In Copenhagen their love had burned so brightly. Here, the light seemed to be getting dim. It was easy to understand why but that didn't mean Maren liked it.

"What will it take to get me going again Maren?" he continued as if he'd read her mind. "To have a goal and be working to achieve it?

Some days I have direction . . . others I feel it's me that's dead and not Hans!"

Maren was growing weary of Peter's self-pity. She had frustrations and problems of her own and the look on her face said so. He'd been so little company to her on this mission of mercy. Who knew? If he'd have paid her more attention . . .

"I think you need to stop feeling so sorry for yourself," she told him abruptly. "Hans is gone and it is sad, but you and I know where he is. You know what the missionaries have taught us. Hans isn't dead at all. He has simply passed from this earth, and gone on to greater things. Peter, you *know* you will be united with Hans once again. You also know that Christ paid the price for the sins of this world, including any Hans had . . . need I go on?"

"No," said Peter lamely.

"Then you know there is absolutely no reason for all this gloom. Here we are in the middle of this beautiful country and I'd liked to have gone riding and seen some of it, or taken a walk . . . something! All you want to do is work at the mill or go off someplace by yourself. Practically the only time we're together is at meals!"

Peter wasn't prepared for this outburst and stared at his future bride disbelievingly. He had never seen such spunk in her. And Maren's compassion toward his mother had also touched the surviving twin. Despite the fog of grief he felt over his brother's death, his dark confusion where Ferdinand was concerned, and the frustration of wanting Maren, Peter had a good look at what life with her was going to be and he liked what he saw.

"One receives a morbid sense of joy out of self-pity," Maren continued scolding, "and I for one am sick of it."

"It's not exactly self-pity," Peter apologized. "It's.. it's . . . well

I guess I have been acting like an idiot. It's like I'm paralyzed or something."

"Let's do go for a walk," he added taking her hand and taking heart. "You are absolutely right. This country is beautiful, the forest paths especially so this time of year. I'm sorry I haven't shown you. I really am."

He took her in his arms and kissed her. "And I have been feeling sorry for myself. Thanks for pointing it out." He kissed her on the nose and then on the lips and held her tightly, not caring if anyone were to come into the kitchen.

They left the house and headed down the road toward Holbaek then off to the left and into the forest. Ferns and grasses grew in profusion yet the ground was clear under the trees. They came to a particularly tall birch where Peter and Hans had at one time built a tree house. Their carved initials were now thickened and black. A small stream bubbled quietly through the area and walking near it Peter and Maren stopped.

It had all been too much; too much of other people's problems, too much of grief and too little time to be alone. Like a carpet, the grass beneath them was soft, green, dry and thick. The forest was peaceful, and beautifully tranquil, only the occasional twitter of birds and the soft rushing of the stream interrupted the quiet. Their kisses were long yet moist and Maren lingered securely in Peter's strong embrace. It felt so wonderful for him to just hold her. She wanted him and he wanted her and both knew it. But the sacredness of the moment would not allow it. Peter held her, caressed her, lightly brushing her hair back.

Together they sat upon the grass. The forest floor beneath them felt like a soft furry rug and the lovers were filled with wonder that was passing between them. It surpassed anything Peter had ever experienced. Heaven and earth and they felt a part of it. Maren lay back upon Peter's arm taking him with her and he felt her long eye lashes brush against his chest. He felt utterly protective of her. Her breathing slowed, his sped up and Maren pulled back from their embrace. "I love you more than life itself Peter," she responded. "But our special time must wait until marriage. I've made a covenant with God, and cannot break it."

"I know that Maren," he said respectfully. "I know."

His passion barely kindled, slowly dissipated. He wouldn't take Maren against her will, and surely not now. There was far more to this relationship. Maren could feel his disappointment, her own was just as keen and she was sorry if she'd let things go too far. She sat up and slowly fluffed her hair, then lay back in his arms.

"I love you Peter," she said with deep sincerity. "Please don't hate me."

"How could I hate you?" he asked, taking a breath. "It's just that . . ." she touched his lips with her finger then gave him a kiss.

"Are you all right?" he asked gently as he put his arms around her.

"As long as you are," she said quietly.

"I am fine," he said. "A bit disappointed I suppose . . ."

"As am I," she sighed.

That was all that passed between them for a time, but sitting there together they felt a bond between them was as strong as steel. If they could withstand the temptation they just had, they could withstand anything.

"This stream feeds our mill pond," Peter commented at length.

"It's not much of a stream," she responded teasingly. "But I guess it's constant enough."

"Only enough volume to fill the mill pond," he said. "Not near enough to turn the water-wheel. But when there is no wind and we open the flood gate, a full pond can run the mill for half a day."

"You love that old mill don't you?"

"I do," he said tossing a stone into the stream. "I love milling. Besides providing food for hosts of people, milling serves humanity with many basic needs."

"Such as . . ."

"Well a mill provides a livelihood for its workers, not to mention their families. Not only that but it provides food for animals. Without milling them down, whole grains pass right on through cattle and pigs providing them little nourishment, on the other hand, grist can be digested. Mills also provide mankind with another basic need," he went on with a twinkle in his eye.

"And that is?"

"News."

Maren looked at him oddly. Men could be so strange.

"As brokers, millwrights and farmers come and go," Peter explained, "they bring information from all around the country . . . also news from Europe and around the world."

"That is a good thing," said Maren, instantly interested.

"Yesterday two grain brokers came in from Frederikssund," Peter continued. "The news they brought was filled with such hope."

"Hope?"

"The government has now fully re-organized under the Venstre party. Most of the Liberals have been ousted from the Rigsdag and the conservatives have taken the majority. The crises amongst our government leadership in Copenhagen appears to be over. Denmark will indeed survive as a nation."

"You had doubts?" she asked

"Serious doubts. Didn't you?" When she didn't answer he went on. "Anyway, a mill is a community center so to speak. I think you can appreciate that."

"Very much so," she said.

Nothing further passed between them for a moment. Then Peter took the conversation down a different path. "I've got some decisions to make Maren," he ventured. They started walking again. "We'll soon be wed . . . and we'll be starting a family." Maren flushed in spite of herself and the cooling breeze felt wonderful against her skin.

"I know," she said softly.

"I wanted a farm for us Maren; someplace near here. And to be honest with you I wanted to work at the mill. I wanted to work there for the rest of my life. But now and with each passing day it becomes more and more obvious that I . . . we could never live around here."

"I didn't even know you'd been considering it Peter. Although it seems so natural . . ."

"Oh I have," he interrupted. "I really love physical labor, and after working at the mill again, I feel so healthy, I'm getting strong again. The thought of being an architect and going soft sitting at a drafting table really troubles me I don't want to waste my education, but I truly enjoy working with grains. The machinery, camaraderie with men, and having my finger on the pulse of Danish commerce . . . I love everything about milling. It's in here with me," he said tapping in the area of his heart with his fingertips. "It's part of me."

"Then what's wrong?" Maren asked.

"I've come to know I could never work around Ferdinand," he added sadly. "I think we'd end up killing each other."

"You don't mean that," said Maren, but not really surprised.

"I do," Peter said dejectedly. "The other day we were in the barn and we both reached for the same shovel. Sparks flew between our eyes that preempted a violence that most certainly awaits." He stopped, then continued. "I'd been wanting to speak with him and when I asked what in the world had gotten into him, he just stalked away. I think the boy hates me Maren. Really I do."

"Have you talked to your mother about it?" she asked.

"She's got enough to worry about right now," Peter said. "I won't subject her to more. If she knew the extent of the rift between my brother and I, it might break her heart."

"Well," said Maren wistfully, "I'm not sure I could live around Krista either."

They had stopped walking and were looking at each other. There was joy in each other's eyes. A bit of fear too. Peter took her in his arms and held her tightly.

"Whatever shall we do Maren?" he said. "Go back to Copenhagen I guess," he added answering his own question.

Chapter 35

Torkil Olsen and Inger Daryberg, both tough as leather and hard as nails, were keenly aware of the evil winds swirling about the Jensen household, namely the silent feud between Peter and Ferdinand. Like the rock of Gibraltar, Torkil was running the mill, the very heart of the estate. And where Catherine was concerned, in reality Torkil knew her every move and anticipated her every need. Inger was his confidant and because of them, Catherine's life had never been more stable. The only loose cog in the wheels of progress on the Jensen estate was Ferdinand. Elias kept that particular cog well oiled but kept himself in the background.

"Do you think Catherine is becoming too soft to manage the estate?" Torkil commented to Inger one day during Peter's visit.

"Fru Jensen is still grieving," answered Inger. "Give her time." Her face brightened a bit. "That girl Peter brought 'as helped. Pretty little thing."

"You like her then?"

"So far," said Inger. "She's not lazy and definitely 'as a mind of her own."

"How do you know?"

“She and Peter were havin’ words . . . she was the loudest.”

“Women can be tough,” said Torkil, with a wink.

“I am worried about things around here though,” Inger said ignoring the gesture. “Fru Jensen ‘as given Ferdinand responsibilities e’ isn’t ready for. And e’ walks around the house like e’ owns the place.”

“He’s no different around the mill,” Torkil said looking toward it. “Definitely feeling his oats; acts as if we work for him. Thinks he could run the whole estate.”

“Humph,” snorted Inger. “ ‘E couldn’t run anything without ‘is mother. The bank still won’t talk to ‘im’.”

“That isn’t true with grain brokers,” said Torkil. “They talk to Ferdinand. Some side up to him thinking they might get a favor. It’s those I watch the closest,” he added.

There were no trees between the mill and the Jensen house, and Inger’s bonnet looked like a signal flag whenever she headed to the water well behind the horse barn. Torkil generally saw her. He saw everything from his vantage point at the second story of the mill and whenever Inger swung her pail in a circle it meant she needed to talk to him.

The workmen also knew the signal and if Torkil hadn’t seen it one of them usually had. “Inger’s swingin’ her bucket,” was a common phrase around the mill. “Off to see your love?” Kev Monsen would tease to which Torkil growled, “Get to yer’ work.”

Between trips to the well and Torkil’s direct conversations with Catherine, he was aware of most everything that went on in the Jensen household. If anyone could handle Catherine’s affairs, he could. She trusted Torkil with her life.

“Ferdinand *and* Peter could manage the estate if they worked together," Torkil was saying. He spoke convincingly but also knew it would never happen. "They could manage easily . . . if there weren't something betwixt them."

"You mean *someone* betwixt them," said Inger acidly. "Two someone's actually; the old man, and that little tart Krista. Between them Ferdinand's so mixed up 'e don't know whether 'e's comin' or goin'. 'er Father bein' over all the stock, and 'im so important . . . puts the misses in a fix I'll tell you; and all because an eighteen-year-old boy can't keep 'is pants on. "

"Catherine and the boy have grown apart," Torkil commented. "More so of late. I wonder what has happened."

"I'll tell you what's 'appened," said Inger. "At first the girl turns Ferdinand's head, gets 'erself in a delicate way, then tries to take over the 'ouse. Struts about and doesn't lift a finger! But that's not the end of it. Ferdinand doesn't like 'er all that much anymore. 'E's seein' a girl in town. Hr Hokensen at the bank saw em' and told Catherine."

"That's five cups of water he's dipped from her pail," counted Kev Monsen from the open window at the front of the mill. "Must be something serious goin' on."

"He'll be in the outhouse all afternoon," hooted Thorn Christiansen who worked at the bolting machine.

"I think the old man is a bigger factor than either girl," Torkil said. "Ferdinand has even begun to sound like Elias."

"You're right there," said Inger, "E's become 'is confederate . . . nothin' but a puppet to 'im."

"But that Krista," added the little housekeeper angrily, "can't Fru Jensen see the girl is merely a gold digger? She needs to send 'er packin', that's what she needs to do. If our misses doesn't come to 'er senses soon, she might well lose control of everything she's built."

"Never happen," said Torkil swishing the residue in his cup before tossing it aside. "It's not even close to that."

"Don't be so sure," Inger said turning on her heel and heading back to her chores at the house.

Catherine wasn't entirely unaware of her employees' concerns. She was as concerned about Ferdinand's haughty and controlling ways, as Inger and Torkil were. Since Hans' death, the heiress to the Jensen estate felt her world slowly crumbling apart. Some days she knew she was losing her grip; and what troubled her most was she didn't care. Drawn inside herself, her grieving seemed as dark and deep as a bottomless pit. Emotionally, she might take years to heal if ever. To her credit, Catherine was fully conscious of the grim and silent struggle between Ferdinand and Peter. In wordless and yet clear communication they had let her know that each felt the other was a threat to him. Polite in her presence, Catherine knew there was a gulf between her sons as wide as a fjord.

Where Ferdinand's attitude was concerned, she also knew the root cause wasn't Krista Holsen. Long and whispered conversations in Elias' sick room always left the boy shrouded in darkness. Greed and control, attitudes Catherine knew only too well. Money was everything to Elias, yet his understanding of it was as narrow as an alley in Copenhagen. Catherine wondered why Ferdinand even listened to him. The boy wasn't stupid so far. He had had a good education. Shouldn't he be able to see by now that his father was merely a parasite?

And why didn't Ferdinand seem to be grieving over Hans? It was all a mystery to Catherine. She wanted to ask him about it but refrained. She was so angry with him having Krista in a motherly way and yet not really loving her, that she could hardly be civil to him.

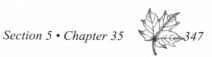

She also thought of confronting Ferdinand about his foolish struggle for position over Peter, but knew he was too immature to understand. By itself that wasn't the issue that troubled her most, it was the sum and total of her youngest son's lack of character. How could she have raised such a child?

Catherine had related concerns, if she were to predecease her husband, Elias would probably have Ferdinand sell the mill and the two of them go gallivanting around Copenhagen. The worry wasn't without foundation, some days her grief over Hans was so sore the heiress felt her heart might stop beating. Catherine actually entertained such thoughts. Because of all that had happened, there were days she wasn't thinking straight, and she knew it. And the house was driving her crazy; the death of Hans had turned the big old place into such a dreary setting. A mausoleum as it were, at least to Catherine. All she could see was the cobwebs in the corners; dust on the tables and all the curtains needing washing. Inger, as meticulous as any Danish housekeeper alive, had let the lethargy of Catherine's grief spill over her. She still made meals, though Catherine ate but little, and Inger saw that the beds were made, but other than the bathrooms and kitchen there had been little serious house cleaning since the death of Hans. Things were about to change, and rapidly.

Her love for Peter notwithstanding, the whole Jensen scene grated upon Maren Carlsen, and in order to keep herself from becoming as depressed as everyone else she threw herself into working Catherine's garden. Raking and hoeing every square foot, going after even the smallest weed, she continued until every clod was broken, every plant hand watered and like little soldiers, lined up for inspection. Marigolds and white daisies surrounded the garden like a halo; green and beautiful. The garden's transformation was having a profound impact upon Catherine.

It started the day she got a whiff of the sweet smoke from Maren's burning pile of weeds and rose-brambles. There was activity about! Day by day from her window she watched as Maren transformed the weed infested garden back to life. It soon became as beautiful and healthy-looking as if Catherine had done it herself.

One day she went for a closer look and was so pleased with the tangle free rose bushes, and the profusion of color she actually laughed aloud. Standing in the midst of it, she felt at one with nature, at one with her God. She felt a profound oneness and peace. Weed-free and watered, the garden began a reawakening in the heiress.

That reawakening was manifest one morning when Catherine had Inger serve breakfast on the back porch of the house. It was cool there, the porch overlooked the garden and enjoyed shade until almost noon. Catherine wanted everyone, with the exception of Elias, present. She had something to say and the porch was the perfect setting.

"You have transformed this setting into a Garden of Eden, Maren," Catherine began warmly. "Only two weeks have passed and look what you've done. I have always loved my garden, loved to keep it up, but in my state of mind it's been so overwhelming. Seeing it like this again has made me feel like a new person." She got up from her chair and leaned over and hugged Maren, then sat down and dabbed at her eyes with her napkin. "Thank you very much," she added sincerely, looking warmly at Maren.

"I've had such fun Fru Jensen," Maren said a bit embarrassed. She was not used to such praise. "I love to get my hands in the soil; it's so different from work in my father's store."

"I do love it out here, don't you Peter?" Catherine deferred, turning her attention to him.

"Very peaceful," he said stuffing a forkful of food in his mouth.

Breakfast was of thin Danish pancakes, fried eggs, new potatoes, sausage and coffee. If not for the fact Ferdinand and Krista were there, Peter would have enjoyed himself immensely. As things were he was somewhat tense.

"I have something to tell you all," said Catherine now addressing the entire table. "Several things actually and I wanted to have everybody together." Ferdinand had his hands folded over his chest and was watching his mother warily, while Krista couldn't take her eyes off Peter. Dull as she was, Krista sensed heavy instructions coming toward the brothers.

"Starting with you Peter," said Catherine as Krista smiled, "I think it's time that you and Maren returned to Copenhagen. You both have been such a comfort, especially you Maren," she patted her future daughter-in-law's hand briefly. "I'm very grateful for what you have done at the mill Peter. The men have been so behind. Torkil tells me you have really made your presence known." She smiled at him, took his hand and squeezed it. "But life goes on," she said decidedly, "and it's high time you got back to your studies."

Peter looked at Maren, then back to his mother. "A garden can do all this?" His eyes were wide. "You seem almost back to your old self, Mother."

"I'm not back to myself Peter," she sighed, "but slowly, ever so slowly, I'm getting there." The look on Catherine's face did show traces of her zest for life returning. She had escaped, though not entirely, from her torpor, her mourning appeared to be under control and she looked like she was ready to get back to work.

War, the loss of Hans and the trouble between her sons had

deeply affected her but not in an altogether negative way. She had aged, but not so much the physical withering of the body, but rather a tempering of soul, an enlightening of the mind. What Maren had done in the garden did trigger it off but just as when she'd lost Kristian, Catherine had reached deep within her own reservoirs of faith and found strength to continue on. An aura of humility seemed to radiate from her that morning, a sense of direction too. Like fine steel from a hot forge, a difficult life had already tempered the heiress, now there seemed even greater strength and depth of character present. Time would show it.

If she'd been kind and fair to people in the past, in the future Catherine would be almost saintly in her associations. If she'd made difficult but wise decisions in the past, the future would show the same. She had the same drive, the same strengths, but carried humility that was born of suffering. You could not be in the same room with her and not feel it.

"You've a bright future ahead Peter," Catherine went on, "and I'll not have you wallowing around in this gloomy atmosphere any longer. You've put too much effort into your schooling to throw it all away."

"Maren and I have been talking about it," Peter said hesitantly.

"It's time to do more than talk," said Catherine feeling his reluctance and sensing he needed an extra shove. "You know I'm not one to waste assets. I've invested heavily in your education and you *must* finish." She turned her eyes to Ferdinand. "As a matter of fact, your brother will soon be joining you." This was all news to Ferdinand. His brow furrowed and the anger in his eyes was immediate.

"At the university?!" he asked. He looked over at Krista in confusion, and perhaps a slight bit of relief.

"At the university," Catherine answered in a warning voice.

"We'll talk about the details later."

Krista threw down her napkin, slid back her chair, and moved immediately toward the kitchen. She had started to cry.

"What am I supposed to do?" she asked angrily as she turned on Catherine, shooting a flaming glare toward Ferdinand who avoided her volley by ducking his head and taking a large bite of pancakes. There were things going on here he really didn't care to understand. All he had wanted to do was fool around in a haystack here and there. The consequences of such, he neither cared about or thought through. This thing of more schooling? He would see what Elias had to say about that. Ferdinand had hated Herlufsholm and everything about it. What he wanted was a freedom with no responsibility.

"You'll be returning to your home young lady," said Catherine pointedly. She said it with mixed emotions. She knew Ferdinand's mind was on other women. If there had been any doubt, the report from her banker confirmed it. A brand new baby would arrive sometime around Christmas, a child her son had sired but felt little responsibility toward. Catherine was sure *she* would love the child, but she had raised her children and would not be raising any grandchildren they produced. And how Nils Holsen would react to her sending Krista home was anybody's guess. She would deal with that issue later.

"The war is over," Catherine went on leaving Krista sputtering and weeping as Inger took her into the kitchen. "Luckily, neither of you young men are in the army or they'd be telling you what to do. But what I've said is said. I'm not one to waste words and once I've set my mind I'm immovable."

Peter did not doubt it, but wondered if his brother did. As far as the estate was concerned it didn't look like things would be quite as Ferdinand was planning. Or did the boy even have a plan? Peter didn't think so but he was sure Elias had plans, disjointed and emotional plans, nothing of substance. He was too dependent upon Catherine.

"Are you sure about all this Mother?" Peter protested. "You've made a very sudden recovery here. I can stay a bit longer. They are still behind at the mill."

"Nonsense," said Catherine. "Torkil's hiring new men. The mill will do fine. Everything here is under control. Nils is taking care of the stock, I'm handling the business, and Inger is in charge of the house . . ."

Upon hearing her name, Inger quickly stepped from the kitchen doorway. "And Ferdinand," she said throwing in her opinion, "we're also taking good care of your Father. You can go off ta' school withouta' care."

Catherine looked over at the plump little housekeeper whereupon Inger ducked back into the kitchen. "In short," Catherine said, "everything here is running smoothly."

"I'm glad to see you back in charge," said Peter very perplexed over her sudden change. He was greatly relieved as well.

"It's about time, don't you think?" said Catherine smiling. "I'm not over Hans, I never will be. But I've got to get busy again. Inger and I must get my house back in order. As orderly as this beautiful garden." She extended her hand and turned to look at its verdant and colorful greenery.

"As long as you don't take too much upon yourself Mother," said Peter.

"Peter," she said, softening and looking at him sincerely. "It's not that I don't want you here. As I said, you and Maren have been so kind, and so helpful, but well . . . I've stated my case." She looked deeply into his eyes to make sure he understood. "I want you to finish your education and that is that," she added firmly. "The sooner, the better. Many options will open to you then, you'll see."

Once he graduated Peter knew Catherine would expect him to apprentice to a master architect. That would be another two-year ordeal and the thought was stifling. But Peter knew if he didn't finish his degree, he'd not only feel like a stranger at home but perhaps an unwelcome guest.

Peter reached over and took Maren's hand. "All right Mother," he said resolutely. "But it will be difficult leaving you and the mill. Very difficult."

"You'll be missed," said Ferdinand wryly. Where he had been squirming in his seat, Ferdinand acted more relaxed. He wasn't going to any school. He had decided that having Krista around to bother him didn't seem all that bad.

"And I'll miss having you around Maren," Catherine said sincerely. "As I've said, you've been such a comfort. Such a blessing."

"I do hope I've been helpful Fru Jensen."

"More than you'll ever know my dear."

Chapter 36

When Peter returned to the university he felt as much a stranger there as he'd been at home. The high ceilings, cold bare walls and stony floors of the university seemed to echo Denmark's defeat. Maps of the country had been removed from classrooms and the rooms themselves held a bleak aura, as if they were ashamed. During the day the halls were somewhat crowded, but the students spoke in low tones and some carried haunted expressions on their faces.

Outside, the university looked about the same. There was some visual neglect, but the war had definitely changed what went on inside. Every lecture was salt and peppered with propaganda and political rhetoric. "We'll build a new Denmark," railed the president of the university, Karl Weinstock, from the lectern in the auditorium. "A Denmark that stands for peace and prosperity!"

"What was lost without, will be gained within," echoed physics professor, Jens Larsen.

There were cries of; "Long live the King," from some professors, and "Long live the constitution!" from others.

Peter, along with other students in his classes, clapped politely but he felt the new wave of nationalism being promoted on campus and in the newspapers, was fraudulent. Denmark had been lucky and Peter knew it. She may have retained her treasured name but that was about all. Only the grace of God had saved her from bondage to Prussia, that and the humiliating treaty signed in Vienna.[6]

October came and went during which time Peter struggled to gain direction. Denmark's defeat coupled with Hans' death and Ferdinand's coldness had left him empty inside. Only Catherine gave him sense of family. He had renewed difficulty concentrating upon his studies and barely passed mid-term exams. Attending church meetings and studying with Mormon missionaries was all that sustained him through these difficult times. That, and Maren's love for him. He couldn't see it, but slowly and ever so surely he was climbing to higher ground.

One evening he made the following journal entry:

'The feelings I have toward my country are a mixture of pride and shame; pride in my Viking heritage, but shame because we lay a conquered nation. One third of our land mass confiscated by Prussia yet politicians and priests are running around congratulating each other . . . I've never seen the likes of it! There is an air of falsehood about and some members of the Rigsdag are even promoting renewed war with Prussia! What's left of our little nation needs to mind its own affairs or have no future at all.

While at home I thought I'd forget the university and work at the mill permanently, but Mother would have nothing to do with it. Her mind is set. Her eldest son will be an architect and she'll accept nothing less, but when I think of life hunched over a drafting board I suffocate. I want something I can get my hands on!

God is my strength and Maren my solace. We have started

meeting with the Mormons again. Hr Carlsen has rented out his back warehouse for worship service. Studying the gospel of Christ helps me better accept Hans' death because I know I will see him again. Still I feel so utterly empty.'

Sometimes man must be knocked to his knees, truly humbled before he will plead with God. In Peter's case, that is exactly what was happening. He needed rest for his troubled soul; he needed light and understanding. And Peter felt he was receiving it, but from a tiny American sect that hardly anyone had heard of? Why wasn't this precious information taught at the University of Copenhagen?

'The Gospel of Christ is a bit like having a baby' one of the missionaries had told him. 'Like a baby is to its Mother, a testimony of the gospel is extremely precious. Like gestation, the journey toward testimony is replete with certain pleasures but much discomfort and struggle. There is a price to pay, but like the study of the gospel a mother-to-be feels guided throughout the process. That guidance is the Spirit of the Holy Ghost.

Worrying about persecution and whether or not the Gospel is true is similar to when the woman frets over whether or not the baby will have all its fingers and toes. Then there's the process of labor; in your case prayer and study, a very difficult thing. And finally birth, a child perfect in every way. It is similar to baptism in the name of Christ. All is well, the gospel is true! You come out of the water spotless and clean like a newborn child.

But there is much more. If the child is not nurtured continually, what happens? It will wither and die. Same with a testimony of the gospel, it must be nurtured or be lost.'

For Peter, there were certain similarities here. His journey toward a testimony of Christ and His true gospel *was* like a pregnancy, a difficult pregnancy. But Peter was making progress, and did feel guided. Insecurity over the future, persecution from family members augmented by the death of Hans, had brought on the travail, brought him closer to the birthing.

Peter set down his pen and fell to his knees, he needed answers.

Outside the dormitory window the sky was robin egg blue and the trees on campus were red and gold, rich with fall colors. Eventually Peter felt his mind slowly clear and like that morning in the mill, a beautiful peace descended upon him. The seed, the fragile plant which had been growing within for years was about to blossom. A radiant light fell upon him, a burning grew within his bosom. His eyes welled up with tears, letting go he felt as calm and serene as a summer's morning. The sweet light and power of the Holy Spirit overshadowed him and several things became very clear. Yes the missionaries had told him the truth; the Church of Jesus Christ of Latter-day Saints was true, yes the Book of Mormon was the word of God. Peter also felt he had a very important mission in life to fulfill. He wasn't sure what it was, but instinctively felt God was leading him and would let him know—eventually.

Feeling confident, free, more relaxed and more joyful than ever before in his life, Peter raised his head, got off his knees, took up his pen and started writing again;

'I have finally come to a decision, a decision I must record. I have decided to be a true follower of the Savior, a disciple. I am merely a man, not a saint, but I am going to serve my God. I am going to be baptized. This decision will come as no surprise to my parents, especially Father; he will probably disown me.

Maren and I have still attended the state church on occasion. Our Savior chapel is just across Norre park, but the meetings are so steeped with tradition and paganism with lighted candles, kneeling up and down, priests in long robes mumbling, there is little comfort for me in it all. Not even in lands and mills or degrees from schools—there is no security in life but God. In the last few months Latter-day Saint missionaries have taught me more about God and His Christ than I've learned all my life. The church has its headquarters in America . . .'

Peter suddenly stopped writing and stared down at the last word to leave his pen. "America," he said aloud. "America . . ." All of a sudden he felt his soul taking fire. The feeling was all consuming. It was electric! The log-jam, which had kept the rivers of his mind from flowing free for several months, was about to break loose. His mother, his legacy and his darling Maren meant everything in the world to Peter but to completely fulfill the measure of his manhood, he had needed something else, a challenge, a goal. And a goal of many facets was beginning to crystallize: Being baptized, marriage to Maren . . . land and occupation included.

The Latter-day Saint Elders had talked about America many times of course. Spoke of it with passion. Boasted of the many cities being settled by Mormons in the western part of America. A gathering to Zion they called it. With all he had at stake in Denmark, Peter had never seriously considered going. The war with Prussia and the fact that the United States was locked in the grasp of civil conflict had all but ended any thoughts he had entertained of immigration.

But things were rapidly changing. Denmark was now at peace and from what Peter had heard from the missionaries, America would soon follow suit.

There was something in the air. What it was Peter could scarcely imagine, but there was something stirring inside him. Something he couldn't quite put his finger on.

"America," he said again, and this time with reverence. "I've got to take a walk," he exclaimed as he placed his quill in the ink well. "This is all too much to take sitting down." He put on his leather cap, left his cluttered room and closed the door.

Down the stairs and into the street, he paused only to touch the pillars near the entry of the university. His face was flushed, his mind on fire and he felt like shouting. As he passed the statue of Niels Steensen (Nicolaus Steno) the famous anatomist he tipped his cap. "Farewell old friend," he said.

Farewell? Ultimately Peter would find Maren, that he knew, but this walk was to be alone. A long walk; much to think about, much to plan. He went the direction of the docks. He felt compelled to see the ocean, compelled to feel its power. Waves crashed against the bulkheads spraying saltwater mist into the air. Seagulls circled ship masts and riggings and searched the beaches. Were their shrill cries signaling a warning? Were they cries of danger? If they were, Peter didn't hear. He was going to become a Mormon, he was going to marry Maren, and he was going to America! He didn't know exactly when or what he would do when he got there or how it would all come together, but in his heart he knew it would.

He wandered the wooden docks and cobbled streets of Copenhagen for hours. On street corners vendors called to him to buy their fish; buy their steaming sausage. From behind their produce stands, women with fresh fruit shouted too. And Peter was hungry but so deeply engrossed in thought he paid no mind. He crossed canals, passed the ornate Church Of Our Savior with its graceful external spiral stairway, passed St. Mary's Hospital with its modern architecture, and even passed the magnificent Chancellery, all without seeing them! Like snowflakes in a blizzard, a thousand thoughts were whirling through his mind.

So deep was his meditation Peter hardly knew where he was. He finally stopped walking near the entryway of Norre Park. The sky had grown cloudy and moving in from the east was a dark section of thunderheads. 'Dear Heavenly Father,' he pleaded silently as his eyes scanned the leafy treetops. 'I can't go to America without Maren. If thou wilt open the way for us to go together, I will serve thee all the days of my life. This I covenant.'

She'll never hear of going, he said to himself. *And even if she wanted to go with me, her parents will forbid it.* Peter took a deep breath, put on a shaky look of confidence and headed toward Carlsen Dry Goods Store. Later, as he neared the door of the store, his forehead wrinkled and his enthusiasm drained away as if someone had pulled the plug. Like a change in the weather his mind clouded over and reality began to settle in.

Maren had seen him coming and went to put on a scarf. "I'm going for a walk with Peter," she said to her father who was poring over the week's ledgers. "Take up for me. I shan't be long."

Lars lifted his eyebrows from behind his accounting book but said nothing. There hadn't been a customer in the store all afternoon. The door slammed and its bells were still jingling as he lowered his head. The tired and aging merchant wondered when his daughter's relationship with the rich young man from Holbaek would ever culminate into marriage. He hoped it would be soon. He paid Maren very little for the long hours she worked, but lately even that was a strain on Lars' purse.

Except for a flock of pigeons clustered on and around an empty bench where two men were playing checkers, the park was deserted; an immense green and gold canyon with few inhabitants. The flower gardens had wilted but, like at the university, the trees were speckled with fall colors and the lily pads covering the pond were tainted with orange and rust-colored hues.

When the lovers finally reached the bridge spanning the pond, Peter took Maren in his arms. "Let's get married soon," he said earnestly, "and I mean very soon." Maren loved this topic more than any other but this day she could sense there was something else on Peter's mind. They kissed but she felt the kiss unusual, hurried, and insincere.

"We can't just yet love," she answered carefully. "You've got to graduate and my parents need me badly right now. Things are hard . . ." She looked at him to see what it was that had him so agitated. Maybe something had come up. "Where would we live?" she asked hopefully.

Maren's soft breath smelled like spearmint and hung lightly about her pretty mouth. She waited for an answer.

"We'll find a place," Peter said nervously. "Maren," he added abruptly, "you know I've been a miserable soul . . . for months. And you know all the reasons; we've worn them out. The war, our government, the state church, architecture . . . my brother's death."

"Is there's something else Peter?" she asked. "Have you grown tired of me?"

"What are you talking about?" he asked incredulously. "Whatever makes you say that?" He took her into his arms again. She was reluctant at first but then slowly melted into his embrace. Her petite softness always moved him with feelings of protective joy.

Maren wasn't always as sure of herself as she'd like to be with Peter. She had been worried that because she wouldn't give in to his desires for something more than kissing that she could lose him. On the other hand her standards were such that if she broke them, she wouldn't be able to live with herself. She looked up at Peter and wondered if he could read her mind. "There's something you don't want to tell me, isn't there?" she said pushing away.

He nodded his head briefly, and looked out over the pond. A chilly breeze blew across the lily pads and dented them in like quilting on a bed. "There's a hint of winter in the air," he said enjoying the cool air, and thinking how to respond.

"Maren," he said turning to her and taking her hands. "My mind is so complex at this moment, that I'm not sure where to start. The only thing I know for certain is that I love you." She showed relief at that, but was still puzzled. "On that you should never doubt. But I don't want to be an architect. I realize that may upset you and I know it will upset my mother, but it's just not in here!" He thumped his heart with his fingertips. "It's just not," he repeated.

"And as for our country," he was testing the water at this point, "With the Prussians still breathing down our backs, I'm not sure Denmark is the place to start a family."

"Whatever are you talking about?" she asked in alarm. "Denmark is our home, it's part of us."

"Was part of us," he said gravely. "That is, was part of me." He hung his head in disgust momentarily.

"Look Maren," he said taking a different tack. "Since the reorganization of our government I think Denmark is safe. The king has taken a neutral position. And in the grand scheme of things what good is Denmark to an ambitious despot like Bismarck anyway? We have few resources and he couldn't force our men to fight against France or Russia, and he knows it."

"I will always be Danish," he went on, "always proud of my roots but since the war, and especially ever since our visit to my parent's home in Holbaek, I'll be honest with you, something has changed within me. Something has been set free. I no longer have *all* my hopes and dreams wrapped up in Denmark and especially in my family's estate. I think I could live anywhere else in the world and be happy."

"Really," she said doubtfully.

"Yes really," he answered flatly. They stared at each other for a moment and although Maren knew he had been building a case for something, she almost feared what he was about to say.

"What would you say if I told you I've finally decided to be baptized a Mormon?"

"I'd be very happy about it," she said without hesitation. "I have almost decided the same thing, but you know that."

"You don't fear your father?"

"Peter, the constitution grants us freedom of religion. And even though father says he will die a Lutheran, he has not stopped me from attending Mormon services. He has told all of his children we are free to choose which church to attend."

"That's a very good thing," said Peter, nodding. "And what about where you will live?"

"I don't know what you mean Peter."

"Does your father care where you will live after you marry me? We have choices there too you know."

She looked at him oddly, there was something exciting in his eyes and it made her tingle, but she wasn't sure she liked what she felt."

"We have choices," Peter went on, but not quite ready to mention America. "We have choices."

Section Notes:

1. It took Bismarck many years and several battles to unify the German states. His war with Denmark was a mere skirmish compared to the Franco-Prussian war of 1870–1871, yet he'd have lost that battle had it not been for a peace treaty he'd engineered between his country and Russia. That treaty removed the possibility of fighting on two fronts. Bismarck's military and political genius impacted all of Europe and more than likely set the stage for the First World War.

2. Apparently the liberals who controlled both houses of the Rigsdag didn't think so, because when the situation over Holstein and Slesvig finally came to a head, it was Denmark who declared war, not Prussia.

3. Christian Julius de Meza a man who may have changed Danish history, and altered the history of the world died a brokenhearted man just one year after his dismissal.

4. The Prussians ended up not wanting the Jutlands and shortly thereafter abandoned them. In 1920 much of Slesvig, or the German spelling Schleswig, was also returned to Denmark. But to show the importance the duchies had to Germany and to add an interesting historical footnote; a deadly German battleship used in World War II was chillingly named the Schleswig-Holstein.

5. The Mormons had in fact created quite a stir in Scandinavia at large and more specifically in Denmark. Throughout the 1850's to the latter part of the 1880's thousands of Danes were baptized and many thousands more immigrated to the United States.

6. Throughout Europe royal families still ruled, but Otto Von Bismarck and Napoleon III would soon lock horns and who knew but their war might put an end to Europe's monarchical system forever. There were those who would have it so. Within three years a book written by a sickly, demented albeit passionately driven fellow named Karl Marx would be published; "Das Kapitol," its title. Dark days lay ahead for Europe's elite.

Section Six

One of a City, Two of a Country

Chapter 37

"Throughout the ages God has spoken to mankind through His holy prophets," the Mormon missionary was saying as Peter and Maren took their place along with thirty-one other listeners in the cramped storeroom. "Moses, Ezra, Nehemiah, Isaiah, Jeremiah, Matthew, Mark, Luke and so on. Prophets testified of the divinity of Christ; they foretold of His coming to earth and also of His crucifixion and resurrection. Prophets have also prophesied of Christ's *second* coming. Prophets are called of God and were ordained by God before the world was created."

"Are you saying that before the world was created God knew Moses?" asked a woman seated on a small keg that had the word "nails" stenciled across the front of it.

"He even knew you Sister Larsen," said Elder Snow candidly. "Everyone please turn to Jeremiah 1: 4."

He waited while those who had bibles found the scripture and then he read it aloud: "Before I formed thee in the belly I knew thee; and before thou camest forth out of the womb I sanctified thee, and I ordained thee Prophet unto the nations."

The Mormon missionary who was speaking that night was a man

about fifty-eight years old. He was of average height, wearing a Prince Albert coat, a derby hat, a neatly trimmed Van Dyke and knew his scriptures. Brother Snow is what he asked to be called, his first name was Elonzo and his hair was, in fact, snowy white; making the association instantaneous. His eyes were a light blue and held the wisdom and light of a kindly old sage. There was also a twinkle in his eye and just a touch of mischief.

He was somewhat pompous, seemingly close to overbearing, but was in fact a kind and decent man, and he wore a bruise on his cheek from a recent beating he'd received during a "street meeting" held on the corner of Norre Park.

"Now, it's all very easy to believe in the prophets of old," Snow went on. "And for two reasons; number one, they are dead." A laugh or two popped up but Snow continued. "And number two, they left behind their writings, which as you know are scripture. Timeless writings . . . as applicable today just as they were yesterday. The mind and will of God as revealed to his holy prophets. Scripture proves the prophets were indeed prophets of God," Snow said without reservation.

Nobody said anything so the missionary continued. "Now if it's all so easy to believe in dead prophets . . . what about a living prophet? What about latter-day prophets? If God spoke to man through His prophets in the past, what about the present? Impossible, right? God has said all he is going to, right?"

The storeroom was twenty feet by twelve, had a ceiling so low Peter had to stoop to keep from bumping his head when he entered. Four kerosene lamps, mounted on thick posts that supported heavy ceiling joists that in turn supported the Carlsen apartment directly overhead, lighted the cozy room. There were also two oilskin windows on the back wall, one on either side of the rear door. The gathered crowd of Mormons and investigators of the church were seated on wooden crates, casks and rickety old chairs lined up in three rows. Some of the people having worked a fourteen hour day stared at the speaker through bloodshot eyes and flushed faces; but were attentive nonetheless.

Fishy smelling clothes, oily caps, hair grease mixed with the scent of dried sweat, moth balls, wool and traces of cheap cologne gave the storeroom in back of Carlsen's Dry Goods Ltd. all the flavor of an old church. And due to the chill outside, the warm and tight conditions were much appreciated!

The storage room was accessed by three doors, one led into the dry goods store itself, another led to an alley behind the store, and the third door was at the top of a stairway leading into the Carlsen apartment. The storeroom was relatively spacious but cozy. A perfect setting for meetings of this sort. Neatly stacked on wall shelves, was a sizable inventory of cloth in bolts, also small boxes containing needles, buttons, snaps, sticks of wax and other notions to tickle a woman's fancy. Two spinning wheels hung from hooks and carefully organized on pegs were spools of thread, and the largest assortment of yarn in Copenhagen. For the shopper's children, there were jars of black licorice and candy sticks awaiting the little hands of future customers.

Lars Carlsen, a hard-working man and thrifty to the core, hated waste and so rented this half empty room to the Mormons because they had no chapels in town as of yet. There *was* a mission office nearby, not three doors down from Our Savior Chapel and passersby were appalled. There it was bold as brass, The Church of Jesus Christ of Latter-day Saints painted on a sign on a white stucco office building. Like David fighting Goliath, the insignificant American sect appeared to be taking on the mighty Folkekirken. It wasn't so; the goal was much, much larger; every nation, kindred, tongue and people, and with Elder Snow's burning testimony of the church he was dedicated to its growth. If one were going to do missionary work, one might as well do it right was his motto. 'Let people know we're out there.'

During the time in question Mormon missionaries were generally married men who had left their families in America, and traveling "without purse or scrip" set off to spread the good news of "The Gospel of Christ" on a wing and a prayer. They slept in barns, haystacks, floors, hallways, and occasionally even beds. As for food they depended largely upon the kindness and generosity of the people they called upon. Even those who were antagonistic and flatly rejected their message about Joseph Smith and his claim of being shown the golden plates by an angel of God, often fed them on the promise that if they shut up about Mormonism during the meal they could eat and be on their way.

Despite the crowded conditions in Copenhagen, people were very hospitable. True, the Danes had their share of selfishness, superstition, poverty, ignorance and moral degradation but culture also abounded. Danish poetry, art, children's literature and symphony orchestra music were without equal in Europe. Indeed the dark ages was giving way to light when Elder Elonzo Snow and company arrived to open a church mission in 1859. Hundreds of Danes eventually believed their gospel message and five years later when Peter and Maren were about to be baptized there were several branches of the church in Denmark and not a few thousand converts.

Inside the Mormon mission office was a small printing press where tracts and choice sections of the Book of Commandments[1]—prophesies of Joseph Smith—were translated and printed for distribution. Small chapels on the outskirts of Copenhagen, Skibby, Randers, and Roskilde, were under construction but funds were scarce and completion a long way off. In Copenhagen proper Carlsen's storeroom did the job. Weekly missionary firesides were held there as well as formal services on Sunday.

Lars Carlsen charged a modest fee for his storage room and paid little heed to the messages presented there. As long as his guests left the place clean and paid the rent on time, he didn't care what they taught. As Maren told Peter, Lars was a fourth generation Lutheran and he would die a Lutheran.

"Prophets and their priesthood authority are the very crux of the matter," Snow continued sincerely. "As I have testified before, I will testify again; Joseph Smith was a Prophet of God. Called, ordained and set apart as God's chosen mouthpiece in these latter days to once again restore the Lord's true Church and Priesthood authority to the earth. Joseph was an unschooled farm boy when he saw God, and barely 21 when he translated the Book of Mormon . . . I know it's an utterly unbelievable claim I am making . . . when I first heard it I didn't believe it myself!" Snow looked incredulous as he said the last, but continued. "I was a staunch Methodist when I first heard that Joseph Smith translated the Book of Mormon from thin plates of gold by the gift and power of God, I read it strictly to prove it false. I told the missionaries the yardstick I would use would be the Holy Bible."

"Well, I read the Book of Mormon my brothers and sisters; I read and I read." A lump formed in his throat and Snow paused briefly, swallowed then blinked away the tears in his eyes and went on somberly. "Holy Scripture it is, the history of God's dealings with the inhabitants of the ancient Americas. It is another testament of Jesus Christ and tells of His visit to the ancient Americas."

Snow then gripped the makeshift podium and spoke from the depths of his soul. "The Book of Mormon is true my brothers and sisters," he said with deep sincerity. "It is the most correct book on the face of the earth.

But don't take my word for it. You in this congregation can find out the truth of what I'm saying for yourselves. Take this challenge—read the Book of Mormon, study it out, and then go to God in prayer. Ask Him." Snow paused again and seemed to be remembering. Tears rolled down his cheeks, he looked above the crowd momentarily.

"It takes a lot of courage to talk to God, do you know it?" he said quietly. "To truly talk with Him . . . it takes a lot of courage." The older Snow became, the closer he felt to God. Often times he felt as if he was talking to an old friend. He didn't tell his audience that but he honestly felt it.

"You can do it my dear friends. Pray to God, ask Him if these things are true; and I promise He *will* hear and answer you." Snow's face was glowing at this point, his eyes were moist, and no one in the room doubted his sincerity.

"If your prayer is genuine, you'll not only find that the Book of Mormon is true but you will find out many other related and important things. Does Jesus Christ really live? Did he ever live? As in days of old, does he speak today through living Prophets; or has what I've said tonight been just so—much—tripe?" To some in the audience it was, and others as tired as they were, did not hear everything, however most were listening. They were there because they wanted to be, and they heard.

Snow then leveled his clear blue eyes at the crowd and bore this solemn testimony: "The Book of Mormon has cost the best blood of this century brothers and sisters; the Prophet Joseph Smith, his dear brother Hyrum, and many others gave their very lives for it. But this Gospel and the Book of Mormon are true and I thank God I know it."

Sitting in the audience, Peter Jensen felt the same. The most profound thing this new church had taught him was that a person could actually speak to God, one on one. Man to man . . . and get answers! Peter had taken the challenge once and for all to find out for himself if Joseph Smith was a true Prophet of God, and he had prayed about it. And in the quiet solitude of his dormitory he had also read the Book of Mormon. Then he had taken the matter to God. Was Joseph Smith a true Prophet? Was the Book of Mormon scripture; was it true?

People get answers from God in different ways. Some get them easily, while most others receive them only after great difficulty, only after a test of their faith. In Peter's case there had been a long struggle. Intellectually he knew the missionaries had told him the truth, but he had not received a firm spiritual witness until just one week previously. Alone in his room he knelt and poured out his heart to God, and didn't he feel a burning within his bosom? He did, a warm and glowing fire, like light from the sun; the Spirit of the Holy Ghost bearing witness that Joseph Smith held the prophetic mantle as Brigham Young did now. Both men were called and anointed, both prophets of God. The Book of Mormon was true and he, Peter, a son of God was to proceed with baptism.

Peter also received other answers that morning: He now knew that the true Priesthood authority of God had been restored to the earth and that this humble, little, American church held that power and authority. Peter also knew God had a work for him in America. Other converts might stay and build up the church in Denmark, but he was going to Zion.

Maren had also reached the decision to be baptized. She had received her confirmation months before Peter and had been patiently waiting for him. But she hadn't received anything regarding America. Off and on she had heard the missionaries talk of it but she had not given it much consideration. Then one afternoon while they were taking a walk through the business district, Peter told her of the experience he'd had while writing in his journal.

"I've had casual thoughts of going to America ever since we first met the missionaries Maren," he said trying to be nonchalant, "I just haven't said anything to you."

At that Maren had stopped walking, frowned up at him and Peter had taken her in his arms. "Listen to me please," he pleaded quietly. "Before you say anything hear me out. When I discovered for myself that the church was true and that I would be baptized, the seed of immigration was also planted in my heart. Then a while back as I was writing in my journal when I saw the word America, I suppose the plant sprang forth. Something quite electric went through me Maren."

He pushed her gently away and looked into her eyes. The love he always saw was still there but if Peter had been honest with himself he could also see Maren was stunned by his talk of immigration. But like a person who fails to listen even when communication is silent, Peter forged ahead. "Our destiny lies in America Maren. I just know it. I could never go home and work on my family's estate, my mother expects me to be an architect, which I'm not sure I want to be and when I think of the opportunities in America . . ."

"Peter," she said stopping him in his tracks. "I'm for taking life one step at a time. Baptism is the subject here at hand. Leaving the Folkekirken! The church of our fatherland. Do you really understand the implications of that decision? Why our parents will surely disown us. I know yours will you. We may know the Gospel is true, but you must admit we still have much to learn about the church, if you understand my meaning?"

"I do understand Maren. I do. It is such a departure from the state church."

"It is and thank heaven," she said glad to have taken him away from any discussion of America. Perhaps he might even forget about it.

They had continued their walk, talking about their decision to be baptized and stopped at a sidewalk café for lunch. Both had so much on their minds that day they hardly saw the pigeons strutting about pecking at breadcrumbs, or the beauty of hanging gardens around them or even the people passing by. But Maren's reminding Peter of the problems he faced with his parents after baptism did take his mind off America, temporarily. Nevertheless, immigration was becoming a passion with him and getting Maren to feel the same way was a goal Peter had subconsciously made with himself.

The day of their baptism a week later, had been calm, scarcely a puff of wind could be felt. Seagulls were gliding quietly above the oceanfront, and the waves rolling in softly across the sand. Maren, dressed in a white gown was completely immersed beneath the sea by Elder Snow. Then Peter, also dressed in white was likewise baptized by immersion.

The day before the weather had been stormy. Like Peter's mind, which had been in turmoil over whether or not to be baptized, the weather was cold, damp, with a drizzling rain. Confusion and darkness were present, his mind felt clouded, and before the day ended Peter felt as if he had wrestled with the devil himself. He had paced the dormitory, knowing he would go through with it only wishing things would be easier. Trouble with his family was one thing, but the word Mormon was fast becoming a dirty word in Copenhagen, and church members were looked upon as something less than head lice. Superstition and ignorance had reared their ugly heads at the rapid growth of the church in Denmark and events such as Elder Snow's beating in Norre Park were becoming commonplace.

Even before his baptism, Peter had been shunned. One classmate, a tall, big-boned and muscular son of a Lutheran priest, had actually slammed him up against a wall. "I'm praying for you Mormon," he growled. "Praying for your damned soul!" Peter could still smell the big Dane's tepid breath, feel the splash of spittle spewing from his mouth, and hear his attacker's stinging words.

The incident left him terribly upset and caused Peter to wonder whether or not he was doing the right thing by becoming a Mormon. That evening the answers to his prayers finally came. Darkness cleared away, joy filled his soul and Peter made up his mind once and for all. He was baptized the next day and as he'd come out of the water, the sun was shining and the peace he felt was indescribable. He knew he had not taken an easy path into the future, but Peter never doubted his decision again.

"Did Christ really live?" he heard Elder Snow repeating. "Does he live today? Re-established upon the earth after a long and dark apostasy, is this church I speak of really the true Church of Jesus Christ, or is this church the church of Joseph Smith?

"You will never know my brothers and sisters, unless you study it all out yourself. Study and then you must ask God."

"The great battles of life take place in the chambers of the mind my friends," he said wrapping it up. "Are you looking for a better life? Are you looking for inner peace? Then I say to you, read the Book of Mormon, and pray about what I've presented. Pray about it. Because what I've taught you tonight is true. This message I leave with you in the name of Jesus Christ, Amen."

"Amen," said the congregation in unison.

Chapter 38

The next speaker was a short, firm and rather plump fellow with a balding head. His name was Elder Richards and he went straight to his subject.

"As most of you know the headquarters of the church is located in western America or Deseret[2] as the land is called. Or Zion[3] as the church has dubbed it. The call brothers and sisters is to gather. Gather to Zion!"

At this point the crowded room came alive with discussion; who would go, who wouldn't. Zion was it? The very word was filled with hope, especially to a people so recently defeated in war. On the other hand, the citizens of Copenhagen had not felt the ravages of war like those on the mainland and most were very content with Denmark. They would stay and build Zion there.

Zion had many meanings. According to latter-day revelation, it meant the pure in heart. The word spoke of Christ and hopes of living around a Christ-like people. But pulling up stakes and immigrating to a strange country, leaving the motherland? Preposterous! The word Zion also aroused fear and great uncertainty.

"Cities are springing up all over western America my friends,"

Elder Richards continued after everyone quieted down, "there are opportunities galore! There's room to breathe out there, everyone that comes gets five acres of land with no other cost than farming it. In Zion there are blue skies, snow-capped mountains, green pines, fertile valleys and abundant rivers; rivers running cold and clear and teeming with fish."

Nobody in the room was asleep at this point and Peter Jensen was on the edge of his seat. So were many others. But not Maren Carlsen. "Why this sudden urging to get us to immigrate to America, Brother Richards?" she blurted out.

The audience immediately hushed. Lamps hissed and fluttered, causing shadows to flit about the storeroom like the skirts of ghosts, and Elder Richards looked at Maren with a bit of surprise on his face.

"And what about the American war over slavery?" she added sarcastically. Maren was somewhat embarrassed to be speaking up this way but she was earnest. "I hear there has been much bloodshed in America and that the worst is yet to come."

"That's what I hear," agreed a young man leaning on the post near Peter. There was an ugly scar on his right jaw caused by a doctor's crude scalpel as he'd dug out an abscess. Elder Richard's keen eyes looked him over sympathetically. If it hadn't been for the scar he'd have been a handsome fellow.

"The church has long encouraged a gathering to Zion," Elder Snow answered for Elder Richards as he joined him at the makeshift podium. "But as America's civil war intensified, immigration became impossible. Southern ports were blockaded and the ports in the north were crowded with military personnel and essential freight. All that has changed."

"I've recently come from America and the war is all but over. Emigration is underway once again. A ship left Liverpool only last month." Many in the crowd looked doubtful and there was whispering.

"There are still skirmishes here and there to be sure," Snow went on, "but the rebels are beaten I assure you. All that's left to do is get them to the bargaining table. By the time our expedition is organized it will all be settled."

"Make no mistake brothers and sisters," Elder Richards took over, "the civil war caused much destruction. There is great poverty not to mention some very bitter feelings, especially in the Southern States. And there are dangers in the land. Roving bands of robbers and thieves are prevalent. A group of former rebel soldiers calling themselves Quantril's Raiders, wreak havoc everywhere they go."

"But you must understand, Zion is in the far western part of America. Well over a thousand miles away from any fighting. It has been untouched by the war. Largely untouched by human hand for that matter."

An over-land trek of a thousand miles was hard to imagine for a people who lived on a relatively small island. Other than looking out across the ocean, they had very little perspective of such distance. The crowd remained skeptical.

"What about the Indians?" A woman in the center asked nervously. "Savages. I've heard they scalp people, bury them alive, and let the ants eat at their heads."

At that the small congregation came alive. War they understood, but the subject of Indians, albeit filled with foreboding, was strange and very unusual to them. They had nothing to relate it to. People talked in twos, threes and fours; and for a while the small storeroom sounded like an auction house. Everyone had an opinion. Everyone had a story and all were filled with the sensationalism of dime novels. "Please come to order," Elder Richards pleaded. "Please." The room quieted, and Richards cleared his throat. "Indian tribes such as the Navajo are peaceful," he began, "as are most of the neighboring tribes out west . . ."

"Don't hold anything back Elder Richards," Elder Snow interrupted patiently. "There's been a little too much sugar coating tonight as it is. Tell them about the Bannocks, the Utes, and the renegade bands of Apaches. Let's don't paint a rosy picture here."

"Right," said Richards somewhat annoyed. "Certain tribes can be very treacherous," he admitted reluctantly. "Whole families have been butchered by these types. Homes and barns have been burned to the ground and livestock driven to the four quarters of the land." Again, there was murmuring. "But this kind of thing doesn't happen very often. As to sugarcoating, I am sorry to admit it brothers and sisters, but your life in Zion will not be without danger, and certainly not without work. Death and difficulty stalks the oceans and stalks the plains."

He let that sink in for a moment. Everyone in the room knew there had been martyrs to the faith and they knew there would be more, but to be slaughtered by savages, or to drown in the ocean? What possible connection to the gospel could that have?

"But hear me now," Richards went on knowing he had thoroughly frightened them. "If you keep the commandments of God, he will bless you. I can tell you story after story where the faithful have been preserved from harm."

"And many stories where the disobedient have brought troubles upon themselves," injected Elder Snow.

Richards looked over at Snow curiously. He wanted to tell him to shut up at that point but went on patiently. "We're not entirely foolish when it comes to dealing with renegade Indians brothers and sisters. For one thing we band together for protection. There are also military outposts, and soldiers to protect you. Furthermore in some cities the saints have built forts. Members of the church have formed militias and *all* men out west must own a gun. It's the law."

"I've never owned a gun in my life," interrupted one man.

"I've never even shot one," said another.

"You'll be taught," said Richards. "But we're getting away from the subject here . . ."

"If what Brother Richards is saying frightens you brothers and sisters," Elder Snow jumped in, "or if you simply don't want to leave Denmark, then it's my advice to stay and help build the church right here. There are dangers here as well as in America, we all know that; but where ever you are, if you die or get yourself killed while in the service of the Lord, for what better cause may I ask?"

"Hear, hear," said a man seated in the back of the room.

Snow looked around the room taking a mental survey. Now that they had heard the good and the bad he wanted to see how many were still ready to leave Denmark. To his astonishment there seemed to be more women than men wearing a look of determination.

"Then again," Snow went on, "some of you might want to brave the robbers and the Indians for the sake of adventure or for owning land in America. Here I must tell you honestly, here I must warn you. If you do gather to Zion, make sure you do it for Christ's church! Not for any dream of riches, or of owning land. The territory is harsh. It's all mountains, deserts, rocks and sagebrush . . . it's a wild and rugged land and needs to be tamed, cleared for use."

"If you think life will be easier in Zion than it is right here, you'll be sadly mistaken. Winters there are just as long, dark, and cold. And people are the same there as here. Some are mean and foul, the very scum of the earth, others are saints and there are those in-between."

"That's right brothers and sisters," Elder Richards injected sincerely. "There are people in America who simply hate us. And the worst of all are the apostates. Former Mormons." There were ripples of discussion at this, but they quieted away rapidly.

"Why are apostates to the cause, worse than people who had never joined?" one man wanted to know.

"Is apostasy common?" Still another asked.

"Why don't those who have left the church or else dropped out simply leave the church alone?"

"These are hard questions," Elder Richards said, but knowing his companion wouldn't tolerate any more sugar coating he answered each as honestly as possible and thought he was doing very well.

When fifteen minutes later a new investigator had a question she knew would stir things up again but she wanted to know and did not care the outcome. The lady's name was Casten Pedersen, coincidentally a long time friend of Peter Jensen's mother. The wife of Otto Pedersen, former Friends of Farmers party chairman, Casten had moved to Copenhagen along with her husband. The two were fighting because Casten was investigating the Mormons and Otto had forbidden it. Their arguing had become so bitter that Casten was considering divorce. She was a particularly attractive lady with striking features, a noble air about her, and her attitude was that of a schoolteacher—inquisitive and thoughtful.

"I want to know about polygamy," the intelligent looking woman stated rather than asked.

If Peter Jensen had been home more over the last few years he might have known who she was. As for Casten, she had only seen Peter as a boy, not the handsome, bearded, adult there in the congregation. And since Jensen was the surname of half the people in

Denmark, an introduction wouldn't mean anything either. They didn't know each other.

Everyone in the room was all ears at Casten's question. Peter, like the members who were present, knew about the practice of polygamy. It was one of the things he had wrestled with prior to his baptism and the question came up every single time a new investigator attended a fireside such as this.

"What do you want to know about the Principle?" said Richards. Church members called the curious institution of plural marriage "the Principle" short for the Principle of Celestial Marriage, and it did give the practice a sort of dignity, if dignity could be given to such a curious and often times inflammatory teaching.

"Everything," is what Casten said as she folded her arms and looked Richards straight in the eye.

"Well there won't be time for everything," said Richards without blinking, "but the Principle of Celestial[4] Marriage is God's law to his Church at this point in time.

As revealed to the Prophet Joseph Smith, the law presents an opportunity of great faith and tremendous sacrifice for the Saints."

"I have my own personal views on the subject and I'll share them with you: The saying, 'The hand that rocks the cradle rules the earth', contains more truth than poetry. Faithful Latter-day Saint women outnumber Latter-day Saint men by a significant margin, and make no mistake, women by virtue of their loving, kind and nurturing ways build strong testimonies of Christ in the hearts and minds of their offspring." A few women looked at each other knowingly while, like Peter, other men were shifting around on their seats.

"As we all well know, Old Testament patriarchs lived the law of plural marriage," Richards continued. "Abraham, Isaac, Jacob and many other righteous men of the day had more than one wife and

God sanctioned it. As he did then, God has divine purposes for imposing the law upon the Church again in this day and time. My opinion is that building up a righteous seed, or better yet laying a strong foundation for His Church is the main reason for the practice of plural marriage, both in Old Testament times and now."

Richards was *not* quoting from the book of Doctrine and Covenants on the exact wording of the law of Celestial Marriage but every eye was upon him. Everyone wanted to hear more so he squared his shoulders and continued. "Even with the potential of safety, unity, strength and joy the Principle can bring, it is definitely not a practice for everyone. Not for base, jealous, and selfish people, that's for certain. And where any of that exists in polygamous marriages, there has been great heartache I can assure you. Truth be known, only a relative few of the saints practice it, however the Principle is open to faithful members of the church and it is legal[5] in America.

Local church authorities must interview those willing to submit to the law, and in many cases brethren and sisters are "called" to join the order of plural marriage. The first wife must agree upon which woman will join a given family and the husband must be willing and able to take upon himself the extra burdens, financial and otherwise, that come."

Peter's mouth was very dry at this juncture. His palms were sweating and he dared not look at Maren or anyone else for that matter. He wondered what other men were feeling.

"The principle of plural marriage," Richards continued, "insures that any good and decent woman can have a God-fearing and honorable man as a husband; a man to love, honor and protect her and provide for her children."

"Not obey?" said Casten Pedersen to which several women snickered, which thing broke the tension Richards felt at present.

"After the first wife approves, the church must sanction the union," he went on much relieved, "and the wedding be performed in the proper place and by the proper authority. All must agree . . . the wives, the husband, and the church. Is there anything else you want to know?"

"How many wives do you have Brother Richards" Maren asked pointedly.

"I have three," he answered directly, humbly.

Silence prevailed momentarily and the tension returned.

"Do you have any other questions madam?" Richards then asked.

"Many," answered Casten astutely. "But this is neither the time nor place."

The whole experience was an enigma to Elder Richards. He had thoroughly expected the obviously refined woman to get up and walk out of the meeting. Beautiful and beautifully dressed, without saying more than a dozen words, the woman had taken control of his meeting. And now she had respectfully given it back to him. She seemed subdued, yet still intrigued. Richards watched as she took a deep breath and adjusted her composure; then he thought he saw just the trace of a smile. Was she about to laugh? He could not figure her out. *Very well,* he thought, *at least she isn't frowning.*

"Now we've given you a glimpse of what to expect in Zion," injected Elder Snow wiping his forehead, "September of next year, this mission will charter a ship bound for the United States of America. The voyage will take from eight to ten weeks depending. From there you will travel by wagon for approximately eleven hundred miles to the valley of the Great Salt Lake. Those of you inclined to emigrate must begin making plans. That being said, are there any other questions? About anything."

"Getting back to the land, what if a person doesn't need five acres?" asked a man seated to Maren's left. "I'm a shoe maker. All I want is a small place for business."

"No problem there," said Snow. "Just refuse the land, or barter your five acres for a plot in town."

"Is my trade needed?" asked the man.

"You must be joking," said Elder Snow. "A shoemaker? Where is a shoemaker not needed?"

"Every trade is needed brother," Elder Richards took up. "Mechanics, tanners, coopers, millers, tinners, black smiths . . . You name it, there is a need. Like you my brother, not everyone farms. I myself am a school teacher."

The young man with the scar, a fisherman about Peter's age raised his hand. "What if a person wants more than five acres of land?" he asked suspiciously. "Can you get more?"

"My friend have you ever seen five acres of land in one place?"

"I've seen a million acres of water," was the reply.

The crowd snickered.

"Do you think you could plow more than five acres of ground and harvest the crop?" Snow asked.

"If my children were hungry, I could plow a hundred," said the scarred and athletic looking man.

Most of the men in the room, Peter Jensen excepted, had seldom seen five acres of land all in one spot. Jammed into the tenements of Copenhagen toiling from daylight till dark on fishing boats, the docks, or at their trades, few had seen a patch of ground any larger than Norre Park.

"To answer your question," said Richards, "if you have a large family you can get more than five acres, but five is all most people want, believe me."

"The only dirt I've ever owned has been under my fingernails," said the man to which laughter again lightly went around the room. "I was just wondering."

Maren wasn't having as much fun as the other listeners. Her brows were knitted and her face a study of anxiety. Peter on the other hand was tingling with excitement. The old wooden box he was sitting on creaked and groaned as he shifted around. "Think of it," he whispered as he leaned over to Maren. "We could have an estate all our own. Not as large as mother's, but . . . land! Ours for the taking . . ."

"What's wrong Maren?"

"I'm afraid," she whispered.

He put an arm around her. "Don't you see what this could mean?" he whispered back. "We could have a place of our own. We'd be free of kings, free of government restrictions. Free of . . ."

"I like Denmark!" she said out loud.

People turned to watch the young couple, and Brother Richards cleared his throat and coughed politely trying to regain the floor.

Maren glared at Richards briefly, then embarrassed she lowered her head, and refused to look at anybody.

Footsteps overhead reminded her of the crowded apartment she currently called home. She was still sleeping with her sister but she loved the coziness of home. She loved her parents too, and if she immigrated to America they would never see the grandchildren. That bothered Maren more than anything.

"Are there any more questions?" asked Snow off-handedly.

"What is it like crossing the great deep Brother Snow?" a man named Nils Peder Nielsen asked sincerely.

"Yes, tell us," asked his wife, Kathryn.

"As you fishermen know, the sea can be a gentle lady or a brutal monster. Ships have improved greatly over the years. They're larger, faster and have better services available. My last trip was almost a pleasure. There was only one death on board and very little sickness. But it's a long and tedious voyage," he added. "You think it will never end."

Chapter 39

The air in the storeroom had become ripe by the time the meeting ended. A closing hymn was sung, a prayer offered and a few people stayed to chat and drink some cold water from a keg outside. But eventually everyone went his or her separate ways.

Maren, of course, was home and with the outside door to the storeroom open, she and Peter were standing in the back alley facing each other. Patchy clouds drifted across the moon, the fall air was crisp, cool, and in the moonlight they could see clotheslines strung from apartment to apartment. Softly tiptoeing across the balcony of the flat next door, a cat stopped to meow while inside the silhouette of an old woman carrying a dish of milk could be seen crossing a lighted window.

"America is about all you think about lately," said Maren. "Am I right Peter?" she added when he didn't answer.

"Yes," he admitted miserably. There was much more there at the moment. The subject Casten Pedersen had opened up for one, but of even more concern and interest to Peter was the discussion of occupations needed in Zion.

Maren just stood there numbly. She had honestly hoped he'd

forgotten about America, but deep down knew he never would. She loved Peter more than life and subconsciously had been struggling with the question of immigration ever since he had posed it.

"Going to America is so right for me Maren," he went on almost pleadingly, "but I naturally have two concerns. The first of course is whether or not you'll go with me . . ."

"And the second?" she asked sighing heavily.

"What I'd do to earn a living once I get there," he admitted.

"What's wrong with architecture?" she asked somewhat irritably.

"A three year apprenticeship," he replied quickly. "Three or four years at slave wages Maren."

"We all have things we don't want to do," she said as she untied her bonnet to let her head cool. "It was getting warm in there," she added as she closed her eyes and rubbed her throbbing temples. "Where I'm concerned . . . I just don't want to leave my family Peter. And I don't really want to leave Denmark."

By her subdued attitude Peter couldn't tell if she'd lost some of her earlier antagonism or not, but he was hopeful, especially at her next statement."But if not architecture, then what would you do to support us?" she asked practically.

"You heard him Maren. There's plenty of land out there. Maybe we could farm . . ."

"What do *we* know about farming?" she asked sarcastically.

He shrugged but quickly recovered. "I know some about it. Look Maren, you know my family has money. I'm not concerned about getting a start. And with Zion growing as it is, maybe I could be an architect. Serve my apprenticeship there."

Maren took in a deep breath and sighed it out. "Why is life so complicated?" she asked him, her head low and shaking back and forth. "Surely you don't expect a decision from me right here and now?"

"My plans all depend upon you Maren. I won't go anywhere without you. Not to America, not anywhere. If staying in Denmark is what you want, then I'll stay."

"You'd be miserable for the rest of your life and you know it," she said weakly. "I can see that." She went to him and he held her.

"It's all so frightening," she said.

"You'll consider it then," he said pushing her gently away to stare into her eyes. The moonlight gave her an angelic glow and Peter knew she was softening.

"Yes," she said with resignation. "I'll consider it. But please give me some time."

"You heard Elder Richards, we've got clear till next September! Oh Maren," he exclaimed. "Just think of it. We'd be pioneering a new land. It would be such an adventure. A new way of life!"

She didn't answer but he took her back into his arms and whirled her around. Then he stopped and kissed her.

"I haven't said yes," she said flustered.

"I'll make you very happy," he said.

"You already do," she answered smiling.

A dense bank of clouds moved across the moon and the sky darkened.

"Maren," came the call from an upstairs window. "It's getting late."

Peter ducked as the window slammed shut. "No snow yet," he teased. "I love you Maren," he added enthusiastically.

"And I love you," she said. Her eyes told Peter she'd go anywhere with him, even to America and his jaunty step down the alleyway revealed his feelings.

"So long my love," he called as he went. "Sleep well!"

Maren watched him round the corner then returned inside the storeroom. She closed the door, locked it and headed sadly, and heavily up the stairs.

As he returned to the dormitories, the night seemed filled with magic for Peter. His life was coming together. At last he was finding direction. He felt exhilarated, emotionally charged and yet strangely relaxed. He knelt by his bed, clasped his hands, lowered his head and poured out thanks to God.

But the next morning while sitting in his room reading a back issue of the Berlingske Tidende, under the headline ***"ENGLISH COMMERCE BRISK WITH EASTERN UNITED STATES"*** the words; ***Update on America's Civil War,*** literally jumped off the page at him. Communication between England and Denmark being more or less constant, with news usually a month or so old still America's war between the states was fascinating, albeit very disconcerting to those who might be thinking of immigration.

"October 19, 1864, Jubal Early launched a surprise attack against Northern forces under command of General Philip Sheridan," the article continued. ***"Thousands killed! Sheridan victorious. Virginia falls!*** Peter read and re-read the details then shaking his head, set the newspaper down and picked up a more recent copy. Under the dateline; November 16, 1864, he read the following, ***"60,000 troops under General William T. Sherman continue to burn their way across Georgia. Atlanta in flames!"***

Where is Virginia? Where is Georgia? Peter wondered as he set the newspaper on his lap. *Is Atlanta as large as Copenhagen? And who is this barbarian William T. Sherman, the Otto Von Bismarck of*

America? Maybe Maren is right, his thoughts continued unhappily. *Why not just stay here. At least our war is over and we know what we are facing. The missionaries may speak lightly of the American conflict but right here under my nose, are printed accounts. It sounds as if their whole country is in flames!*

With the humiliation and aftermath of Denmark's war with Prussia still underfoot, Peter briefly began to question his sanity about going to a war torn land. But then picking up the newspaper he continued to read and when his eyes scanned the last paragraph his discouragement began to dissipate and once again he took to heart. ***"The death knell is sounding all across the Southern States. With ammunition is short supply, Rebel forces on the brink of starvation are surrendering wholesale, or melting away into the forests. It won't be long until they all lay down their arms. The civil war will soon be finished."***

Immigration for dozens of church members from Copenhagen and elsewhere in Denmark was still months away and because of America's war and other discouraging factors, many recent converts would drop their plans to immigrate. Some might even apostatize. Peter knew all that but nothing was going to stop him. Once again he became firm in his resolve. Civil war, or no he would remain steadfast in his decision to go to America. Like no other time in his life, he had direction.

From that day on his enthusiasm for study catapulted to great heights. Peter still lacked enough credits to graduate but as Christmas 1864 approached he found himself at the top of his class.

As for Maren, she still couldn't get comfortable with the idea of leaving Copenhagen, much less Denmark! The charming old city, with its busy streets and quaint shops, held her captive like a princess in a castle. Maren was in love with the parks, in love with the shops and the bustle of city living. It was all so civilized! To cross a vast and turbulent ocean, then travel thousands of miles in a dusty and dirty old wagon to settle in a new and raw land were huge and terrifying thoughts to her. She could scarcely entertain them. Peter's dreams were her nightmares.

Lars Carlsen had taken his daughter's joining the Mormon Church fairly well. Was it the rent the Mormons were paying on the storeroom? He'd never admit it. No Lars was fine with his daughter being a Mormon, but then one evening as he and Maren were closing up, things came to a head over the issue of immigration.

The store was quiet, Maren and Lars were straightening up after finishing with a rash of poor customers buying needles, thread and buttons. "I hate selling buttons," said Lars making small talk. "The bloody little things take more time than anything and net us so little money. But we must carry them I suppose."

"Oh we need to carry them all right," Maren said sagely and when he didn't comment she swallowed and said, "You know Copenhagen is very crowded Father. Lots of poor, and otherwise . . ."

"You couldn't tell it by the number of customers today," he interrupted. "But what are you saying?"

"Well, oh . . . well—it's just that Peter has been thinking—that is we have both been talking about . . ."

He looked at her curiously. "What is it girl," he demanded.

"Oh I might as well come out and say it," she said lowering her head. What Maren wanted that evening was her father's advice regarding immigration, not necessarily his permission but for the next ten minutes Lars Carlsen listened as his daughter poured out her heart. Yes, she and Peter were thinking about going to America. A rich, vast country brimming over with opportunities, but she was afraid, confused. Could he, her father guide her, could he tell her if what she and Peter were thinking about and talking about was a good thing?

"The missionaries tell us we could own several acres of land Father, and would not have to pay a single farthing for it. All we have to do is claim it, work it and just live there. And the job opportunities Father, opportunities beyond anything we might imagine here in Denmark."

As she rambled on, Maren knew she was trying to persuade herself *and* her father at the same time. "Peter and I could get a farm," she continued. "Build a home of our own. A nice, large one." She almost said, 'and you and mother could come and visit' but knowing how ridiculous that would sound she hastened on. "We'd have room for several children—what would you think of it Father?"

At first Lars had been patient, nodding and shaking his head when appropriate rubbing his chin; now he was staring at Maren as if she were crazy. And just at that moment the bell on the front door jingled. Good thing as Lars was about to explode in a rage. An elderly, wealthy customer and her two granddaughters came in. "Good day Hr Carlsen," the old lady said as she began milling about the store.

"May I help you find something? Said Lars walking away from Maren hoping to cool himself off.

He didn't even remember taking the wealthy woman's money when she left, and now it was just about closing time, the last customer, again an elderly woman, had just walked out. Tired from a long day on his feet, and having little in the register to show for it, the shopkeeper decided to confront his daughter head on.

Maren was now near the front of the store absently folding some cloth she had just shown the old woman. She was humming quietly, somewhat nervously.

"Had you put your mind into it Maren," Lars said sharply as he grabbed the cloth from her hands, "you could have easily sold this piece to her! Lately, all you do is daydream!"

"She claimed it was too coarse Father," Maren apologized, "but she really didn't have any money. I could tell it."

"You were still daydreaming!" shouted Lars. "You didn't wait on her 'til she was almost out the door."

"You've been daydreaming ever since you came back from Holbaek and started up with the Mormons again. Speaking of whom," he roared, "they must be out of their minds. Can't they read the papers; America is still at war! The whole stinking, uncivilized place is in an uproar. Do you know they have so many kinds of money, people are killing each other over it! Bartering that's all they do. Mormon idiots! I should never have rented them the storeroom!"

Her father's words stung like salt in the eyes, but all Maren could do was listen. Everything was out now, there was nothing to hide and where it all went, heaven knew.

"And what in the name of might is the matter with Peter Jensen?" Lars continued to rail. "Is he insane? Leave his inheritance!?"

"Oh, that's all you care about him!" Maren the shouted back, surprised at her instant ire. "Greed Father. It shows all over your face!"

Lars slapped her face so fast it shocked both father and daughter. "You'll not talk to me that way young lady!" he bellowed. He wasn't a strong man but Hr. Carlsen's blow knocked Maren off balance and left fingerprints on her cheek.

Her ears were ringing, her head felt numb and her eyes hurt. Maren whirled away. She grabbed her shawl from the coat rack and stormed out of the store. She didn't stop her rapid pace until she'd reached the center of Norre Park. There she took a seat on a park bench, buried her face in her hands, and sobbed.

When Maren finally wiped her eyes and began to look about herself, her cheek was still burning from the slap. There were a few pigeons strutting around, and in the flowerbeds the foliage of summer looked withered and dying, just like Maren's spirit. But overhead a mighty oak seemed to be standing guard over the injured girl. "I will never be treated like a child again," Maren said under her breath, and taking heart she clenched her fist. "And I'm going with Peter," she added determinedly. "I'm going to America."

As soon as the word America left her mouth Maren felt her heart glow within her breast. Just as Peter had done, she'd received confirmation. Immigrating to America and settling in Zion was the right thing for her to do. Maren's answer came from God and there was no denying it.

After a time she returned to the store and started in where she'd left off, folding rumpled cloth and straightening shelves. There were no further words between she and her father. Lars too had calmed down and was very glad to see his daughter. Glad she'd returned, but there was a great sadness about the merchant as he watched the graceful girl out of the corner of his eye. Lars knew for certain his little bird was about to leave the nest.

Chapter 40

December 18, 1864 the University of Copenhagen closed its doors for the Christmas holidays. A week after that, with his personal effects packed in a trunk and Maren sitting at his side, Peter Jensen, the would-be immigrant to America, was headed home. That is, he was headed back to Holbaek. Were it not for Catherine, Inger, Torkil and the mill hands Peter might very well have spent his holidays in Copenhagen. He couldn't wait to see his mother and enjoy the holiday festivities, however he could hardly stomach dealing with Elias, Ferdinand and Krista again.

Maren finally told him she'd also decided to go to America, the day after her confrontation with her father. Her reasons for leaving Denmark were as complex as Peter's. Being with him was paramount but like Peter she had obtained the spirit of gathering to Zion. Maren also had a strong testimony of the Book of Mormon, of Joseph Smith as a Prophet of God, and she loved the Gospel of Christ. These things were undeniable. Marriage to Peter was a certainty and Maren wanted to live amongst the Latter-day Saints and raise her children in a new clean land. A land of mountains, lakes, rivers, springs, clean water and air. Away from crowded conditions! Once Maren had made up her mind to leave Denmark, Copenhagen looked more and more dreary as the days progressed.

Maren had become very close friends with Gunda and Claus Wangsgaard, the newly called west side Branch President and his wife; and was working with them in fund raising projects to aid the poorer members of the Church who were likewise planning to immigrate. Maren had great compassion for the downtrodden and found under Hr. Wangsgaard and his wife, an organized way of serving. Under their direction, she started a quilt making society; ladies who set up their quilting-frames in various homes and then sold their production on consignment in Lars Carlsen's store. Lars knew the money would be used for immigration, but didn't believe Maren would really leave Denmark. 'When push comes to shove, she will change her mind,' he had told his wife.' No Lars didn't mind selling the quilts; with winter coming on the demand was great and so were profits.

"I'm sure Mother will give us her blessings Maren," Peter was saying as their rented buckboard bumped along the country road towards the Jensen estate. The way was clear. There were a few patches of snow here and there and pockets of mud and ice made the road interesting, but so far winter had been relatively mild. Rails were complete all the way from Copenhagen now, and after arriving by train in Holbaek Peter had scoured the town and had finally rented the jolting, spring-less conveyance from the town's blacksmith. The buckboard's wobbly rear wheel, and primitive suspension gave the old wooden relic a personality all its own, especially around curves.

"And I'm equally sure mother will give me money for passage, and for a good start in America," Peter went on.

"You really think so?" said Maren doubtfully.

"I'm sure of it," said he flipping the reins. Like steam from a small train, his breath chuffed out in steamy vapors. The temperature was hovering around zero and with the wind now in their faces, it felt much colder. Peter had on his greatcoat and Maren an indigo blue woolen coat with matching hand muffler.

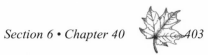

"Oh, I do hope you're right Peter," she said with little enthusiasm. "It would make it all so nice. Your mother and I have become such friends."

"And that won't change regardless," Peter said naively. "Think of it Maren," he went on, his voice loud enough to be heard over the thudding hooves and churning wheels. "Our own estate in America! Why, we'll have cattle, horses, pigs, chickens . . ."

"And children," she interjected.

"And children!" he agreed as he put his arm around her. "As many as you like! But Maren," he added, suddenly becoming very pensive, "Perhaps I'm sounding too worldly."

"It's not wrong to want a better life Peter," she said more loudly than she wanted. "I, too, want to spread my wings. Do you think I want to spend my entire life in Father's store?"

"We're going to America for Christ, Maren," Peter reminded her. "To serve in His church. To live with a people who share our beliefs and who are working together in a grand cause. We can never forget that."

"I know Peter," she sighed. Sometimes he was too devoted. She wished he wasn't so serious all the time.

Hearing her sigh he quickly altered his course. "I truly want to help build Zion, Maren; but I also want to help make the desolate valleys we've been told about, blossom like the rose. Help build a city, one like Holbaek, a clean place for people to live!"

"That's what I want Peter. And at our home I'm going to have a beautiful garden. One just like your mother's."

The frosty countryside was passing in review at a fair pace. Trees were naked of leaves. The hard winter months of January and February were waiting in the wings; meanwhile, as Peter and Maren bumped semi-pleasantly along, one would think they were discussing a walk on the beach, or a boat ride up Holbaek Fjord, not of putting an entire ocean between family members. Not the permanent uprooting of untold generations.

Peter didn't mind taking risks. The harsh realities of his planned venture had broken many men and women. But Peter chose not to dwell on the stories of doom regarding ocean travel he had heard. Wasn't it true that no vessel carrying Mormons had ever sunk? Ship captains liked having Mormons aboard; although some were obnoxiously self-righteous, they were industrious, never drunk and disorderly, and they brought luck to the voyage.

As the carriage arrived on the Jensen lands, the first thing that came into view was the gristmill tucked against the hillside, north of the large house. Its wind-wings weren't turning but the sight of its substantial presence made Peter's heart swell.

"Get up," he urged the team. "Get up there!"

The buckboard reached a gate in the fence about a hundred yards from the house where a man stood holding a shovel. He looked as if he'd been digging a posthole.

"I saw you coming," was his greeting. "Thought I'd see to the gate."

"Thank you very much," called Peter. "You're new here aren't you?"

"I've been here two months now. My name is Parkinsen. Bradley Parkinsen. And you must be Peter?"

"I am," said Peter enthusiastically.

"Your mother's been expecting you for a week now, master Jensen. And how are you madam?" Parkinsen said tipping his hat toward Maren.

"Fine thank you sir," said Maren a bit nervously.

"Your mother is down at the stables," Brad Parkinsen told Peter.

"Thank you," he acknowledged, "I'd like to surprise her. Could you please see to our buckboard?" he then asked as he stepped down and reached up to Maren. "Park it in front of the house. I'll unload the luggage in a while."

"Right sir," the man said as he stiffly mounted the seat. Although he should have, he didn't offer to unload the luggage. He was a listless fellow, his coat was dirty, moths had been at it, and Parkinsen looked like he'd been leaning on his shovel far more than he'd been digging with it.

Peter and Maren crossed the fence and walked the distance to the corral where they saw Catherine and Nils Holsen standing near a young colt. Peter wondered if Krista Holsen was still lingering about the place. If he hadn't had his head so high in the clouds, he'd have realized that whether she was around or not, her pregnancy was coming to a rapid conclusion; and that he, Peter Jensen, would soon become an uncle.

Catherine was wearing a heavy dress and coat, high button shoes and her hair was pulled back in a bun. Her face was flushed and there were loose strands of hair blown about her head; but rather than looking exuberant which she usually did when out of doors, she appeared bone tired.

"Peter! Maren!" she exclaimed and her face lighted as she saw them. "I've been expecting you for days."

The colt, which Nils held securely by its mane, had moments before been caught in the gate by its head and rear leg making extradition nearly impossible and definitely dangerous. Catherine, who'd been coming up from the mill, had heard its frightened whinnying. She and Nils, who also heard the colt's cries, had to nearly take the gate apart to free the frightened animal and now Nils was stroking its neck soothingly.

"Take the colt to the barn and give him some oats," Catherine told him.

"Yes Madam," said Nils. "Welcome home Peter.. and Miss Maren," he said nodding their direction.

"Thank you Hr Holsen," said Maren as she watched Nils lead the colt away.

"My goodness Peter," Catherine exclaimed. "What took you so long to get here? The University closed a week ago."

"I know Mother," he said kissing her on her rosy cheek, "but I had some things to finish up. By the way," he added with much enthusiasm, "my marks this semester have me at the top of the class."

"How wonderful," Catherine said. "But of course, I expected nothing less."

"How is Father?" Peter asked hesitantly.

"Elias is much improved," Catherine said. "Much improved."

"And Ferdinand . . ."

"He's fine," said Catherine somewhat coolly. "We've had our problems. I couldn't get him to start back to school, but with you and Hans gone, I didn't try very hard," she paused, "he's a lot of help when he wants to be . . ."

"And how are you Maren?" she said quickly changing the subject, walking over to hug her. "You seem a bit shaky."

“It’s nothing Fru Jensen. Just glad to be out of that bumpy wagon.”

“It has got a bad wheel,” Peter explained then turned to see the buckboard just cresting a slight incline near the house. “I need to fix it while I’m here or it may not get us back to Holbaek.” He wanted to ask her about the new man, but really didn’t care and would get to it only when it came up.

Are things all right at the mill?” he then asked as he looked across the fields toward the ancient structure. The mill’s wind wings were now turning slowly in the breeze and the two men working outside looked like dwarfs in a fairy tale.

“We’re still making flour,” Catherine replied proudly. “But we’ve come to the end of the season. There’s been such a demand this year that the farmers are emptying their silos. We’ll soon be forced to shut down.”

“But never mind that. Let’s go to the house and see everyone.” She had regained her worn composure, but Peter was worried about his mother. Not knowing just how he would approach the subject of leaving Denmark, he was hesitant to enter the house. They were home for the holidays weren’t they? Best to leave the subject alone for a few days. He and Maren had earlier agreed to take it slowly. Let the holidays progress, then at just the right moment, perhaps when everyone was merry with wine, sort of mention it. But knowing his mother as he did, Peter knew it would be better to come right out and tell her then and there and be done with it. Worry about Elias later.

“Mother,” he said awkwardly. “I need to talk to you . . . about a rather important matter.”

Catherine thought she knew exactly what her son wanted to discuss but as disheveled as she was, she wouldn’t hear it just yet.

She wanted to share her son and Maren's joy but not while she was wearing grubby old work clothes.

"Is everything alright?" she asked teasingly.

"Of course Mother, but . . ."

"Peter," she said cutting him off. "I don't want to talk about anything serious just yet. Let me get out of this old coat, wash up and put on a clean dress . . . besides your father ought to be in on this conversation too. Let's go to the house."

"But . . ."

Catherine had already started walking. "Come on," she said happily. "Your father will be so glad to see Maren. Lately he's been talking quite a bit about her."

Chapter 41

Catherine led the way down a narrow trail of flattened grass, a trail bordered by high grasses bent and coated with a light brush of snow. The walk left their shoes wet and muddy and by the time they reached the house, Peter felt ready to talk to his father. Ferdinand, just up from the mill, was standing on the porch to greet the trio and his attitude was one of mock formality.

"Peter," he said ceremoniously. "What a pleasure to have you back. And Maren," he said taking her hand and kissing it. "You're becoming just like family." Ferdinand still acted as if he owned the house rather than just residing there, and for a brief moment Peter felt like striking him.

"I will soon be a member of the family," Maren blushed. "That is . . ."

Catherine put an arm around Maren and hugged her. "I'm so excited to have you here Maren. I'm afraid I wasn't much company last visit."

"And how is the university?" asked Ferdinand with all the haughtiness his father displayed on occasions such as this. He took Peter by the arm and started to lead him inside.

"Not so bad," said Peter, pulling away. At the moment he'd lost all enthusiasm for leaving Denmark. *How can I do this thing?* he thought bitterly. *Leave my portion to the likes of my little brother? He's still plotting to take it all. I can see it in his eyes.* Peter had to reach inside himself for resolve. This wouldn't be as easy as he'd imagined.

"Now you all go in and see Elias while I freshen up," said Catherine cheerily. "I won't be long."

The trio entered the living room leaving Catherine to retire upstairs to her room.

"Ah Peter," said Elias as he entered the living room and sat in the chair closest to the fireplace. He had just retrieved a stein of beer from the kitchen. "How are you?"

"Fine sir," was Peter's reply as he walked over and took his hand. "Just fine."

Elias had been up and dressed for an hour and though his graying and well-combed beard hid much of his face, it still reflected a prideful demeanor. Taking a seat across from his father, Peter could also sense the old familiar air of intimidation.

"The new man said you'd arrived," Elias said as he took a sip of warm beer, "and I see you've brought your young lady . . ." He coughed then added, "so nice to have you back again my dear." He remembered Maren but had momentarily forgotten her name.

"Would you like something to drink?" he said motioning to the kitchen. "Ferdinand, get them some wine . . ."

"No, thank you," said Maren politely. "I'll get something later." Ferdinand hadn't moved.

"How do you like our Christmas tree?" Elias asked. Having gotten up late he had not yet become inebriated and was in a merry

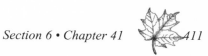

mood. "As usual, Catherine and Ferdinand did a fine job, don't you think?"

"It's lovely Hr Jensen," said Maren sincerely.

"It is," Peter agreed.

Normally there were pine branches, colored ribbons and tinsel hanging all about the house but the tree seemed to be the only vestige of the season. The walls, rafters, and woodwork were without decoration or color and, like the Ghost of Christmas Future, the spirit of Hans seemed to be lingering about. Peter felt the old depressed atmosphere returning.

Ferdinand took the chair nearest his father leaving Peter and Maren to sit on the velvet couch across from them. Ferdinand looked a little tense and for the life of him Peter couldn't understand why. A moment ago he'd been strutting around like a peacock. Now he acted nervous as a cat.

"How was the trip Peter?" Elias asked.

"A bit jarring," Peter answered. "There must have been a lot of rain this year. The roads were quite rough."

"I hope it wasn't too hard on you my dear," said Elias solicitously. "She's such a lovely girl Peter."

"Thank you," said Maren embarrassed.

"So how is your health, Father?" Peter asked.

"Only fair I'm afraid," answered Elias. "My doctors have been very worried." He broke into a light spasm of coughing. "Since the war, and Hans' death, I've been on a steady decline."

"I'm so sorry Hr Jensen," said Maren.

There wasn't a thing wrong with Elias Jensen's ego and the touch of feminine interest caused him to rally instantly. "Ah but with

Catherine's constant fussing over me and with Ferdinand's help around the place," he looked at Ferdinand and nodded, "I've managed to survive."

Actually Elias seemed fairly fit. So far he'd only had one glass of beer and was actually being pleasant. As Peter judged, it was only Catherine who showed signs of wear since the last visit home, and it seemed so unfair.

"Are your parents well my dear?" Elias asked Maren as he shifted in his high backed armchair and coughed again.

"They are Hr Jensen," she answered. "And they send their best."

"It's a wonderful time of year, isn't it?" Elias went on to no one in particular. "So much good will in the air. Peace on earth. Don't you agree Ferdinand?"

"Absolutely," said Ferdinand without emotion.

"Nothing like it Father," said Peter uncomfortably.

"Yes, yes," Elias went on. "Not much snow so far." He covered his mouth to cough. "But cold enough for a fire—and such a festive time of year. You should enjoy your stay young lady."

"Ferdinand, please tell the new maid to bring in some coffee. Do you mind?"

"Of course not," said the younger brother rising from his seat.

"What happened to Inger!?" Peter blurted out.

"I've had to let her go," said Ferdinand over his shoulder.

"*You've* had to let her go?" Peter demanded.

"We've made some changes around here," said Elias firmly.

"A new grounds keeper, I can understand," said Peter still in a state of amazement. "But Inger is family!"

Very shortly a pretty flaxen-haired maid carrying a silver tray with a pot of hot coffee and service for five, followed Ferdinand back into the room. She set the tray on the coffee table, poured everyone a steaming cup then without saying a word but nodding to Elias, she left the room. A light came on in Peter's mind. No wonder his mother looked so care-worn. With Inger gone Catherine probably felt another member of her family had died. The reason the old house had lost so much of its warmth and charm was very clear.

The living room was quiet as everyone sipped their coffee and just as Peter was about to probe further regarding Inger's removal, Catherine came in.

"I've been involved with that smelly little colt most of the morning Peter," she explained briskly. "It feels so nice to be clean again."

Catherine was wearing a soft cotton dress and like Elias, she was graying but more thin than Peter ever remembered. She was too thin. Although she was smiling, and her eyes still carried the confidence they'd born since the night she had worn her beautiful necklace, Catherine's countenance held a pained expression and again, she looked very tired. Her daily struggle with Elias, the loss of Hans, and now Inger had definitely taken their toll.

"You appear well today Elias," she said placing her hand upon his shoulder.

"I am my dear," he announced, "I awoke rather strong in fact," he managed before a cough took his voice.

"Splendid," Catherine answered as she sat down next to him. She poured herself a cup of coffee, sipped it, then closed her eyes and waited as its warmth began to penetrate her weary body. Peter couldn't tell what kind of mood she was in, but what Catherine said next took things right down to business.

"So bring us up to date Peter. What have you and Maren got to tell?" she winked. "As if I didn't know."

"W–well," he began, "there's not much to say. We had an uneventful trip home."

"We did," Maren quickly agreed. "The countryside had every sign of a heavy winter coming on. Thank heaven we had no breakdowns."

"Before we go any further," said Peter trying to regain composure. "I'd like to know what happened with Inger. The house seems so cheerless without her blustering around. It's like we've lost another family member."

"Let's just say we all stopped seeing eye to eye," said Ferdinand trying to be aloof.

Except for Elias slurping his coffee the room went suddenly quiet, then Catherine sighed heavily. "I didn't want to go into all this just now Peter but there's no time like the present I suppose." She turned to Ferdinand and taking an envelope from her apron said, "Ferdinand, take this voucher to the mill and give it to Ole. Peter has a right to know what's been going on and in your absence I'll explain. Furthermore, I think he has something sensitive he wants to discuss, with just your father and I."

"As you wish Mother," said Ferdinand irritably, his attitude suddenly that of a butler or a maitre`d at a hotel. He snatched the envelope from her and stuffed it in his pocket.

"I don't think it necessary that he leave," protested Elias. "What must be said can be heard by all."

"It's all right Father," said Ferdinand haughtily. "I'll be back in a while."

Peter could see the anger in his brother's eyes but he was much more comfortable when Ferdinand had left the house. Catherine was also visibly relieved.

"After you went back to school Peter," Catherine began, "my health took a turn. It started with my trying to force Ferdinand to join you at the university. It was such an ugly scene. But he wouldn't go and so I decided to give him a great deal of responsibility around here. I made him an overseer . . . of a sort. Then, frankly speaking, I lay in bed for two weeks. It took that to get feeling better." She shook her head. "I didn't know emotions could do that to a person."

"Inger didn't take to receiving orders from Ferdinand and left us about a month ago. She wasn't fired mind you, and we do keep in touch. Furthermore, I'm stronger now and Ferdinand doesn't know it but I'm about to put things back the way they were."

At that Elias gave Catherine an angry look. He'd been delighted with Inger's leaving. A few years previously he'd made advances toward the stout little maid and she had not only stomped on his toes with her wooden clogs, she had kicked him in the shins and slapped Elias' face. Ever since the incident he had hated her. The new maid was not only as dainty as Inger was bulky, but as pretty as she was plain. Pleasant scenery for an old man's aging eyes. Unfortunately the girl avoided heavy work such as scrubbing floors, stuffing mattress ticks with new feathers or washing clothes. Other than cooking, setting out coffee or tea, and dusting here and there, she was practically useless. Catherine wasn't amused.

"The main reason I asked Ferdinand to step outside Peter is so I can explain something else to you. It seems our young father to be has taken quite an interest in the new maid and because of it he and Krista Holsen are not speaking."

"That's not exactly true," Elias interrupted.

"Oh, yes it is Elias, and I'll not be told otherwise," Catherine rebutted sharply. “Here Krista’s stomach is as turgid as a bloated cow’s and there has yet to be a wedding! Don’t tell me our young bull hasn’t been sniffing around other pastures. We’ve a grandchild coming any day and it’s high time its immature father takes hold of his responsibilities!” Catherine had to pause to calm herself. It was plain to see she was not about to make herself sick again. She closed her eyes a moment, then continued.

“I’ve been too burdened with grief to push the issue,” she said turning her attention toward Maren. “First I sent Krista home, then I allowed her back in the house . . . then this new maid situation. If I can just get Inger back, and Ferdinand and Krista married, I’m sure things will be all right.”

No one spoke, and Maren stared at her wooden shoes.

“They will have to live here after the baby comes, until I have a house built for them,” Catherine added wearily. “But one way or the other our new little maid will be gone. And I hope you can hear me,” she shouted toward the kitchen.

Peter couldn’t help but smile. To see the old fire rising in his mother was a very good sign. He caught Maren’s eye and winked. So far Elias remained silent.

“So that’s what’s been going on Peter,” Catherine concluded. “Ferdinand overstepped his bounds where Inger is concerned, but rest assured I’ll have her back. Probably by next week. Now I hope that satisfies you.”

“It does Mother. And I’m very sorry for the strain the situation has caused you.”

“No sense crying over spilled milk,” Catherine said changing the distasteful subject. She was still highly agitated. “Now tell us. What are your plans? It’s Christmas time. Why not?” She wanted to say, have a wedding but Catherine checked herself.

She watched both their faces picking up a signal she couldn't decipher. There was to be a wedding, that she believed, but when? There was definitely something in the air where Peter and Maren were concerned, and Catherine wanted it out.

"You've been too hesitant Peter. What is going on?"

'Why ruin a perfectly good evening? He thought. He looked at Maren and then at the floor. "I might as well get it out Mother. As you say, no time like the present."

"I'm afraid what I'm about to say will cause you further grief Mother. But say it I must." The scene was suddenly void of any joy at all and when Peter tried to continue his voice failed him. Had a pin dropped, it could have been heard clear across the room. If she could, Maren would have crawled under the table. As it was she was picking at her coat as if there were lint on it.

"This wasn't how it was supposed to be," said Peter spreading his hands. "Where to begin?"

"What you have to say can't be any worse than what I've just told you," Catherine quipped trying to lighten the atmosphere. "Is there going to be a wedding or not?"

Elias coughed and cleared his throat, but didn't say anything.

"Most assuredly," said Peter. Maren nodded.

"Thank Heaven," said Catherine obviously relieved. "I can already see Maren's wedding dress. What could possibly be troubling you?"

Maren smiled nervously at that and Peter continued. "You know I love Maren. I love her more than life itself. And I love you Mother . . . Father," he added hesitantly. "I know in many ways I've been somewhat of a disappointment to you. But I've tried to be a good person and bring honor to our family."

Elias nodded slightly but Catherine's brow wrinkled. "What could you be talking about?" she asked.

"My past letters for instance," said Peter. "They've been somewhat damning where government and state church are concerned. I realize I have been quite radical. But I'm past that now. Our country is on the mend and I fully support our leaders. Especially the King."

Elias cleared his throat again and coughed. "I'm glad to hear that my boy."

"Hans' death caused me so much grief," Peter went on. "But it has actually been pivotal for me. You also know my love for the Mormon Church. Actually the Church of Jesus Christ of Latter . . ."

"Your letters have been very clear," Elias interrupted sharply.

"What you don't know is that I was recently baptized," Peter went on. "I am now an official member of the Church."

Elias' face went purple then gray, but oddly enough he didn't speak. Peter wondered if he could.

"We've expected it," said Catherine trying to sound matter-of-fact.

"But I want to tell you why I did it Mother. Father." Neither parent said anything. Both were waiting for the other shoe to fall, and they knew it would.

Peter continued. "First off where is Hans? Do we know? Do we really know?"

"Why he's in Heaven of course," grumbled Elias with growing anger. Catherine sat poised, patiently listening. She sensed Peter was about to upset her terribly, but she loved him, was proud of him, and believed she could handle anything.

"I didn't know where Hans was for certain," Peter continued as if not hearing Elias. "But the Mormon Church's teachings have helped me understand perfectly. I not only know where my twin brother is, but also my baby brother. I now understand the true meaning of life. I know why I'm here, I know where I came from, and also where I'm going after I die."

Elias' temperature had not cooled during Peter's brief discourse but he knew if he started arguing that he might become gripped in a coughing spell that would render him useless. It had been so long since Peter had had any dealings with the Lutheran Church it was no wonder he had apostatized. Elias had also stopped attending, his own attachment had waned, but pride kept his eyes and ears closed to anything new where religion was concerned.

Peter drew a deep breath and let it out, then with deep conviction continued on. He spoke from his heart, with honesty, sincerity and without guile. "I also know that the Book of Mormon is the word of God. It is a companion to the Holy Bible. Pure scripture. I know it Mother, Father. I know that the Gospel of Jesus Christ as taught by the Church of the Latter-day Saints is true! And I will do anything I can—anything—to help strengthen the Church and perpetuate the Gospel of Christ."

"All right, all right, enough of this," said Elias impatiently, harshly. "So what," his tirade was interrupted by a short spell of coughing. "what are you trying to say?"

"Just this," Peter continued doggedly, "because of my love for the Church and my deep desire to support it, I.. that is we," he said looking at Maren and she smiled and met his gaze straight on, ". . . have decided to join with others of our faith who are immigrating to America."

Like the death of Hans, the word America pierced Catherine's heart like a dagger, rendering her weak as a kitten. She lowered her head and began to weep. Her body felt leaded and for a brief moment, she seemed unable to move anything but her head.

"Next September," Peter forged ahead, "there's a boat leaving Copenhagen. Maren and I plan to be on it."

"You what?!" croaked Elias as the words finally sunk in. "Leaving Denmark?! Are you mad? Surely you can't be serious! This is the most preposterous thing I've ever heard!" Rising from his chair, he shook his fist at Peter. All fear of a coughing spell had left him. "How in God's holy name could you do such an asinine thing? You'll be the death of us yet!" He sat back down, coughing and clearing his throat.

"We'll come back for visits," Peter offered feebly.

"You will come back for nothing!" scolded Catherine as she raised her head. She clenched her fists. "You are not going Peter! What about your schooling? What about the mill? What about *me?!"*

At that Catherine began to cry. She covered her eyes with her hand and her shoulders were shaking. Nothing she could do or say would dissuade her son from his plans and she knew it. But she could never accept it, and the frustration made her furious.

"You are the eldest son," Elias strained struggling to stand again. "Half heir to this estate . . . to the milling business . . . and you're leaving it? What have these damned fanatic Mormons promised you?!" He was livid and before Peter had a chance to speak Elias turned on Maren.

"And you, you city wench, you actually support this madness?"

Peter was on his feet instantly and face to face with Elias before he had time to breathe. "I won't have you talk to her that way!" he shouted. "Say another word to her and I'll break every bone in your sick old body!"

"Peter!!" Catherine shouted. "Stop it! Both of you stop it this instant!"

Maren wanted to run from the room, but stayed glued to her chair. In her mind she was praying.

"And please sit down," Catherine pleaded. "Both of you. We need to talk this out."

Peter immediately complied, but Elias remained on his feet till his legs began to tremble. For a while, except for some shuffling sounds coming from the kitchen, the room remained silent. Catherine sat with her head bowed and hands clasped firmly together. The whole thing seemed so unreal to her. She'd always known once a child got married, parents saw less of them, but immigrate to another country? In her wildest dreams she never thought she would have to deal with such a thing.

Finally she raised her tortured face then stood and went to the window to stare at the mill. Presently, she turned to face her son. "I have something to say to you Peter." She paused and chose her words. "I do not agree with this desperate measure. It rests very heavily with me to think there'll be oceans and continents dividing our family. I understand your past frustrations with the state church and the Danish government. I can even accept your being baptized a Mormon. Your father and I knew it was coming . . ."

"But to leave Denmark? To throw away your future in architecture and to leave your homeland? Not only is it wrong, it's reckless. You can't possibly know the consequences! Whole generations will be affected."

At that Catherine grew deathly earnest. "I'll not support your actions Peter. There is no possible way!"

"But Mother," Peter said desperately. "You don't understand."

"I understand perfectly!" Catherine countered sharply. "You are selfish and totally ungrateful. Look at what we've done for you—food, shelter, an education. A good life. A very good life! Why, you're not going to America for your religion, you are going to please yourself! An adventure . . . that's how you look at it. A holiday perhaps. How can you be so foolish?"

"I'm not going to please myself Mother," Peter said sincerely. "My desire is to please God. I believe I'll be engaged in His work. And I am grateful for my education," he added. "Very grateful."

"You can serve God right here in Denmark!" Catherine stated loudly. "You don't have to go traipsing off across the globe with a bunch of religious fanatics."

"They're not fanatics Mother," Peter said firmly.

"Peter!" Catherine said in a voice so loud it shocked even Elias. "I'm not going to argue with you! I want you and Maren to leave this house! Leave this very instant! And do not return until you come to your senses!" Catherine was shaking from head to foot as she said this. Not since the night she'd worn her beautiful necklace had Elias seen her in such a fervor.

"B–but Mother," Peter stammered.

"Leave!" Catherine shouted again. "And furthermore Peter, as long as you maintain this silly notion of leaving Denmark I'll not send you another farthing! And you Maren!" She said pointing a menacing finger at the trembling girl. "How could you go along with this? Have you any idea what it would do to your parents?"

Maren couldn't answer. All she could do was cry. Peter put a protective arm around her. "I won't allow anyone to attack Maren, Mother," he said respectfully. "Verbally or otherwise, not even you. Come on Maren," he added pulling her up. "We are leaving. We're leaving and we won't be back!"

Elias had gotten out of his chair and was feebly holding out a hand. "Excuse me Father," Peter said moving Maren firmly but gently into the hall and out the front door. Catherine made no move to stop them.

Ferdinand was on his way back to the house and upon hearing the shouting had quickened his pace. "What's going on here?" he demanded as he came up to Peter. "Where are you two going?"

"I hope you like it here brother," Peter said as he helped Maren onto the buckboard then climbed aboard himself. Their arrival had been tense from start to finish. The new man had not removed their luggage from the buckboard, nor had Peter and there it sat. Peter helped Maren on with her coat and left his own upon his lap. "It's going to be all yours one day."

"What are you talking about?"

"Gid-up" Peter said just as Catherine came out of the house. As she watched her impetuous son whip his team toward Holbaek, she was torn in half. Part of her wanted to call him back and part didn't. "What has happened to this family?" she sobbed mournfully as Elias joined her and Ferdinand. "What have I done? Dear Father in Heaven what have I done?"

The three Jensens were a diverse assortment of emotion as they stood watching the prodigal son speed away. Catherine appeared as if her heart would break, Elias' face was a study of bitterness and anger, and Ferdinand wore a smirk.

"Should I go after them?" he asked artificially.

"You might," said Elias.

"Let it be," said Catherine as she wiped her eyes. "They'll come to their senses." Then shaking her head she repeated, "surely they'll come to their senses. What could a religion possibly teach to make a person give up so much?"

Chapter 42

It was well past dark when the discouraged young couple finally returned to Copenhagen. Exhausted by the day's events they had stayed at Goteberg Inn in Holbaek then a day later were back in the capital city. Norre park seemed a dark and a foreboding place. The lighted street lamps surrounding it gave the trees an eerie and depressing look, a look that matched Peter's mood exactly.

"I'll get a job at the docks," he was saying to Maren. "I'll work like a dog, until I've earned enough to pay for our passage to America. We may have to go as passengers in the steerage, but we're still going!"

"Do you think they're hiring at the docks?" Maren ventured.

"I do," he answered. "I don't know what they pay but loading ships is how most of my classmates get their books and tuition,"

"Where will you stay?" Maren said shaking her head sadly.

"I've still got another week or two at the dorm," he answered as they approached a bench near a street corner. "But there are rooms to let all over town. Let's sit down for a minute."

The trunk they'd been carrying had become heavy and when they reached the bench Maren dropped her end with a thump. “I still have a little money,” Peter said as they sat down, “I’m going to have to stretch it if it’s going to last. Something I’m not used to,” he added.

“I have some money saved,” said Maren without hesitation. “You can have it all if you need it.”

It was the Christmas season but two more miserable souls weren’t to be found in all of Copenhagen. Had things gone as planned, by this time they’d be tucked into soft feather beds at the Jensen estate awaiting the Julifred. Peter and Maren had planned to stay throughout the holidays, enjoying themselves to the fullest, then somewhere during the visit gently break the news that they were planning to leave Denmark. Catherine would have been sad, of course, but in time she’d have gotten used to the idea. Getting her to pay his passage and a little extra for support while Peter got himself established in America would have taken a little doing, but Catherine would have done it and life would have gone merrily along its course!

It all looked so ridiculous now.

Peter looked over at Maren. “Are you still committed to go with me?” he asked.

Yes,” she answered firmly, but sorrowfully. “Going to Zion has come to mean as much to me as it does to you, Peter. I just can’t see how it will happen now. Even with all the quilts the ladies have made and sold we’re a long way from what’s needed. Now the number is larger.”

He took her in his arms. “Don’t worry Maren. I’ll make it happen. I’ll find the money.”

“It’s a long walk back to the university,” she said as he held her. “Especially with a trunk. And the dormitories are probably locked. Perhaps Father will let you sleep in the storeroom tonight.”

"It won't hurt to ask," said Peter not really caring.

Peter did ask Lars if he could stay the night and to his credit the shopkeeper agreed. Carlsen may have been totally against his daughter's leaving Copenhagen with Peter, but his hope that they would change their minds, that plus being a decent man, he couldn't make himself refuse.

After bringing down a few blankets and helping Peter arrange them on a straw tick, Lars headed upstairs. "Sleep well young man," he said as he chuckled to himself. "Breakfast is at six."In the dimly lit storeroom Peter was laying on the lumpy makeshift mattress gloomily observing the beams which supported the Carlsen apartment above. They resembled thick prison bars. "Thank you Hr Carlsen," he said as the door closed.

Weeks passed, winter pressed its iron grip around Denmark and by mid-February Peter Jensen's money had all but run out. He had secured a part time job loading cargo on ships but trade was slow therefore wages small. Peter had also rented a cheap one room apartment near the docks and unlike his cheery little dormitory—which he had lost due to high rent—the apartment was old, had a low ceiling and its walls were water-stained plaster, brown and coming off in patches. Maren had brought in a porcelain bowl and a chunk of lye soap for washing, also some blankets and towels.

A yellowed painting of a ship an earlier tenant had left, hung off center on one wall and the other three were bare. There was an old dresser, a kerosene lamp, a chair and Peter used his trunk for a table. The apartment had one oil-skin window, a door which had to be forced open and a low fireplace provided heat. Included in the rent was enough coal for each month, if it was used sparingly.

As often as he could Peter ate meals with the Carlsen's and when he did Fru Carlsen's genuine Christianity shone through. She always made plenty of food and usually sent leftovers home with Peter. Lars knew it and didn't care. He was always sullen with Peter, eating his meals with as few words as possible. In spite of what he thought was Peter's stupidity the shopkeeper liked him but would never show it.

"I'm earning four rigsdalers per day as a longshoreman Maren," Peter was telling Maren during a lunchtime visit she paid to his dreary little dwelling. "It's enough for books and rent but not much toward our passage to America."

"I've been able to put a little money away in a sock," she said smiling at him. "But it's hard to save much. Ever since we returned from Holbaek, Father started holding back some of my wages for room and board."

They were sitting on his wood floor, leaning against the rear wall. Maren had brought Peter a smoked herring sandwich and two green apples and was curled up next to him listening as he took the last bite of his apple, which happened to be the core as Peter had eaten the entire thing.

"Charging you rent?" said Peter wiping his mouth. "That's pitiful!"

"Oh I don't know," she returned. "He doesn't withhold much and ever since the war business at the store has been slow.

"Humm," he said. "Just as long as he's being fair to you."

"He is."

"You know Maren," Peter went on, "there are days my mind is so black with worry about money I can hardly think straight. But then I'm still fairly confident it is the Lord's will for us to go to America."

"I feel the same way," she said.

"Well then," said Peter liking what he heard, "if we can't afford passage this September, then perhaps next."

"I think we'll have enough in six months or less," she said leaning up to kiss him.

Neither of them recognized it at the time but there was something truly exhilarating about going it on their own, so to speak. Peter was no longer obligated to his parents, and enjoyed not having to answer to them. And Maren, by paying for her room and board, also felt certain independence.

"Your father is very sullen lately," said Peter making small talk. "I've had many meals at his crowded table and he barely speaks."

"Except to try and talk us out of going to America," she said.

"He is wasting his breath Maren. We're going."

"Have you heard from your parents?" she asked changing the subject.

"Not a word," answered Peter dejectedly. "I wrote and told them that although I'm no longer living in the dorms at the University, I'm determined to finish my education. I also let them know my graduation looks certain, but so far the mails have brought nothing. Danish stubbornness is legend you know."

"I know," she sighed. "I've got to get back to the store Peter," she added kissing him again. "Help me up."

He stood and pulled her into his arms. "And I've got studies," he said looking over at a pile of books waiting for him on his trunk. It was a wonderful thing holding her. He felt so complete. Peter bent to kiss her. "Thank you for lunch," he said. "The apples refresh my mouth."

"Aren't I clever," she said and kissed him back.

"You are, and I don't know what I'd do without you," he said kissing her on both cheeks and then passionately on the mouth. "You are my strength. My reason for putting up with all this."

She looked around the dreary one room, then back at Peter. "A bit of white wash certainly wouldn't hurt. "Maybe we could do it Saturday."

"Maybe," he said going to the door and yanking it open. The door squawked as it cut the half circle groove deeper into the floor. "You better get going Maren. I can feel your father's disdain all the way from the store."

"I am a little late."

They kissed again, and Maren stepped lightly from apartment and down the stairs. Peter followed her to the street and watched after her until she reached the end of the block. He then returned inside and sat to his journal.

'March 13, 1865,' he wrote. *'Lars Carlsen has stooped to charging Maren rent for room and board. He's doing it to try and stop us from saving for America. But it doesn't matter. We'll come up with the money for our tickets one way or another. —Lars' wife on the other hand does all she can to help Maren and I. Fru Carlsen sets a fine table and were it not for her leftovers I'd be starving. She goes about her life rather quietly and is a kindly but uneducated person. She has a great deal of common sense however and I won't mind at all being her son-in-law. —My life at present is a bleak situation, but there is hope. With each church meeting Maren and I attend, the missionaries teach us more about America. It's a goodly land, a promised land. The Book of Mormon says it's a land choice above all others . . .'*

Peter had much to write in his journal that afternoon and with little money and nowhere to go he did. As hopeless as finances appeared, he ended the entry with his intended plans for immigration still in tact. *'Will September ever come?'*

It was true Peter had received nothing in the mail from Catherine, but his lack of interest in the family was also apparent. Peter had completely forgotten about Krista Holsen's pregnancy and that by now Ferdinand would be a father. Krista and Ferdinand's child, a girl they named Anna, had in fact been born early in January. Colic and ear infections had kept the child screaming since birth but regardless of her disposition she was beautiful. Well-formed with dark eyes and a head full of light brown hair, when she wasn't crying, she could steal the heart. Catherine loved her dearly. But because of Ferdinand's involvement with the new housekeeper, he and Krista were estranged and fighting bitterly. The baby spent most of her time at Nils Holsen's and Ferdinand was very pleased with the situation. He'd take a childless and buxom maid to a controlling woman with a screaming child any day.

On May 30, 1865, Copenhagen's papers heralded the news that on April 9, 1865 General Robert E. Lee, General in Chief of the armies of the Confederacy, had met with Ulysses S. Grant at Appomattox Courthouse. Virginia had surrendered. The American Civil War was over! And, scarcely six days had passed when more news arrived. On April 15, 1865, American President Abraham Lincoln was shot to death by an assassin while attending the play; "Our American Cousin."

"It's a country filled with murderers and thugs," Catherine told Elias after reading the headline and handing him the paper. "It's a savage land that our son thinks will be paradise!"

"Yes," Elias commented dryly. "The so-called United States will be decades rising out of its quagmire. If ever."

"Look here at the bottom of the article." He pointed to a column, pausing to cough. "It says Negro men might soon be granted suffrage in America." Another brief coughing spasm hit him. "Next thing you know American women will be voting."

"Heaven forbid!" said Catherine sarcastically.

About the time of this fascinating little exchange a similar one was taking place in Lars Carlsen's apartment in Copenhagen. Once again Peter was having a hearty dinner with the Carlsen's. The newspaper bearing the headline of Lincoln's assassination lay at hand and had Lars all in a heat.

"No less than a fool would immigrate to such a barbarous country," he said as he threw his spoon to the table. "They just shot their president for heaven's sake! The one man responsible for freeing their slaves and reuniting the country and he's murdered in cold blood. Such things just don't happen in Denmark."

"Are you forgetting the marches upon the castle Father?" Maren said without looking up from her meal. "King Christian might easily have been assassinated."

The wind was taken from Lars' sails for a moment with that. He knew full well that during the war some of the protesters that had stormed the palace were armed. Given half the chance any one of them might well have shot the king.

"It wasn't the same thing at all," he said angrily firing back. "The protests were all in the open. While this, this," and he held up the newspaper and shook it, "this was all done under secrecy. All under the cloak of darkness."

"Just like that damnable religion of yours," he murmured giving vent to what was really bothering him. "Must be a very secret doctrine you people teach. All it brings is trouble. Look at this article." He pointed to a headline in the lower corner of the same newspaper. "Mormon missionaries[6] banned from preaching in Skibby. Worshippers at St. Michaels Cathedral disturbed by secret meetings held by the Church of the Latter-day Saints." "There you have it," he said triumphantly, and smacked the newspaper with the back of his hand.

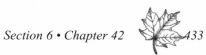

"Our meetings are open to all Hr Carlsen," said Peter standing and wiping his mouth. "You know that. I've invited you many times. May I please be excused," he added dropping his napkin near his plate. "You know Elder Snow and Elder Richards very well by now. There is nothing secret or sinister about either man or what they teach."

"That may well be true," Lars admitted. "But why all the uproar over the Mormons? Why are they continually in the newspapers?"

"Most of the uproar is coming from the inside the Folkekirken," said Maren wisely. "Priests are losing members of their congregations. People should follow your example Father. Let them worship how, where or what they may." She quoted Joseph Smith on that but Lars was agreed since he was in fact a free thinker. He truly believed people must be free to choose, especially where God was concerned.

"As long as they don't cause me any trouble, the Mormons can continue to rent my storeroom," was all Lars had to say on the matter as Peter donned his cap and left.

June found Peter hard at work at the docks and even harder at his studies. His books, plus the long hours at the docks were taking a huge toll. With little sleep and poor diet, his face took on a gaunt expression. He had dark circles under his eyes, his cheekbones were showing and some days he felt his heart was racing. He could still light up Maren's face with a smile, but inside he was sick with worry. Passage to America cost ninety Rigsdalers per individual and September was rapidly approaching. He had forty saved, needed one hundred and eighty but would get it if it killed him. And it may well yet.

Graduation on June 20th of 1865 was a sterile affair. Wearing a long black gown and a proud but somber expression, Peter stood in line in the auditorium with the rest of his classmates. Maren was there and clapped as he received his diploma. Later as families gathered in pubs to celebrate lavishly with their graduate, she and Peter took a quiet walk near the docks. Behind the moored wind-ships with their tall masts and rolled sails, the ocean loomed vast and foreboding. Swelling here, rushing there. Gulls shrieked as flags from various countries whipped in the breeze. The Dannebrog and the Union Jack were the most prevalent in the forest of masts but one ship displayed the Stars and Stripes of America! Peter pointed in its direction.

"One day soon we'll be boarding one of those Maren," he said as casually as if saying let's climb aboard a buggy for a drive around the city. "Do you think America needs another architect?"

She laughed. "Oh I'm sure of it Peter. I have all the confidence in the world, and one day you might design us a mansion."

"Better I build us one," he said taking her in his arms and kissing her. "You will want everything just so. You will never be happy unless you get to say where the kitchen and the closets go." He laughed at that. Maren had already told him what she wanted in a house.

She laughed and kissed him on the lips. "I'll help you Peter. I can paint and put down clay tiles. It will be such fun . . ."

They started walking again, passing a café that overlooked the water. The lights and gaiety inside spilled out over the dock. Peter had barely two rigsdalers and eleven skillings in his pockets. He could only dream and wonder at the menu and fine food offered inside. Earlier while seated on a park bench, he and Maren had shared a ham sandwich and some sliced cheese.

"I am so fortunate," he said at length. "It's not every day a person graduates from a university in this country. There were only seventy-eight of us who finished their course of study."

"You are fortunate," she agreed. "And it's a shame your Mother and Father weren't there to share the joy of the event."

"It was a shame," he agreed. "They might have taken us out to a proper dinner. But how can one blame them?"

"If only they understood," said Maren. "You haven't let them down at all, Peter. Especially your Mother. You've done exactly what she wanted."

"I will yet make her proud of me," he said determinedly. "Who knows what things I, that is we, might do in America."

"Who knows what we might do for the gospel of Christ," she said reminding him of what was behind it all.

"Who knows," said he said somewhat sadly. "Who knows?" Then a certain confidence overshadowed Peter and he cast his gaze out over the ocean. "But let me here quote our friend Soren Kierkegaard . . ."

"Quote on good sir," said Maren.

"To venture causes anxiety," he stated seriously, "but not to venture is to lose one's self . . . and to venture in the highest sense, is precisely to be conscious of one's self."

"And we are venturing forth in the Lord's work," Maren concluded for Peter.

"That we are," said he.

Chapter 43

"Welcome," said Elder Richards. "Please come in and find a seat. There are plenty this evening, the proprietor, our host Lars Carlsen recently cleared out some old inventory."

It was true. Lars had made a big sale to an exporter for thirty bolts of linsey-woolsey—a not so popular blend in Denmark—which had been in his storeroom for over a year, and had taken out the racks that held it. After the sale, the entire lot was shipped to England where it had come from in the first place! With the cloth and racks gone there was room for an extra row of chairs.

Seated on the front row was Claus Wangsgaard afore mentioned Branch President for Copenhagen's west side and the man Maren had worked under during the quilt-making effort. Claus was a brick maker, a barrel-chested and powerfully built fellow with arms like logs. He looked like a brawler but unless he or his beloved Gunda, who was with him that night, were threatened he was a man of peace. An imposing and very serious figure, Claus was an infrequent visitor to the meetings in Carlsen's storeroom and he had not met Elder Richards.

"Du taler godt Dansk, broder Richards," he said "hvor kommer du fra?" (You speak our language very well brother Richards, Where are you from?)

Knowing he was being tested Richards offered his hand answered Claus in Danish. "Jeg er oprindelig fra New York, men dette er min tredie missionstur til Danmark, broder?" (I'm originally from New York, but this is my third mission to Denmark, brother?)

"Wangsgaard," said Claus.

"Min første tur til Danmark var I 1850, broder Wangsgaard. Jeg boede mos en familie pa en gard og der lærte jeg at tale Dansk." (My first trip to Denmark was back in 1850, brother Wangsgaard. I lived with a family on a farm. They never joined the church but they taught me the language.)

Claus beamed. Proud to be Danish and proud of the Danish language he was impressed Elder Richards spoke so well. The two were to become fast friends.

Elder Snow was the main speaker, he also spoke excellent Dansk, and there were thirty-five people present; including eight children. Snow was in his glory. The gospel was his life and he loved a good crowd. Elder Richards gave a few announcements, a hymn was sung, an opening prayer offered then Snow stepped to the podium.

"Instead of a prepared text for tonight," he began pleasantly, "I thought I might open the floor for questions. Things have been so exciting lately, we have chartered a ship for the September voyage and we've had several baptisms. Later tonight we'll have some time for testimonies, but first are there any questions . . . questions about anything?"

"A doctrinal question," said Casten Pedersen getting right down to cases. The beautiful woman was still investigating the church and still had no idea that Peter Jensen was her dear friend Catherine Jensen's son. "A friend of mine says Mormons believe a person can work his way into heaven. Is it true, or do you believe in being saved by grace, or in salvation by good works? Or both?"

"You always have such good questions, Sister Pedersen," he said respectfully. "The Atonement of Jesus Christ assures salvation to all mankind. It also assures that all mankind will be resurrected. The Atonement of our Lord is unconditional; Salvation is a free gift to *all* and neither our works nor lack thereof has a single thing to do with it."

"So why do anything?" asked the intelligent looking young lady sitting next to Casten. "Why not eat, drink, and be merry as they say?"

"Young lady," said Snow smiling, "you have just gone straight to the heart of the issue. As I said, salvation is free, all mankind will be saved, and all mankind will be resurrected. I think that's why so few people take the gospel message seriously by the way. They are not really afraid of hell, or that there is a hellish existence after they die."

"So why do anything? Why have good works?" He looked out over his audience not really expecting an answer. "You do good works because it makes you happy that's for certain, and God gives you blessings for your works. But it goes much, much further. What you are asking about young lady is eternal life; and eternal life is an extension so to speak, of personal salvation."

"The process begins with *faith* in Christ, then continues by personal *repentance* and then *baptism* by immersion for the remission of sins. Now you are on the path that leads to eternal life." Snow knew he had lost some of the audience with that and so opened his Bible to 1 Corinthians chapter 15 verse 41. "There is one glory of the sun, another glory of the moon, and another glory of the stars: for one star differeth from another star in . . ."

"Shusssh!" interrupted a man seated on the front row. "There's something going on outside!"

Snow abruptly stopped talking and turned to see shadows, the silhouettes of several persons moving across the oilskin windows.

"Look there," blurted out the woman who had asked the last question. At that exact moment a burst of obscenities erupted from outside. Someone started banging on the door while others began pounding on the outside walls. A fist came through one of the oilskin windows and the hair on the back of Peter's neck stood up. His mouth went dry as a desert. "Blow out the lanterns," he shouted hoarsely. "Blow out the lanterns!"

Elder Snow quickly extinguished the lantern on the small table next to him while two other men threw themselves against the door in a vain effort to hold it shut. All the other lanterns were extinguished making the storeroom smoky and as dark as night. Meanwhile with banging and shouting resounding, women grabbed whimpering children and crouched behind chairs and boxes. Little else was accomplished before the back door came crashing in.

"Mormon pigs!" shouted a large bearded man who was wielding a club. Silhouetted in the dim outside light was a longshoreman Peter recognized as a fellow with whom he had recently unloaded a boat with. The man was strong as a bull, dumb as an ox and nobody to tangle with. He had the mentality of a criminal and generally arrived on the docks suffering from hangover, bruises from brawling or both. Peter in his over-zealousness for the gospel had once shared his testimony with him and had received such a horrific string of filthy epithets that he feared working with the man.

The burly longshoreman muscled his way in, followed by a surge of men swinging clubs and shouting obscenities. The table next to Elder Snow's lectern was smashed whereupon the lamp crashed to the floor spilling warm kerosene in a puddle. Chairs were overturned, people knocked about and amid yelling, screaming and thuds of fists and clubs, women cried, men cursed and children's terrified screams salted the air.

"Fanatics!" one man roared as he struck Claus Wangsgaard down. "Mormon swine!"

"Polygamists," shrieked one of the more informed mobsters as he swung a heavy stick at a chair behind which an eight-year-old girl was kneeling. His blow smashed the chair in pieces taking a chunk of the girls' cheek in the process. Blood spewed from the wound like warm water. Meanwhile another five men surged through the door and met strong resistance from the Mormons as many were men.

Claus Wangsgaard had gotten on his feet, taken a heavy blow to the shoulder, then struck his attacker square in the face knocking him cold to the floor. Claus then grabbed another mobber who was wrestling with Gunda and began choking him.

Most people were either bleeding or else knocked insensible and Olef Fredricksen, a tailor, a gentleman, father of seven children and as good a man as ever walked the earth, would die three days later from a fractured skull.

Peter Jensen, who'd been struck repeatedly in the face, pushed Maren into a corner and like a lion protecting its mate, stood slugging it out with anyone who came near. "I baptize you in the name of Joe Smith!" a mobster shouted as he swung an iron pipe at him. Peter raised his arm to protect himself and felt it shatter under the blow. Blinded by pain he pulled Maren to the floor and received several kicks in the face, head and back before losing consciousness.

Short-lived as the brawl would be, the putrid smell of stale alcohol mixed with blood, smoke and kerosene permeated the air. The doorway was so jammed that nobody could get inside or out and outside with lighted torches mobbers were howling like demons. Inside, the mob had run into more than they'd bargained for. Mormon men, most of whom were also working class, exchanged blow for blow with the intruders while women intent upon protecting the children, tore handfuls of their tormenters hair and scratched their faces.

Just when it looked like the storeroom might burst at the seams, a flood of light erupted from the top of the stairway to the Carlsen's living quarters and Lars Carlsen, musket in hand rapidly descended. An earsplitting explosion thundered amid the tumult and a lead ball struck a ceiling beam. Splinters of wood flew in every direction.

"Get out of here!" Carlsen shouted as he stood midway on the stairs.

As badly as he was shaking, and dim as it was it would have taken him twenty minutes to reload the musket. He'd forgotten his powder horn anyway. One shot was all it took however and the intruders plunged pell-mell through the back door. Those hollering outside were certain someone had been killed and went scattering down the alley. Mobbers and Mormons alike struggled to leave the storeroom and shortly, in the distance the shrill sound of the constable's whistle could be heard.

Smoke hung thick as fog in the storeroom and the smell of burnt gunpowder assaulted the nostrils. Women and children were crying, lanterns were lit revealing injured people laying about like so much scattered kindling. Three were members of the mob, and two others, one with both his eyes blackened and the other with a broken jaw had barely made it through the door only to faint just outside. Peter had a compound fracture of the forearm, his face and back were bruised and bloodied and like a slave who'd been whipped, he lay moaning on the floor. Elder Snow, Elder Richards, Claus Wangsgaard and one member of the mob were arrested for disturbing the peace and everyone else was sent to their homes.

"I'm lucky this old relic didn't blow up in my hands!" Lars

barked after he and two other men had helped Peter and Maren upstairs to lie on a mat in the apartment. Lars was still shaking and sweat beaded his balding forehead as he put his musket back over the mantle. He mopped his forehead with a towel and began to pace, his wooden clogs clopping on the floor like a cooper's mallet. "With my luck I'd have killed somebody and could right now be sitting in jail with your friends!"

"Who were those people?" he demanded.

"How should I know Father?" Maren whimpered. Her hand had been crushed by an attacker's heavy boot. She was sick with pain and white as a sheet. "It has become very unpopular to be a Mormon. Lately we've had many threats." She rolled to Peter's side and started to cry.

"There'll be no further meetings on this property," Lars said angrily. "Not by anyone! I don't need money that badly, and I won't endanger this family because of your strange religion!"

With two children clinging about her apron Fru Carlsen was preparing to bandage Maren's hand. "Please lower your voice," she said to Lars. "You're scaring the children."

"Ever since the war, Denmark has become a nation of cowards," she added as she bit into a cloth and tore off a strip. "Citizens who sneak around at dark and strike women and children with clubs! What about our so-called religious freedom? Why, there's no enforcement whatever!"

Maren was stroking Peter's tousled hair with the fingers of her good hand, shaking her head as she looked at his swollen face. He was breathing but not totally conscious. "Thank you for protecting me," she said and placed her cheek against his.

Lars was very touched as he watched them. He knew Peter and Maren loved each other. Even though he felt they were wrongly captivated by the spell of Mormonism he had to admit the religion had a very positive effect upon them. Other than tonight, they seemed enlightened, happy and at peace with themselves. Lars loved his daughter as he loved life. During the last year she had been such an unfailing support to him. He came over and knelt by her touching her cheek gently. "Maybe we should leave the country with them Mother," he said sighing.

"Maybe we should," Mrs. Carlsen agreed.

Chapter 44

The next day Peter was out of his head with fever, moaning constantly with pain, and had to be taken to a hospital where his broken arm was set. He was still barely conscious of his surroundings. Later on that same day Lars Carlsen found himself on a train to Holbaek and later still, on a horse riding toward the Jensen estate. The sun was setting when the dry goods merchant finally arrived at the house of Catherine and Elias Jensen. It hadn't been hard to find. Everyone in Holbaek knew of the gristmill, many had worked there.

Lars felt very uncomfortable as he viewed the spacious fenced-in property. How could one family own so much land? He sighed with envy. Here was wealth. Real wealth. He led his horse up the road through the gate then lashed the reins to a post. He'd no sooner done so than he was greeted by the new grounds keeper and taken to the house.

Inger, back at her post and in full vigor, met them at the door. "The gentleman wishes to see Fru Jensen," said the groundskeeper making no reference whatever to Elias. "And 'e shall, if 'e'll give me 'is name," said Inger.

"I'm Lars Carlsen from Copenhagen," said Lars. "Maren Carlsen's father."

"Oooh," said Inger. "Do come in sir."

Inger left Lars in the hall turning his hat in his sweaty hands and less than two minutes later Catherine appeared. The dismal shadow of Elias shuffled in behind her.

"I'm Maren Carlsen's father," Lars began when he saw them.

"Yes, yes of course," said Catherine.

"Pleased to make your acquaintance," Elias said shakily. He'd been drinking heavily the night before and was still feeling the ill effects.

"Let's sit in the living room Hr Carlsen," said Catherine anxiously. She'd known something was wrong the moment Inger found her but was trying not to act alarmed. "My husband isn't feeling well."

"I'm fine," coughed Elias sourly but allowed his wife to take his arm anyway.

"So tell us," said Catherine trying to hide the concern in her voice. "What brings you to Holbaek?"

"I've got a bit of bad news," said Lars coming straight to the point. "Your son has been beaten."

"Oh no!" gasped Catherine.

"He's not doing so good madam," said Lars soberly. "He's in and out of consciousness. My wife and I thought you should know."

"What in the world happened to cause such a thing?" said Catherine in great alarm.

"It was one of their church meetings," said Lars. "A mob gathered outside to protest. One thing led to another and the mob crashed the door. Peter got it badly but he protected Maren. He's pretty bruised and has a broken arm. His back is also hurt."

"Where is he?" questioned Elias.

"He's in the hospital . . ."

Inger brought in some coffee and the hot dark brew made Lars sweat all the more, but he welcomed something to do with his hands. He then related the events of the riot in his storeroom. How he chased off the intruders, the arrests and so forth. Afterward the conversation settled into a discussion of Peter and Maren and their going to America with the Mormons. Shared heartache brought the strangers quickly together and before they knew it they were talking as old friends.

"They're so very foolish," Catherine said sadly.

"Reckless is more like it," said Elias. "Across an unfriendly ocean and then traipse off into some godforsaken wilderness!"

"Since they told us about it," said Catherine in a slightly milder tone, "we've done some studying. Did you know the western part of America is little more than desert and rock?"

"All Peter and Maren talk about are the mountains, trees and rivers," said Lars.

"Those fool Mormons have got them thinking it's a fairy land," said Elias acidly. He coughed briefly and wiped his mouth with his hand. "A land flowing with milk and honey."

"They have so much right here," added Catherine dismally.

"And a lovely place it is too," Lars complimented.

"We planned upon building a house for them north of the mill," Catherine went on. "It was to be a surprise after Peter graduated. We thought that . . . Oh I can't talk about it, Hr Carlsen. I've been so upset. Young people will never know what they do to their parents!

When they came here for Christmas, instead of saying something to dissuade them, something loving and kind, I flew off the handle and told them to leave."

"I've argued with them for hours on end about staying in Denmark," said Lars trying to ease Catherine's anguish. "Nothing like this has ever happened in my family. My married brothers and sisters all live within a few blocks of each other."

"Is that so?" said Elias appeasingly. Just as he had Maren, he judged Lars to be a commoner. Catherine on the other hand felt a kinship toward the obviously devoted father.

"Could we offer you a bed for the night Hr Carlsen?" Catherine asked. "We've plenty of room and the hour is drawing late."

"I'll just get a place in town," said Lars. He was twirling his hat in his hands again. "That way I can get an early start without disturbing anyone. I must get back to my business."

"We'll be in Copenhagen day after tomorrow," Elias said knowing full well it would be Catherine who made the journey.

"Hr Carlsen I insist you stay," interrupted Catherine. "We have more room in this old house than we ever use. Inger will prepare a bed for you and you'll have all the privacy you require. We can leave early, after I've set things in order. Elias you've been too weak to travel. I'll take Ferdinand when I go."

"Well," and he coughed twice, "whatever you say my dear. I really haven't felt my best Hr Carlsen."

So Lars gratefully accepted the offer to stay the night and next day he, Catherine and Ferdinand took a train to Copenhagen. They'd made the entire trip without incident and rejecting Lars' offer to reciprocate on lodging, Catherine and Ferdinand took a room in a downtown hotel. The next day after seeing the crowded and less than clean conditions of the hospital, Peter's good mother quickly determined that home would be a better place for her son to recuperate.

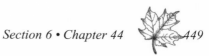

In addition to his broken forearm he had several cracked ribs, a broken finger and bruises on his face and head. Bloodshot and blackened, his eyes were almost completely swollen shut. Peter was barely recognizable, but he was lucid and aware of his surroundings.

Catherine paid the hospital, then making up a bed in a coach she'd rented, sat across from Peter holding his head while Ferdinand drove the horses. Row after row of run down apartments and dilapidated buildings greeted them as under Peter's guidance the coach made its way to his apartment on the wharf. Wandering the streets were sailors in striped pantaloons, greasy hair and wind burned faces. The area stunk of fish, rotting and otherwise, and humorless longshoremen hung about while fishermen and riffraff from the four corners of the earth clustered inside and around the pubs. Warm beer flowed freely from spigoted wooden casks and fights were as common as flies.

"Now you lie quietly Peter," Catherine ordered as she climbed out of the coach. "We'll only be a moment. Ferdinand tie the horse to that lamp post."

"Yes Mother," he said and then followed Catherine inside the building.

"What a horrible little hole he's crawled into Mother," Ferdinand observed after he and she had walked upstairs and into Peter's flat.

"It's not so bad," said Catherine as she scanned the bleak apartment her eyes resting upon Peter's open journal that lay upon the bed. She smiled to think that he still kept it then picked it up to read the last entry.

Ferdinand was snooping around peering into a small larder where

Peter kept bread. He looked out the window. "Not a bad view," he said sarcastically.

"Oh that I could rewrite his life," Catherine lamented as she shut the journal. "I'd certainly change the last few chapters." She placed the journal inside Peter's trunk and as she did Catherine noticed a Danish translation of the Book of Mormon lying on a folded shirt. Taking the book in her hand and randomly flipping its pages she came upon a passage[7] Peter had underlined in ink.

"And when ye shall receive these things, I would exhort you that ye would ask God, the Eternal Father, in the name of Christ, if these things are not true; and if ye shall ask with a sincere heart, with real intent, having faith in Christ, he will manifest the truth of it unto you, by the power of the Holy Ghost. And by the power of the Holy Ghost ye may know the truth of all things."

The passage struck Catherine in a most profound and peaceful way . . . "*ask God if these things are not true*." She read the passage again then quietly closed the leather bound book and placed it in a bag she was carrying.

"Let's just get his clothing Ferdinand," she said impatiently. "I'd like to be on the train before dark."

A drunken man pushed past Catherine and Ferdinand as they later emerged into the hallway with Peter's now loaded trunk. Down the dirty, narrow, staircase he weaved. Catherine and Ferdinand couldn't get past him but once they were finally into the street both took a deep breath of air and let it out in a gust.

"How could you stand it in there Peter?" Catherine demanded as she entered the coach in flurry. "I feel like my skin is crawling with vermin!"

"The rent was cheap Mother." He winced as she rearranged his pillows. "And it's close to my work."

Catherine looked out her window and down the docks. A huge freighter laden with ropes and rope ladders was moored next to several smaller skiffs and struggling up the gangplank a crew of men were rolling a large wooden keg. "My son the dock hand," she said with a hint of pride and disdain.

Peter was seated lengthwise on the tufted and buttoned leather seat and his arm was tightly wrapped against his side in preparation for the bumpy ride ahead. "It takes several days to load a ship like that Mother," he said noticing her interest in the activities on the freighter. "Pickled halibut casks are heaviest of all and once you get them into the hold they must be nailed to the floor."

"I'm sure of it," she said turning her attention toward him. "Loose in a storm, a barrel like that could crush a man like a grape."

"Or smash a hole in the side of a ship," added Peter."All set down there?" Ferdinand called.

"Yes we're all ready," Catherine responded. "Go by the Carlsen's place Ferdinand," she called up to him. "I'm sure Peter would like to say good-bye to Maren."

"As you wish Mother," Ferdinand said wearily.

The coach rolled away under the indignant stares of the street people hanging about. Smirks and scowls crossed their faces as they nodded their heads knowingly. The well-dressed woman in the coach obviously owned the tenement she'd just walked out of.

After a brief visit with the Carlsens and a few quiet words between Maren and Peter, the Jensen coach rattled and bumped its way along the cobbled streets of Copenhagen. The weather was sultry and the air blowing in the open windows much appreciated. Periodically Catherine reached across to wipe Peter's brow with her handkerchief, or else give him a sip of water from a flask she had brought along. The roll of nurse fit her like a glove.

Peter felt weak as a kitten. His face was pale and he grimaced with pain at each jolt of the coach. But he was so gratified to be reunited with his family that nothing else mattered. "I thought you had dispelled me for good Mother," he said at length.

"Nonsense," Catherine answered somewhat sharply. "I have been angry with you. Hurt to think you'd actually want to leave Denmark. And your family for that matter! And you haven't changed your mind about it have you?"

The sound of horse hooves, jingling chains, slapping leather and rolling wheels surrounded the coach as she waited for Peter to answer.

"I'm not sure what to think anymore," he said at length. "Those men who beat me hated us Mother. They truly hated us."

"And all the Church teaches is love. Love towards mankind. The pure love of Christ. I'm not giving it up," he added resolutely. "I still love the Church. It's the Lord's Church and I know its teachings to be true . . ."

"Stop it!" said Catherine as she clenched her fist, struck her own knee and turned to look out the window. *The Lord's Church indeed! A narrow little sect was more like it,* she thought brokenheartedly. Tears formed in her eyes then trickled down her cheeks. Buildings, shops, and people seemed to scurry past, but Catherine scarcely saw them. Women carrying baskets snooped the markets while children played tag at their skirts but the streets may as well been empty as far as Catherine was concerned. Whatever spell the Mormons had cast upon her son was strong. It caused the heiress to Peter Rasmussen's fortune great concern. and yet a certain personal introspection.

"I'd like to tell you about the church Mother," her wayward son added, "and about the Book of Mormon . . ."

Catherine shook her head and frowned at him. "Let's just leave it Peter," she said cutting him off. "You need to get some rest."

They reached the train station and for the balance of the trip to Holbaek scarcely a word passed between them. Catherine had shut her mind to any further discussion. After they boarded the train she pulled down the window shade and closed her eyes. The light powder on her face was streaked with tears and she slept now, spent from emotion. Eventually Peter also dropped off. He slept fitfully, waking now and again only to drift off into fevered insensibility. Ferdinand was indifferent to the whole thing.

At Holbaek, Torkil was there with the family coach. He greeted Peter putting him instantly at ease by grabbing him by the chin of his beard and then smacking him lightly on the cheek.

"Careful," said Catherine. "He's a bit banged up."

"He'll be alright," said Torkil confidently.

Ferdinand drove, enjoying the feeling of power one gets from commanding a fine team of horses. He was also enjoying the view. "Why would anyone want to leave such a beautiful country Torkil?" he said over the racket. "Peter's got to be crazy." The terrain was rushing past them in such a blur that Torkil closed his eyes.

"I don't know why a man would leave it all young Ferdinand," he said wistfully. "Some people are just adventurous I guess. And in a way," he added as he opened his eyes and scanned the horizon, "it's them I envy most."

Chapter 45

"You just lie here till you're stronger," Catherine said as she fluffed a pillow and tucked it behind Peter's head. They'd made it to the house before dark and Inger had helped get Peter situated in his room upstairs. The long ride had caused his arm to bleed and Catherine had just changed the outer bandage. Peter's old room was very orderly now, empty of youthful artifacts and the bed, which was made up with fresh linen, felt cool and comfortable in the warm August evening.

"Thank you Mother," he said looking at her through swollen and blood-shot eyes. "Thank you for everything."

She kissed the bareness of his cheek just above his beard before turning down the lantern.

There would be many trips into Peter's bedroom during his rehabilitation and Catherine prayed that as his body mended he'd gain his sanity as well.

Days passed. Peter was soon up and about and everyone in the Jensen household spoke civilly toward him but there remained a rift in the family. The weather, the mill, the animals and crops were all part of everyday conversation, but nobody touched the subjects of religion or immigration. Catherine even began to fantasize that Peter had forgotten about leaving Denmark. That he'd stay, marry Maren and build himself a house nearby so that she, Catherine would always have easy access to the grandchildren.

Peter could remain a Mormon if he wanted, why there was even a small congregation of them in Holbaek. Catherine had seen a hand painted sign on a small building last time she was in town. "The Church of Jesus Christ of Latter-day Saints" it read." The increasing presence of this fledgling American religion was an major irritant to Elias, a small one to Catherine and yet she couldn't help feeling interested. Reluctantly at first and then with growing curiosity, Catherine began reading the Book of Mormon she'd found in Peter's trunk.

Meanwhile the more he healed, the more restless Peter became. He had a few discussions with Elias, but each was full of dissension and ended with father and son as far apart as ever. His arm still splinted and in a sling, Peter escaped the house to wander the estate. He felt like a wounded soldier with a strong desire to re-enter the battle. Often he would visit the mill to stand outside and watch its huge wind wings turn steadily in the breeze. At lunch he'd talk with Torkil and the men. How good it was to be with them again; to laugh at old jokes and to discuss the year's grain crop and new procedures if any. Peter knew he belonged in milling. He belonged here. Or did he? How could a rational person be racked with so much indecision? He began to wonder if he was rational.

"You can't go on like this my brother," Ferdinand told him one morning as he found Peter leaning against the horse barns.

"What do you mean?" asked Peter defensively.

"You've been home four weeks now, and you wander about like a little lost sheep. I've been watching you. Don't you think it's time you sat down with Mother and talked about your future?" For a moment Ferdinand sounded like the respectful younger brother he'd once been and Peter eyed him distrustfully.

"What would we talk about Ferdinand? My coming home to live?" Peter had been chewing the sweet base of a straw of grass and spat it on the ground.

"You might start with your religion," Ferdinand chided. "Now that you see what people think of it, you might get some advice. And since I'm the one who brought it up," he paused, looking his brother in the eye. "I thought Mormonism was supposed to make people happy. It seems to me all it has brought you is misery."

"You don't understand little brother," Peter countered. "Mormonism has made me happy. In here, where it counts." Peter held his chest where his heart lay. "I can't help it if there's so much ignorance and hate in Denmark."

"All right so you're happy being a Mormon," Ferdinand said sarcastically. "Why all the indecision?"

"I didn't know it was so obvious," said Peter with a sigh.

"Ha," said Ferdinand.

"It's about going to America," said Peter candidly. "Before being beat up by that mob, I held no indecision. I was quite certain of my course in life. It was all mapped out."

"But the hate I felt that night. The ignorance! Part of me says I should stay in Denmark and speak out against religious bigotry. Go right back to Copenhagen and stand up for what I believe. Teach anyone who will listen to open his or her eyes!" He looked at Ferdinand's bland demeanor. *How would I ever reach the likes of him,* he thought glumly. *Still he is my brother, I ought to try.*

"The other part tells me I must leave the country," he went on. "Go to Zion and help build the church . . ."

"Peter, I'm not the least bit interested in what you're saying,"

Ferdinand interrupted. “You keep your religion and I’ll keep mine. Even Mother and Father have forgiven you for becoming Mormon; I’m not sure I have or that I care. But why must you leave Denmark?” he added half-heartedly. “Why not stay and help around here?”

“Because there is something compelling me to leave Denmark,” Peter answered emphatically. “I don’t know what it is, but I don’t belong here anymore. I can’t describe it but every time I think of America I feel whole. Truly whole.” Peter folded his hands and stared at his brother as if looking for confirmation.

“I can’t imagine what’s made you so crazy in the head Peter,” said Ferdinand as he slumped against the barn. “Why would you want to leave all this? It would take two lifetimes to have as much.

“But then,” he added ignobly, “if you really must go to America, then do it. Get it out of your system. It may tear Mother apart—on the other hand,” he added as if talking to himself, “lately she seems quite at peace concerning you. Go talk with her. You’ll see what I mean.”

“I don’t want to upset her again,” Peter said decisively. “Last time I mentioned America she went berserk. You should have seen her reaction.”

“Like I say Peter,” the younger brother said as he pushed away from the barn and started to walk away, “Mother seems to have mellowed about you recently. I don’t know what it is. She’s even been more tolerant of me, and considering all the trouble I’ve put her through with Krista and the baby . . .”

“Anyway,” said Ferdinand skirting the subject. “Go talk to Mother, you’ll see what I mean.”

“Maybe I will,” said Peter somewhat touched that Ferdinand had finally said something decent to him and that he had said it in a decent way. *Maybe there is hope for the boy after all,* Peter thought.

Ferdinand was smiling sardonically as he walked toward the house. "What a fool he is," he said to himself.

That evening Peter was out on the upstairs balcony that overlooked the courtyard. He was seated with his arms folded and seemed to be staring at his feet.

"Would you like some company?" Catherine said as she approached from behind. She placed a hand on his shoulder and rubbed his cheek with the back of it. "You look lonely."

"I guess I'm missing Maren," Peter replied. It was the first week in September, nearly a year since Catherine had ejected him from the house, and yet it seemed like just a few weeks had passed by. Like the past year had all been a dream. The moon was up and the sky streaked with thin gray clouds. It was chilly and Peter had a blanket over his lap.

"Your arm is healing nicely," Catherine said touching his sling gently.

"It's about ready to come out of the splint," he answered. "I'm finally able to grip with my hand." He demonstrating by taking hold of the iron railing.

"Mother," he said looking at her intently. "I'll probably be returning to Copenhagen soon. I've got to be about my life . . . and I do miss Maren."

"You needn't be in such a hurry," Catherine answered gently. "And what will you do? Start an apprenticeship?"

"I don't know," Peter said, a little cautiously. "At first I'll probably go back to the docks. Things are always busy there and . . ." he didn't finish.

Catherine sat next to him. "My son, a common laborer. The very idea." Peter looked at her sheepishly. "I need money," he said.

"You won't earn much loading ships," she said patting his hand.

"Not for a while anyway. You better consider being a draftsman. You still have one good arm you know." He smiled at that.

"Peter," she went on intently. "What could I ever say, or do for that matter . . . to get you to change your mind about leaving Denmark?"

He looked at her sorrowfully and took her hand. "Mother, I'm so very grateful for all you've done. Grateful for your having me home, nursing me back to health, especially when I've upset you and Father so badly. I love you more than words can say, but please, please understand. I must follow my destiny . . ." Catherine didn't comment only sat there looking proudly at him.

"There's a boat leaving Copenhagen harbor in less than three weeks," he said presently. "I plan to be on it."

There was another long pause as Catherine let the fatal words sink in. This boy . . . This man! Why the madness? And yet something tingled inside her. What an adventure it would be! She shook her head in despair.

Peter sat anticipating a salvo of anger but instead his Mother rose and cradled his head in her arms. She was crying softly. A tear rolled down her cheek and dropped from her chin into Peter's hair. He could feel it trickle down his scalp. "I've been reading your Book of Mormon," she said quietly. "I found it in your trunk."

Peter opened his eyes in amazement. He was also humbled. That his mother or anyone else in the family would one day find what he'd found, was the thing he'd prayed the hardest for, and expected least. "I thought the book was still in my flat," he said as he turned to look at up her.

"What an unusual and interesting book it is," she went on. "And the sweet peace I feel when I read it! The love of Christ flows from nearly every page. If only it were true. And for your sake," she added, "I pray it is." Her eyes were shining and Peter could feel his mother's love. "If it is true, it may ultimately change this wicked world we live in Peter. I've never read anything so filled with hope!"

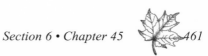

"It is truly a remarkable book Mother," said Peter looking her. "And it is true. As crystal clear as a flawless diamond. It's the most true and correct book on earth."

"Then you actually believe it is scripture?" Catherine asked as she looked at him steadily. "That prophets were among the people of ancient America?"

"I do," said Peter sincerely. "And yes, that prophets were among the people then and that a prophet leads the church today."

"And you also believe that Christ went among them and taught them his gospel, and that they kept their records on gold plates?"

"Yes."

"Which Joseph Smith later obtained from God and translated?" Catherine had never taken her eyes from Peter's. The things she'd read had struck her mind so profoundly she had to know the truth about them.

"I do," said Peter sincerely.

"My dear son," Catherine exclaimed. "If only I had such faith."

"Mother," said Peter taking her hand and holding it against his cheek. There were tears in his eyes and he was so full of emotion he could hardly speak. "I love you so very much. Thank you. Thank you for trusting me enough to look into what I've been telling you."

"Curiosity is what it was," said Catherine smiling. "But your book *has* given me some insight. Insight I've never had before. I feel I know myself better—who I am, where I came from and where I'm going. The book has also helped me face the terrible situation between your brother and Krista Holsen."

"There's no chance of reconciliation between them?" Peter asked.

"There's no love there Peter," said Catherine sadly, "and it has almost killed me. Krista now refuses to let me see the baby," she added with deep hurt in her voice. "She's using the child as a weapon."

"You remember Nils Holsen, Krista's father?"

"Of course I do," said Peter.

"I had to terminate him," said Catherine.

"What happened?"

"Krista had gone to him with lies, saying I was mean and impatient with the baby. That I'd whipped her of all things! In fact Krista has spanked the child often and spanked her hard. Slapped her little face too. The little dear, with her ears all full of pus and she not able to hold down her food. Life has been unkind the to the poor little thing ever since she arrived."

"Things became so heated between Nils and I over Krista's lies and the way *she* was treating the baby that Torkil had to step in. Thank heaven he was near at hand. I was afraid there would be violence. Now Nils and Krista have gone to the law. Your brother and I must stand before the magistrate on Tuesday." Catherine should have been furious; instead she was soft and very vulnerable. Sorry over what had happened and wishing she might have handled things better.

"And all over an innocent baby . . ." she shook her head sadly.

Peter didn't know what to say.

"Money is what it's about," Catherine stated flatly, dejectedly. "It's all Krista ever wanted from us. Ferdinand was simply the means to an end."

"I'm so sorry Mother . . ."

"Peter," said Catherine shaking off her emotion, and changing the subject. "Once again, you've been so restless since you've been home. I've wanted to talk to you about all this but every time I get myself free of your demanding father you've wandered off somewhere."

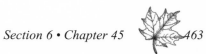

"Father can be demanding," said Peter following her track for a moment. "I've tried to spend a little time with him since I've been here, but it's either, get me this or go get me that . . . and when we do sit down to talk he goes off some political or religious tirade."

"It has always been that way hasn't it?" said Catherine. Then she checked herself. "He's not well Peter. And I don't know that he ever will be." It wasn't exactly true but it's what Catherine told people. It made her feel better. Tuberculosis had done its damage to Elias that was true, but he was healthy enough. Back to his pleasant old self, living in the lap of luxury without so much as lifting a finger and sticking barbs into anybody who got near him. To Catherine's horror, he was even getting somewhat frisky again.

"It's so odd," said Catherine thoughtfully, "reading your Book of Mormon has also helped me better deal with your father. Reading it lifts my spirits. I actually see things in a different light." She sat down again. "I even understand you better, Peter. But I must admit there's much I don't understand about your religion."

"Such as?"

"Well . . ." she said pointedly. "I've heard the Church teaches polygamy. Is that true?"

Peter was dumbfounded. How could his mother know about Mormon polygamy and speak so calmly? "A small number of church members do practice plural marriage," he said as matter-of-factly as possible. "That is true Mother. I don't fully understand the doctrine myself, and do not intend to practice it, but what you've heard is true."

Her eyes rolling back in a look of bewilderment, Catherine leaned back and shook her head. "Then why does the Book of Mormon say a man must have but one wife?" she asked leveling her stare at him. "I read it with my own eyes."

"It's a long story Mother," said Peter slowly, "but celestial marriage is a commandment of God through a modern day prophet. The order has a divine purpose and God has imposed the teaching to his children at various points in history . . ."

"We don't have time for this right now," she interrupted him somewhat impatiently. "Let's set this troubling piece of the puzzle aside for the time being. In fact," she said pointedly, "let's leave the topic of your impractical religion altogether and be practical for a moment. If you are going to America, then I want to know what you'll be facing. From what I've read, their war was far more horrible than ours. Most of a million men were killed, or else wounded. Can you imagine?!"

"I can't," Peter said woefully.

"And the country's rails are all torn up," she went on. "How on earth are they shipping things? Things such as grain? Why the whole nation must be starving . . ."

"They're not starving Mother. At least where I'm going they're not. People look out for each other in Zion. It's a clean new land, with room to breathe, not the crowded conditions of Copenhagen. People there have farms that support large families. Maren and I want a large family by the way. Lots of grandchildren." Catherine smiled when he said it. A melancholy smile, but in her mind she could actually see those children.

"We also want a farm of our own," said Peter. "A place as large as ours here . . ."

Old and new ground was covered as Peter and Catherine lingered on the balcony. They discussed the American scene thoroughly. They even discussed the tremendous growth of the Mormon Church not only in Denmark, but Norway, Sweden and England. They discussed Kierkegaard and how his philosophy was changing Danish politics. They discussed the king, Bismarck's attack on Denmark, and the subsequent loss of Holstein and Slesvig. Their discussion ultimately led to Hans' untimely death and Catherine cried tears she'd held in for months. Her grieving had never quite been satisfied and sensing it, Peter let her pour out her heart to him.

They talked about Indians. Catherine had gotten hold of a tattered and sensational novel about the American West and every page was dripping in blood. Gunfighters riddled with bullets lying dead on dusty streets, and painted savages wearing nothing but loin cloths ransacking wagon-trains and scalping pioneers.

Eventually Catherine rose from her chair, stiff from sitting but satisfied, willing to face the inevitable. She was losing another son, only this time death was not the cause. Catherine took comfort in that. No, this time life was involved and unlike the grandchild Ferdinand had sired, Peter's children would be wanted. She might never see them but at least they'd be wanted by her son and Maren.

"You know I've always had faith in God," she said after a while. "And as to your leaving Denmark, I'm going to leave that burden in his very capable hands. I certainly can't shoulder it." She stared into Peter's eyes. "This is really what you want then," she stated more than asked. "This will truly make you happy? To take a young girl off into an untamed wilderness, a barren place in the middle of nowhere? And there start your family?"

"Yes Mother," Peter answered with conviction. "It is truly what I want."

Chapter 46

Catherine lowered her eyes and was shaking her head. She then lifted her gaze and faced her son squarely. There was sadness in her voice but a definite pride as well. “If this is what you truly want, then, so be it,” she said. “This thing appears to be greater than both of us.” With all her defenses gone she added, “and financially speaking, I’m going to help you . . .”

“W–what did you say?”

“I said I’m going to help you.”

“It’s not necessary mother,” said Peter knowing he didn’t mean it.

“Do you think I’d throw you to the dogs?” said Catherine. “Long before this talk, I had decided to help you. What you are planning is so extreme Peter. So extreme. But if you must go, then I will help. It may be my last chance to ever do anything for you.”

He said nothing, but waited for her to continue.

“It sounds to me that all of America is filled with barbarians and ruffians, and nothing I’ve said diplomatically or with passion has convinced you otherwise.” Catherine was almost back to her old self. Whatever had happened to soften her had dissipated somewhat.

"How much money do you think you'll need?" she asked pointedly. "And how pray tell, will you carry it safely in such a hostile land?"

"I think a few hundred rigsdalers will see me through Mother," Peter answered naively. "That is until I get established. I hear there isn't much use for money where I'm going. People barter for what they need."

"Let's go downstairs," said Catherine smiling and extending her hand. "I'd like some coffee and a little breakfast. It's almost morning and we've more to discuss."

The stairs creaked and squawked like an old man with arthritis as Peter and Catherine descended. Elias snorted in the middle of his snoring then continued sawing away. The house would be asleep for at least another two hours and as Catherine and Peter entered the kitchen all was quiet.

"Early morning is my favorite time of day," said Catherine, "though I've usually had several hours rest," she added as she lit the two overhead lanterns and turned up their wicks. She looked around. Everything was neat and tidy. A starched white tablecloth, pots and pans hanging from the rack, and on the larder freshly baked bread lay covered with a cloth. Inger was definitely back.

"Inger will be taking the day off," said Catherine taking an iron skillet from its hook. "She went to visit her mother. What shall I cook for us?"

"Ham and eggs," said Peter enthusiastically. "I'll stir up the fire."

"Inger beats me to the kitchen each morning," said Catherine yawning. "The coffee is always ready before I get up."

Coals from the day before were still glowing under gray ashes in the iron stove and Peter took an iron crank and worked the grating. He then added a few lumps of shiny black coal, worked the bellows and soon the smells of hot metal, boiling coffee, and ham sizzling in the pan filled the room. The meal and coffee revived them and mother and son continued their discussion.

"There's a great lack of confidence in America's currency as I understand it," Catherine was saying, "Confederate money is virtually worthless while the value of Federal money varies widely from place to place. You simply can't trust a country's banking system in time of war."

"You and Maren must have the means to obtain your needs . . ." Catherine was almost talking to herself. "And you say bartering is what the Mormons do?"

Peter nodded. "We won't starve Mother. I'll have five acres of land to plant. And someday I'd like to buy more land," he added as he finished his eggs and set his plate aside. "As I said, I'd like a place as large as here."

"And well you should," said Catherine. "Half this estate would have gone to you."

Peter looked pained. "I may come back . . ." he began.

"You'll never return to Denmark," Catherine said with finality. But not wanting a single ounce of ill feelings to spoil their time together, she took a breath and paused a moment to sip her coffee. "A mother knows these things," she added calmly.

Peter sat silently holding his warm mug as the air of dissension dissipated.

"I have a plan that will fulfill my intentions for both yourself and Ferdinand," said Catherine at length. "But you must never reveal what I'm about to do."

"I don't understand," said Peter.

"Remember no one is to know," repeated Catherine smiling to

herself. Then rising from her chair, "Wait here," she said quietly. "I'll be back shortly."

She left the warm and pleasant smells of the kitchen and in her stocking feet, stealthily walked through the quiet house. Peter heard the door to the study creak open, then nothing but silence.

When she returned, Catherine had an impish look on her face. Sitting at the table, she placed a beautifully carved wooden box in front of her astonished son and opened the lid. The treasure she exposed took Peter's breath away. Lying against the red velvet lining of the jewelry box was the necklace Gustav Hanse had crafted for her so many years ago.

"Your inheritance," she said lifting the sparkling masterpiece with both hands and placing it gently on the table. Sparkles of light reflected from the lantern and danced on ceiling and walls. The tabletop glittered with light. Each golden oak leaf and each gem seemed to make their presence known. How much brighter they would shine in daylight!

"Mother," gasped Peter, "whatever are you talking about, it–it's your necklace!"

"That it is," said she as she carefully arranged it in a golden and glittery circle.

"And now as I said it's your inheritance. If you're going to America, I want you to be able to live as you've lived here. You are to take this necklace with you and, as you need money, remove a stone or pull off a gold leaf." Catherine's demeanor told Peter she meant what she said. She was extremely earnest.

"I couldn't possibly do such a thing Mother," he protested. "The necklace is a work of art."

"Mere trinkets and metal," Catherine countered austerely. "Now hear me out Peter. This piece of jewelry means nothing to me. It may

have once, but now it only reminds me of foolishness. I don't go to parties anymore. I hardly ever go to church. Things and their values change as a person ages."

"But I thought women loved fancy jewelry," argued Peter.

"Some do. I don't," she said flatly. "The necklace is worth approximately a quarter of a million rigsdalers Peter, and I know of no other way to pass to you that which is rightfully yours. Like the prodigal son you will receive your portion while your parents are still living. Ferdinand will receive his, the land and all the outbuildings, when your father and I have passed on. Because you are leaving, it's the way it has to be and it is fair."

"There are practical reasons," she continued. "The necklace will be easy to conceal. I'm going to sew it inside the lining of your coat where it will rest under your arm. That way you'll always be aware of it and until you reach your destination, simply guard the coat as you would your life. Never take it off except at night, then sleep with your arms around it!"

"Any good jeweler will be able to assess the value of the gemstones and the gold leaves, sell the necklace in whole or in part. When you need money you'll have it."

Peter was thunderstruck. He actually thought Catherine had lost her mind. "I need money Mother," he said sincerely, "but . . . this is a king's ransom!"

"Our Viking ancestors carried similar treasures you know," she said half-ignoring him. "Only they didn't bother to conceal them." Catherine half chuckled to herself. "I'm beginning to feel as reckless as they. As reckless as you! Perhaps it's the Viking in us."

"But Mother . . ."

"This has been no easy decision on my part Peter," she continued soberly. "I've stewed over this for weeks. One day Ferdinand will own everything I have in Holbaek because you've forsaken it. But," and she raised her hand to stop any further argument from him, "you have never disappointed me Peter, not really. So why should you not receive equal to your brother?"

Peter could see her mind was made up and he wanted to give Catherine the assurance her gift was greatly appreciated and that he would honor it. "I'm so very grateful Mother," he said with tears in his eyes. "Unlike the prodigal son, I will not squander my portion. I vow to use it wisely. It's just so much . . . so very much." His face suddenly filled with worry. He drew a deep breath and blew it out.

"Don't be too concerned," Catherine said lightly. "You'll know what to do with it. Soon you'll have a family, then you'll know what real responsibility is."

"Take my necklace to America. Turn it into land. Build some barns and fill them with hay and animals. Build Maren a fine home and have some children. I want grandchildren Peter, many grandchildren. Who knows one day I may cross the ocean and come to visit . . . this Zion or whatever you call it."

Before either of them realized it, a faint orange light appeared on the eastern horizon. It was the dawning of a new day, and in the mind of Peter Jensen, the dawning of a bright new life. He hadn't been so excited since he'd first decided to immigrate to America. On the other hand his soul was humbled. His mother had just placed a huge responsibility upon him and he was determined never to let her down.

"We've been up all night," he said smiling as he put his arm around his mother.

"We have," Catherine nodded. "But a lot of healing has taken place Peter. Strange that I'm not tired."

"Nor I," said Peter. "Just some ragged edges."

The yellow-orange sunrise was gradual. Birds in the tree outside the open kitchen window flitted about the branches and twittered quietly so as not to be disrespectful. Then, as shafts of light illuminated their leafy perches, they burst forth in song.

Catherine had something else to say to Peter and her words reflected her noble and prudent soul. Even though she'd always been frugal where running her business and the affairs of her father's estate were concerned, she'd always been generous with people. Generous to a fault. These were the reasons she had kept good employees such as Torkil Olsen and Inger Daryberg for so long, and also why she had attracted enemies such as Krista and Nils Holsen.

"Peter, your life will cross many paths. As undeserving as some may seem, never forget your fellowmen. Use this necklace to bless those in need. Use it to help those who'll help themselves. Be generous. I'm not saying throw your money away, but I am saying be a steward over what God has given you." She took his hands in hers and squeezed them tight. "You can never get ahead of Him. I know you understand what I'm saying."

"Mother," Peter said feeling the weight she'd laid upon him as heavy as the weight her own father had laid upon her many years before, "are you really sure about this? There is a small fortune here."

"I'm sure Peter. What possible good is all this wealth doing sitting in a box? Locked in a closet? I've not worn the necklace in years and never intend to again."

"Now you listen to me," she said firmly. "This is no casual gesture I'm making here. I happen to know exactly what I'm doing and I trust you to follow my instructions. This necklace is going to America. It will be used for good, your own, and many, many others. I feel it. I know it." Tears came to her eyes as she considered her last words. "I know it," she repeated.

Catherine then rose from the table. She placed the necklace back in its box and closed it.

Peter's hands were trembling and he interlocked his fingers together to hold them still. "Now remember," Catherine told him before leaving the room. "No one but you and I are to know about this." Again her father's words echoed in from the past. Peter closed his eyes and nodded. "In due time, I might tell your father and Ferdinand, but that is entirely up to me."

"I'm going to put this away for now," she said taking up the jewelry box. "I'll accomplish my plan of concealment later." There was an air of majesty about the matriarch of the estate as she left the kitchen and walked quietly to her father's old study. When she returned she said, "it has been a long night Peter. I'm going up to bed for a while."

"I love you Mother," he said standing to embrace her. Even though his large stature dwarfed Catherine, Peter felt insignificant in her presence. She was a strong-willed individual, but then so was he. Two runs of stone, mother and son; each had a good heart and each loved the art of milling; the craft that had given each so very much. They knew it would be the last time they would share a moment like this and they savored it, drank in the beauty and hopelessness of it.

Peter had dreams of returning to Denmark one day. Triumphant of course. But Catherine was a realist. As with grain so with life; under her son's husbandry, some of her assets would be sewn in America and grow amidst the tares of life. She was intensely proud of Peter's courage and prayed that through him her bloodline might thrive amongst the Mormons, prayed the harvest would be bounteous. On that she could only trust in God, but she knew her son would never return to Denmark and her heart was breaking.

Pushing gently away from him, Catherine touched Peter's face with both hands. "When you see Maren," she said as she looked wistfully into his eyes. "Tell her I love her. Tell her I support the decision of going to America. Tell her to fear nothing, there are wonderful and exciting things ahead of you—children to rear, and lives to build.

Now go make your plans Peter. God is with you."

SECTION NOTES:

1. The Doctrine and Covenants is a publication of the Church of Jesus Christ of Latter-day Saints containing the prophecies of the Prophet Joseph Smith as well as a relatively few revelations by other Church Prophets including: Brigham Young, Joseph F. Smith, Wilford W. Woodruff, and Spencer W. Kimball. Known as the Book of Commandments at the time of the novel this important book is considered scripture by members of the Mormon Church.

2. Officially established in 1830, by 1847 the Mormon Church had moved its headquarters from Nauvoo, Illinois to Salt Lake City, Utah. Salt Lake City was one of several cities established within a vast and empty territory the Mormons called *Deseret*, a Book of Mormon word, meaning honeybee.

3. Zion: The kingdom of God on earth. Because of their fundamental Christian values and odd, to the world at large, beliefs such as; polygamy, the temple rites of uniting families together for time and all eternity and vicarious works for the dead such as sealings and baptisms; the Mormons as their enemies called them or the Latter-day Saints as they called themselves had been brutally persecuted. Hostile neighbors and mobs had driven them from: New York, Ohio, Missouri, and finally from Illinois to the valleys of the Great Salt Lake and western America. Time and again their homes had been burned, livestock stolen or else driven off and the people compelled to abandon livelihood and business and flee for safety.

In 1846 a mass exodus from Nauvoo, Illinois began in which the exiles traversed over a thousand miles of wilderness to re-establish their church and community life in western America, their Zion. They came on horseback, mules, and rode in wagons, but most simply walked. Once they arrived, rather than have the Saints, as they were called by Brigham Young, church president, congregate in a single location as they had in the past, they established cities throughout Utah, California, Nevada, Arizona, New Mexico, Texas, Colorado, Wyoming, Idaho, Washington, Oregon, and Montana. Some church members were asked or that is "called" to establish settlements as far away as Canada and Mexico. Over three hundred Western American cities, not the least of which was Salt Lake City Utah were originally settled by Mormons.

Called Zion for a brief time, Salt Lake City became Church Headquarters and for a while was the largest of all the new settlements. Located in a huge, rock-strewn desert the fledgling city was a virtual wasteland surrounded by mountains to the north, east, and south and on the west by a mammoth brine-filled body of water called The Great Salt Lake. The lake was a remnant of the mighty Pacific Ocean, left behind centuries ago as the waters receded, and its dense repository of minerals and salt made it the "Dead Sea of the Western Hemisphere."

The endless flat lands surrounding the lake were alkaline therefore useless for growing crops, however a large acreage of deep black earth near the center of the valley and below the foothills proved enough to sustain crops and gardens for the early settlers.

There were many valleys in the Utah territory surrounded by mountains. All were rocky, desolate etc., and like the Salt Lake Valley would have to be wrenched away from Mother Nature, not to mention native Indians, and voracious insects. But tedious years of backbreaking toil eventually made the desert valleys blossom like the rose.

At the time of this story the vast area in question was totally remote and virtually unpopulated. There were no railroads, for that matter few, if any, roads, and habitable only after hiking hundreds of miles and climbing mountains the heights of which staggered the faint at heart. From 1847 until by 1865, nearly 100,000 Mormons had settled the area and more were coming. Even so opportunities were few and food was scarce. In the words of one early settler, a doctor named Priddy Meeks; "in 1848, the valley from a human standpoint presented nothing better than extreme suffering if not starvation. The Saints were scattering hither and thither. Some went back to the states, and some to California, while the mass of people were eating anything they could get. Some eating the hides off cattle, some eating wolf, hawk and crow; some eating the flesh of cattle that had been dead for some time. And while all this was going on, it looked like there was a splendid chance of going stark naked." "If this is Zion, where is hell?" remarked many pioneers upon their arrival.

4. The revelation on celestial marriage as given to the Prophet Joseph Smith is today recorded as Section 131 of The Doctrine and Covenants.

5. Plural marriage was legal in the United States until a series of laws were passed including the "anti-bigamy law" of 1862, which was deemed unconstitutional. In 1874 the constitutionality of the "anti-bigamy law was tried and because of an illegal jury, the Supreme Court threw out the first case. But the constitutionality was tested and proven in January of 1879 and fines of $500 plus two years at hard labor were levied. Then, the passing of the Edmonds-Tucker Act in March of 1887 providing for the disincorporation of The Church of Jesus Christ

of Latter Day Saints put additional pressure on those individuals having more than one wife. Massive arrests and the seizing of church property put the Mormons under severe hardship, but it wasn't until September 25, 1890 that a revelation called "The Manifesto" was presented by then Church President Wilford W. Woodruff suspending the law of celestial marriage.

At that juncture the church officially ceased teaching the doctrine of plural marriage. Members everywhere including countries where plural marriage *is* legal, such as Pakistan, are forbidden to enter into the practice. Since 1890, any members violating Church and Federal laws prohibiting plural marriage are excommunicated.

6. Foreign proselytizing from various religions was at its peak in Denmark during that fall of 1865. Not only Mormons, but Seventh Day Adventists, Catholics, Methodists and Baptists were working to increase their numbers. But no sect was as successful as the Mormons. There were branches of the church springing up in principal cities all over Denmark and consequently priests from the State Church were growing alarmed. Their craft being shaken at the roots, flaming sermons regarding apostasy erupted from their pulpits. Sermons laced with hate spewed forth and certain members of their flocks reacted, often times with violence.

Spurred on and sometimes led by "men of the cloth", mobs most of who were recruited from grog shops, roamed the streets looking for street meetings and other religious gatherings. Many of the men were drunk and cared less about religion; they were merely looking for something to do to put a little life into their otherwise dull existence. Inflammatory newspaper articles fanned the fires and often times proselytizing activities had to be curtailed for the safety of members of the church.

7. Moroni 10: 4–5.